The Dreaming

Walks Through Mist

Kim Murphy

To Yvonne,
Best wishes,
Kim Murphy

Published by Coachlight Press

Published by Coachlight Press January 2011

Coachlight Press, LLC
1704 Craigs Store Road
Afton, Virginia 22920
http://www.coachlightpress.com

Printed in the United States of America
Cover design by Mayapriya Long, Bookwrights Design

Library of Congress Catalog Number: 2010910414
ISBN-13: 978-0-9716790-9-2

*to Aunt Janice
and Phoebe*

Prologue

NO MOONLIGHT ALIGHTED MY PATH TO AID ME. Halting to catch my breath, I focused on the night sounds. Branches, with rustling leaves, creaked in the wind, a screech owl trilled a mournful melody, and midges hummed past my ear. Upon hearing rushing water, I reasoned that I could follow its course and escape those who sought my death.

Unless the hounds were sent aft me, the advantage was mine. Unlike my pursuers, I had been taught to move swiftly and silently through the forest. Reaching the bank of the stream, I kicked off my leather shoes, for they were a hindrance. I dipped my toes into the water and felt the cool and slippery moss-covered rocks. Near me, a fish splashed. On the path behind me, I heard a familiar voice, hailing me and assuring me that no harm would come to me.

For a moment, I turned, contemplating whether I should continue on or turn back. Always steadfast in his devotion, Henry would not harm me. But was he alone? My back stung from the whip's lashes. Like spiders waiting in their webs, those close to him could have spun a trap.

He called to me once more. I quivered with irresolution, when a voice inside me urged me to continue forward. Though my life with Henry had ne'er been true, I feared what lay ahead.

"Do not fear it. You will be reunited with what once was."

'Twas *his* voice. So many years had passed that I had nearly forgotten the sound of it. Unashamedly, tears sprang into my eyes. Disregarding those who followed me, I called out to him in the tongue that had been forbidden to me for so long.

"Forward," he urged.

Heeding his advice, I forded the stream. The water churned around my feet whilst fish kissed my toes. Near the middle, the water swirled about my waist. I slogged through it and reached the far bank, when suddenly I was lost.

Trees were everywhere. I stumbled my way through the gigantic roots. Ne'er having felt confused and alone in a forest, I cried, "Where, my love? Where am I to go?"

Raging shouts came from the opposite stream bank. My heart pounded at their nearness. If I did not seek refuge, the mob would be upon me. I could now see their torches, and my breaths quickened. In the breeze, my beloved whispered, and I followed his voice 'til an elegant white hound stood afore me. I now knew what I must do.

The dog's body was made for coursing, but he kept a slower pace in order to guide the way. Deeper and deeper into the forest we traveled. I sought shelter in a dark opening within the roots of an immense oak. Instead of blackness surrounding me, a thick mist engulfed me. The clammy dampness upon my skin raised the hairs on my arms. The hound was my salvation, and I latched onto his leather collar.

On and on I faltered through the fog with the dog tracing a huge circle. I felt the rough, bare wood of a rocking and swaying ship neath my feet. A wave of nausea overcame me, and I clutched my stomach with my free hand. The hound failed to break stride. Onwards.

From a nearby branch, a crow cawed. Suddenly, I thought of a tiny lad vanishing in a similar mist, ne'er to be found again. Assured that my pursuers would reason that I suffered from the same fate, I continued walking along the arc.

When my beloved's voice returned, I signaled the hound to halt. He kept going, and the loving voice faded. With a twinge of remorse, I thought of Henry. He, too, had loved me. A love that I could ne'er return, for my heart had always belonged to another.

The mist grew thinner, and *he* whispered in my ear for me to follow the light. Up ahead, I spied what looked like thousands of torches. As I emerged from the fog, the dog vanished. I blinked in disbelief. How could so much light be possible in the night sky? I scanned about me. Lights upon lights, swarming with people. And clattering noise. I pressed my hands to my ears to block the racket. The thoroughfare had a surface the likes of which I had ne'er seen. *Where am I? Which lights should I follow?*

I stepped into the road to escape. More lights chased aft me, blinding me. I froze in my path, deafened by a piercing sound and sudden screeching. The earth trembled, and I was flying afore striking the pavement. I closed my eyes to the pain. *Soon, my beloved, I will join you.*

1

Lee and Shae
Near Richmond, Virginia

L EE CROWLEY FLASHED HIS BADGE and police identification at the receptionist behind the emergency room desk. "Detective Crowley to see Dr. Miller," he said to the woman.

"Right away, detective." Dark circles beneath her eyes hinted that the night shift had been a long one. She put in a call to announce his arrival.

Sympathetic to the feeling, Lee stifled a yawn and wandered away from the desk. Coughs and groans from waiting patients filled the room.

"Detective Crowley. I'm Veronica Metcalfe." A fiftyish nurse dressed in blue scrubs motioned for him to follow her down the corridor. "Dr. Miller will go over Jane Doe's injuries with you. The patient is white, in her late twenties to early thirties, and was brought in after being struck by a 2005 Toyota Camry on Route 5 a few miles from the I-295 interchange. She's about five feet two inches and 105 pounds. Even though she's petite, she's muscular."

Lee transcribed the details into his notebook. "Muscular, as in she works out?" They turned the corner to another corridor.

"I've never seen anyone like her. No, it's more like she's worked every day of her life—heavy, hard work."

He made note of her comment.

She continued, "Her hair is strawberry blonde, and her eyes are blue green. Her ears are pierced, three times each, and she was wearing copper earrings. She's got scars on her right forearm from what appears to be a former fracture. She has tattoos circling her upper arms and on her breasts and thighs. She has stretch marks, so we know she's given birth. A tooth is missing from the upper-right side of her mouth. She has incomplete syndactyly of the third and fourth digits of her left hand."

Lee stopped writing and waved at the nurse to back up. "English, please."

"Syndactyly is webbing between the fingers or toes. All human fetuses start out with webbing, but in some cases the digits fail to separate during development. Jane Doe has fleshy webbing between the knuckles of her middle and ring fingers, as well as the second and third toes on her left foot. Frankly, I was surprised to see it."

"Why do you say that?"

"Because in her case, it would have been an easy operation to have fixed as a child." She continued with her report as Lee made note of her comment. "She had no ID and was wearing unusual clothing."

The officer at the accident scene had also noted the victim's clothing in his report. "In what way was it unusual?" Lee asked.

"The garments don't look modern. I'll show you what I mean." They turned into the lab.

The victim's clothing had been cut away in the emergency room, but fortunately, the hospital staff had spread the garments out for the blood to dry. Lee examined the clothing without touching it. He was no expert on women's fashions from other eras, but the simple cloth undergarment would have been white, if it hadn't been covered in blood. There was also a long gold skirt and metal eyelet holes in the top with laces that had been cut away for the victim's treatment. "She must work in a colonial tavern or living history program."

"No doubt," the nurse responded, "but when she was brought in, she muttered a foreign language."

Lee donned gloves and carefully collected the clothing in a bag. He tagged it, in case it would be needed for evidence at a later date, before tossing the gloves into the trash receptacle. "What was the language?"

"No one can make sense of it," came a deep bass voice from behind them. "Detective Crowley, I'm Dr. Jack Miller." The doctor, a bald man in a white lab coat, shook Lee's hand. "If you'll step into my office, I'll go over Jane Doe's injuries."

They took an elevator to the next floor. Except for a file folder with x-rays, the doctor's massive oak desk was spotless. A computer with a flat-panel monitor sat on the highly polished surface. Miller hit a key, and numerous images of a skull popped onto the screen. "My patient has an amazing constitution. She has a minor skull fracture." He pointed to the trauma on the screen. After another click of the keyboard, he switched to an image with a view of a ribcage. "She also has two broken ribs. She may be older than we originally believed because I see the beginning of osteoarthritis in her legs and hands. Other than that, she came away from the accident with minor contusions and lacerations, but . . . ."

Lee picked up on the doctor's hesitation. "Go on."

"She's been whipped and possibly beaten—recently."

The doctor was finally getting to why he had been called in. "As in assault or consensual sexual bondage?"

"In my professional judgment, the former. She had healed scars on her back that indicated it wasn't the first time either."

A simple traffic accident with a nameless victim was definitely turning into an assault case. Lee wondered if she might have been abducted as well. "Was she raped?"

"There was no evidence."

"If she's conscious, I'd like to see her."

"I thought you might. She's conscious, but heavily sedated. I couldn't tell how much of her apprehension of our proceedings was due to pain or disorientation." The doctor escorted Lee to the intensive care unit.

The woman's short stature left abundant empty space at the end of the bed. An IV tube trailed from her forearm to the saline solution. Her hair had been tucked under a medical cap, but reddish blonde tufts were visible. Lee observed the roots were the same color. She was a natural redhead.

"Ma'am."

Her eyelashes fluttered. At first, the blue-green depths revealed fear and grogginess. As her eyes focused on him, she relaxed.

He showed his badge. "I'm Detective Crowley, ma'am."

"*Netab?*"

Her inflection told him that she had asked a question. The language was guttural, and for some reason, he felt he should recognize it. It wasn't German or any of the other European languages he had heard before. He pointed to himself, then presented himself with an open-handed, non-threatening gesture. "Dectective Crowley." He pointed to her. "And you are?"

She lightly grasped his hand. "*Netab.*"

The doctor spoke up. "Whatever she's saying, she's comfortable with you. She hasn't exhibited any similar feeling toward the rest of us."

The fact that he had instantly gained the woman's confidence would certainly help his investigation, but he couldn't bring in an interpreter if no one could figure out what language she was speaking. *Start with the basics.* "I'll get a sketch artist and finger printer in here, and we'll see if we can identify who she is and what's happened to her. Bring me a map."

"A map?" the doctor asked.

"You heard me. Bring me a map of the world. Let's start by finding out where she's from."

"Of course, detective." Dr. Miller relayed the order to one of his assistants.

Was it his badge that had eased the woman? "We're going to do all we can to try and find out what happened," Lee said.

She tilted her head slightly. Did she understand?

"I'm Detective Crowley," he said one more time. "You are?"

She muttered a string of unintelligible sounds with the words coming faster in a frenzied frustration.

"I'm sorry, ma'am. I don't understand."

She leaned forward and traced a line with her fingertip across his cheekbone. "*Netab.*"

Did she think he was Hispanic? Few correctly guessed his Indian heritage upon meeting him. Lee was relieved when the nurse brought an atlas. "Point to where you're from."

With the curiosity of a child, Jane Doe watched with round eyes as he slowly turned the pages of the book, letting her study each map in detail. He flipped a page, and she ran her hands along the paper and flared her nostrils as if taking in the scent.

"The West Indies?"

"*Tangoa.*" She took the book from him and began turning the pages on her own. A quarter of the way through the atlas, she stopped and frowned. She jabbed a finger to the page.

Lee looked at the map. "England?" With Jane's red hair and blue eyes, she could be English. She *did* comprehend what he was saying. He'd check with Immigration Services. Whatever had happened to her had terrified her to the point of losing normal communication.

Relieved when her last patient had closed the door to her office, Shae Howard eased into the leather chair behind her desk and looked over the following day's schedule. Kay Hood, her bulimia patient, was scheduled for 10:00 a.m. Right after Kay, she had a new client, suffering from depression. After lunch, she had three patients.

The phone to her direct line rang.

"Dr. Howard," she answered.

"*Shae, I was wondering if you could take a look at an assault victim for me.*"

She let out a tired breath. "You could start by saying hello, Lee."

"*Hey. Now that we have formalities out of the way, Jane Doe was hit by a car, but she was assaulted before the accident. She speaks a foreign language that no one has a clue about, yet she pointed to a map of England. I think she understands us, but whatever happened, she's so shaken that she's reverted to what must be her native language. So far, there's no trace of her via immigration. Her fingerprints aren't on file, and it'll be a few days before we get DNA analysis.*"

Same old Lee—right down to business. "In a case like this, hypnosis is a long shot."

"*I realize that, but I have no leads. The department has approved it, if you're willing to give it a try.*"

"How was she assaulted?" Shae asked, fearing the worst.

"Some bastard took a bullwhip to her. And it wasn't the first time."

That definitely wasn't the answer she had expected. "Then you think she may have been abducted and escaped, rather than it being some sort of domestic dispute?"

"Yes."

In spite of their past, Shae trusted his hunches. He was a good cop. "Where is she?"

He relayed the details, and she jotted them down on notepaper.

"That's all the way across the city," she said. "With traffic at this time of day, I'll be there in forty-five minutes. Thirty if I get lucky with the lights. I also need to give Russ a call that I'll be late."

"Thanks."

The line went dead. Shae put in a quick call to home and got the answering machine. She left a message for her live-in boyfriend, saying she'd be late. After gathering together the files that she would need for the morning, she stuffed them into her briefcase, locked her office, and went down to the parking lot. Luck was with her. She hit mostly green lights and made it to the hospital in forty minutes. Dr. Miller showed her to his office, where she could review Jane Doe's files. Lee joined them when she was nearly finished reading.

"For some reason," Dr. Miller said, "the patient seems comfortable in Detective Crowley's presence."

Lee was over six feet tall and had an athletic-cop build. Women were often drawn to him. While his black hair and brown skin were certainly attractive, a woman needed more than earth-shattering sex in her life. She dealt with patients learning that painful lesson the hard way all too often, as she had. "We may be able to use that to our advantage," she finally said. "I'm ready to see the patient. Detective Crowley, I'd like for you to accompany me. Since she's comfortable in your presence, you can introduce us."

Lee nodded. He'd never really been much of a talker.

She hated seeing patients for police investigations. It was a one-time examination, which made a doctor/patient rapport an impossibility. In addition, the session was videotaped on the chance it might be needed in court for evidence.

Lee opened the door for her.

With a corner sofa, the room at least gave the appearance of a comfy lounge rather than a sterile exam room. Nurse Metacalfe escorted the patient into the room. Jane Doe was dressed in a hospital gown and wore her light-red hair pulled away from her face. Upon seeing Shae, Jane's eyes widened as if she were a predator's prey. *What had happened to the poor woman that would make her so afraid?*

Lee took his cue and introduced them. "This is Dr. Howard. She's a friend."

At the sound of Lee's voice, Jane relaxed. *"Netab?"*

"Netab," Lee replied. "She wants to help you remember what happened."

Lee's inflection had strangely matched Jane's in a perfect copy. Finally, Jane glanced warily from Lee.

Shae motioned for Jane to have a seat on the sofa. "We're going to have a little chat and get to know each other better. If you still have difficulty remembering what happened, I'll see if hypnosis can help you recall, so Detective Crowley can find whoever it was that did this to you. Do you understand?"

Shae lightly touched Jane's elbow to guide her to the sofa. The woman flinched but offered no resistance. The nurse left the room, and as Lee strode for the door, Jane drew her knees to her body. Pain reflected in her eyes as she did so.

Unless Shae gained the patient's confidence, there would be no interview nor hypnosis. "Lee, I think you had better stay."

Without an acknowledgment, he seated himself at the opposite end of the sofa.

"There's no reason to be afraid," Shae said to Jane. "Detective Crowley will remain with us."

Gradually, Jane stretched her legs and began to look a little less haunted.

What was it about Lee that comforted Jane?

"Detective Crowley investigates crimes," Shae said. "He wants to know what happened to you, which is why he called me. I'm a psychologist, and I use hypnotherapy when I think it will help. We're both here to help you, so you can ask either of us any questions that you might have."

Jane muttered in a language unfamiliar to Shae.

"Do you speak English?"

Jane merely stared at her in confusion. Lee had stated that she seemed to understand, but Shae had her doubts. She'd try a different tack. Some sort of two-way communication was necessary if she was going to use hypnosis. "The important thing is that you're safe here. No one can harm you further. If you'll do what I say, we can recover your memory so that you may begin healing. Will you do as I say?"

No response.

"Do you understand what hypnosis is?"

Jane stared blankly at Shae.

"Lee, can I speak with you privately?"

He nodded, but before leaving, he bent down to Jane and spoke to her in a soft, gentle voice. "We'll return shortly."

Jane uttered no response, but Shae spotted immediate relaxation and trust. Such a pity that Lee had no knowledge of how to induce hypnosis. *Was Jane responding to his words?* No, it was more like an instant connection. Once outside the room, she left the door cracked so they could keep an eye on the patient without her hearing their discussion. "If she can't communicate, I can't use hypnosis. I must be able to explain to her what it is."

"She does understand you," he insisted.

"How can you be so certain? It appears to me that she's responding to you."

"Okay, call it another hunch, but I'm certain she understands some of what we're saying. Try again—please."

Shae was aware how much he hated cold cases. "I don't like jeopardizing a patient's mental health for a hunch."

"Why do you think I called you? Because I *know* you'll get the leads I need without endangering anyone."

Damn him. He knew exactly how to hit her where she was vulnerable. If she could somehow communicate with Jane Doe, not only would she help Lee, but she would pave the way for the patient's healing as well. "All right. One more time, but if we're not successful, I don't want to hear anymore about it."

"Agreed."

"I presume you'll accompany me? It must be that no-nonsense authority figure thing, but she relaxes when you're around."

He motioned for her to proceed before him. "After you."

Upon returning to the exam room, Shae drew in her breath. Slow and easy. It was going to be tough finding Jane's comfort zone. "Sorry for the interruption. First, let me explain. Detective Crowley was called in on your case because you've been whipped by someone. He wants to know who did this to you so this person can't hurt you or anyone else again."

Jane glanced in Lee's direction. Maybe she *did* understand.

Taking her cue, Shae continued, "Whipping another person is against the law, and Detective Crowley wants to arrest him. Do you understand?"

"De-tect-ive . . ."

Shae thought she had detected a hint of an English accent. "That's right, and I'm Dr. Howard. I'm a psychologist trained in hypnotherapy. Detective Crowley thought hypnosis might help you remember what happened, but we can sit here and chat for a while if you prefer. Can you tell me your name?"

Jane muttered in the guttural language once more.

"That's fine. We'll come back to your name when you feel more comfortable. Do you know where you are?"

Jane shook her head.

Good! She understood.

"You're in a hospital. The doctors treated your injuries. Most importantly, you're safe. Whoever hurt you can't reach you here nor harm you again. You can have a comfortable rest while your body heals. The doctors and nurses will see to that. I, on the other hand, am a doctor who helps people with emotional injuries. You've endured a trauma from the accident, and I'm here to help you. If you listen to what I say, I can help you, and in turn, the two of us can help Detective Crowley. Will you listen to what I say?"

Jane glanced at Lee. He gave her a nod.

Shae was beginning to doubt that the patient's trust in Lee was due to his badge. It was more like she knew him.

Jane faced her again. "Aye."

Scottish? Shae wondered. "Through the use of hypnosis," she said, "I can help you recall what happened. Contrary to what you might have seen on TV, hypnosis doesn't control your mind. You won't go to sleep, nor will you be stuck in a trance."

"Trance?" Jane asked.

"Yes, hypnosis is a trance-like state of the mind, but it's never permanent. Your attention will be more focused, but you will be relaxed so that you can calmly tell us what happened. Shall I continue?"

"Aye."

"You will be in complete control. Do you understand?"

"Trance." Jane closed her eyes.

"Good. Relax. Breathe in. Now out. Breathe in and hold for the count of three. One. Two. Three." Shae went through several breathing exercises with Jane. She was hopeful. The patient was responding. "Imagine a bird. Can you see it?"

Jane's eyes remained closed. *"Ussac."*

Some sort of bird, Shae presumed. "Now I want you to imagine your right big toe." Shae continued the relaxation script through Jane's foot and leg. "Think of a boat. You're riding on a gentle wave. The wave reaches your left foot and leg." Waves and waves, until she led Jane through every part of her body. "You may feel a pleasant tingling sensation from the tips of your toes or in your fingertips. It's growing stronger as your entire body is bathed in the glow. You're now drifting and floating in peace. Now, can you tell me your name?"

Jane responded in the guttural language.

"Can you tell me your name in English?"

"Phoebe Wynne."

The patient had most definitely spoken with an English or Scottish accent. Yet, somehow it seemed different. Shae couldn't quite put her finger on why. Lee watched Phoebe with growing interest. Thankfully, he knew his place and remained silent.

"Phoebe, I'd like for you to think about before the accident. Someone whipped you. Can you describe who did it to you?"

Silence.

Shae needed to use another approach. "Phoebe, where are you from?"

"Dorset. When I was a lass of nine years, Momma and I sailed on the *Blessing* to James Town."

Jamestown? Phoebe had uttered the name as if it were two distinct words.

"Was this in celebration of the recent anniversary?" Shae asked.

"Nay. Poppa was on the *Sea Venture.* She wrecked during a hurricane. We thought Poppa had been lost at sea."

Phoebe's memory was most unusual. Shae had to remind herself the purpose of the session was to discover Phoebe's assailant. Still, the memory could be leading somewhere, and if the patient could remember the date, they might have a birthdate to go with her name. "When did you arrive in Jamestown?"

"1609. Momma thought Poppa was dead. We ran off the following February during the starving time."

2

Phoebe Wynne

NOT A HORSE NOR A DOG roamed the colony. Even the rats scurried for shelter to avoid capture from hungry hands. A walking skeleton—Master Littleton—dug his grave, lay in it, and prayed to be taken. Master Collins committed the greatest of sins. He hated his wife and killed her, saying that she had died. Then he cut her up, salted her, and fed upon her to satisfy his hunger. For his crime, the men heaped faggots around a wooden stake.

Sullen and mute, Master Collins marched to the stake in shabby and dirty clothes. He paused briefly when he reached the circle of broken sticks and knelt in prayer. He arose and placed his back to the stake. Half a dozen men wound ropes about his body and a chain around his neck. The torch was applied. For a moment, smoke billowed. Sparks flew into the air, and the wood crackled.

Almost immediately, his breeches caught fire. Though his flesh must have been scorched, he uttered no sound. Flames crawled upwards on his clothing. With a sudden convulsive jerking on the ropes, Master Collins turned his head from the rapidly increasing flames. A cry pierced the air. "Oh my God! Let me go!"

In an attempt to prevent me from viewing the spectacle, Momma seized my hand. "Come, Phoebe."

Amongst Master Collins's screams came the smell of roasting flesh, followed by a musky odor. I was so weak from hunger that my knees nearly buckled. Momma tugged on my hand once more and nearly lifted me from the ground to keep me moving. The men were distracted by the burning, and no one observed us slipping out the wooden gates. Soon, we were away from the fort. As we neared the snow-covered forest, a man with brown skin painted with black geometric patterns stood afore us. He wore a breechclout, deer hide leggings, and a mantle draped in duck feathers. His crown hair stood upright. Whilst the right side of his head was shaved, his black hair, tied in a knot and adorned with fowl feathers, stretched the length of his back on his left side. Bird's claws hung through each of his ears, and the same black patterns decorated his face, making his expression look more fierce.

With their bows at the ready, other warriors joined him. I had ne'er seen Indians up close afore. Their frames towered over us, casting imposing figures. I clung to Momma's skirt, hoping the wool fabric would make me invisible.

"Please," Momma said, sinking to her knees. "My husband is dead, and I have naught to feed my daughter. Do what you will with me, but spare her."

Even though they hadn't understood a word she uttered, they lowered their bows slightly. The first warrior stepped forward, lifted Momma's thin hair, and let the strands fall slowly from his fingers as if he were curious about her blonde curls. Though her face remained stern, I felt her shaking legs neath her skirt as I shrank further into the folds.

The warrior spoke in his Algonquian tongue and drew Momma to her feet. The other warriors lowered their bows and moved away from the colony. With a wave, he indicated for us to follow. Momma had only heard ghastly tales of savages. She had no way of knowing that Paspahegh warriors rarely raped, nor did they kill women and children, but she obeyed. Her head remained high. She pretended to be unafraid. With that simple gesture, we followed them to their town.

3

Shae

"INDIAN WARRIORS, JAMESTOWN! I half expected to hear a tale or two about John Smith and Pocahontas thrown in for good measure."

Normally, Lee wasn't the sort to ruffle easily, but Shae watched him pace the length of Dr. Miller's office, then back again.

"I warned you that hypnosis would be a long shot," she said.

Calming, he halted by Dr. Miller's desk. Thankfully, the doctor had loaned them the use of his office so they could speak in private. "You did," Lee finally agreed. "What caused her to make up such a story?"

"Confabulation. Phoebe has completely fantasized details of her trauma into a pure work of fiction. She needs therapeutic treatment, not forensic analysis. I suspect it lends some insight as to why she's comforted by your presence."

"Proceed, doctor," he said with interest.

"You look very similar to her description of a Pa . . . Paspa . . ."

"Pa-spa-*hay*. They were a tributary tribe to the paramount chief, Powhatan."

"You sound like a textbook," she said. "Where did you learn about them?"

"My parents had me read about all of the Virginia tribes—to teach me about my heritage. For all the good it did," he grumbled.

Amazing—all the years they had known each other, he had never shared the fact that he had read about the tribes. She was getting distracted. "Phoebe trusts you because you look like a Paspahegh warrior."

He straightened his tie. "I guess I had better trade in my suit for a loincloth."

"Lee, don't dismiss her. You were right for me to continue, but her mental state is fragile. The warrior is some sort of symbol, most likely for someone she knows. Whoever he is, she feels protected by his presence. It's why she trusts you."

His eyes were the color of burnt almond, and they grew piercing as he met her gaze. "I have a name, if it's her real one. I've already put it through to the dispatcher, but if that turns up empty, I have nothing more to work with."

And Phoebe would most likely be turned over to a psychiatric hospital, unless she could function in transitional housing. The patient struck Shae as one who might not do well in either environment. "Let me know if anything turns up."

"I will." Lee strode for the door.

"Lee, I'm going to ask Dr. Miller if I can take over her case upon her release."

He faced her. "Getting personally involved, Shae?"

"No, but she needs someone to help her work through her trauma. I don't want to see her cast off to some state hospital."

"Sounds like personal involvement to me."

"Of course you would think so, since it's so easy for you to turn off emotions."

Lee opened his mouth to protest.

She continued before he had the chance: "I'm sorry, I shouldn't have said that. I guess after all these years, I still find myself vulnerable to slinging a petty jab on occasion. I merely don't want to see Phoebe lost in the system. Someone cares for her and is looking for her. Unless they step forward, who she is and what happened to her are locked away in a troubled mind."

"And you, doctor, have ulterior motives. You seek a published paper from treating such an unusual patient."

She resisted the urge to respond with a biting retort. "I'll admit a paper would be nice, but it's icing on the cake. I truly believe I can help her. I've got a few favors to call in. I think I can get her placed in transitional housing. She deserves a chance."

"I'll see what I can do on my end."

"Thanks, Lee. By the way, you haven't said how you've been."

His expression softened slightly as he lowered his detached detective's mask. "I'm fine."

"And Linda?"

"We split six months ago. You know the score—long hours and wondering if she'd get the call late at night saying I was lying dead on some dark street."

She did understand—all too well. Shae suspected that was the reason why they were better friends now than when they had been married. "I'm sorry it didn't work out."

"The story of my life. What about you?"

"Pretty much the same. Russ and I—"

Lee's cell phone rang. "Crowley," he answered. "I'm on my way. Have to run, Shae."

He shot out the door before she could say goodbye. She shook her head with a knowing laugh. Nothing had changed. No wonder he had lost yet another woman.

4

Phoebe

THE WARRIORS ESCORTED MOMMA AND ME to a town of arched houses covered by woven mats. Upon our entrance to the town, the Indians sent up a joint shrill cry, terrifying the two of us with their noise. I clutched Momma's skirts that much tighter. A warrior in a feathered headdress introduced himself as the *weroance* Wowinchapuncke and made a speech. We understood not a single word he uttered and feared the worst when he finished and motioned for us to follow four women.

The women, wearing leather mantles for warmth, took our hands and led us towards the river.

Momma's free hand gripped my shoulder as we traveled a path cleared from brambles. "Everything will be fine."

Her trembling hand signaled a different story than her words. I had overheard tales in the colony how the Indians cooked children and ate them, as Master Collins had his wife. "Momma," I cried.

"Not now, Phoebe."

We reached the river bank, and the women stripped us of our woolen clothing, including our shifts.

Momma kept her eyes focused forward so as not to view the men, women, and children lining the bank, watching us.

Again, the women took our hands and led us into the water. I already shivered uncontrollably from the winter day, but the ice-edged river water was downright freezing. Momma struggled to reach me. Two women clamped their hands around her arms and held her away from me, whilst the masses on the bank burst into laughter. Momma howled like a crazed bitch protecting her pup 'til one of the women said in English, "No hurt."

Numbness spread, tingling my feet, but the women began to wash us. Dunked underwater, I panicked and flailed my arms, for I could not swim. The women scoured and scrubbed. The cold water bit into my flesh. When I was allowed to rise, I choked for air to fill my lungs. Briefly, I saw a long-legged white hound on the opposite bank. I gasped for another breath, and when I reopened my eyes, the dog had vanished.

Released from the water, we were offered fringed leather aprons similar to what the other women wore. Momma's face remained pinched, but she smiled and spoke to me calmly, so as not to alarm me. I cried, and Momma hugged me to her bosom. Though I could not understand their words, the Indian women spoke in soothing voices whilst giving me gentle touches.

When I stopped weeping, Momma dried my tears. Once again, the women held out the garments.

I fingered the fringed skirt. Momma reassured me that I should try it on. The doe hide was soft against my skin, and I relished in its warmth. At such a young age, I discovered great joy in this new game of dressing like an Indian. Momma blanched when the women demonstrated that she was to keep her right breast exposed, but she ne'er flinched. They spread mantles over our shoulders, and Momma quickly covered herself.

The women draped shell beads around our necks. I marveled at my necklace, for I ne'er had any jewelery so fine. Surrounded by Indians, we once again traveled the path, down which the women escorted us to a house. Inside were turtle shells, gourds, clay pots, and woven baskets filled with items that I knew not what they were. Wooden frames with mats similar to the house coverings and draped animal skins served as pallets. An open fire crackled in the middle with a smoke hole cut away in the mat above it.

One woman took a mussel shell and motioned for me to sit on a mat near the fire. Momma nodded for me to follow her instructions. Cross legged in front of the fire, I did as I was told, savoring my newfound warmth. I screamed when the woman brought the shell near my head, fearing she was about to scalp me.

"No hurt," she repeated.

Momma hushed me. "Phoebe, it shall be all right."

The tremor in Momma's voice had faded, lending me assurance. I sat still as the woman grated the shell near my scalp, shaving the forepart and sides of my head. She left the hinder section long, winding my hair into pretty plaits.

Momma was next. The women cut her hair short all around. When they were finished, they showed us to the door. Outside, the drums beat the rhythm of a heartbeat. Indians had gathered with the warriors still painted black. They danced in a circle around the fire to the tempo of the drum.

One of the women showed me the steps. I followed her lead. At first, I was awkward, and Momma faltered. Round and round in the circle I went, 'til I no longer required instruction. The beat quickened. I picked up my pace. Faster and faster, I absorbed the drumbeat, only halting when I fell into a heap from exhaustion.

My heart pounded within my chest, and when the Indians sent up the shrill cry, I joined them. I was now Paspahegh.

5

Shae

"PHOEBE?"

Coming out of the hypnotic state, Phoebe blinked. "Did I tell you what you had hoped to hear?"

"You did fine." Shae wished she had some idea where the woman's story originated from. With Lee's help, she had checked the local living history sites and restaurants that employed costumed staff. No one had claimed a missing employee nor the possibility that Phoebe might have been a former employee. None of Lee's checks had turned up anything either. "Dr. Miller says you're well enough to be released today."

"Released?" As though she were a child, everything seemed new to her.

"You can go home."

"I may need your help to find my way."

Thankfully, the staff had agreed to keep Phoebe hospitalized for a couple weeks, giving Shae the time to find her patient a room in transitional housing. She dreaded what would happen to someone in Phoebe's delicate frame of mind in a state hospital. "That's what we're trying to do. I'd feel better about releasing you from the hospital if you could remember the details of the accident and if it was related to who whipped you."

Phoebe placed a hand to her throat. "I recall naught."

Shae highly suspected dissociative amnesia and fugue, even though no other personality ever appeared than the one named

Phoebe. She had gained no information following standard protocol with a clinical interview. Only hypnosis revealed glimpses into what troubled Phoebe, and Shae was convinced that continued treatment would get to the bottom of the matter. But it was going to take time. She only hoped that whoever had beaten Phoebe wasn't lurking somewhere, waiting for another opportunity.

Shae held out a canvas shopping bag. "Your dress was ruined in the accident. I thought you might like to try this on."

Phoebe peered inside the bag and withdrew a long-sleeved, chive-green dress. Her eyelashes flickered in bewilderment. "Where are the stays?"

"There are undergarments in the bag. I guessed your size. I hope everything fits."

Puzzled, Phoebe stared at Shae.

She truly doesn't know. Shae decided she should consult with her live-in lover, Russ, who was also a practicing psychologist. He had experience in treating amnesia patients. "Here, let me help you," she said.

She assisted Phoebe with her hospital gown. The lacerations on her back from the whip were scabbed but healing. How long would it take for her mental wounds to heal? Shae unpacked the undergarments from the bag.

Phoebe held up the brassiere in confusion. "Instead of stays?" she asked with her left brow raised.

"Instead of stays. This might not be such a good idea right now. You'll likely hurt your back. The dress should be less confining and more comfortable." Without further comment, Shae helped Phoebe dress. While the below-the-knee dress was a plain one, the chive color accented Phoebe's strawberry-blonde hair, which fell to the middle of her back. Shae ran a brush through the woman's locks. She truly looked part of the twenty-first century now, rather than the seventeenth, and was quite attractive.

"Once the doctor has your paperwork ready, I'm going to take you to the house where you'll be staying."

"House?"

Maybe this wasn't such a good idea. "You do know what a house is?"

"Aye. Will Master Crowley come to see me?"

"Lee is a detective. Unless something new turns up regarding your case, he won't be following up."

Another bewildered blink.

Imagining Lee as a Paspahegh warrior, Shae struggled to keep her professional demeanor and not laugh. Then again, if he had chosen a career other than police work, he would have blended right in as an authentic-looking tour guide at one of the historic sites. Young female visitors would doubtless be more intent on what lay beneath his loincloth than local history. Shae attempted to rid the vision from her mind and said in as even of a voice as she could, "I won't make any promises that he'll agree, but I'll speak to him about paying you a friendly visit."

"Thank you, Dr. . . . ."

"Please, call me Shae."

"Shae," Phoebe repeated with a growing smile.

"And call Lee by his name. He might split a gut if you called him Master Crowley."

"I shall. I don't wish to inflict any bodily harm upon him. Thank you for warning me."

"Split a gut is a figure of speech. He won't physically burst."

"That's good to know." Phoebe's wide eyes exhibited total innocence. She was perfectly serious. While Shae had studied dissociative identity disorders at the University of Virginia, to actually be confronted with a bona fide case was a different matter altogether. All that counted was Phoebe *believed* she was from the seventeenth century.

The door opened, and Dr. Miller walked into the room. "Good morning, ladies. Phoebe, I'm giving Dr. Howard a prescription in case you experience pain over the next few days. Even though your constitution is remarkable, I expect you to take it easy and rest for a couple of weeks. I've never seen anyone heal as quickly as you, and I have no doubt you'll be feeling normal quite soon. If you're still unable to recall where you're from when it's time for a follow-up exam in ten days, Dr. Howard will find a suitable physician for you. If you notice any regression or new symptoms, feel free to call me or Dr. Howard. Any questions?"

Totally perplexed, Phoebe stared at Dr. Miller.

"I'll see that she gets settled and follows doctor's orders," Shae said.

"Thank you, Dr. Howard. A nurse will be in shortly to escort you." He gave them a smile before leaving the room.

Phoebe focused on Shae. "I've told you where I hail from."

"You have," Shae agreed. "But we have been unable to locate your family or anyone who knows you. Immigration has no record of a Phoebe Wynne from Dorset, and Lee hasn't found any clues about you or anyone you've mentioned."

A nurse, wearing cartoon rocket ship scrubs, entered the room with a wheelchair. "I'm your ride out of here."

Phoebe's eyes became fixed on the metal contraption. She stood her ground.

"It's all right, Phoebe," Shae reassured.

Phoebe touched the wheelchair with her index finger, then withdrew it quickly, as if it might bite.

Shae patted the seat. "You sit in it."

Phoebe glanced at her, and Shae nodded for her to continue. The frightened woman cautiously sat in the wheelchair. Her back remained as stiff as a board, and her hands gripped the arm rests like she was afraid to let go. When the nurse started to wheel Phoebe from the room, Shae thought Phoebe might shoot straight out of the wheelchair.

"It's all right," Shae said once more. "If you don't mind, I'll go pull the car around front."

A hand clamped around Shae's wrist.

Shae met Phoebe's gaze. "The nurse will wheel you to the door, and I'll be there to greet you."

"Do you vow?"

"I promise."

Phoebe let go.

"I'll see you out front." Shae went ahead and collected her Acura. The nurse walked through the door with Phoebe as she pulled alongside the curb. Shae opened the passenger door.

Again, Phoebe failed to move. "One of those hit me."

"It's a car. It'll transport you to your new home." Shae waved for Phoebe to get in.

Phoebe got to her feet but remained in place like a stubborn mule.

"It's like a carriage without horses."

Phoebe blinked. "I see no sail like a ship. What propels it if there are no horses?"

Phoebe's comfort zone in the seventeenth century seemed complete. *Delusional?* She didn't quite fit that diagnosis either, confounding Shae. The sooner she consulted with Russ, the better. "A gasoline engine. Now get in."

Although obviously confused, Phoebe complied.

Shae strapped Phoebe into the seatbelt.

Phoebe pulled on the belt in puzzlement.

"It keeps you from flying through the windshield if I brake too fast. Now just sit back and pretend you're in a carriage." Shae went around to the other side, slid in behind the driver's seat, and started the engine. Phoebe clutched the armrest.

Shae drove away from the hospital. "Relax. Cars are less wild than horses."

"I shall honor your word." Phoebe gave her a hesitant smile but settled back into the seat.

Good, she had gained the patient's trust. When Shae had a chance to glance in Phoebe's direction, she saw Phoebe staring at the passing streets and cars in wide-eyed amazement. It was if she had never seen a city before.

"Where do all of the people hail from? I have ne'er seen so many."

The time had come to play along to strengthen Phoebe's trust. Shae might be able to gain insight beyond what Phoebe recalled while under hypnosis. "Virginia has changed since the seventeenth century. There are over seven million people in the state."

"State?"

"Colony. Phoebe, you're in the twenty-first century."

"The twenty-first..." Phoebe placed a hand to her chest. "If you speak the truth, wouldn't I have passed on?"

Shae stopped at a red traffic light. "The fact that you're here says you're very much alive. Your memory is playing tricks to safeguard the traumatic experience you've been through. When we uncover what really happened, I'm certain the rest of your memory will return. But it's all going to take time, so I'm hoping you'll allow me to continue your sessions now that you've been released from the hospital."

"If it will give you the answers you need, I shall continue. I'm curious to discover how I came to be in the twenty-first century."

You and me both. The light changed to green, and Shae started driving again. "Then you believe me?"

"How else can I explain all of the people, cars, and . . ."

They passed a towering building, and Phoebe gaped.

"It's a multi-storied building called a high rise," Shae said.

Instead of fear, Phoebe exhibited curiosity and fascination. Once in the residential area, Shae halted the car in front of a square, red-brick building from the turn-of-the-twentieth century. The sidewalk was also brick, and the steps leading to the two-story house had black wrought-iron rails. Identical houses adjoined the structure along the block.

"This is your new home." Shae led the way up the steps. Inside, the entryway had a finely polished oak floor and a stairway with a wooden rail leading to the second floor. The wallpaper was a pastel peach stripe.

A woman in her mid thirties with a bob hairstyle greeted them. "Welcome to Colwell House, Phoebe. Shae has told me about you. I'm Valerie Evans." Valerie stuck out her right hand.

Phoebe stared at Valerie in uncertainty.

Valerie grasped Phoebe's hand and shook it. "Colwell House is named after our founder, Rebecca Colwell. After being on the streets and homeless for two years, Rebecca was able to get a decent paying job and return to society . . . ."

Shae tuned out the welcome speech. Suspecting there were many scenarios that she hadn't considered, she hoped Phoebe would be able to adapt in this environment. Valerie was one of the best social workers. Phoebe couldn't be in better hands during this delicate emotional stage.

Valerie started the tour of the house and led them into the parlor. A velvet sofa sat near a shuttered bay window. Lamps with fringes and high-backed chairs completed the small but homey room.

"The women often meet here in the evenings," Valerie explained. "There's a modern kitchen in the back of the house. Over here is the dining room."

They stepped into the adjacent room. An African-American woman most likely in her late teens had a two-year-old girl clinging to her arm. "I'm Meg." She offered a welcoming smile, and continued setting plates on a white linen tablecloth with embroidered edges.

"Phoebe's going to be taking Kayla's room," Valerie said. After Meg and Phoebe greeted each other, Valerie returned her attention to Phoebe. "All of the women get to know each other very well here. Our goal is to get the women on their feet and successfully into society within two years. Let me show you to your room."

Valerie led the way up the stairs to the second floor. The room at the end of the hall was sparsely furnished. It had a brass bed with a fireplace, desk, chair, and a couple of lamps.

Phoebe tested the mattress. "It feels softer than straw. Where do you tighten the ropes?"

Valerie exchanged a glance with Shae. "I'm not sure I understand."

"Beds in the twenty-first century don't need to be tightened," Shae said. She had briefed Valerie on Phoebe's case before bringing her to Colwell House, so Valerie nodded in understanding.

Phoebe glanced around the room. "Where shall I find the piss-pot?"

Shae sighed. Her work was cut out for her.

6

Phoebe

M Y MIND WAS A WHIRL. How could I possibly be in the twenty-first century? Yet I couldn't deny what I had experienced. Carriages propelled without horses, tall buildings reached to the heavens, and there were mobs of Englishmen with peculiar accents. Where were the Paspahegh? Only Master Crowley resembled them, but he did not seem to comprehend the Algonquian tongue. Mayhap, he was Monacan and spoke Siouan instead. Still, he was attired like many other men I had seen upon my arrival and spoke fluent English.

Even the language differed vastly. 'Twas English, I had no doubt, but sometimes I had difficulty understanding the words, and Shae hadn't been the first to grimace when I inquired about the pisspot. Was it my question that bothered them, or the manner in which I asked? 'Twasn't the first time I had been immersed in a strange culture. I would shoulder my burden bravely as Momma had upon meeting the Paspahegh warriors.

On the eve of my arrival at Colwell House, Valerie gave me a list of rules for conduct. Though Momma had taught me to read simple sentences, the manner of script was squatter than what I was accustomed to. "I cannot read this," I admitted.

With a pinched smile, Valerie motioned for me to have a seat at the table.

I did as she instructed.

"I'm the housing coordinator. Meg is the resident manager. I interpret all of the house rules. If there's any conflict, feel free to talk to Meg, but ultimately, the decisions rest with me. We expect to maintain a community atmosphere here. You will be on a thirty-day probationary period."

"Have I unknowingly violated your rules?"

"No," Valerie explained. "All residents are given a probationary period to see if they can follow protocol. There will be no overnights during this period and curfew will be at ten each evening. You look puzzled."

"Where would I go for an overnight?"

"Some of the women have boyfriends, which leads me to another rule. All male guests remain in the entryway or living room and nowhere else in the house. You must announce to the rest of the house when you have a male visitor, and he must not stay any longer than thirty minutes. Visiting hours are from 9:00 a.m. to 8:00 p.m...."

My mind blurred as she cited the rules, half of which I did not comprehend.

"I need you to sign at the bottom." She thrust a writing device into my hand.

I stared at the cylinder-shaped instrument that looked naught like a quill. "I do not know how to write."

"Phoebe, have you had any formal education?"

"My momma taught me to read."

"Then you were home schooled?"

"Aye, and I count my blessings that Momma could read as well as she did. Most lasses weren't taught at all."

Valerie muttered under her breath. "This is going to be more complex than any of us thought."

"I am a hard worker," I proclaimed on my behalf.

"I have no doubt." She patted my hand in reassurance. "We give everyone a fair chance at Colwell House, and the first thing we're going to do is assign you a tutor. We'll have you reading and writing in no time."

I had never dreamt of anything so grand. I used to pick up Poppa's prized books, inhaling the leather and opening the covers, all the while wishing I could decipher more than a few sentences here and there on the pages. I looked forward to discovering the secrets of this new world and sharing my memories while under *hypnosis* in order to learn how I had come to be here.

Aft Momma's and my adoption by the Paspahegh, the warrior Silver Eagle, who had rescued us from James Towne, shared his hearth with us. Momma remained melancholy for she still believed that half-clad, body-painting Indians must be godless savages. In the night, she clutched me to her bosom and sang me a lullaby, as if to reaffirm the reality of the world we had left behind. Too young to understand her fear, I grew to accept these people as my own and quickly learned their Algonquian tongue.

Silver Eagle was more of a gentleman than those in James Towne who professed to be such. He had lost his wife the previous year in childbirth, and whilst warriors oft masked their feelings, he doted on me as if I were the daughter he had lost. He called me Red Dog because of my fondness for one of the town's hounds. The dog preferred to trail aft me instead of being with its pack.

The Paspahegh loved children. Unlike the English, they had no apprenticeships, nor did they administer harsh punishments. A child learned by example. In spite of the tribe's acceptance of us, Momma resisted casting off her English name, Elenor, and continued calling me Phoebe.

The women taught us how to weave mats and baskets, gather food and firewood, and grind tuckahoe for bread. Back in Dorset, Momma had practiced the way of family physick by gathering herbs and treating neighbors' ailments. Amongst the Paspahegh, a young woman by the name of Snow Bird showed Momma the native plants, and Momma's knowledge expanded.

Like Momma, Snow Bird was a gifted healer. She carried her son in a cradleboard upon her back. I oft watched aft him as he toddled round us, examining everything with inquisitive eyes. I felt much the same and delighted in making our discoveries together. For Momma, 'twas endless work during much of the daylight hours, but she ne'er expressed discontent with our plight. We had food to eat and were no longer starving.

In the eves, the people of the town oft gathered for dancing and singing. Near the entrance to our house, Silver Eagle played a flute with a hand-carved bird's head. Momma clutched my hand and whisked me past him to our pallet.

"Why do you fear Silver Eagle?" I asked her.

"There are things you cannot yet understand."

"He plays the flute for your ears, Momma. He grieves for those he has lost and wants to be made whole again."

Momma bent down, kissing and hugging me. "For a child so young... Phoebe, ne'er forget how much I love you. 'Tis not because he is a savage."

I stamped a foot in protest. "Do not call him that!"

"I beg forgiveness, my daughter. I am trying to protect you."

"Me?"

Hearing our disagreement, Silver Eagle entered the house with the flute still in his hand. His English was equal to Momma's Algonquian, but he had obviously detected something amiss in our tones. "I would not hurt you. Either of you," he said, glancing from me to Momma.

"Phoebe, what did he say?"

Though I was not yet a fluent speaker, I translated as best as I could.

Momma closed her eyes and attempted to hide her tears. "Do you not understand? I would shame you amongst your own people." She lifted my left hand to reveal my conjoined fingers. "I have borne a daughter who bears the witch's mark."

Silver Eagle towered over Momma and me, creating an imposing, frightful figure.

Careful to keep my malformed fingers from plain view, I withdrew my hand from Momma's grasp and hid it behind my back.

Silver Eagle bent upon his knees, and I could not meet his piercing gaze.

"Red Dog," he said, "allow me to see your hand."

Still not realizing that he would ne'er strike me, I held my hand to him out of fear.

He gently touched the webbed flesh betwixt my fingers, and a smile slowly spread across his face. " 'Tis a blessing from Ahone."

"Ahone?" I asked.

"The Creator. You alone must discover the meaning of your gift."

Gift? No one had ever referred to my deformity as anything but a curse of the devil. I spread my fingers, studying my gift, afore planting a kiss on Silver Eagle's cheek. He smiled and embraced me.

No longer afraid, Momma joined us. Soon afterwards, she took the name Mother of the Red-Haired Lass.

7

Shae

AFTER HER LATEST SESSION with Phoebe, Shae watched Russ with interest as he read over the mystifying woman's file. His brow wrinkled in a pensive way that it often did when he was concentrating on something. She kissed him on the cheek and quietly sat on the sofa. Unable to get comfortable, she fidgeted. "Russ?"

He held up a hand for her to be patient.

She sat back, watching him intently. *Was that a gray hair in his beard?* She smiled to herself. A touch of gray added character. She looked forward to discussing their respective days over a glass of burgundy and Russ's specially prepared fondue beef. She'd worry about the calories when she stepped on the scales in the morning.

Russ frowned, and she leaned forward, hoping he'd finally say something. "Well?"

"In a moment." Finally, he looked up. "I believe your diagnosis is correct."

"So what do I do about it? She'll talk about how she's getting along at Colwell House, but otherwise, she only responds to hypnosis."

"Dissociative cases can be very difficult. Have you tried getting her to recite her phone number or street address while in a hypnotic state?"

"I have," Shae replied. "No response. Everything takes place in the seventeenth century."

Russ checked the file once more. "You may need to think outside the box. Call Lee."

"Lee's done everything the police can. Her picture is plastered all over their databases. He's checked the missing persons and unidentified files. Nothing. No one seems to know Phoebe Wynne or care that she's missing."

"I didn't mean on a professional level."

She studied his face to see if he was serious. There were no signs that he was joking. She gave a sarcastic laugh. "Great idea. If I know Lee, he'll want to do more than chat."

"You've got a very troubled patient who's no doubt been assaulted in her recent past. Lee sees worse things on the street. Your patient has exhibited comfort in his presence. According to this . . . ," he said with a motion to the file, " . . . she asks about him. I think he can behave sympathetically to her situation to help you learn who she is and where she's from. Not only that, he's got the investigative training to spot things others might miss." He handed her Phoebe's file.

She squirmed with indecision. "I can't."

"She's your patient," he agreed.

"She is, and I think it would be a mistake involving Lee."

"Just be honest with yourself as to why you don't want to call him. Would you say the same if he wasn't your ex?"

Probably not, but she couldn't admit as much to Russ.

"What are you really afraid of, Shae?"

"Stop playing psychologist!"

He laughed. "I've obviously struck a nerve."

To prove him wrong, she picked up the phone and started dialing. "So help me, if I have to read him the riot act . . ."

No longer laughing, Russ said, "He might be able to break through to your patient."

Russ was right. She wouldn't have hesitated asking for anyone else's help. Lee came on the line, and she swallowed. "It's my turn to ask a favor." When she explained Phoebe's requests to see him, he readily agreed. She had another session with Phoebe later in the week and asked that he see her soon after. If she made progress in the following session, she could call him again and let him know the whole arrangement was off.

8

Phoebe

A FT MOMMA CAST OFF her English name, she continued her study of the native herbs and their healing values. Snow Bird guided her and, in turn, questioned me to see how much I had absorbed. "If you are to be a healer," she said, "one day soon, you will be tested."

At the time, I did not fully understand her words. To hide my fear, I went over to where Snow Bird's son, Crow in the Woods, played in the sand and sat aside him. Though my Algonquian had surpassed his two-word sentences, he could already imitate many bird calls, as well as sounds of barking dogs and animals in the forest that I knew not what they were. As soon as he was capable, his mother would give him a child-sized bow for him to contribute small game for the cook pot.

I watched Crow in the Woods scribble lines in the sand with his fingers and overheard Momma's laughter. She was coming to know the Paspahegh and regard them as friends. When Snow Bird mentioned Silver Eagle, Momma's face reddened. Not only did he play the flute for her ears, he brought her fowl and fish for the cook fire. Of late, I had noticed her exchanging glances with him.

The women gathered their herbs and placed them in deer-hide satchels afore returning to town. I agreed to watch Crow in the Woods for Snow Bird whilst she checked on the whereabouts of her husband. When I returned to our house, Momma sat cross legged afore the fire with an empty expression upon her countenance.

In Dorset, she had used a candle to focus on the flame for her travels that she referred to as the dreaming. 'Twas the first time I had witnessed her enter the realm since arriving in Virginia. I waited quietly 'til she blinked with recognition. She smiled upon seeing me. "I confessed to Snow Bird about the dreaming. She says some of the Paspahegh have visions too. I no longer fear I will be accused of witchcraft."

"What did you see?" I asked.

"That I shall marry Silver Eagle. 'Tis right, my daughter, for you need a loving father."

Momma hadn't spoken of Poppa since leaving the colony. With a shiver, I sought to blot out the memory of him.

9

Lee

TWO DAYS LATER, OUTSIDE Colwell House, Lee parked along the
street. Although uncertain whether Shae's request for him to
see Phoebe was truly wise, he strode along the brick walk. He'd
seen so many people not playing with a full deck, he could write a
book. So had Shae, but her job was to placate them, while his was to
haul their asses off the street. He knocked on the door, and a teen-
aged black woman with a young child gripping her leg answered.
"You must be Detective Crowley."

"I'm off duty now. Call me Lee."

She opened the door for him to enter. "Meg. Please come in,
Lee. I'll get Valerie."

She showed him to the parlor and motioned for him to have a
seat. He made himself comfortable in a high-backed chair. Of all of
the transitional and halfway housing in the area, Colwell was definitely one of the best. It tended to have the highest success rate as
well. The women who made it to Colwell were the lucky ones. Shae
must have called in some powerful favors to get Phoebe in. Usually,
the wait list was a year or two long. Too many times he had been
called in to investigate murders by abusive husbands or boyfriends
due to housing shortages.

When a petite, brown-haired woman entered the room, Lee
stood. She introduced herself as Valerie and gave her report. "I've
already told Shae I'm not certain this is going to work. Phoebe really thinks she's from the seventeenth century. At first, I thought,

'How harmless can that be?' The other women are also supportive, but this afternoon, she tried to help cook lunch."

"Isn't that a good thing?"

"Normally, yes, but she started a fire in the fireplace instead of using the stove."

At least Phoebe was original. Lee struggled not to laugh. "Was there a fire anywhere else?"

"No, but—"

"Then I don't see the problem. If she wants to do hearth cooking, what's the harm?"

The stress lines on Valerie's forehead faded. "She made something called pottage. It was a thick soup with peas, eggs, and spices. It didn't taste half bad."

"You see, she's expanding everyone's horizon. Bear with her and show her how things are done. I'm certain she'll eventually reveal something of her past."

"I hope so."

"Meanwhile, I'll take her off your hands for a few hours."

"I think it'll be good for her. Except for the sessions she's had with Shae, she doesn't know what to do with herself. Besides the women she's met here, she doesn't know anyone. She seems to be a stranger in a strange world. I'll go get her."

"Thanks." Lee reseated himself. If only the background checks for Phoebe Wynne had returned with some clues as to where she had come from or who she really was. *Stop thinking like I'm on duty.* He was a visitor to Colwell House on personal time. Dinner and a movie with Phoebe might turn up something to help Shae. Where did he take a woman who thought she was from the seventeenth century? A pub or somewhere more exotic?

Wearing a black, knee-length dress, Phoebe entered the parlor. "Master Crowley."

Definitely someplace more exotic. Lee stood. He was almost a foot taller than Phoebe, and her red hair seemed to shimmer against the modest black dress that flattered her curves. "Please, call me, Lee."

"Lee," she responded softly. "Shae warned me that you might *split a gut* if I failed to use your Christian name, but I have difficulty recalling your customs. They are informal to the English, but very different from the Paspahegh."

The Paspahegh. Right. Still debating whether she was one hell of an actress, or if she truly believed her words, he held out his arm. "Let's talk about the differences over dinner."

She grasped his arm, and he escorted her to his 2003 Thunderbird. He opened the car door for Phoebe and adjusted the seatbelt for her. She nodded that she understood.

Once they were on the drive to the restaurant, she asked, "What tribe do you hail from?"

He raised an eyebrow. The usual ice-breaking question tended to be about his profession. "I'm not certain. I was adopted by a white couple in their late forties who had finally given up hope of ever having kids of their own."

"Your parents cleansed you of your heritage?"

"Not exactly. It's a long story." As a detective, he had the knowledge and means to dig past the red tape to help identify his birth parents, but he often thought his adoption had been on the shadier side, especially since he had been born a few years before the laws protecting Native American children had gone into effect. If that were the case, nothing would be gained by bringing shame to his parents. "My parents went to great pains for me to read about my heritage. The books were nothing more than words and didn't make much sense. Then, when we went to family reunions, I always stuck out like a sore thumb in the family photos. All of the kids called me 'Injun' or 'redskin.' "

"Then you are much like I am. I, at least, have an inkling from where I hail."

"I hadn't thought of it that way, but you could be right." How had Phoebe turned the tables on him? Wasn't *he* supposed to be the one asking the questions? Lee pulled the T-Bird around the back of an Italian restaurant. Curious as to what Phoebe's reaction would be in the new environment, he showed her the way inside. A waiter seated them at an isolated booth in the corner.

He picked up his menu and glanced at it.

She copied him. "Lee, I cannot read this transcript. What is it for?"

Although unconvinced she was illiterate, he explained, "It's a menu. It tells what food the restaurant serves."

A smile of comprehension crossed her face. "In the ordinary, the innkeeper recites the menu."

Maybe he should have taken her to the pub. "Let's start with what sort of food you like—beef, chicken, fish—"

"I like fish."

"Salmon with white wine sauce, it is," he said, taking charge, "and I'll have the lasagna. There, now that's settled, would you like me to order wine to go with the meal?"

"Aye."

The waiter returned, and Lee ordered. While they waited for their food, conversation turned to an uncomfortable silence. Normally, he wasn't tongue tied when having dinner with a beautiful woman, but what did one say to someone who thought she was from the seventeenth century? Questions about John Smith or Pocahontas would come across as condescending, but if there was a chance that he could break her theatrics . . . .

Phoebe saved him the bother. "I'm certain Shae has discussed the results of my sessions with you."

"Actually, she hasn't. That would be against doctor/patient confidentiality. Except for the initial investigation where I was present, I know little else. She merely thought if I got you away from Colwell House for a few hours that it might trigger your memory beyond your sessions with her."

"You remind me of those I once knew."

The Paspahegh. Had he pretended to be white for so long that sometimes he actually believed it?

"I fear I've said something that ails you," Phoebe said.

With a shrug, he took a sip of water. "It's not important."

She gave him a knowing smile, which unsettled him more than it should have. It was almost as if she could instantly read him. Even Shae had only the most basic ability. How could someone he had barely met understand where his head was at?

The waiter returned, and Lee, relieved, focused on their meal.

Over dinner, Phoebe filled in the details of her sessions with Shae. Nothing in her mannerisms indicated that she was lying. Still not totally convinced by her performance, he uncovered no clues to her true identity or who had whipped her. She might be protecting a jealous spouse or boyfriend. He'd certainly seen it often enough. In that case, the jilted significant other would likely rear his ugly head again. He needed to make Shae aware of the potential danger.

During the meal, Lee noted that Phoebe gripped a fork like a toddler, and when she asked for a taste of his lasagna, she chose to use a spoon. Although she was left handed, the webbing between her fingers didn't appear to be the reason for her awkwardness. She managed her spoon with the usual dexterity. Whereas with the fork, she seemed to lack skill.

She reached for another bite of his lasagna. "Do you have more than one wife?"

"Excuse me?" he asked, wondering if he had heard correctly.

"Shae said you are a good *cop*. She informed me that your duties are similar to a sheriff. I presume that makes you a good provider. Such Paspahegh men oft have more than one wife."

"How do the men keep the women from bickering?" he asked, without thinking.

"Separate houses."

He laughed at Phoebe's seriousness. She came across like a walking history book. Her story was outlandish enough that she might believe she was telling the truth. Instead of a costumed historical interpreter, she could be a history professor specializing in seventeenth-century Virginia.

She helped herself to more lasagna. "You aren't married?"

He shoved the plate across the table. "Take as much as you like. No, I'm not married."

Using the spoon, she scooped another portion to her mouth. "I have ne'er tasted anything like this afore. Then your wife died?"

The waiter returned, and they declined dessert. Phoebe was enjoying the leftover lasagna too much for anything sweet. When the waiter left the table, Lee responded, "I thought you knew. Shae and I are divorced—since about seven years ago."

Her brow furrowed. "Divorce is allowed?"

Okay, play along for now. "Virginia is no longer part of England, and let's just say the laws have become a little more relaxed since the seventeenth century."

A growing smile appeared on her face. "English women are allowed freedom. I think I shall like your century."

The waiter brought the check in a padded holder. Lee tucked several bills inside. Phoebe gave him another questioning look, and he explained, "I need to pay the bill. Certainly people of the seventeenth century used currency?"

She picked up a twenty-dollar bill and inspected it. "We paid our bills by barter or with tobacco."

"Tobacco?"

"The *kwiokosuk* grew and used it for ceremonial purposes. The English sought it for profit. It became the currency in the colony."

"Who are the *kwiokosuk?*"

"The priests."

Interesting. She seemed to know more about the Natives than he had read on the subject. Lee checked his watch. They had spent nearly three hours in the restaurant with Phoebe relaying her life in the seventeenth century. There wouldn't be time for a movie after all. He got to his feet and held out his arm. "Ma'am." She laced her arm through his, and by the time they reached the steps of Colwell House, Lee debated whether to give her a goodnight kiss. "I enjoyed the evening," he said.

"As did I."

Definitely intrigued by the woman who claimed to be from the seventeenth century, he said, "I have Sunday off. If you'd like, I can show you some of the sites."

"Thank you, aye."

Lee decided to forgo the kiss. Phoebe Wynne, if that was truly her name, had enough emotional baggage in her life right now without him adding extra stress. He bid her goodnight and left it at that. The first thing he intended on doing was checking the accuracy of her history.

10

Phoebe

IN JUNE, MOMMA MARRIED SILVER EAGLE. Well known throughout the Paspahegh as a brave warrior, he showed us that he was a worthy provider. Upon his return from hunting trips, I squealed with delight and greeted him like other daughters.

On one homecoming, he cradled a bloody beast in his arms. Afore reaching him, I halted. If I went no closer, I did not need to see what he held. *"Nows,"* I said. Father.

"Come quickly."

With reluctance, I did as he asked. My hound had deep gashes upon his shoulders and a flap of skin hanging from his back.

"A bear," Silver Eagle explained. "I shall relieve him from his misery."

"Nay! You mustn't. I can save him."

"You will only prolong his suffering." But Silver Eagle relinquished the dog to my arms.

The beast gave a pitiful howl from the jostling.

"Thank you, *Nows.*"

Silver Eagle said naught as I carried my beloved hound to our house. Outside, Momma waited beside a boiling pot, hoping to have fresh meat to add for our meals.

Near the fire inside, I laid the dog upon a woven mat. Due to my youth, my knowledge of physick was limited. "Momma, please show me how to heal my hound."

With a frown, she bent beside the forlorn beast and washed the blood from his wounds. I followed her example. Taking deer sinew for thread and a bone needle, she showed me how to stitch the gashes, whilst she sewed the flap of skin into place. The hound moaned.

Day and night, I tended him. I cupped my hands for him to drink, and I fed him a little meat from my stew. Silver Eagle watched over my shoulder but ne'er said a word. I was too young to understand that I would learn a valuable lesson about life and death, regardless of the outcome.

To my delight, the hound refused to die. When I passed my hand over his coat, he feebly wagged his tail. As I did so, his vigor strengthened. Little by little, he mended, and afore long, he traveled by my side once more.

With a smile, Snow Bird nodded. "You have touched the animal's spirit."

The test, and I had passed. Together, she and Momma taught me in the ways of *wisakon.* The art of healing.

11

Shae

AFTER FIVE SESSIONS, Shae was no closer to discovering who Phoebe was or where she had come from. Sitting across from Phoebe, she jotted down a few notes. "At this point in time, I can't say where your 'memories' are coming from. When we get close to the answer, I think we'll both know. Now, how have you been adapting to Colwell House?"

"They treat me well, and I am learning much about your century."

Phoebe's progress report had matched Valerie's. The outlook was promising, and Shae was hopeful Phoebe would work through to the source of her problems. "Valerie told me that you had a visitor the other night."

"Lee took me to the ordinary for a meal. I tasted something called laz . . ." Phoebe's brow furrowed. "Lazan . . ."

"Lasagna?"

"Aye. He said the two of you used to be married."

The last thing Shae wanted to do was dredge up the past with a patient. She *had* loved him. "That was a long time ago. We were high school sweethearts."

"High school?"

"Secondary eduction." The frown on Phoebe's face warned Shae that she remained puzzled. "We were fifteen when we first dated but waited until after college to marry. We're better friends apart than we were together."

"I think I understand."

Shae believed that Phoebe did understand. "I'll see you on Monday. Be sure and give me a call if you have any difficulties over the weekend."

"I shall," Phoebe replied with a growing smile. "Valerie says she will teach me how to use the phone soon. I'm fascinated that a person can talk to another over a distance from a little box."

Pleased to see Phoebe's enthusiasm, Shae escorted her to the outer office, where Valerie waited.

While Phoebe was a willing and compliant patient, it might take months or years before they finally uncovered what had happened to her.

12

Phoebe

DURING THE SPRING, a new governor, Lord De La Warr, had arrived in James Towne. He threatened paramount chief Powhatan to return all English captives. Believed dead, Momma and I were not amongst those thought to be prisoners. In reality, few were held against their will. Like us, others left destitute in the colony had sought refuge with the Indians. The paramount chief ignored Lord De La Warr's demands, which would set forth the governor to campaign against the Indians as he had previously done with the Irish.

Afore the harvest, Momma and I bade Silver Eagle, along with several other warriors, goodbye as they departed on a hunting trip. Two days later, the sound of a drum woke me at sunrise. The beat signaled hospitality. Momma was already at the door, peering out, when I joined her. Like us, curious neighbors sought to identify the drummer. Lulled into the gesture of good fellowship, some elder warriors and women moved towards the drummer and the men standing in a line next to him.

Upon the realization they were English, I felt my heart race. "Momma, have they come to take us back to the colony?"

Momma hushed me in a frightened whisper. "This has naught to do with us."

I immediately gripped her deerskin skirt and watched the greeters come within a few yards.

"Ready! Aim!" Muskets raised. "Fire!"

All at once, they fired, and men, women, and children fell. Panicked screams surrounded us. Amongst piercing shrieks, Momma seized my hand.

The musketeers shot another volley afore the surviving aged warriors had recovered from the deception and sent off a flurry of arrows. Like Momma and me, other women and children took flight. Behind us came the sounds of clubs striking metal and screams of pain and rage.

Armored soldiers appeared from every direction with swords and torches. Longhouses were afire. The stench of smoke assaulted my nostrils 'til nearly smothering me. Momma half dragged me in her haste to escape. In front of us loomed a soldier, waving his sword. An elder with a tomahawk charged at him. In one quick motion, the steel cleanly sliced off the warrior's hand.

Momma screamed and unintentionally released my hand. On my hands and knees, I scrambled for safety. I was alone now. Aside me, smoke billowed and flames licked. Houses everywhere were ablaze. Nearly succumbing to the heat, I crept along the ground. I cried for Momma and covered my ears in an effort to silence the dying wails. Tears streaked my cheek. With the wind fanning the flames, I coughed and sputtered. I could move no further. My head swirled from the smoke filling my lungs when a wet tongue licked my face. Grateful to see my hound, I wrapped my arms about his neck, and he led me through the blinding smoke.

The smoke drifted, and I spied a young lad. Having lost his Momma, he crawled along the ground, not knowing where to go for safety. I bundled him against me and held him 'til his cries quieted, hoping the soldiers would not find us again.

Far into the day, I watched the embers and smoke dance upwards into the sky. Whilst the screams and shooting muskets and pistols sounded less and less often, I heard throaty sobs and anguished moans. The lad stirred, and I wiped the grimy soot from his face. Only then, did I recognize that he was Crow in the Woods. The duty to keep him safe had fallen upon my shoulders.

He babbled about his hunger. I rocked him, trying to comfort him, all the time praying that Momma or Snow Bird would find us. Near sunset, the crying and painful groans continued to surround me. Upon nightfall, I huddled with Crow in the Woods in my arms next to the hound for warmth. I could no longer keep slumber at bay.

When I awoke, Crow in the Woods had wandered off. I heard his muffled cries in the darkness and attempted to follow him. "I'm coming, lad." In the soft moonlight, branches and brambles scratched my arms and legs. Ignoring the pain of my cuts, I pressed onwards. "Where are you, Crow in the Woods?"

I stumbled through the darkness 'til totally engulfed by mist. Like a beacon, the long-legged white dog that I had spied moons ago stood on the path ahead. My hound made no sound of alert. He failed to even bristle from the other dog's presence. Naught more than a blurry shape, the dog sauntered off. I followed him, but the mist got thicker. The lad's cries came from within.

"Crow in the Woods!"

Staggering through the mist, I could not locate the lad. His whimpers came from everywhere and nowhere at the same time. I had no guidance. I stretched my arms afore me and fumbled my way around, making every attempt to find him. Suddenly, as if stepping through a door, the mist vanished, and along with it, Crow in the Woods's cries. He was gone.

"Phoebe!"

"Momma?"

"Phoebe." Upon reaching me, she swept me into her arms. "I thought I had lost you."

"Crow in the Woods, Momma. He's over here." I tugged on her hand. We searched and searched for the lad in vain.

Amongst the deaths, the *weroance*'s wife had been brutally murdered, and her children, slain. The Paspahegh were shocked the English would seek bloodthirsty vengeance against innocent victims in such a cowardly manner whilst the majority of the warriors were off hunting. Momma and I feared the tribe would cast blame on us for having hailed from Dorset. We needn't have worried. Our adoption had been complete. They accepted us as Paspahegh.

Upon the warriors' return, they sought to avenge the deaths. In spite of their heroic measures, the Paspahegh tribe and town vanished to the circle of time. Silver Eagle had become much like us— an immigrant to another tribe.

* * *

At Colwell House, I numbly went about my daily chores and sat
quietly through supper, whilst the other women chatted. My session
with Shae had revealed the death of the Paspahegh. Ne'er afore had
I a bed chamber to myself. Ne'er afore had I been more relieved as I
shed my tears in solitude. Snow Bird and Crow in the Woods were
dead.

"Phoebe?" came Valerie's voice from behind the closed door.
"Are you all right?"

I dried my tears afore opening the door.

"What's wrong?"

"All of the Paspahegh are gone."

"The tribe that you said adopted you?"

I barely could move my head, but I managed a nod.

"Phoebe, that was four hundred years ago. Come." She took my
arm and led me to the stairs.

Four hundred years? My mind still had difficulty grasping how
much time had passed. Even more so when only a short time seemed
to have passed since I had held Crow in the Woods in my arms.
" 'Twas my fault that he died. My momma found me, but I lost
Crow in the Woods."

Valerie repeated that everything had happened long ago. We entered the kitchen where Meg's daughter, Tiffany, sat at the table
coloring, whilst Meg prepared tea. I checked the knobs to see if the
coil was "on," as I had learnt by burning my finger. It needn't be a
brilliant orange to boil water.

"It'll be ready in a few minutes," Meg said.

Tiffany was around the same age as Crow in the Woods. I swallowed uneasily at the realization.

Again, Valerie led me to the dining room. "I picked up some
books at the library today."

A former Colwell House resident, Mrs. Sedgwick, tutored me
in reading, writing, and mathematics, but Valerie supplemented my
education with what she called "day-to-day living." And I could
ne'er resist looking at books.

She opened one and said, "I want you to tell me what the animals are."

Her instructions sounded simple enough. She showed me a picture of a wolf.

"Wolf," I responded.

"Good." Then she pointed to a picture of a bear, deer, bobcat, cardinal, and heron. On and on . . . 'til a page contained a long-necked, spotted beast, and the next, a striped horse.

Grasping the book, I remarked that I had ne'er seen such incredible creatures. "Surely, they are imaginary."

"The giraffe and zebra are from Africa."

"Aye, and sailors oft spread tales to drive fear in many a child's heart."

"They're real, Phoebe. We'll take you to the zoo when it gets a little warmer to show you. Here, let's look at these."

Oak, poplar, bloodroot, and coneflowers—I knew them all. On a few, I could only recall the Algonquian names, but I convinced Valerie I was familiar with them when I explained their medicinal uses. Then, as with the beasts, she showed me plants I could ne'er have envisioned. One looked like a green tree with huge arms covered in sharp needles.

"This is a saguaro cactus."

Another had sword-shaped leaves with a towering stalk of yellow flowers.

"This is a century plant."

I could only imagine what their medicinal uses might be. "Where do such magnificent plants grow?"

"In the Southwest." Valerie showed me a map. "Here's Virginia. New Mexico and Arizona."

I pored over the map.

Meg joined us with a platter of cups and a teapot. She poured some tea, setting a steaming mug in front of me. "I see that Phoebe has her nose in a book."

Valerie had purposely distracted me, and I was thankful. With each passing day, my fondness for her and Meg grew. To my knowledge, I had seen but a few Africans. I was even more surprised that

Meg had not traveled the ocean, but originally hailed from Virginia. She was studying to be a nurse, and I had instantly liked her.

"Where's Carol?" Meg asked.

Valerie's brow furrowed. "Out, where else?"

"I believe she's ill at ease by my presence," I said.

Meg giggled. "She's with *Kevin.*"

"Meg," Valerie said in a firm tone. "We only speak kindly about the other women."

Meg quickly apologized, but I was already aware of Valerie's consternation. Carol used all of her overnight privileges to accompany her sweetheart.

"Phoebe," Valerie said, changing the subject, "I promised to teach you how to use the phone. Who would you like to call?"

"Lee. I would like to thank him for taking me to the ordinary."

"Lee it is." Valerie went into the entrance hall, where the phone sat atop a round table. "All calls are limited to fifteen minutes. No long distance calls, and no incoming calls before 7 a.m. or after 9:30 p.m. You can make outgoing calls until ten."

Precise hours by the clock confused me. "I shall only make calls with guidance 'til I learn how to tell time better."

Valerie chuckled. "You'll be fine, but I have to inform everyone of the rules." She opened the phone book. "You search for a person's number by looking up their last name first." She flipped the pages. "It's alphabetical. A, B, C . . . ."

I followed her finger as she went down the page.

"C, r . . . Crowley. Now, first name. Can you find Lee? Again, they're alphabetical."

I traced a finger through the lines, sounding out the names as I went. "Carl, Dale, David, James, Lester, M.L. There is no Lee."

"I should have guessed that he'd have an unlisted number. It was a good exercise for you anyway."

"What is an unlisted number?" I inquired.

"His phone number isn't in the book."

"I cannot call him?"

"Normally if a person has an unlisted number that would be correct, but I have his cell number." She added a number on the cover at the back of the book and handed me the phone. "Okay, call him."

Uncertain what I must do, I put the phone to my ear as I had seen others. "Hello?"

"No, Phoebe. First, you need to dial the number. See the numbers on the keypad? Touch each one in the order I've written them down."

Carefully, I checked each number and did as Valerie directed. She put the phone to my ear. " 'Tis making an odd sound."

"That means it's ringing."

"Ringing?"

"Crowley."

Lee's voice took me by surprise, and I nearly dropped the phone. 'Twas almost like he was in the same room aside me. "Lee?"

"Phoebe?"

"Valerie has shown me how to use the phone. I wanted to thank you for taking me to the ordinary."

"You're welcome. I'm looking forward to seeing you on Sunday."

"As am I." As we talked, I sensed a connection. I had from the beginning. I knew not the source, nor whether he experienced it too. I only knew my spirit would not be complete 'til I understood why.

Aft the attack on the Paspahegh town, Momma and I sought refuge near the falls with the Arrohateck tribe. The following winter, the *weroance* Wowinchapuncke was slain. Silver Eagle remained with the warriors in an assault on James Towne. From the cover of the forest, the warriors taunted the lieutenant in the blockhouse. Accepting the challenge, the lieutenant charged with his full force. The warriors released their arrows afore the soldiers were able to fire their muskets. The slain English lay upon the ground, taking on the appearance of pincushions.

Warriors frequently told of their battle tales around the fire in the eves. Whilst Momma listened with interest, her pinched face showed discomfort upon hearing the deaths of kinsmen. But what could we, a mere woman and her daughter, do to change the ways of men? 'Twas in their nature to wage war or make peace, leaving the women to grieve their deaths or suffer at the hands of the enemy.

In spite of constant warring betwixt the Indians and English, we rejoiced during the season of the earing of the corn. Momma gave birth to my brother, Sly Fox. The Arrohateck provided no wet-nurses, 'less a woman's milk failed or a child's mother had died. As with so many customs of our birth country, Momma threw her preconceptions aside and nursed my brother herself.

Life with the Arrohateck was akin to living with the Paspahegh. Here, I met Sparrow Hawk. His hair was as yellow as Momma's and his skin nearly as pale as mine. Unlike Momma and me, he did not hail from James Towne, and he knew not a word of English. His mother was Arrohateck, and only whispers were spoken of his father. At the time, I was too young to understand that his mother had been raped by a European on a voyage previous to settlement. I knew not whether the perpetrator be English or Spanish, as the Arrohateck described him as *tassantassas*. Stranger.

From the beginning, Sparrow Hawk took a fancy to me. I presumed the reason being that my pale skin looked akin to his. With the way he stared at me, I realized that 'til Momma's and my arrival, he hadn't seen any other Europeans up close. With a childish infatuation, I returned his attention by attempting to be near him whenever possible and dreaming of the day we would marry. Soon, he would undergo the *huskanaw,* the rigorous rite of passage to becoming a warrior, and I feared my dream would shatter. A warrior would no longer show interest in a mere lass, and his eyes and thoughts would turn to women instead.

Like most lasses who had not reached their moon times, I had cast my garments aside and ran about naked. Though more sensitive to the extremities of cold and heat than the Arrohateck, I adapted quickly and turned cartwheels alongside the other children.

Early in the fall of the leaf, sailing ships appeared on the Powhatan River. Many eyes exchanged nervous glances at the latest development, and the warriors secretively watched the English erect a fortification on a precipitous peninsula. One morn, I gathered herbs for Momma with another lass of my age, Bright Path, when several of the lads, including Sparrow Hawk, passed us with their bows in hand. Curious, we followed them into the forest, trailing a safe distance behind.

The path went past marshlands, where I spied herons fishing and waterfowl diving. Bright Path remarked that the lads had not noticed us tracking aft them. "Hush," I said to her. "We do not wish for them to see us."

She covered her mouth to muffle her words. "Why do you wish to follow them? Because of Sparrow Hawk?"

Everyone was aware of my fancy for Sparrow Hawk. Once again, I told her to hush, but it was too late. The lads rushed towards us with their bows ready. " 'Tis only us," I said, waving a signal there was no danger.

The eldest of the five lads, Towering Oak, glared at us in a attempt to give the fierce impersonation of a warrior. He failed miserably, and I nearly doubled over in laughter. Now, Bright Path warned *me* to hush. Even Sparrow Hawk did not indulge me and sent me a penetrating stare. I sobered from my laughing fit but had to bite my lip to keep myself contained.

"You will return to town," Towering Oak ordered, "unless you wish to return to the English."

Bright Path bolted in the direction we had come, but I was not afraid of idle taunts, for I had suffered far worse. About to protest, I caught Sparrow Hawk's gaze.

"You are acting like a small child, Red Dog," he said.

His words pierced me like an arrow striking through my heart. "You are correct. I apologize for my behavior. I have shamed myself." I turned in the direction of town.

When the lads were satisfied that I no longer had any temptation to pursue them, they returned to their goal of glimpsing the English fort. Saddened by my actions, I perched on a knoll above the cattails and watched the herons fish. I had no recollection of how long I had sat there, when one of the birds raised and exchanged my gaze. I had seen many a heron afore, but it was almost as if this one communicated with me.

Water beaded on blue-grey feathers. A pair of black plumes extended from just atop its eyes of a mostly white face, and I studied the perfection of Ahone, the Creator, and fully understood Silver Eagle's teachings. On stilt-like legs the large bird waded through marshes, searching for fish. Once prey was discovered, the sharp yellow beak speared them.

Aft a while, the heron and its mate took flight with massive wingspans. With their departure, I was filled with a great sense of dread. Closing my eyes, I shivered. In the distance, I heard Indian war cries and gunfire from the English fort. I raced towards town as fast as my feet would carry me.

Soon, shouts sounded behind me, and three of the lads caught up with me. "Towering Oak," one said, gesturing to the other lads.

I stopped and looked around. Sparrow Hawk had Towering Oak's arm over his shoulder. "We must get him to the *kwiocosuk*," I said.

Sparrow Hawk caught up with us and gently lowered Towering Oak to the ground to rest. "Your mother has trained you in *wisakon.*"

My heart thumped. "I cannot. I'm only a lass."

"You must. He may not reach the *kwiocosuk* in time."

"Was it caused by a musket?"

Towering Oak swallowed but managed a weak shake of his head.

As I bent to check Towering Oak's wound, I breathed a sigh of relief. Because of their limited knowledge with muskets, even the *kwiocosuk* had difficulty treating matchlock wounds. And I did not have the experience of Momma.

Towering Oak's arm was swollen to his shoulder. His breath was shallow and his eyes half-closed. Like a true warrior, he did not cry out. I examined his arm and could find naught wrong with his shoulder. I followed the line of bruising and found two red puncture holes upon his hand. 'Twas a snakebite. "What type of snake?"

"Red adder."

Once again, I was relieved. Though the bite of the adder could indeed be dangerous, 'twas less risky than the vipers. "Please," I said to the two nearest lads, "run and fetch my mother and the *kwiokosuk.*" The two lads charged off. I looked to Sparrow Hawk. "I require your knife."

Without question, he handed me a bone knife. I tested its sharpness on my finger. Blood dripped. I should have known better than to question, for he and Towering Oak would soon become warriors.

I met Towering Oak's gaze. He nodded that he was ready, and I made two small incisions over the fang marks. I lowered my head and sucked the poison from the wound. I thanked Ahone for Towering Oak's good fortune.

When I finished sucking out the poison, I quickly gathered some moss to pack the wound and slow the bleeding. "I shall collect some snakeroot."

"Thank you," Towering Oak responded in a weak voice.

Grateful for the opportunity to redeem myself, I was pleased that Towering Oak no longer saw me as a wayward lass. "The bite will bring you much pain," I warned him.

At this, he showed no fear. I turned in search for snakeroot and passed the marsh. The heron had returned. With its appearance, I realized I had gained full acceptance in my new home.

13

Lee

ON SUNDAY AFTERNOON, Lee pulled his T-Bird alongside the curb at Colwell House. This time, Valerie answered the door. "Lee," she said, as she showed him to the parlor.

"No more hearth fires?"

"None. In fact, Phoebe's taken a great interest in how we cook. She wants to learn how to make lasagna."

He must have hit on something that Phoebe had enjoyed in the past, but how useful was the fact that she liked lasagna?

Valerie frowned.

"What's wrong?" he asked.

"The women here are helping, and Phoebe's tutor has already made tremendous strides. She can read some of the letters, but she has significant difficulty. We had her eyes checked just to be certain that wasn't the problem. They're fine, but she had to read the kindergarten eye chart. Even then, she didn't recognize all of the symbols. I tested her here. When it comes to Virginia plants and animals, there's no fooling her. She recognizes everything. She even knew the Carolina parakeet. But foreign animals like elephants and tigers, it's like she's never seen them before."

"I thought Shae explained to you that Phoebe truly believes she's from the seventeenth century. Even I'm beginning to think she may not be lying."

Valerie chuckled. "Shae warned me that you're a cynic."

He shrugged. "It goes with the job."

"How do you explain she doesn't slip on anything? No one can be that precise."

"Right now, I can't give you an answer. As soon as I figure it out, I'll let you know."

Her brow furrowed in confusion. "There is one thing..."

"And that is?"

"She has no problem shaving legs and underarms. She also likes to bathe, daily. A shower won't do. Weren't people a bit reluctant practicing hygiene in the seventeenth century?"

He smiled slightly. Phoebe's actions were in perfect character with her story. "I presume you mean white folks? Many Native people bathed frequently and shaved, even back then."

A slight blush filled her cheeks. "Sorry, I didn't mean to offend you."

"None taken."

"Good, and thank you for your help. I know Phoebe enjoyed talking to you on the phone. I'll get her."

Lee mumbled his thanks, and Valerie left the room. If his idea of taking Phoebe to a historical park with costumed interpreters didn't bring answers to the light, he doubted that anything would. Her historical facts seemed to check out. But if he could locate them with a couple of hours on the Internet, what could someone do who had studied the era intently? If she were a fraud, he wouldn't be so puzzled. Alarm bells clanged in his head when he was near fraudsters. Maybe Shae was right. Something so traumatic had happened to Phoebe that she had retreated into a safer world—one that she was obviously very familiar with.

Phoebe, wearing a light green dress, entered the parlor. "Lee, I've been looking forward to our afternoon together."

"Me too," he responded. "The March wind makes it a bit chilly out. You might want to grab a jacket."

"I shall be fine. I've fared much worse."

"I'm sure you have. I only meant—"

"That you were being polite. When I lived with the Indians, we bathed every day in a pond or the river, *regardless* of season."

Lee was a little embarrassed that she had overheard his conversation with Valerie, but he couldn't help but think of ice cold water on his—

No, he wouldn't go there. "I see. Very well."

The corners of her mouth tipped into a grin.

Touché. He held out his arm and escorted her to the T-Bird. This time, she managed the seatbelt by herself. Once behind the wheel, he pulled away from the curb and headed out of the city.

As high rises faded behind them, Phoebe spoke of her sessions with Shae.

While he had read about the annihilation of the Paspahegh, her story made the words come to life. He fought the building anger that he carefully kept in check. How was the Paspahegh's plight any different than the Trail of Tears or Wounded Knee?

Then, she told him about being taken in by the Arrohateck. *Convenient,* Lee thought. Neither tribe had survived to modern day, so no one could dispute her story. He listened patiently.

After several miles, he exited the freeway, traveling past the usual section of gas stations, strip malls, and restaurants. He turned off the main road, where four lanes became two.

Uncertain what to make of her continuing story, he asked, "Is it because I look like I'm Arrohateck that you trust me?"

"You remind me of Towering Oak."

The curious teenager who had checked out the English fort with his friends and wound up getting bitten by a snake. Years before, he'd had his own close encounter with a copperhead and was tempted to inquire what had become of the boy. Instead, he remained silent. Shae had warned him to let Phoebe tell her story in her own time. The road passed a swampy area.

"A heron." Phoebe pointed at the stilt-legged gray bird fishing in the water.

Lee parked the car and showed her to the wooden viewing area. The trees surrounding the swamp had buds of spring on them. A couple of red-eyed brown ducks paddled by. The one which Lee presumed to be the male had brighter plumage. "I'm not familiar with the species."

"Wood ducks."

A flock of Canada geese honked while landing in the water.

"What are the geese doing here this time of year?" Phoebe asked.

"I'm not certain I know what you mean. They're always here."

"They should have flown north by now."

Now he understood, but how did he explain? "Times change. Some fly north, but most are residents now."

She frowned. "That's sad."

Had he really lost all touch with nature working and living near the city? In his mind, he heard Shae's voice suggest that his actions were avoidance behavior. He could count on Shae to be his conscience. The suburbs kept him from thinking too much about the circumstances of his adoption. "We should be continuing on."

When they reached the car, Phoebe asked, "As the sheriff, do you send people to jail?"

He got inside and started the T-Bird. "I'm not the sheriff. Shae merely used that example to help you understand. I work for the county police department as a detective—the violent crimes unit. I was originally called in on your case because of the beatings you had suffered." When she added nothing to his statement, Lee decided not to press the issue. "I'm no longer working on your case. There were no leads."

"I don't recall what happened."

"That's why Shae is helping you."

After Lee drove a couple of miles, they arrived at a wooden fort. He paid for their tickets and checked the map for the walking tour, while Phoebe browsed the colonial and Indian trinkets in the gift shop. He joined her as she picked up a pewter mug, stared at it, then abruptly returned it to the shelf. "Remind you of something?" he asked.

She shook her head.

"Why don't we take the tour first?"

Once outside the gift shop, they took the path leading to the fort. Phoebe drew closer and clung to his arm.

Intrigued by her reaction, Lee reassured her. "It's all right. Everything is a replica."

"Replica?"

"A copy. It's to give us an idea of how people lived in Virginia in the early 1600s."

Her lock on his arm loosened slightly. They stepped into a mockup of a coastal Indian town. A dugout canoe was near the entrance. Phoebe touched it, looking like it reminded her of something.

A blond-haired man in a fringed deerskin shirt and pants greeted them. "Dugout canoes were widely used by the Indians. They made them through burning and scraping."

Phoebe's eyes widened, and she began speaking rapidly in the guttural language she had used on the first night in the hospital.

"English," Lee reminded her.

"If I'm not mistaken," the costumed interpreter said, "it sounds like Algonquian. Ma'am, have you studied with the tribes?"

Algonquian? That was an interesting discovery.

The interpreter eyed him. "And you, sir, are you . . . ?"

Suddenly annoyed, Lee gave his best stereotypical Indian pose by standing rigid and crossing his arms. "I don't speak Algonquian, and I left my tomahawk at home."

"I meant no insult," the interpreter apologized. "I merely thought the young lady might be your student. Virginia Algonquian hasn't been spoken in at least two hundred years, so I concluded you must be from one of the northern tribes who still uses an Algonquian dialect."

Relaxing, Lee thought it best they move on. "Apology accepted, but my friend is a student of history. Thank you." He grasped Phoebe's arm and led her down the path toward the longhouse covered in woven reed mats. "Why did you suddenly slip into Algonquian?"

"At first I thought he was Sparrow Hawk, but Sparrow Hawk would have ne'er dressed in such a manner. He would not have worn a shirt, and he wore a breechclout." She giggled. "Like all warriors, he kept his hair long on the left side and shaved the right."

"Ah yes, I seemed to recall reading about hairstyles. It kept their hair from getting caught in the bow string."

"You know of the Arrohateck?"

"The Paspahegh, Arrohateck, Kecoughtan, Nansemond, Pamunkey . . . About thirty tribes were tributaries to the paramount chief, Powhatan. The surviving tribes' troubles continue today."

"How can you know so much, yet not know which tribe *you* belong to?"

"Long story. Should we continue with the tour?"

She agreed to his suggestion. At least he had a lead by narrowing down the language she had spoken.

They moved toward four houses of various sizes. Bent saplings formed the frames, which were then lashed and covered by the woven mats. At the door, Lee tested the strength of the structure. Solid.

"The houses are quite sturdy," said a woman dressed in deerskin similar to the previous interpreter's. She stepped aside for them to enter. "They remained standing after a hurricane last year."

Inside, animal skins hung from walls and covered raised pallets. Bowls were made from turtle shells, gourds, and clay. There was an assortment of woven baskets and bone needles. In the center, rocks formed a circle where a fire should have been. Another interpreter wearing glasses sat on a raised pallet made of mats. She twined fibers to make cordage.

Lee picked up a clam shell scraper. The books he had read as a child must have infected him. Everything seemed familiar.

From behind him came Phoebe's voice. "Where is the fire? To let it go out is bad luck."

"We're not allowed to burn now," one of the interpreters responded. "Because of the drought, the governor hasn't lifted the burn ban."

"Why would the Arrohateck abide by an act of the governor for something as important as a fire?" Before the interpreter could respond, Phoebe grasped the fibers from the woman's hands. "Your chore would hasten if you held the fibers in your hands like thus." She held separate fibers in her fingers and twisted them into cordage. After a couple of minutes, she produced twice the amount of cordage that the interpreter had already made. Phoebe handed the fibers back to the woman. "Only an elderly Englishman would wear spectacles."

An insulted expression crossed the woman's face.

"Phoebe . . ." Lee guided her from the longhouse. "Maybe this wasn't such a good idea," he said under his breath.

"Should I not correct their errors?"

"Actually, if it were up to me, I'd make certain you got a job here, but it might be best to save your comments for me."

They followed the path from the Indian town to the English fort. A cluster of wattle and daub houses stood at the opposite end. As it was chilly and still early in the season, no one tended the gardens. A cloaked woman carried a wooden pail of water toward one of the houses.

"The houses are not practical in this climate," Phoebe muttered.

"So what else is new?"

A group of men dressed in armor and wearing helmets entered the field with swords at their sides and carrying muskets.

Suddenly ashen, Phoebe froze. "We must leave now."

Lee checked the tour brochure. "It's a militia demonstration."

Her voice filled with terror. "Nay, we must leave. We're not safe."

"All right. We're going." He took her hand and guided her away from the presentation. A musket went off behind them. Phoebe nearly dragged him to the safety of the car. At least they had a lead as to what troubled her.

14

Phoebe

THE ARROHATECK RESISTED THE INTRUSION of the growing fortification by shooting arrows into the fort. Silver Eagle was
amongst the more daring when he joined a band of warriors one
eve. They shot arrows through all of the doors and escaped unharmed. None of these actions dissuaded the English, and the Citie
of Henricus was established. As time went on, an uneasy peace descended betwixt the Indians and English, for the paramount chief's
favorite daughter, Pocahontas, had married Master Rolfe.

And curious lads grew into men. Not only did Towering Oak
survive his snakebite, he and Sparrow Hawk went through the
huskanaw, a grueling ordeal held in the wilderness. Upon reaching
their warrior status, they took men's names. From then on, Towering Oak became Lightning Storm, and Sparrow Hawk was called
Two Wolves. Bright Path reached womanhood afore I and, to my
disappointment, married Two Wolves.

Upon reaching my fourteenth season, my moon time began.
Like all Arrohateck women, I isolated myself from the men, for
their hunting prowess could be harmed by blood from the womb.
In seclusion, the women found relief from heavy day-to-day work.
Because no other women had their moon time, no one joined me.
From the time Momma and I had been adopted, I had ne'er been
alone afore.

Momma and the other women brought me venison stew and
instructed me in the ways of womanhood. Whilst I had oft heard

the grunts and groans of Momma and Silver Eagle mating, from the beginning, I was taught that it was impolite to watch. I oft wondered if they were in agony and why anyone would partake in such an activity.

The women assured me the act could be most pleasurable. Upon hearing their confessions, Momma blushed. I saw longing in her eyes, and when the other women left, I asked, "Momma, do you miss the colony?"

Tears misted in her eyes. She clutched my hand. "Phoebe . . ."

I couldn't remember the last time Momma had used my English name. "We could return for a visit," I suggested.

Her grip grew tighter. "We can ne'er return. Their ways are different. They would put me to death for abandoning the colony."

"Why would they execute you for choosing the chance of life o'er certain death?"

She wiped the tears from her eyes and patted my hand. "We shall not speak of it again. Suffice it is to say, their ways are different. You are a woman now, and you shall marry soon."

Aft Momma left, I set to work on my *huskanasquaw* dress. It was made of the softest doeskin with fringes. I decorated the dress with tiny seashells and colored beads. During the ceremony, I would be joined by other lasses who had made the transition to womanhood, and take my adult name.

Over the next two days, the women continued to bring me food and teach my lessons. Sleeping little, I worked tirelessly on my dress. On the third eve, I heard the beat of the drum, and the hound arrived at the door of my hut. He trotted over to me and licked my hand, whining for a scrap of meat.

When I handed him a piece of turkey from my stew, his legs lengthened. Only then did I recognize the hound as the same one that I had seen on two previous occasions. Realizing he was a spirit, I feared him. The dog now stood thigh high and was a magnificent, sleek white. His legs were well muscled, and his frame was made for coursing. His ears no longer drooped about his face, and he had a long, pointed muzzle. Only in Dorset had I seen such a fine specimen. He hunted with landed gentry.

The dog hastened away from the hut. Fearful of what he might show me, I huddled in a corner. He soon returned to my side and uttered a pitiful whine. I covered my ears 'til I could bear it no more and agreed to do his bidding. Faster than the wind, the dog raced through the woodland with his feet barely touching the ground. He halted near a steep bank along the Powhatan River. I saw my town burning. Momma and Silver Eagle lay dead. Standing over their bodies was a bearded man in a helmet and armor. *How could that be?* There was peace.

But the sleek hound led me away from the scene of destruction 'til I stood in the forest. The mist was so heavy that I could barely see. Swirling around me, the fog grew thicker and thicker 'til I blinked. I was surprised to find myself still in my hut, very much alone. The experience must be what Momma underwent during the dreaming. She had warned me that her initial journey occurred upon reaching her first moon time, as it had her mother afore her. The Arrohateck believed such visions were passage betwixt worlds.

Disturbed by the vision, I curled on my mat-covered pallet, drawing my legs to my body. *What could it mean?* Totally numb, I lay there, unmoving, and did not speak of it when the women brought my meal the next morn.

Aft the other women had left the following eve, Momma lingered behind with vexation on her face. "You're troubled?"

I trembled and closed my eyes. "I had a 'dream.' The English were making war on the Arrohateck."

"Hush, Phoebe." Momma took me into her arms like she had when I was a small lass and rubbed my back. "There's naught to fear. We're at peace."

As a woman now, I was determined not to cry and drew away from Momma's bosom. "Why did we come to Virginia?"

"Your Poppa wanted a new life for us. You bear the witch's mark, and I feared for your life."

Momma rarely spoke of my dead father, for I had long ago accepted Silver Eagle in that role. Only now was I coming to the full realization that James Towne had been part of Paspahegh land. To see things as a woman was to view them in a contrasting perspective. My dream had warned me. There would be more war. "I'm pleased that you chose to flee."

"I was forced to," Momma replied softly. "You would have starved had I not."

"Then you long to return?"

"Not to the colony, but Dorset. I wish to see the land of my kinsmen one last time."

To my memory, England was naught but a distant land. I recalled men working in hayfields with scythes. The voyage remained more prominent in my mind. Day after day of rolling waves. I was banished below deck, ill to my stomach amongst the smell of manure from the horses. All eight of them were consumed during the starving time. "I will find a way to grant you your wish."

A hint of a smile crossed Momma's lips. "You're speaking like a child once more. I shall leave you 'til the morrow. You must prepare for the *huskanasquaw*."

I returned to my bead work, and Momma gave me a parting kiss on the forehead. Soon aft her leaving, the white hound reappeared. Aware that he was a spirit, I was less affrighted than afore and followed him, seeking the message that he chose to show me. Mayhap, he would tell me the previous vision could be avoided. As we began our journey through the forest, the mist returned. Wave after wave, the fog rolled to engulf me. Up ahead, I spotted a light. With the dog in the lead, I traveled towards it.

Upon reaching the light, I arrived at the town. Relieved to see the town hadn't been destroyed, I felt my body sway to a drum beat. I wore my fringed doeskin and a seashell necklace. The other Arrohateck lasses who were to become women wore their *huskanasquaw* dresses. Aft a feast, there was more dancing.

During the courtship dance, Lightning Storm asked me to join him. Even though my skin was pale, he fully accepted me as a member of the tribe. I had never dreamt that he might love me. The hound barked, and the mist captured me once more. I took a deep breath, again finding myself in my hut.

Lightning Storm would become my husband, and at the *huskanasquaw*, I would become Walks Through Mist.

15

Shae

PHOEBE DIDN'T BLINK, AND SHAE WONDERED if she should bring her out of the hypnotic state. They wouldn't get to the bottom of what troubled the woman if she halted the sessions anytime they became uncomfortable. "Did you marry Lightning Storm?"

"Aye. Aft he proved his love for me to my father."

Shae reminded herself that everything was an imaginative story from the depths of Phoebe's mind to cover the pain she had been through. "Your father?"

"Silver Eagle. 'Tis the Arrohateck way. A warrior must prove his love afore a father gives his blessing to marry his daughter."

"I see." And Lee reminded Phoebe of Lightning Storm. That was enough for one day. "Phoebe, you will wake up in a few moments. When you do, you'll be relaxed and content. I'll count backward from five. When I reach one, you'll feel totally refreshed. Five—you feel the boat riding the gentle waves. Four—as the waves return through your body, you maintain the glow of peace. Three—the waves reach your eyes bathing them in soft light, ready to awaken you. Two—you open your eyelids. One—wake up."

Recognition entered Phoebe's eyes. "I had forgotten how much I had come to love Lightning Storm."

Shae didn't know whether to be angry or glad that Lee had taken Phoebe to the historic park. His description of what had happened gave her an added glimpse into what troubled the woman, but they were making so little progress. "Lee says he reminds you of Lightning Storm."

"Aye."

"In what way? His looks?"

" 'Tis more than his appearance. Neath his exterior, I sense the heart of a warrior."

As Shae feared, Phoebe was most likely falling for Lee. She needed to talk with him. If he followed his usual pattern of getting involved with a woman for six months, then splitting, Phoebe would be devastated, maybe beyond repair in her delicate state. "I'll see you on Friday, Phoebe. Again, don't hesitate to call me if you need to talk to me before your next appointment." She wished she could get Russ's firsthand observation on her patient. She could— discretely. "In fact, my friend Russ and I are having a little get-together a week from Saturday. Just a few friends and neighbors, if you, Valerie, and any of the other women from Colwell House would like to join us."

"What is a get-together?"

"A small party." Confusion remained on Phoebe's face. "A gathering of people where we talk, eat plenty of food, and listen to music. I'll be certain to have a selection of seventeenth-century music."

"I should like to join your *get-together*. Would you like for me to help with the preparations? I'm familiar with cooking for feasts."

"I appreciate the offer, but Russ is a gourmet cook. He'll see to all of the details."

"Gourmet?"

"He's an expert at cooking. We'll talk socially at the party. Meanwhile, we'll have another session here on Friday."

"Thank you, Shae."

"You're welcome." Shae escorted Phoebe from her office and informed Valerie of the party plans. After returning to her office, she checked her schedule. Her next patient was due in half an hour. She picked up the phone and dialed Lee's cell number.

"*Crowley.*"

"Lee. Shae here. I was wondering if we could meet to discuss Phoebe's case?"

"*Sure. She's all right, isn't she?*"

Had there been concern in his voice? Maybe she was making a mountain out of a molehill. "She's fine, but I'd prefer to discuss her case face-to-face, rather than over the phone." They agreed for him to drop by her office around six.

During the afternoon, Shae met with three more patients. As usual, Lee was late. She reviewed files for the following day. By 6:25, she picked up the phone to call Lee, when he walked into her office dressed in a tie and dark-brown business suit, signaling that he was still on duty.

"Sorry I'm late."

Shae motioned for him to have a seat across from her. "Spare me the reason. I know you had some all-important case. Let's just discuss Phoebe."

Without comment, he sat in the chair she had indicated.

"Lee, I'm concerned."

"So am I. The bastard who took the whip to her is still out there. Without leads, we don't know anymore about her than we did a month ago."

"That's not what I mean."

"Then what?"

"I know Phoebe has been sharing what she recalls here with you. Obviously I can't discuss what I've learned in the meantime, but I know you're aware that you remind her of someone she once knew."

"So?"

"Do I really need to spell it out? Someone that she once *knew.*"

The wrinkles of confusion faded from his forehead. "I was only doing as you asked," he reminded her.

Even though he was well trained at keeping his anger in check, she detected his annoyance. "I merely meant that because of your resemblance to someone that she loved, she has transferred the feeling to you. She's in a very delicate state. I don't think she can handle any major disappointments."

His brown eyes pierced right through her.

Now *she* was annoyed. She hated his habit of stonewalling when he was pissed. "Come on, Lee. We've known each other too long for this kind of game."

He stood. His voice remained firm but calm when he spoke. "That's precisely why I didn't answer. You wouldn't have summoned anyone else that you had asked for help to your office. I'm not officially on Phoebe's case, nor is anyone else in the department because there is no case. Her story intrigues me. Even though I agree with you that it will lead to answers about what happened, I'm not constrained by your psycho-babble. I'm all too aware of her delicate mental state, but thank you for pointing out the obvious, doctor. I think you know me well enough to tread carefully, but should my relationship with Phoebe develop beyond the casual, quite frankly that's between us."

"You're right," Shae agreed, hating to make the admission. "I wouldn't have called anyone else to my office. I would have warned my patient of potential hazards. I took advantage of our past, and I'll keep groveling until you tell me to stop—"

He waved for her to continue.

"All right. I'm sorry. Are you happy now?"

Finally satisfied, he smiled. "You have obviously learned more about the teenage boys that tried to reach the fort in your session today, or you wouldn't have called me. Since I don't look anything like the white guy, it must be the other one who got bit by a snake."

Because of doctor/patient confidentiality, she couldn't acknowledge him, but she could make amends. "Russ and I are having a little get-together. If you happen to be off duty a week from Saturday, you're welcome to join us. Phoebe will be there."

"Are you certain you want me to attend? I just might sweep her off her feet, and she might miss Colwell House's curfew. Then, she'd be forced to spend the night with me."

She met his gaze. "If any of the women from Colwell House miss curfew, they can stay with me. Valerie will be attending though, so I'm sure she'll see they get home on time."

"Damn, you know how to spoil everything. I had visions of rescuing several damsels in distress."

"I think I'm sorry I invited you."

He laughed. "You can always change your mind."

"I won't stoop to rudeness just because we used to be married."

"Then I trust I won't be receiving anymore calls reminding me of Phoebe's delicate nature."

"You won't." Shae rose from her chair. "I hope you'll continue to tell me what you find out about Phoebe. Confabulations from a patient's mind usually show some traces of normal life without the fantasy. Until she works through the seventeenth-century events, I'm mystified what to do to help her."

"I'll do anything I can."

"Thanks, Lee. I may have overreacted, but I do appreciate your help."

He nodded. "Is everything okay otherwise?"

"It is. That's why Russ and I are throwing a party."

"You haven't finally decided to tie the knot?"

"No, not yet. Trust me, I'll let you know if and when it happens."

He took out his cell phone. "I need to get back to work."

"Talk to you later."

He gave her a hasty goodbye before leaving the office. Shae stuffed her files into her briefcase, along with her laptop. Much calmer after talking with Lee, she realized the answers would come in time.

16

Phoebe

AFORE THE WEDDING FEAST, Lightning Storm and I joined hands. A chain of shell beads was broken over our heads, and both families partook in ample helpings of venison and fish. During the rite, Momma had tears of joy in her eyes. Upon my birth, I'm certain she had ne'er dreamt such a life for me. And with each passing day, I grew to love Lightning Storm all the more.

Like my adopted father, Silver Eagle, Lightning Storm provided me and his widowed mother with plentiful game. He stood much taller than I—my head barely reached the top of his broad chest. Like all warriors, his black hair was shorn so that it stood upright on the crown of his head and shaved on the right side. He knotted his long hair on his left side, adorning it with beads and copper. Serpent's teeth hung from his ears. He was passionate about everything in life.

With my red hair, pale skin, and freckles, I feared that Lightning Storm would find me unattractive. I needn't have worried. He was enchanted by my differences from the other women and, like the other Arrohateck, he believed my left handedness and conjoined fingers were a sign from Ahone. When I coupled with him for the first time, I comprehended the words the women spoke afore my *huskanasquaw*. He could be delightfully frolicsome, and he prided himself in showing me how many ways he could give me pleasure.

My friend, Bright Path, had taken the name Singing Woman, and now that we both had gone through the *huskanasquaw*, our friendship renewed. I aided her in scraping a stretched deer hide, and she asked me what it was like to live amongst the English.

" 'Tis like a dream, Singing Woman. We crossed the Great Waters when I was nine seasons."

Singing Woman stopped scraping the hide and picked up her toddling daughter, hugging her to her breast. "I sometimes fear that Two Wolves will hear the call."

"He knows naught of that life. He is Arrohateck and has you and a beautiful daughter to care for."

My response seemed to satisfy Singing Woman. She placed the child on the ground and returned to her scraping. "Do you ever regret that Two Wolves married me?"

"Nay. I'm very much in love with Lightning Storm."

"Good," she said with a smile.

As we continued to speak and scrape the hide, my hound approached us with a milky foam covering his muzzle. "He must have a caught a toad," I insisted.

Singing Woman knelt to pet the dog. He snapped, biting her hand. She yelped.

"Let me see." I inspected her bleeding hand. The hound had ne'er been a vicious sort, and I was startled by the depth of my friend's injury. The bite had gone to the bone.

"I shall collect some moss to stop the bleeding," I said.

"Walks Through Mist, he has the madness."

"He caught a toad," I demanded.

"During the full of day when conditions are dry? Try to give him a drink of water."

Terrified, I poured some water into a bowl from a gourd. Bending down, I presented the bowl to the hound. With difficulty, he lapped at the water, then choked. The English had another word for the madness—hydrophobia.

17

Lee

ON SATURDAY AFTERNOON, LEE GOT A BREAK in his caseload and headed away from Richmond on I-95 south. He puzzled over Phoebe's case. After making a few calls to the local university, he had located an old professor of his, who might be able to verify whether the language she spoke was indeed Algonquian. Unfortunately, with spring break coming up, she was out of town.

Before reaching Petersburg, he turned off the freeway and parked in the lot of a nursing home. Neatly manicured trees and flower gardens spread over several acres. The brick building with colonial columns was leaps and bounds better than the rundown facility he remembered when visiting his grandmother, but the care center remained a warehouse for the elderly.

He clenched his hand. After his mother had nearly burned her house down from leaving the tea kettle on too long once too often, he had been left with no choice but to move her here. Even now, he recalled her sobs at being told the news.

Lee went inside. The hall had hospital-like polished floors. Such a sterile environment. The hardworking staff did their best, but to grow old alone and forgotten was an undignified way to end life.

He turned the corner. Before reaching his mother's room, a staff woman called after him to wait. "Excuse me, who are you here to see?" The pouty-faced woman stared at him.

"My mother," he replied dryly.

Her eyes narrowed in disbelief. "Your mother?"

Each time there was a new staff member, he repeated the same scenario. "Just tell Natalie Crowley there's a crazed Indian dude lurking outside her door ready to scalp her." He handed her his police identification.

Her face turned beet red. Without an apology, she returned his ID and about faced down the hall.

Lee knocked.

A weak voice answered.

He poked his head into the room. "It's me, Mom."

His mother's frail, bone-thin form sat in a wheelchair beside the window. Cloudy eyes looked in his direction. "Lee?"

"Would you like to go outside?"

A faint smile appeared on her wrinkled face.

"I'll get something warm for you to wear." He went to the dresser and grabbed a drab navy-blue sweater.

After helping his mother with the sweater, she insisted they bring along a photo album. He hated going through family pictures, but it was the one thing that seemed to give her pleasure. Lee rolled the wheelchair into the afternoon sun. Robins trilled and mockingbirds scolded. Daffodils bloomed. He parked the wheelchair in the warm sunshine and sat on a bench beside her.

A gnarled, knobby hand reached over to him. "How have you been, Lee?"

Relieved that he had hit a day when she was lucid, he answered, "I've been busy, like usual."

"I saw Shae the other day."

Aware that Shae was the daughter his mother never had, he was pleased she visited regularly. "That's good."

She leafed through the photo album, skipping over the family reunions and opening the pages to a wedding photo. "Shae was a beautiful bride."

Since shacking up with Russ, Shae had put on a few pounds, but he kept that thought to himself. "Give it a rest, Mom. We've been divorced for a long time."

She drew an exasperated breath. "Lee, I was only hoping that someday you might remarry."

"Not likely."

"Then you're not seeing anyone?"

How did he explain Phoebe? He had plans for taking her out to dinner later. "I didn't say that."

"Can't a mother hope?"

"You can hope all you like, but it won't help it come to pass. It took me two years to regain my head after Shae left. I don't care to repeat the experience."

"Your father and I were married for over forty years."

"I'm glad you and Dad made it 'until death do us part.' Can we change the subject now?"

With a slight laugh, she patted his hand. "You're just like your dad—stubborn as a mule."

Right. Beyond being a cop like his dad, he had very little in common with him. Fortunately, the rest of their visit went smoother, and he brought her up to date on his hectic schedule since seeing her the previous week. She had the usual worry that he was working too hard, but at least she didn't digress about Shae or him getting married again.

When he wheeled his mother back to her room, they met the staff member who had stopped him on his way in. "As you can see," he said to the woman, "my mother still has her hair."

She scowled, but huffed off.

"Lee, I thought I had taught you better manners than that."

Even after raising an Indian child in white society, she saw the world as being color-blind. At eighty-two, she wouldn't change. While he couldn't think of a way to get her out of the accursed nursing home and care for her himself, he could grant her some respect. "You did, Mom. I shouldn't have said that."

Over a Mexican meal of beef fajitas and refried beans, Lee contemplated the latest development in Phoebe's story. At least now he had confirmed the significance of his resemblance to someone she cared for. Phoebe hadn't sent any cues that her trust was anything beyond platonic, but knowing that she believed she had been married to a warrior by the name of Lightning Storm warned him that he needed to maintain his distance. Had he really missed discovering his own heritage so much that he was beginning to buy into her story? Silently chastising himself, Lee was uncertain what to say.

"Singing Woman was my best friend," Phoebe said, dipping a tortilla chip in salsa.

The expression of delight on her face told him that she loved sampling new cuisines while confiding her story. What had Shae called it? Confab— *Fantasy*. What part of Phoebe's story was reality? Maybe she *was* married to a Native American, and they had frequented ethnic restaurants. A lot of people did that sort of thing. Or was Shae's concern a valid one? Phoebe intrigued him, and maybe he was a stupid prick falling for a pretty face. "Phoebe, in my job I must collect evidence in order to prove my case."

Her brow furrowed in confusion.

"For instance, if someone is murdered, the body is examined to determine how and why he was killed. I try to find the murder weapon, hoping that once we put all of the clues together, I can discover who the murderer was. I often have to think like him so I can figure out where he might have fled to after the murder. But in every instance, I must have physical evidence, or my case will be thrown out of court when it goes to trial. Do you understand? I want to believe your story, but there is no evidence."

She reached across the table and gripped his hand. "Sometimes the answers are not what we seek, but they enrich us all the same."

"What in the hell does that mean?"

"Would you like to learn the dreaming?"

Too much like his own tactics. He hated it when people answered questions with a question. "The dreaming?"

"My spirit guide can help show the way."

The conversation was getting weird. Lee checked his watch. It was nearly nine. "I might not get you back by curfew. Another time."

She smiled, as if seeing through him. "You're afraid?"

"I'm not," he insisted. "You weren't listening. Yes, I often follow my gut, but it's while looking for leads to uncover the evidence. What you're asking is to take a leap in faith for something that makes no sense."

Phoebe got to her feet and tugged on his hand. "Then what harm is there in trying? I shall call Valerie. I have had exemplary conduct, and my chores are covered at Colwell House. She will understand my desire to spend a night away."

So much for a respectable distance. Confused by her actions, he stood. Although she had never struck him as naive, her face seemed oblivious to the insinuation. Maybe it was her disordered thinking. "I don't think this is a good idea," he said.

"I would like to teach you. Please, allow me the honor."

"Okay, you win." He placed a few bills in the check holder to cover the meal and tip. He grasped her hand and led her to the darkened parking lot. Stopping beside the T-Bird, he handed her his cell phone. "You can call Valerie while I drive."

"Does this work like the house phone?"

"Mostly." Once inside the car, he flipped open the phone and showed her how to dial. After a twenty-minute drive, they arrived at his apartment. Normally, when escorting a beautiful woman to his home, he was eager with anticipation. With Phoebe, he had no idea what to expect.

He opened the door to the living room with a wide-screen TV filling the far wall. Off to the side were glass doors leading to the balcony. Clothes were strewn across the sofa, and a clutter of beer cans overflowed in the recycling bin. "I'm rarely home," Lee explained, loosening his tie. "I have a cleaning woman come in once a month, but as you can tell we're nearing the end of the month."

Phoebe smiled politely but was drawn to a dreamcatcher hanging on the sliding door. "What is it?"

He handed it to her so she could inspect it further. "It's a dreamcatcher."

She held the sinew-webbed hoop, while running her other hand down the trail of beads and feathers.

"It's Ojibwe, but many of the tribes have adopted them now. A dreamcatcher is supposed to protect children from nightmares."

"I'm not familiar with the Ojibwe, but you do not believe in its magic."

Had her statement been a question? "I've got arrowheads, a Navajo blanket, a Lakota medicine staff, a medicine pouch from who knows where. Someday when we have more time, I'll show you the collection. My parents thought they'd give me a sense of heritage."

Phoebe pointed to the beads, grouped in fours. "White, red, yellow, and black represent the four winds amongst the Arrohateck. The Ojibwe must be similar."

Lee looked at the dreamcatcher as if never having seen it before. "The four winds?"

"Each morn I face the sun and give thanks to Ahone. I hope that he is nearby, but he has other tribes to attend to. I must face in each direction so that he hears my prayers."

Ahone was the Great Spirit. That much he knew, but the rest . . . . They were getting sidetracked. Lee replaced the dreamcatcher on its hook on the door. "You said that you can show me evidence your story is real. If you like, I can get you something to drink first."

"Nay. We should begin. It may take awhile to reach the spirits."

"Just let me get into something more comfortable." He took off his suit jacket, and Phoebe gasped.

Her eyes were wide with terror. She stared at the gun on his hip.

"What did those bastards do to you?" he asked. "It's part of my profession, Phoebe. No one will hurt you. I'm locking the gun away."

Lee cursed at himself for not thinking. He went into the bedroom and locked the Glock in a metal box. Phoebe shouldn't be left alone for too long. He quickly changed into a T-shirt and jeans. By the time he returned to the living room, she sat on the sofa.

"I'm sorry, Phoebe. I didn't mean to scare you."

She got to her feet. "I beg forgiveness for my childish fears. I know that you would not hurt me."

They stood two feet apart, and Lee resisted the temptation to take her in his arms and comfort her. He took in her scent. Her perfume wasn't the sickeningly sweet type that women often wore, but something herbal that he couldn't quite identify. Something seductive. "Phoebe, I don't think this is a good idea. I don't know how they do things in the seventeenth century, but we're alone in my apartment. I won't be thinking about spirits, but you. If that's what you have in mind, I can get you back to Colwell House before curfew."

"I haven't agreed to fornicate with you, but you are a warrior. Are such thoughts wrong? You may have them initially, but they shall pass. Trust me, Lee Crowley, and I shall guide you to the spirit world to collect the required evidence."

Her soothing voice mesmerized him, casting a spell over him. His body was already reacting. With some reluctance, he agreed. "Where?"

"Here shall do."

"I better close the drapes. The neighbors might get the wrong idea."

After he had returned from the chore, she had an amused grin. "Your propriety is much like that of the English."

For some odd reason, Lee didn't think her words had been a compliment. "I wasn't raised by the Paspahegh or Arrohateck, but God-fearing Irish-Catholic parents, okay?"

"Though you attempt to jest, I sense sorrow."

Her remark cut him to the quick. She saw right through him. How could a muddled patient of Shae's have that effect on him? "My parents did their best, but they never reached what was within my heart."

She nodded in understanding. "Mayhap you will learn why. Do you have a candle?"

"Of course." He went into the kitchen and from the drawer got a candle and holder that he used for emergency power outages. "I doubt the Arrohateck had many candles."

"My momma used candles in Dorset. I don't have any flint. Please light the candle, then turn out the lights."

Lee wondered why he had agreed to this. He set the candle on the table, lit the wick with a match, and switched off the main light. "Why do we need to sit around in the dark and stare at a candle?"

She sat next to the table. "The candle should help you focus."

The soft candlelight framed her face in a sensuous glow. Lee imagined himself bending beside her and touching her silky skin. He let out a slow breath and had no idea how he was going to concentrate on anything but the woman before him. What had happened to a respectable distance? "I'm contemplating whisking you off to the bedroom."

"I agreed to guide you through the dreaming, not share your bed. Although—"

"Although? Does that mean I can whisk you off later?"

"It means naught."

"All right. You win. But even you agree that my thoughts are normal."

"Aye." Phoebe motioned for him to sit across from her. "But thoughts do not necessarily become fact."

So true, he thought in disappointment. He sat on the floor. "Now what?"

She held out her hands. The webbing between her third and fourth finger of her left hand caught his eye.

"Does it bother you?" she asked as if reading his mind.

"No." To prove his word, he grasped her hands.

"The English thought it to be the witch's mark."

"And the Arrohateck?"

"Lightning Storm assured me that it was a sign of luck. Now, look into the flame."

If he did as she asked, he might be able to think of something besides exploring her body. He stared at the flame.

"I have described my guardian spirit," she said. "Together, we seek him."

Lee heard a ticking clock from the kitchen and Phoebe's soft breathing. He continued to stare, and the sound from the clock seemed to grow louder. Unable to resist any longer, he moved close enough to kiss Phoebe, but she placed a hand between them, stopping him short.

"Absorb the flame. Let it become part of you."

Once more, he was reseated across from Phoebe and looked at the flame. He kept hearing the clock ticking away. If he hadn't locked the Glock in the bedroom, he could have blasted the damned thing. Five minutes passed. He heard neighbor's voices on the stairs outside. Ten minutes. A car pulled up to the entrance. Half an hour. A horn blared on the street. After an hour, he was ready to give up. "Nothing. I don't think the spirits are coming tonight."

"Because you have not absorbed the flame. Feel its heat."

Absorb the flame. The only heat was between his legs. "What in the hell do you mean?"

"Hell hath no place on our quest." She tightened her grip on his hand. "I shall be along on your journey. Try again."

Of all the senseless, asinine.... He stared at the flame. "If I had some idea of what I'm looking for, I might have better luck."

"Has Shae e'er hypnotized you?"

"Once. She was just learning the technique, and I foolishly allowed myself to be her guinea pig."

"Guinea pig?"

"Never mind. To make a long story short, I came out of the trance too quickly and had a doozy of a headache. She learned from her mistake and takes her time with patients."

"You should not be left with head pains, but what we are seeking is much the same."

And what he didn't add was that Shae had hypnotized him in the hope of making him a more attentive lover. What could he say? They had been in their early twenties, and he hadn't yet learned the finesse of not rushing. The hypnotic hangover cured his quick trigger on that night.

Lee nodded that he was ready to try again. With Phoebe across from him, he focused on the flame. She no longer held his hands, but it was as if they were touching all the same. He reached for the candle, but Phoebe's blue-green eyes drew him back. If anything was hypnotic, it was her eyes. They held secrets beyond what he could imagine. Her eyes reflected like pools of water, holding and captivating him. Around him swirled a heavy mist. Clad in a loin cloth and moccasins, he stumbled through the thick fog. Finally, the mist thinned, and he reached a forest clearing.

He was lost. Normally not the sort of person to panic, he had frequent nightmares of being in the forest. Muzzle flashes surrounded him. Why couldn't he draw his gun? Then he wandered aimlessly through the trees. Looking for whom?

"Lee."

It was Phoebe's voice. Unable to locate her, he continued walking. Brambles cut his arms.

"Lee." Up ahead stood a white greyhound. Beside the dog was Phoebe, dressed in a long green skirt, laced top with metal eyelets, and linen cap.

She ran to join him, throwing her arms around his neck. His mouth pressed against hers in feverish kisses. They sank to the ground. Clinging to each other, almost desperately, he pushed up her skirts and shift. She arched to meet him.

"No!" Covered in sweat, Lee blinked back the image. He suddenly felt sick to his stomach. The nausea passed, and he glanced around. He was in his apartment, not the forest.

"Lee? You appear unwell."

He focused on Phoebe's concerned face. Slowly, he got to his feet. "Are you trying to tell me that I'm Lightning Storm?"

"Nay. I don't control the dreaming, but *you* are the reason why I'm here. Of that, I'm certain. We must decipher the symbols and discover their meaning together."

Unsettled by the sensations, he needed time to think. "You can have my bed tonight. I'll sleep in the den."

"You no longer wish to fornicate with me?"

Was she offering what he had sought? What he had envisioned? *Resist the primal urges and think with my head.* "Not until I understand what's happening."

She sent him a teasing smile. "I shall see you on the morrow, Lee Crowley."

He didn't trust himself to show her. "The bedroom is through the dining area and all the way to the end of the apartment. The bathroom is right off the bedroom. Goodnight, Phoebe." Thank God he had a change of clothes in the den, and the apartment had a second toilet. He'd shower at the station. If he went near the bedroom, his resolve would be hopeless. She had totally bewitched him.

18

Phoebe

Aft I returned to colwell house the next day, Valerie said little to me. She scrutinized me as I performed my chores. I felt like a small child, wondering if I had unwittingly committed a violation of the house rules. This time period, the twenty-first century, the more I learnt about it, the less I seemed to understand. If only I could discover how I had come to be here.

The Arrohateck had taught me patience. All my answers would come in the proper time.

I joined Meg and one of the other women, Carol, in the parlor where they watched TV. People seemed to be painted upon a canvas as though they lived inside a box, yet unlike a canvas, they moved within the container. The first time I saw the screen, I checked behind the box to see where the people hid, only for the others to laugh at my confusion. I had heard tales of fairies and thought mayhap this was their world.

Meg moved aside me on the divan, and she broke into a wide grin. "Well . . . ."

"Well, what?" I asked.

"Last night. Details," Meg said, giggling.

Carol came closer. "I think I'd be afraid of doing it with a cop."

Uncertain what they were talking about, I asked, "Doing what? Lee and I had dinner."

Carol rolled her blue eyes. "C'mon, Phoebe. You spent the night with him. Dinner doesn't take *that* long." She left the room in disgust.

"Don't worry about her." Meg patted my hand. "She's jealous. *Kevin* can't compare to Lee. Tall, brown, and handsome. He doesn't have a brother, does he?"

"I don't think he knows. He's adopted."

"Too bad, but lucky you. And don't worry about Valerie, she'll get over her bitchy mood when she realizes Lee's not like Kevin."

I now comprehended their words, and though I admitted to myself I had been tempted, I said, "Lee and I didn't fornicate. He needed proof that I hail from the seventeenth century. I showed him the dreaming."

"The dreaming?"

For whatever reason, I trusted Meg. I went on to tell my friend about the dreaming. Her eyes grew round, and I suddenly worried. Momma had warned me of neighbors in Dorset who pretended to be friends, only to cry witch.

One moon aft Lightning Storm relieved my hound from the madness, Singing Woman became sullen. Few Arrohateck complained of pain, but as her friend, I knew something was amiss. When she developed a fever, I treated her with dried wild quinine flowers in a warm drink. The English would later discover the same plant as a beneficial treatment for malarial fevers that they and the Africans had brought to Virginia.

For Singing Woman, my medicine was inadequate. In my heart, I knew the madness had spread, but I continued to care for her as if it were an ordinary fever. She partook water in carefully measured sips, and Two Wolves told me that she awoke at night, screaming in terror.

The *kwiocosuk* brought Singing Woman to the sweat house made from stone to purify her. I removed my deerskin apron afore entering the sweat house. At the center was a shallow pit that contained the heated rocks. Prayers were given to join Singing Woman's mind, body, and spirit. An offering of tobacco was made to appease the vengeful spirit Oke.

As we sang and prayed, the spirit dog appeared afore me. I followed him through the now-familiar mist. To my astonishment, he led me to Two Wolves's house, where Singing Woman was tied to her pallet by deer hide straps. Struggling against the leather, she roared in anger. When I tried to give her some water, she choked, unable to drink. Like the hound, she foamed from the mouth.

I spoke softly, but her screams of terror intensified. Finally, I took her hand and held it. Her muscles relaxed slightly. For a brief moment, I spotted clarity in her eyes.

"Walks Through Mist, please take care of my baby," she said.

I squeezed my eyes shut against the tears. "You're not going to die, Singing Woman."

"Vow to me."

"I vow."

With my vow she released her burning rage, lashing fierce words at me once more. Even Two Wolves's warrior stance could not hide his grief as her eyes rolled up in her head. Her muscles quivered violently. *How much longer?*

When the fit ended, her eyes showed confusion. Two Wolves clutched her hand. "I thought you had taken the path to the afterlife."

A blissful smile appeared on her lips. "I saw my father."

I struggled not to cry when Two Wolves asked, "What did he say?"

"I will soon join my ancestors."

Though her voice had been weak, I mulled over her words. Would I see my English father, who had been lost on the *Sea Venture,* upon my death? I shivered. My mind had blotted out what he had looked like. I turned to give Two Wolves and Singing Woman a few precious moments alone.

But as I left, the time Two Wolves had been granted was lost as swiftly as it had appeared. Behind me, Singing Woman raved as the madness engulfed her being. Numbness spread throughout me. I prayed for an end to her suffering, and the spirit dog returned me to the sweat house.

19

Shae and Lee

IN NERVOUS ANTICIPATION of the party, Shae stepped onto the scales and closed her eyes. *Might as well get it over with.* She peeked. Two pounds heavier than the last time. "Ugh."

"Shae?" Russ entered the bathroom. "I thought you were ready. Guests will be arriving soon."

She got off the scales and glanced in the mirror. Since living with Russ, her face had become rounder, and she'd gone up a dress size. Soon she'd be checking the racks for the next size. And her hair had that frizzled, dishwater look.

"Earth to Shae. You look great."

She blinked, finally seeing Russ in the mirror behind her.

"Stop obsessing about your weight," he said.

She turned and gave him a quick peck on the lips. "And you know exactly what a girl needs to hear. Did you have a look at the seventeenth-century recipe book I found online?"

"I did. I doubt too many would find boiled mutton and roasted neat's tongue appetizing."

"Neat? Dare I ask what that is?"

"Cow," he replied. "Even so, I think roast tongue has gone out of fashion. I hope you're not too disappointed that I bypassed such delicacies." He drew her into his arms.

"I'm glad you did," she murmured, and they kissed. With a sigh, she stepped back. "Save that thought for later. I'll be right there."

Shae quickly changed. Satisfied that a loose-fitting blouse hid the extra pounds, she hurried into the living room. After putting on a CD of recorder music, she checked the hors d'oeuvres.

Russ had prepared a vegetable tray and homemade dips, a fine spread of mini crab cakes, beef wellington, steak on garlic toast, and wild mushroom tart for the vegetarians. For dessert, he had made a sampler of cheesecakes.

"Everything looks fabulous." Shae gave him a bear hug. "Oh, there is one thing—I forgot to tell you that Phoebe was a little quiet earlier in the week. I don't know what the problem was, but she refused hypnosis. Her session the other day was back to normal, but she wouldn't tell me what was bothering her before."

"Stop worrying about Phoebe. I'll talk to her when she's here. Now relax."

Easier said than done. Before she could respond, the doorbell chimed. The first guests were her next-door neighbors. Soon after, she ushered a few more neighbors through the door. Half an hour later, Phoebe and Valerie arrived. "I'm so glad you could come, although I was hoping we'd have a larger turn out from Colwell House."

"The other women had an array of activities planned," Valerie replied, and then she beamed. "Phoebe has something to show you."

Shae glanced from Valerie to Phoebe. Phoebe withdrew a note-pad and pen. In awkward, scrawling letters, she wrote her name and handed the paper to Shae. Shae clapped her hands.

"Wonderful!"

Pleased with her success, Phoebe gave a broad smile, and Shae congratulated her again.

"What do you think of the music?" Shae asked.

"Very pleasing."

"Let me introduce you and Valerie to Russ and the other guests." After a round of introductions, Shae mingled and made certain everyone had plenty to eat and drink. More guests arrived, and she welcomed them in.

During a quiet moment, Valerie approached her and Russ and glanced between the two of them. "Umm . . . ."

"If it's about Phoebe," Shae said, "you can say it in front of Russ."

"I can see to the other guests," he suggested.

Valerie waved that his leaving wouldn't be necessary. "Shae, I've debated all evening whether to tell you, but I thought you should know that Phoebe spent the other night with Lee."

Shae shot an "I told you so" look to Russ. Phoebe's preoccupation earlier in the week suddenly became crystal clear. "That must be the reason why he hasn't shown his face this evening." Calming herself, she took a deep breath. "Thanks for the heads up, but there's nothing I can do about it other than to warn Phoebe this isn't a good time for her to be involved with someone. If I do anymore, then it would be on a personal level rather than a professional one."

Valerie nodded in agreement. She opened her mouth to say something further, but closed it again.

"You wanted to say more?" Shae asked.

With a glance at Russ, Valerie swallowed. "If you don't mind my asking, why did you divorce him?"

"I've heard this one," Russ said. "I think it's time I have that chat with Phoebe."

When Russ headed in the direction of Phoebe, Shae took a sip from her wine glass. "Take a look around you. I invited him tonight, with Russ's blessing. He thought Lee might be able to help with Phoebe because she trusted him. See where trust got me?"

"Are you saying he had an affair?"

"God, no." Shae gulped her wine. "If only life were that simple. Everyone would have understood my reasoning if he had been a philandering husband. He was caring, devoted, and loving to me, but there's another side to him. He's distrustful to the point of being cynical and paranoid."

"I'm afraid I don't understand."

"After college, he went into law enforcement. From the beginning, he was a natural for the job. I decided to go onto grad school. Instead of waiting to see if we could survive as a couple apart, we foolishly got married. After all, we had been together since we were fifteen. We naively thought love could solve everything."

Shae bit her lip before taking another sip of wine. "After I finished my doctorate, he was promoted to detective. So not only did I have to contend with his dark side that few knew about, but also the job. When he was a patrol officer, I was buried in my studies and able to pretend he did nothing more than write speeding tickets and help little old ladies whose cars had broken down. After I finished my dissertation and had a real job myself, I had more time on my hands. I met him at the station one day for lunch. He was on the phone and couldn't join me right away. On his desk was a photograph of a nude woman who had been brutally raped and murdered."

Shae closed her eyes. That woman's blood splattered on the wall would stay with her until her dying day. "When he finished on the phone, he simply filed the photo away. That was it. He was ready for lunch. Get a couple of beers in him, and he has no difficulty talking about dismembered bodies, yet he can't go to the Lobster Shack for a meal because he says it smells like decomposing bodies."

"Certainly as a psychologist you realize the stress police officers are under."

"I do, but we lost all of our friends who weren't cops or married to one. He sizes up people upon meeting them and has amazing recall of height, weight, age, features of their faces, or any other distinguishing mark. And let's not forget how he watches people like a hawk, waiting for them to do God knows what." Shae gulped another breath. "I realize that stress goes with the job, but he gets an adrenaline rush from the excitement. I got to the point where anytime he strapped on his gun, I panicked that he might not be coming home. He shrugged my fear away with a joke that he was more likely to be hit by a speeding truck than shot in the line of duty."

Valerie squeezed her arm. "Thanks for sharing. I know that must have been difficult for you. I'll keep my eye on Phoebe, but underneath it all, he could actually be a decent guy. A little troubled perhaps but who isn't? Compared to some of the guys the women bring to Colwell House, Lee sounds like a prince."

"He hasn't kept a steady relationship since our divorce. Wouldn't you think after seven years . . . ?"

A smile emerged on Valerie's face. "You're the psychologist."

In frustration, Shae bunched her hands. "You know it's different when analyzing one's own life."

"It'll come to you, in time, but if Phoebe has taken a liking to him, you may have to face a clash of the professional and personal."

Shae glanced across the room at Phoebe, where Russ stood talking to her. "That's why I consult with Russ. He'll help me keep that distance."

Valerie nudged Shae. "Speak of the devil."

A guest had opened the door, and Lee entered with a bottle of wine in his left arm. Even off duty, he knew how to dress. He wore navy Chinos and a two-toned gray T-shirt that flaunted the muscles in his arms. The shirt was a little on the long, baggy side. Aware that he chose the fashion to conceal his off-duty weapon, Shae pasted on a smile and went over to greet him. "Lee, I'm glad you could join us."

Before he could respond, one of the neighbors held up his hands and shouted at Lee, "I didn't do it!"

Laughter filled the room. Even Shae hated the cliché, but Lee took the joke in stride, as if it had been hugely original. "Good to see you again, Fred. Now, about that unpaid ticket . . ."

Fred's face reddened. "I'll take care of it first thing Monday." He walked away in a huff.

Shae snickered to herself. "Checking up on my neighbors?"

"I didn't," Lee insisted, handing her the bottle of wine. "Do I apologize for being late or do you take it for granted?"

"Thanks," she said for the wine. "Let me get you a beer. I think you know most everyone, so make yourself at home."

"It *was* my home at one time."

Fortunately, they usually refrained from barbed insults, and she took his comment with no hard feelings. She just had to maintain her cool when it came to Phoebe. She placed the bottle of wine on the table with the others and poured him a beer. He had already sought out Phoebe, and Russ returned to her side.

"Well?" Shae asked.

"There's no doubt. She believes she's from the seventeenth century."

"And he knows we're watching. All of that cop training. It's almost like he has eyes in the back of his head."

Russ snorted. "You're not keeping your professional decorum."

"I'm not?" She held up the beer that she had poured for Lee. "If I was getting personally involved, I'd walk over there and 'accidentally' spill this down his pants. See what I get for listening to you. Help us with Phoebe, indeed."

"Calm down, Shae, and just take him his beer. Unless you'd prefer that I do it."

"I can handle it." She studied Phoebe and Lee a moment, thinking they made an unusual-looking couple. He towered at least a foot over Phoebe. Deep in conversation, he nodded while she spoke. He had always been a good listener. Maybe she was getting bent out of shape for nothing. If they were lovers, they certainly weren't flaunting it. She moved in their direction and handed Lee the beer.

He muttered his thanks. "Phoebe was telling me about her session the other day."

"She's making progress. I thought it best to reduce her sessions to twice a week, but I'm sure she's already told you about it."

"She has."

Shae focused on Phoebe. "Are you enjoying yourself, Phoebe?"

"Aye," she answered, nibbling on a piece of cheesecake. "I have ne'er been to a gathering like it."

If Phoebe continued to indulge herself with lasagna and cheesecake, she'd put on a few pounds too. *Like me.* Shae sighed. "I'm pleased you're having a good time."

Phoebe met Lee's gaze and beamed.

He returned Phoebe's look with one Shae recognized—one that used to be reserved for her. "I should be seeing to my other guests," she said. "I'm glad you could make it, Lee."

Throughout the evening, Shae kept herself occupied by mingling with guests. She noted that Phoebe never left Lee's side. When Shae finally made her way around to them again, a neighbor was deep in a one-way conversation with Lee, complaining about several encounters he'd had with the police. Was it any wonder Lee preferred the company of other cops?

"Lee," Shae said, "there's a call from the station. Feel free to take it in the den if you like."

He sent Shae an appreciative smile and grasped Phoebe's hand. "Thanks, Shae."

"You're welcome." She joined Russ again.

"Shae?"

Valerie's voice came from behind her, and she turned.

"I need to be leaving. Thanks for inviting me."

"And Phoebe?"

"Lee says he'll see she gets home. I reminded her that should she decide to stay out, house rules are no more than two overnights a week."

"Lee's a stickler for the rules, and he knows Phoebe isn't ready to function in society on her own. He's also good at uncovering clues. I think Russ was right," she added with a squeeze to Russ's hand. "Lee may actually be an asset in helping to figure out where she came from. Besides . . . I think he likes her."

"That may be . . ." Valerie frowned.

"You're still worried."

"I worry about all of my girls."

"I'll talk to her, and I want to thank you, Valerie."

"For what?"

"For giving a tough case a place to stay until she gets her head together."

"It's been my pleasure. Everyone likes Phoebe. She may do and say some strange things, but she's hard working and eager to learn. I just hope she doesn't try to soar before she can fly."

Shae picked up the paper where Phoebe had scrawled her name. *So do I.*

As during the previous occasion, the candle was on the coffee table. Lee stared into the flame. *Don't think of Phoebe.* The flame was part of him. *Absorb it.* Over and over, he repeated the words in his mind. Across from him, Phoebe's eyes flickered like brilliant jewels, urging him on. The candle's flame wavered with tiny wisps of smoke, tendrils reaching for the ceiling. The smoke formed the mist, and like before, he plunged into a thick fog.

Phoebe was beneath him. This time, he had no desire to break the trance. He shoved up her skirt. They came together feverishly, as desperately as two lovers who had been separated for far too long. She cried softly as they clung to one another. Was he Lightning Storm, as in the previous vision? He didn't care. He clutched her hips against him. On the edge, he could no longer hold back.

Caught up in the pleasant afterglow, he held and kissed her. "Lee . . ."

It was *her* voice, but he couldn't let go—not yet. He kissed her again, and she parted her lips, while her hands stroked the length of his back.

"Lee, there's more to see."

Her gentle voice broke the spell. Conscious of the flame, Lee drew away.

Phoebe grasped his hand. "There's more for you to see. Pray, continue. I vow you shall not lose yourself."

For the moment, he felt satiated. "Was it real?"

"In our minds. For we are connected."

Lee agreed to continue. Once again, he focused on the flame. When the mist drew him in, Phoebe stood beside him in the same long green skirt with laces and metal eyelets, as on the previous occasion. Next to her was the white greyhound.

The soft leather of deerskin brushed against his flesh. Long hair on his left side touched his shoulder and extended to the middle of his back. He was seeing the world through Lightning Storm's eyes. Phoebe was noticeably pregnant. With some reluctance, he touched her abdomen.

She pressed his hand against the growing child in her womb. Beneath his fingertips, the baby wriggled. *What could it all mean?* He had wanted children with Shae, but she had been too busy building a career to take the time. *Regret? For what might have been?* He held Phoebe close.

Lee blinked and the mist vanished. The candle had burned to a nub. *How much time had really passed?* Drained of energy, he felt like he had pulled double duty. Even with Phoebe beside him, he couldn't break the wave of exhaustion. "I don't understand."

"You shall in time."

"And us? Phoebe, it seemed real."

Her gaze met his. " 'Twas as real as you wish to make it."

What in the hell was that supposed to mean? "That's not an answer, and you know it."

" 'Tis the best I can give. You, alone, must decipher the meaning."

Had his feelings toward Phoebe been Lightning Storm's or his own?

"You need rest," Phoebe said. "The experience can be all consuming 'til you are more practiced."

She turned, and he grasped her hand. It trembled beneath his grip. "Don't run."

A smile appeared on her lips. "I could ne'er run from you, Lee Crowley, but I fear I shall end up as I always seem to—alone."

He tightened his grip on her hand. "You're not alone."

"My faith was rectified when I met you."

He only hoped he could live up to that trust. He had failed with Shae.

Lee hadn't visited campus in nearly fifteen years. Woods surrounded red-brick buildings. Blossoming dogwood trees lined sidewalks and buildings. He entered the hall housing the linguistics department, located the office of a former professor, and knocked on her door. A woman with brown hair, peppered with a touch of gray, answered. "Detective Crowley, I've been expecting you." She ushered him into her office.

"Please, call me Lee. I'm not on an official investigation."

"Lee." She motioned for him to have a seat, before taking her place behind the desk. "I'm Ellen Hatfield. What can I do for you?"

Thankful that she hadn't recognized him as a former student, he took a digital recorder from his pocket. "I was wondering if you can identify the language." He switched on the recorder to Phoebe's voice reciting numbers and saying a few phrases in the language she had used in the hospital.

"Algonquian."

"You're certain?" He switched off the recorder.

"Yes, but I don't recognize the dialect." Her brows knitted together. "It doesn't sound like Ojibwe. Would you like me to try and identify it?"

He handed her the recorder. "There's about forty-five minutes on here."

"Can you give me some background? You said it wasn't an official investigation."

"I was originally assigned to the case. A white female in her late twenties was brought into the hospital. She had been beaten and whipped. At first, she only spoke this language. In six weeks, we know little more about her than we did then. While she also speaks English, she reverts to this language when under stress. The case remains open, but no one seems to know who she is or where she came from. A couple of translators didn't recognize the language."

"Not surprising. Few translators are familiar with Native American languages. It may take me a few days, but I'll see what I can do."

Lee handed her his card. "I appreciate your help."

"I'm happy to do it. By the way, you seem to have done well since leaving school."

So much for her not recognizing him. "I'm surprised you remember me. English wasn't one of my better subjects."

"As I recall, a lot of subjects weren't your better ones."

He shrugged. "That's why I'm on the streets and you have a desk job."

She laughed. "Good seeing you again, Lee."

"Same here."

"I'll give you a call when I have something."

"Thanks." After a quick goodbye, Lee went out to the T-Bird. Phoebe was indeed capable of speaking a Native language. She certainly didn't have any Indian characteristics herself, but, then again, many in the local tribes had been mixing with other populations for almost four hundred years. He'd wait for Dr. Hatfield's analysis before drawing any conclusions.

20

Phoebe

SOON AFT SINGING WOMAN'S DEATH, I lost the child I carried. I painted my face black and wailed my sadness. I was almost seventeen seasons afore I was with child again. When my due date drew near, Lightning Storm accompanied me downriver in a canoe to stay with Momma 'til the babe was born. Except for brief gatherings, I had seen little of Momma since marrying Lightning Storm. She and Silver Eagle greeted us and held a feast in our honor.

Both Momma and Silver Eagle were beginning to show their age. Momma's gray hairs hid neatly amongst her blonde locks, and Silver Eagle, a warrior nearing forty, would soon become an elder. My half brother, Sly Fox, had grown tall and lean and would go through the men's initiation, *huskanaw*, in another year or two.

During the feast, Silver Eagle spoke softly to Lightning Storm. I suspected something amiss. The men were trying to protect me from overhearing, and I spotted tears in Momma's eyes. Later, when I was alone with Momma and the other women, clearing bowls and leftover food from the feast site, I asked, "Why do the men speak in hushed voices?"

"Pocahontas has died in England."

In spite of my youth, I understood the consequence of her words. Peace betwixt our people would soon end, and Momma and I carried division within our hearts.

The other women gathered round us, reassuring us that we would always be welcome amongst the Arrohateck. But Lightning

Storm and Sly Fox would be drawn into the English wars. *How was this really any different than other hostilities?* I reminded myself. Men oft warred amongst themselves. Lightning Storm already had scars that proved himself in warfare.

Ordinarily, the Indians did not kill innocent women and children. The English oft held no such qualms. I thought of my vision afore my *huskanasquaw*. Would it finally come to pass? I felt like a lass once more. "Momma, I'm frightened."

I spotted fear in the other women's eyes and chastised myself for voicing my childish fright aloud. All of the women felt the same. Whilst the Arrohateck men were expert bowmen, they had no guns, cannon, or horses.

21

Shae and Lee

DURING THE PREVIOUS SESSION, Shae hadn't resorted to hypnosis, and Phoebe had talked about her pregnancy. Because Phoebe was speaking on her own, Shae felt they had made a significant step forward. This session Phoebe had regressed. They were back to using hypnosis. In such a complex case, she wasn't surprised by the reversion, but she still had no clue as to where Phoebe's "memories" were coming from. It was almost as if Phoebe Wynne had walked out of the mist she mentioned while under hypnosis. "I'm sure none of this is easy for you, but I think each session brings us closer to what's troubling you."

Phoebe's eyebrow arched slightly. "Learning to manage in this century is what ails me, doctor."

"Yes, of course," Shae replied, worried that Phoebe might be considering withdrawing from her sessions. "We're working on that too, but it's all going to take time."

"Of that, I am aware." Phoebe sighed.

Shae detected something wrong. "Is something else troubling you?"

"Nay, I am such a ninny. I so looked forward to sharing my new-found memories with Lee."

Treat her like any other patient. "Why can't you?"

"He is working on a *case* and will be unable to have dinner with me this eve."

Shae comprehended all too well. And there would be many more nights of eating alone. "Why does that make *you* a ninny?"

"An Arrohateck woman does not depend on a man to entertain her. Men are oft away on hunting and fishing ventures."

As Shae had feared, Phoebe was falling for Lee. "Phoebe, I need to maintain a professional distance when it comes to Lee, but there is one thing I must tell you. It's something I would say no matter who he was. Lee may remind you of Lightning Storm, but he can never be him."

"Aye. I'm wary, and I shall heed your warning."

"Good. Then perhaps you're disappointed because you only have a few friends and social outlets right now. I know you're frustrated that it's taking so long to find the answers that you require to get on with your life, but again, time is on your side. It will help you."

"Life has taught me patience."

For that much Shae was thankful. Other patients might have been suicidal, and she would have been referring them to a psychiatrist. But Phoebe was a survivor. "I'll see you next Tuesday. Don't forget to call me if you need anything before then."

On Saturday afternoon, Lee parked the T-Bird in front of Colwell House. By the time he had gotten off duty on Thursday, he had already been awake for nearly thirty-six hours. When he knocked on the door, Phoebe was the one to answer. Her face brightened upon seeing him, and she quickly ushered him to the parlor. "I was pleased to receive your call."

"I have three days off," he said. "Of course, I spent most of yesterday sleeping, but I'm your humble servant for the rest of the weekend."

"Shall I inform Valerie that I may be away for my allotted two nights?"

Direct and to the point. He liked that, but with Phoebe it might not mean anything suggestive at all. He didn't care. "Why not? I'll be happy to wait if you'd like to get a few things together."

"I shall return posthaste."

Her voice seemed happy, and her step was lively as she left the room. He made himself comfortable on the sofa. From the kitchen, he heard a clatter of dishes and women's voices, chatting. A soft tread of footsteps headed toward the parlor, and Valerie poked her head in. "Lee . . ."

He stood. "Valerie."

She entered the parlor. "Phoebe's upstairs, getting ready."

He detected hesitation in her voice. Everyone at Colwell House most likely thought he and Phoebe were lovers. "You don't approve."

"It's not that I don't approve, but—"

"You can save your breath. I'm sure Shae—"

Valerie signaled a "T" for timeout. "Actually Shae has said good things. It's nothing personal. I'm the same with all of my girls. Many of them have come from very bad relationships. You're a cop, for God's sakes. You've seen the bodies of the ones who weren't lucky enough to make it here."

Her name had been Marcia—his first case as a detective. Her husband had avoided hitting her face to hide the bruises. "I have," he agreed. "If you think I should leave—"

"You would, wouldn't you?" Valerie shook her head. "No, I only want what's best for my girls. Right now, I think you're instrumental in Phoebe's mental health. She's happy after seeing you, so stay. I just worry that you may find her problems too much to deal with after all of the other pressures you encounter each day, not to mention the risk of your job."

He sighed. "I'm more likely to be struck by lightning than die in the line of duty."

"Shae said 'speeding truck,' but thanks for indulging an old mother hen. Not all guys take my nosing into their affairs kindly. I wish you would visit sometime when Carol's boyfriend is here. He hasn't done anything overt as of yet, so I can't send him packing, but I sensed trouble from the moment he walked through the front door."

"I can do a background check, if you like."

"That won't be necessary, but I pray that I'm wrong."

Out of the corner of his eye, Lee detected movement. Phoebe entered the parlor. "I'm ready. Where are we going?"

"How about something relaxing for a change? A walk through a park, perhaps?"

Phoebe's smile let him know that his plan met with her approval. Valerie bid them goodbye as he escorted Phoebe to the door.

"I thought you were packing a few things," Lee said.

She held out a small grocery bag. "I have."

Everything she owned. He chastised himself. He had momentarily forgotten places like Colwell House depended on donations. "Would you like me to carry it for you?"

"I have no deformities. Pray do not behave as if I'm a gentlewoman."

She was a feminist in any age.

"As you wish." He showed her to the car and automatically turned down the police radio chatter upon starting the engine.

Once they were on I-95, she relayed what she had uncovered during her Thursday session with Shae. Afterward, they sped along the freeway, and Phoebe stared out the window at the countryside as if absorbing every detail.

"Has it changed drastically?" he asked.

"Aye. I could ne'er have fathomed high rises or cars, but the woods... What happened to the woods?"

"A lot of the forests have been cut down since the 1600s. There are over seven million people in the state now."

She glanced over at him in shock. "When I feel I'm beginning to know this century, I discover I have yet much to learn."

"You're doing fine."

She returned to gazing out the window. "Do all men hide their weapons as you?"

Lee exited the freeway onto a side road. "Not everyone carries weapons in this time. It's part of my job. Because of the risks I face each day, I always prepare myself for the worst. I've heard of too many off-duty officers shot because they had left their pieces in the car."

"A warrior would always take his weapons with him as well."

"Then I guess I'm in good company." Still, he was all too aware that she feared his Glock. It wasn't the same fear he had spotted in Shae's eyes when they were married. Something had happened to Phoebe—something involving a gun where she or someone she cared about had been a victim. All of his training told him to ask questions. Shae claimed the opposite in Phoebe's case. For the moment, he resisted.

Once outside the park, he brought the car to a halt in the designated lot. He escorted Phoebe along the hilly path. In the gentle April breeze, new spring leaves blew. Phoebe's eyes lit up upon seeing the aviary and focused on the heron. "Why are they kept in a net enclosure?"

"They have nowhere else to go. All the animals here have had injuries that prevent them from living in the wild."

She frowned. "I have much in common with them."

He grasped her hand. "I brought you here to cheer you up, not make you sad."

She smiled. "I'm not melancholy, for I'm with you."

Lee could no longer restrain himself. He bent down and kissed her.

Phoebe touched her lips. "Are such displays of affection acceptable in public?"

"Within reason."

"I shall look to you for guidance."

He kissed her again, more deeply this time, and she eagerly reciprocated.

Beside them, a throat cleared in annoyance. A stooped, elderly woman sent him a scorching look.

"My apologies, ma'am." He attempted to keep a straight face. "Didn't mean to offend you." Hand-in-hand, they traveled up another hill to the next enclosure. A bear lazed by a pond, and a gray fox paced the length of its enclosure.

"The red fox was brought from England," Phoebe stated, "because the gentry found the gray fox too sly to hunt."

"Phoebe," Lee said, hoping his frustration wasn't evident, "because of Shae's advice, I'm restraining myself from asking any serious questions, but when you tell me trivia . . . Sorry, I need to be more patient, but the next thing you'll be telling me are tales about Powhatan, Pocahontas, and John Smith."

"Wahunsenacawh."

Another history lesson. "I'm fully aware that Wahunsenacawh was Powhatan's familiar name."

Her brow wrinkled in confusion. "Then why did you mention their names? I met Captain Smith once, but he sailed for England shortly aft my arrival. Pocahontas—"

Lee kissed her once more, cutting off her sentence. "You really don't understand, do you? I'm trying to help you."

She pressed a hand to his chest. "Don't be afraid to ask what is in your heart. You have shared the dreaming with me. You know me better than anyone in this time."

Next to his brown hand, Phoebe's pale skin almost seemed translucent. "How can I know anyone else when I don't know who I am?"

"If you share the journey with me, we shall discover the answers together."

Why was everything she said cryptic? "We're a lot alike. I—" Lee caught himself. He had almost revealed more than was comfortable and immediately switched to a detached police officer's stance. "Usually we can trace people through their ID, fingerprints, or DNA. But there's nothing on you—anywhere. You almost have me believing that you *are* from the seventeenth century."

They continued along the tree-lined path. "I thought the dreaming would show you that I'm being truthful," Phoebe said. "What other evidence do you require for proof?"

He clasped her hands and faced her. "Phoebe, I can usually spot someone very quickly when they're not telling the truth. I know you're not lying, but there has to be a rational explanation. People simply don't travel through time."

"Then why would I have no memories of my time here afore being struck by the car?"

He had blown it. She had been opening up to him, trusting him, but as usual when a woman got too close, he shoved her away. "I don't know. That's Shae's expertise. We're here to help you find the answers."

In silence, they went up and down the hills, viewing bison, otter, and deer. After lunch, they toured the Japanese garden. Phoebe delighted in seeing the stone lanterns, arched bridges, and water lilies, but she failed to share with him as she had before.

A pergola marked the entrance to the next garden. Wisteria climbed the colonnades and rooftop trellis. For some reason, while walking along the cement path, Lee imagined what the way would be like in the mist. When Phoebe gripped his hand, he envisioned her pacing the length of a palisade like a caged animal. In the night, he crouched low and signaled his location to her with the call of the crow. *Lightning Storm?*

A whippoorwill responded.

Phoebe's grip tightened, and Lee shook his head and blinked. The colonnades came into view. "What just happened?" Lee asked. "I saw you pacing and called to you, like a crow."

"You have not witnessed enough to understand." She sank to the path and cried. "I thought I'd ne'er see Lightning Storm again."

As was Russ and Shae's tradition on Saturday night, Russ had prepared a romantic candlelit dinner. The blackened salmon with chipotle squash and mango rice had more than filled Shae. Yet . . . she had been unable to resist having a slice of hazelnut torte. Sprawled in misery on the sofa, she felt bloated.

Russ set the coffee cups on the table. He sat beside her and rubbed her back.

She groaned. "I shouldn't have had the torte. After all these years, you'd think I'd learn."

"I'll get the antacid."

He got up, but she caught his arm. "Don't leave."

"I thought you weren't feeling well."

Feeling better just having him near, she ran her fingers through his beard. "I'll be fine, if you—"

He leaned down and kissed her, while touching her in the places she liked. The phone rang, and Shae started to get up.

"Let it ring," Russ said.

"What if it's a patient?"

He kissed her again. "If it's anything urgent, they'll leave a message."

With the phone ringing in the background, Shae wrapped her arms around his neck and kissed him.

The answering machine picked up. *"Shae . . ."*

At the sound of Lee's voice, Russ broke their embrace and grumbled, "You'd better answer, Shae. If the ex calls, I'm sure it's something all important."

Detecting his annoyance, she drew him to her once more. "Lee can wait." Then she overheard Phoebe's name. She shifted her mindset and rushed over to the phone. "Lee, I'm here. What's wrong?"

"Phoebe's not well. She keeps crying but won't tell me what's wrong."

"Where are you?"

"My place."

That was a good thirty minutes from her. "Can you meet me at my office?"

He assured her that he could, and the phone went dead.

"Would you like me to go with you?" Russ asked.

"I'd appreciate your company." She kissed him on the cheek. "Thanks for being understanding."

Normally, the drive to her office was a good twenty to twenty-five minutes, but in the evening with little traffic, she arrived in fifteen. Lee already waited, and as she got out of the car, he helped Phoebe. Shae unlocked the door and switched on the lights to the outer office. Phoebe had streaked cheeks like she had been crying.

"Phoebe, are you all right?" Shae asked.

No response.

"Russ, can you stay with her while I find out what happened?" He nodded, and she motioned for Lee to follow her into the main office. She turned on the lights and faced him. "Well . . ."

He began by recounting his visit with Phoebe to the local city park.

Shae paced the length of her office, then back again. "I warned you about bringing her memories to the surface too suddenly!"

"How was I to know that a walk through a garden would trigger something traumatic?"

She stopped pacing. "You told me to butt out of your personal affairs. I did, but Phoebe is *my* patient. Her personal life is my professional concern."

"I know what you're thinking."

Sometimes she just wished for once that he'd lose his cool, but no, he stood across from her with his detective's poker face and every appearance of being calm and collected. "What am I thinking?"

"That Phoebe and I are more than friends."

"I've seen the way you look at her."

"So? I haven't slept with every woman I've had sexual thoughts for. Shae, I'd be lying if I said I haven't been tempted, but we're not lovers."

She calmed slightly. She had never known Lee to lie. "Not . . . ?"

"No, and I avoided the historical parks like you suggested. While she has shared memories with me, I thought a trip to the park would be relaxing for her."

She waved at him to back up. "Shared memories with you? What do you mean? I thought she was merely relaying what came to her as a result of our sessions."

He motioned for her to have a seat. Shae took the chair behind her desk, and he sat across from her. "She showed me some sort of ritual. Don't ask me to explain it because I can't. All I know is that I was drawn in and shared part of what appeared to be her life in the seventeenth century."

Uncertain whether she liked the idea of what he might be suggesting, Shae asked, "What kind of ritual?"

"She said that it was similar to hypnosis. She had me light a candle and told me to absorb the flame. I was as skeptical as the look you're giving me, but when I finally concentrated, I viewed the seventeenth century as myself and Lightning Storm."

Coming from anyone else, she might have doubted the story. "The explanation is actually very simple."

"Please enlighten me."

"It's not just similar to hypnosis. Phoebe knows how to induce it. She planted the suggestion in your mind."

His forehead wrinkled. "But it seemed so real."

"Think about it, Lee. When you've called me in for forensic hypnosis, the session is taped so everyone knows that I didn't ask any leading questions. You're not the easiest subject, but contrary to what most people believe, just about anyone can be hypnotized as long as the hypnotist knows what he or she is doing."

The lines on his forehead faded. "Makes sense."

It also likely explained how Phoebe had recalled Lightning Storm without a session.

"Just one question," Shae asked, "did you see anything that might help?"

"If it wasn't real, how can what I remember help?" His expression became pensive.

Aware that he didn't trouble easily, Shae had to say something quickly. "Because what she planted in your mind is an extension of her own."

"Nothing, really, except that she loved Lightning Storm."

His statement didn't surprise her. If only they could discover who the real Lightning Storm was.

"A word of caution," Shae added, "before I have you send Phoebe in. I don't think it's a wise idea to indulge her further. I think she may be channeling her trauma through you to help ease the pain. You remind her of someone she obviously cared about, so she sees you as a strong shoulder. It would be healthier for her to work through it herself. I know you like to play the tough guy, but the emotional stress could cause a strain on you as well."

"Worse than what I see each day, doctor?"

"Lee, please . . . everyone has a breaking point."

He cracked a grin. "Then I guess I'll have to relieve my stress in other ways. You're blushing, doctor. I bet you haven't told Russ about the way we used to—"

"Shut up." Silently cursing him, she took a moment to compose herself. "I really should speak with Phoebe now."

On his way out of the room, he laughed.

"One more thing . . . ," she said.

He reached the door before facing her.

"Thanks for doing the right thing by calling me. I'm sorry for yelling at you earlier."

He gave a nod and left the room. Before long, Phoebe appeared in the doorway. Shae motioned for her to step into the office. "Are you feeling any better?"

Phoebe approached her and sat in the chair vacated by Lee. "I had a momentary ill feeling. Naught more."

Shae watched Phoebe with concern. "It looked more than momentary."

"Aye, I felt poorly. 'Twas not like reliving the memories in your office. They're shadowy, and I always have a feeling of wellness afterwards. Instead, whilst visiting the park, I faced memories we have yet to discuss and had the need to escape."

"Post-traumatic stress. Hypnotherapy hasn't triggered the same reaction because I make certain to suggest that feeling of wellness before bringing you out of the hypnotic state. You accept the suggestion, which helps us here. Your reaction in the park tells us your memories are just under the surface. You can give yourself the same suggestions to avoid similar reactions."

"I shall try," Phoebe agreed.

"Good. Now, what's this I hear about you using hypnosis on Lee?"

"I have not."

Shae sat on the edge of her desk. "He said that you performed some sort of ritual."

" 'Twas not hypnosis."

"Then what was it?"

"My mother was a cunning woman."

"A what?"

"She practiced the art of physick, but some brabbling tongues in Dorset labeled her a witch because of me." She spread her fingers to reveal webbing. "I am left handed, and it bears the devil's mark. 'Tis why Poppa insisted we sail for Virginia. From the moment I can first recall, Momma showed me her ways. The Indians embraced our gifts, rather than fearing us. Like my mother and her mother afore her, I'm a cunning woman."

"What exactly is a cunning woman?"

"I use herbs for healing. Sometimes I call upon the spirits for their guidance."

"How does a cunning woman relate to Lee?"

"With my aid, he summons the spirits. In a way, he is much like me. He has no knowledge of who he is or where he comes from. Through the spirits, he seeks the answers."

In all the time they had been together, Lee had rarely spoken of his adoptive status. How could she have missed the signs that he had no sense of past, while Phoebe saw them upon meeting him? Uncertain what to make of Phoebe's revelation, she returned her concentration to her patient. "Phoebe, I think it's best if you refrain from using rituals to find out what happened right now. I'm concerned you might remember something traumatic, and I'd be unavailable. Here in the office I can make certain that you recall things in a controlled manner."

Phoebe made no comment.

22

Phoebe

I PONDERED SHAE'S WORDS again and again. Why should I not participate in the dreaming with Lee? Momma had counseled me that neighbors in Dorset thought the dreaming was a pact with the devil. Did Shae feel the same? Witch trials had been held for lesser charges. Had her words been a warning?

For dinner, Lee brought me to a place that served *American*, and I sampled beef pot roast. Whilst the meat was finely seasoned and pleasant tasting, 'twas not dissimilar to the stews I had oft cooked during my time with the Arrohateck. How I longed to return to that world, for 'twas the last time I had felt truly happy. But I could not deny the connection to the man who sat across from me. I had yet to visualize the hows and whys, but something bonded us. In time, I would uncover the answer, but I feared he would pull away from me afore I understood the significance. More importantly, did he believe I had led him astray?

Throughout much of the meal, he seemed melancholy. He spent more time spearing the peas on his plate than consuming them. All the while, I studied his face. Like an Arrohateck warrior, he failed to display his emotions easily. Lightning Storm was much the same, yet as his wife, I was familiar with his thoughts. In that regard, Lee differed. I was certain he would open to me if given half the chance.

"You do not need to bring me to the ordinary every time we are together. I am capable of cooking."

A hint of a smile crossed his lips. "Using a stove?"

"I have learnt," I proudly assured him.

"Listen, Phoebe." He placed his fork to the side of his plate. "I'm sorry about today. I shouldn't have taken you to the park."

"There is naught to forgive, for you have done naught wrong. How could you have known that a visit to a park would cause me distress? Shae says that overall, 'tis good for me to confront my fears. I am unlikely to recall what happened 'til I do, and she has given me advice on how to best recover from my fears in the future."

"That's good."

His dark-brown eyes told me what I needed to know. "You're dubious."

His brow furrowed. "I'm uncertain what to believe."

I delighted in the fact that he was honest, a trait worthy of a true warrior. "More than anything, I wish to give you the proof you desire, but Shae has told me that I should refrain from the dreaming."

"It's probably for the best." His voice had been abrupt, and as if noticing it himself, he softened his tone. "If you like, I'll return you to Colwell House."

I finally understood. 'Twas not my initial fear. Though he would ne'er admit as much, he was afraid. Certainly not of death, for he faced it everyday, but exactly what, I had yet to uncover. "I do not wish to return to Colwell House. You vowed to be my humble servant."

His brow slackened, but his jaw remained taut.

"Lee, you have no obligation to me. I shall return to Colwell House if that is your wish."

"I don't know what I want. Part of me says to forget this whole farce." He threw some currency on the table to pay for our meal, stood, and helped me to my feet.

Whilst I did not totally comprehend his words, I gained the essence of his meaning. "And the other part?"

He muttered something unintelligible and escorted me to the car. Such vehicles still frightened me, and I oft had nightmares of one striking me as upon my arrival. Lee drove faster than Shae or Valerie, and the car itself had some sort of stick betwixt us that he called "gears." He gripped the stick and moved it about as he drove. I felt certain I was observing a manly ritual but had no comprehension to its meaning. I gathered his actions might be similar to men racing horses to see who had the fastest. But Lee ne'er traveled with other cars, and he ne'er seemed to win anything, except for being the first to reach a red light. And when that happened, he uttered blasphemies.

To my surprise, we returned to his apartment, not Colwell House, and as we went up the steps, I felt something anew, something pulsing. I could not recall anything similar, except in my visions of Lightning Storm. My heart had known as much upon meeting Lee in the hospital room. Still, I had held back my desire, for I was uncertain whether a woman of this time held any freedom.

He closed the door behind us and made simple conversation.

"Can I get you anything?"

"Nay," I said.

"You're welcome to use my room again."

Afore he could turn from me, I grasped his hand. Mine was so much smaller that his surrounded my fingers like a glove. And the strength of his muscles—he could crush my hand if he so wished. But neath the warrior's exterior was the gentleness of a newborn fawn. "Can you not feel it?" I whispered.

"Phoebe . . ." His voice had gone soft, and he swallowed noticeably, whilst withdrawing his hand from my grip. "I don't think it's a wise idea."

Mayhap, I had misjudged the time. "I'm familiar with the ways of men. I don't expect you to love me. I feel so . . . alone here."

He placed a hand under my chin, tipping it upwards, 'til our gazes met. His eyes were a shade lighter than Lightning Storm's. "How many times do I have to tell you that you're not alone? Don't you see? I *would* love you."

I finally understood, and my breath quickened with his response. "Why fear it, when we should embrace it?"

He traced a finger over my lips. "Because I haven't loved anyone since . . ."

I nearly twittered with amusement. He was making comparisons similar to my own. "And I have not loved anyone since Lightning Storm."

"But what if...? What if you vanish the same way you appeared?"

I pressed my hand against his hip, where he kept his gun safely tucked away from roving eyes. Though touching the gun and my subsequent thoughts brought terror to my heart, I said, "And what if a bullet should pierce your heart? The circle cannot be complete without traveling the path."

He nodded that he understood but drew away. Fearful that he was leaving, I crossed my arms and hugged myself. I *was* alone. He turned back, and his mouth met mine in a burning hunger. My arms went around his neck, and he picked me up in his arms and carried me towards the bedroom. "You don't know how long I've been holding back," he said.

Once inside the bedroom, he set me down so that I stood next to him. He helped me remove my dress, but I, on the other hand, had no clue about men's garments from this time. His shirt was similar to my dress, with no buttons or laces, but he was more than a head taller than I.

Seeing my difficulty, he stripped off his shirt. His scent was neither fetid, like that of so many of the English of my day, nor slightly musky, like that of the Arrohateck. I luxuriated in his masculine smell. Unlike the Indians of the seventeenth century, he wore his black hair cropped short. His chest was hairless, and my fingertips traveled down the broad expanse of his muscles until I reached the leather strap that held his gun. I withdrew as if I had been scalded.

"I'm sorry," he quickly apologized. He went through a ritual that I had never seen a colonist perform. He removed something called a magazine, checked the chamber, and locked the gun away in a box. "I hope I haven't ruined the mood." He took my hands and kissed my fingers.

"Guns frighten me," I said with a tremble. "But I know not why." I had meant to relish the moment, not engage in dreary conversation. "My fear is gone now, for I am with you."

My reassurance was all he needed to hear. Aft another kiss, he slipped my petticoat over my head, and my momentary fright vanished. I had refused to wear the binding garment that Shae had called a bra aft leaving the hospital. I slipped off my underdrawers, and he stared at my nakedness. For a long while, he looked at my breasts, and the serpent tattoos coiled around them. His gaze lowered, following my midsection to the swell of my hips. He looked at the red hair betwixt my legs and the snake tattoos circling my thighs.

He reached for me and touched the tattoos upon my breasts in a way that was reminiscent of Lightning Storm's caresses.

Again, I forestalled. Valerie had shown me how to work a zipper, but I had little practice. In my desire to view all of him, I got the zipper of his trousers stuck. He gave a nervous laugh 'til, in my haste to unjam the zipper, it caught his underdrawers and came just shy of hitting his male member.

"I think I had better see to it," he said, "or the mood *will* be spoiled."

"Aye. I'm a bit clumsy."

His face creased in annoyance as he struggled with the zipper. Unable to resist touching him, I caressed his back. Soon, he was free of his trousers, and he drew me into his arms. We fell to the bed together, laughing and kissing.

I could not recall the last time I had lain with a man, and I reckon that was the reason why I had a moment of hesitation. Instead of entering my person immediately, he explored my skin with his lips and fingertips, putting my mind totally at ease. I reciprocated with teasing strokes of my own. He reached into the chest of drawers beside the bed and withdrew a package.

As he opened the package, I stared at him in puzzlement.

"It's a condom and keeps you from getting pregnant."

How could a little, flat device . . . ? I had visions of performing some sort of incantation. "Better than my herbs?"

"Trust me. It's more reliable than herbs."

"*More reliable?* I have knowledge of some potent herbs." When he unrolled the condom over his *pocohaac,* I couldn't help but giggle. How similar it was to a scabbard for a sword. I could not fathom many men willing to sheath themselves for the sake of preventing babes. My arms encircled his neck for being so thoughtful.

Only then did I realize the magnitude of his need. His kisses became more feverish than afore, and in one swift move, he clutched my hips and thrust inside me. His intensity signaled that it had been awhile since he had last bedded a woman. I opened wider, allowing all of myself to him so that we could join each other in body and spirit.

23

Lee and Shae

WHEN LEE WOKE, HE FELT TOTALLY AT PEACE. Beside him snuggled Phoebe. He had no idea where she had come from or who she really was. Why was he drawn to her? Her tales of the seventeenth century were fanciful at best, but for some reason, they intrigued him to pursue further. And the visions. How could he explain them? Dismissing them as hypnosis seemed all too simple.

There was something more—at the back of his mind. It was like an out-of-focus view through a camera, but when he tried to adjust the lens, the photo got fuzzier. What in the hell was wrong with him? He wasn't normally the sort to have sex with a woman and fall in love. Yet, he had.

In his arms, Phoebe trembled. She stirred in a nightmare. He brushed the hair away from her face and held her. In her sleep, she muttered in the guttural language that she often resorted to when stressed. *Algonquian?* He hadn't heard from Ellen Hatfield and made a mental note to call her.

Finally, Phoebe breathed easy again. She opened her eyes, and a radiant smile appeared on her lips.

"Good morning," Lee said, taking in the sight of her unclad body.

Her smile widened, and she touched his face as if checking that he was real. "I feared you would be gone when I awoke."

"Not a chance." He gave her a lingering good-morning kiss, when the phone rang. In frustration, he cursed under his breath and reached for it. "Crowley."

"Lee." It was his partner, Ed Bailey's voice. *"Holt wants to talk to you."*

Holt? A moment passed for Lee to mentally shift gears to a black woman who had been raped. Her case had gone cold nearly three months before. "Does she remember anything new that will help?"

"She won't talk to me—only you. She's here at the station."

Unless a minority victim specifically preferred a female officer, he was often the detective of choice. Lee sighed at the idea of being dragged out of bed with a beautiful woman on Sunday morning. Even worse, he was leaving for a definite maybe that the victim could recall something that *might* help the case. "I'll be there as soon as I can." He hung up the phone and turned to Phoebe. "As much as I'd rather spend my time with you, I need to return you to Colwell house."

She traced her hand along his arm. "Do not despair. I understand."

In all the years he had been married to Shae, he had never heard those words. Maybe that was what went wrong between them.

On Monday morning, Shae received a call from Lee. He wanted her to consult with a rape survivor, at the victim's request. Three months had passed since the assault, and Lee had no new leads. Shae psyched herself for the interview in her drive across the city. She'd have to take extensive notes from the victim before even considering hypnosis, on the chance the case would eventually be tried in court. Her thoughts turned to Phoebe. At least there had been no more emergency calls over the weekend.

Upon Shae's arrival at the station, Lee briefed her on the case. The interview would be in the two-room suite typically used for polygraph exams, with several police officers behind the one-way glass. She hated the cold, sterile environment. After conducting an extensive interview with the victim, she began the hypnotic session. She decided to use an induction like a TV screen, so the victim wouldn't directly relive the assault but would watch it from a distance. For two grueling hours, the victim relayed what had happened to her in graphic detail. By the time the session concluded,

Lee had already put a trace on a license plate number and called for a sketch artist.

Emotionally and mentally exhausted, Shae was thankful when one of the officers guided her to a chair and handed her a cup of coffee, while Lee and a female detective saw to the victim. Shae had no idea how long she sat there before Lee appeared.

"Thanks, Shae," he said. "I know how much you hate investigative interviews."

"If it helps give you some leads, then it's worth it. I think I prefer amnesia victims though."

He smiled slightly. "Phoebe remembers exactly who she is. She's just missing some of the details."

Still numb, Shae was in no joking mood. "Right. She's a cunning woman from the seventeenth century."

"I think she could be telling the truth." His eyes had grown mischievous, in a way that she remembered when he used to look at her.

"My God, it's worse than I thought. You've fallen for her. What happened after . . . ? On second thought, don't tell me, but it's not like you to sleep with someone, then fall in love with her."

His expression sobered. "I did with you."

She noted that he hadn't denied his involvement with Phoebe. "Very funny. We were barely seventeen, and you know how adolescent hormones distort emotions."

"I'm not laughing."

"Lee, stop it. I don't care to relive the past."

"I'm not. You brought up a point that was untrue."

"Fine. So you love Phoebe. Now what? She has deep psychological issues that are going to take years to deal with. She may never get better."

"Are you worried about me or her, doctor?"

"Both of you, you fool."

"Then save your breath for Phoebe. I can take care of myself."

"Like hell."

A uniformed officer approached Lee and handed him a report. After reading it, Lee crumpled the paper.

"What is it?" Shae asked.

"The tag number was from a stolen car."

All too familiar with his frustration in dealing with a cold case, Shae knew he wouldn't exhibit any emotion on the job, but he would at home, curled up with a six pack. Or in bed with Phoebe. Although she felt relieved she had left the life of a constantly fretting wife behind her, she worried how such a lifestyle might affect Phoebe's delicate constitution.

Shae checked her watch—nearly seven. "Is there anything else you'd like me to do?"

He waved at her to leave. "Go home to Russ. I'll call if need be."

"Lee..."

He glanced over his shoulder.

"Take care of yourself."

He gave no response and vanished down the hallway. Shae took her cell phone from her briefcase and dialed home. When Russ picked up the phone, she said, "I'm on my way. And yes."

"Yes?"

"I'll marry you." The phone dropped on the other end.

"I've asked how many times? Why the sudden change of heart?"

"As a psychologist, I'm all too aware that people often make the same mistakes again and again, but while working on this case with Lee, I realized the two of you are like night and day. I'll be home as quick as I can fight my way through the traffic, and I expect the champagne to be chilled."

"Yes, ma'am."

After a quick "I love you" and a "goodbye," she returned the phone to her briefcase. Pleased with her decision, she debated if she should tell Lee. Later—after she had a chance to celebrate with Russ.

24

Phoebe

B Y THE TIME LIGHTNING STORM and I returned up river, messengers had already delivered the word of Pocahontas's death. Peace betwixt the Indians and English had been tenuous at best. Some said the paramount chief suffered intense grief over the loss of his favored daughter. Instead of experiencing joy at the birth of my son, Dark Moon, I feared what lay ahead. His skin was brown like Lightning Storm's. Only his blue-green eyes gave the secret of his heritage away.

Lightning Storm reassured me. The Arrohateck would always accept the two of us. Of that, I had no doubt. He misunderstood my uneasiness. I feared the glimpse of the world the spirit dog had shown me many seasons afore.

Like all Arrohateck women, I carried Dark Moon on a cradleboard whilst I performed my chores. When he cried in hunger, I suckled him. Unlike Momma's reservations with Sly Fox, I held no qualms other than to satisfy my son's needs. By *taquitock*, fall of the leaf, I gathered herbs for my medicines and nuts for food for my family. I was comforted by the other women working around me, 'til I heard Yellow Butterfly cry out in pain.

I made my way over to Yellow Butterfly, who braced herself against an oak tree. She had tripped in a hole and twisted her ankle. With the aid of two other women, I eased Yellow Butterfly off her feet with the tree supporting her back. I unwrapped her legging. Her ankle was already swollen and severely blackened.

Without being told, the women gathered the materials for a litter, whilst I collected moss for a compress. Fearing that Yellow Butterfly's ankle might be broken, I cut a cedar branch and splinted her lower leg. I packed her ankle with moss and grass afore wrapping her leg with a pliable sapling branch. Satisfied that her leg would be fine 'til we returned to town, I went down to the stream to fetch water.

I spotted four bearded Englishmen, wearing armor and carrying muskets. I backtracked my steps, hoping they hadn't seen me.

A firm hand latched onto my arm. My fists flew, but a man with reddish-brown hair caught my forearms. With all of my strength, I fought him. I nearly broke his grip, when a gap-toothed man joined him. They pulled the cradleboard from my shoulders and Dark Moon fell to the ground. Unable to answer my babe's cries, I continued to fight the two men. A rough hand seized my arm and twisted it behind my back. Now there were three. They were so close I could smell their grimy stench of unwashed flesh. I was surrounded. They held me so tight that I couldn't move.

The gap-toothed man forced his tongue into my mouth, whilst another fondled my breast. A gunshot went off.

A fourth man with long dark hair joined the group. "Gentleman, we are to return this one untouched. She's English."

The other men howled with laughter.

"She doesn't look English," said the gap-toothed man. He pressed his mouth to mine once more, gagging me with his tongue.

"I said leave her!"

He obeyed, and the man with dark hair approached us. "I am Captain Henry Wynne," he said. "You will not be harmed."

Moments passed for me to translate his words in my head, for I thought in the Algonquian tongue. I looked to Dark Moon crying in his cradleboard. "Please," I said in broken English, "let me fetch my son."

"Indians do not travel alone," Captain Wynne replied. "The other women can take care of the child. We aim to bring you in, Phoebe Knowles."

"I'm Walks Through Mist."

"From now on, you shall be known by your English name. Your father awaits you." Captain Wynne placed a blanket around me to hide my bare breast.

My father? But he had died aboard the *Sea Venture.* I struggled as the men led me away from Dark Moon. As a consequence, they lashed my wrists with hemp. I kept looking over my shoulder for glimpses of Dark Moon, straining to turn back to him. Soon, his cries faded. With me as a prisoner, the men walked two miles through the forest afore arriving at the Powhatan River. A small wooden sailing ship that the men called a pinnace waited near the bank.

"Master Knowles," Captain Wynne called to announce our arrival.

A man with streaks of gray in his blondish-red hair descended the plank of the pinnace. I gasped. I had tried my best to forget him. There were deep wrinkles near his eyes that hadn't been there the last time I saw him, but I easily recognized him. "Poppa," I said weakly.

Tears entered his eyes. "My God, Phoebe, what have the savages done to you?"

At first, I was unable to find my tongue and muttered my distress in Algonquian.

"From now on you shall speak English," he commanded.

All Arrohateck women were taught from a young age they might be taken captive by another tribe, but the English *were* my tribe. "We thought you had died at sea, Poppa. The Paspahegh saved us from starving at the colony. I have a husband, and you have a grandchild. His name is—"

"That life is behind you."

In Dorset he had ne'er shown me any affection, but he wrapped his arms around me.

The thought of ne'er seeing Lightning Storm or Dark Moon again pierced my heart. I could not return his embrace. I also feared Lightning Storm would retaliate if he found me. He was no match for English guns. I had to find a way to gain the confidence of my captors and escape on my own.

25

Shae

SHAE UNCONSCIOUSLY HELD HER BREATH as Phoebe blinked. The session had uncovered more information than she could have anticipated. Although Phoebe still recalled everything taking place in the seventeenth century, Shae found the abduction by her father highly significant. Future sessions would likely uncover that he had been abusive. He might have even been the one to have whipped her. "We've made a lot of progress this time. How is everything else?"

Phoebe took out her notepad and started writing. Her concentration was intense when forming the letters. With a proud smile, she handed Shae the note.

The letters were smoother and less scrawling as on the night of the party. "Your writing certainly is improving. Wonderful, Phoebe." Shae checked the list of Phoebe's accomplishments. "Cooks on a stove. Good. Vacuuming. Running a dishwasher. Laundry, using a washing machine. These are all good." She set the note aside, wondering if she was ready to take on the topic both of them had been avoiding. "Okay, Phoebe, I'd like to move onto something else. I presume everything went well after you left my home the other evening."

Phoebe frowned, as if uncertain whether to disclose her relationship with Lee.

"You appear troubled."

"I'm not," Phoebe insisted.

"In this room, you may say anything you wish. It stays between the two of us, unless you tell me otherwise."

Phoebe stood. "I must leave."

"Phoebe, if it's about Lee, I had already guessed. It's all right. I can maintain my professional distance."

Phoebe reseated herself, clenching her hands together on her lap. "What is your conjecture?"

"You tell me. Do you love him?"

"Aye. I have since meeting him."

The truth didn't bring the flood of emotion that Shae had expected. With an untroubled sense of focus, she truly could help her patient. "Does your love stem from the fact that he reminds you of Lightning Storm?"

"Whilst it's true Lee is much like Lightning Storm, he also differs vastly. I cannot explain better 'til I understand myself."

"It'll come to you in time."

A slight smile appeared on Phoebe's face. "Thank you, Shae."

Not only had they broken through some of Phoebe's frustration, they had made significant progress in discovering who she was and where she was from.

26

Phoebe

WEDNESDAY EVE CAME TO PASS AFORE I saw Lee again. As usual, he collected me at Colwell House. Instead of taking me to the ordinary, he brought me to a smoke-filled tavern. Even in the colony, the custom had confused me. The Arrohateck used tobacco for ritual purposes, not for everyday smoking. Here, youth and elder, men and women inhaled cigarettes.

The tavern served "burgers and fries," and a metal box played music that caused me severe ear pain. Perplexed by Lee's selection, I watched everyone carefully and soon realized that using one's fingers whilst eating was considered acceptable in this establishment.

I dipped a fry in a red sauce as Lee had done and tasted sweetness mixed with a salty potato. Intrigued, I tried another as he told me about his week since our parting on Sunday. He was growing comfortable in my presence, and I delighted in that fact.

In turn, I wished to wait 'til we were alone afore revealing my latest remembrances. Aside from that, I had naught to contribute to the conversation, as I had only performed mundane chores and attended menial tutoring. I was painfully aware that, in this society, my level of schooling could be accomplished by any six-year-old child.

Detecting my melancholy, Lee reached across the table and grasped my hand. "It's going to take time."

" 'Til then, I'm a lost soul."

He gently squeezed my hand. "I'll help you through it."

I longed to be taken into his arms. Only then could I pretend that my nightmare journey was anything but.

"I'm a lot like you," he said.

His voice had been solemn, and I sensed his need to convey the story. "Because you were adopted?"

He shook his head. "It wasn't important."

He had come close, but a warrior would reveal his thoughts in his own time. For me to question afore he was ready would be disrespectful.

"Lee!" came an overly loud male voice. A man with puffy brows and a cleft chin, but a kind, smiling face, struck Lee on his shoulder like he was a comrade, then winked at me. "I see why you haven't been hanging around here much lately."

Lee stood. "Phoebe, I'd like for you to meet my partner, Ed Bailey. Ed, Phoebe Wynne."

Afore I knew it, several other detectives gathered round our table. Some had women on their arms. There was also a female detective amongst the group. All hailed me a hearty greeting, and I finally understood why Lee had brought me to the tavern.

They inquired about my accent.

"I'm English," I replied. More questions. "Aye, I'm from Dorset." On and on, and I feared that I might say something that would distress Lee, as I had no wish to make him an object of ridicule. Afore long, the group dispersed, except for Ed.

Ed seated himself in the chair aside me. "Why haven't I heard a word about you before now? Lee doesn't bring just any woman here." He glanced from me to Lee.

"The time never seemed right," Lee responded with a shrug.

Ed's grin widened, and his eyes twinkled. He began telling me tales of the cases he had worked on with Lee. "We were trying to nab a suspect that had run into the woods. I ordered no one to fire, unless absolutely necessary, so we could flush him out. Next thing I know, Lee's blasting away, cursing that he had missed him. I repeated my order, but Lee kept swearing and blasting. Turned out that he was shooting at a copperhead."

"The goddamned snake had coiled around my leg. Nearly scared the shit out of me."

With a laugh, Ed added, "We apprehended the suspect, but the snake got away."

A special bond existed betwixt these men that I had seen amongst warriors. Either would lay down his life for the other, and their stories reminded me of those told round the campfire. As Ed recounted another tale, a man walked by with tattoos of skulls, candles, and flames on both of his arms in an array of reds, greens, and yellows.

"Phoebe?" Lee asked.

"I have ne'er seen a man with tattoos afore—only women. Warriors paint—"

"It's quite common around here," Lee quickly interrupted.

Ed sent me a look, not quite understanding, when a thin man with sunken eyes walked up to our table. He pointed a finger at Lee. "Crowley . . ."

Ed tensed his hands, whilst Lee calmly sipped his ale.

"Going to ignore me like the drunken redskin you are? Everyone knows Injuns can't handle their liquor."

Ed started to rise, but Lee grasped his partner's arm, signaling him to stay where he was. Lee shoved back his chair, and stood. "Good to see you too, Snyder. I presume your cheery hello is to let me know you've been released. I appreciate the warning. I'll know to watch my back now." He sent the man a fierce stare.

The sunken eyes looked from Lee to Ed, and now a gathering group of detectives. He slunk off under their watchful eyes.

Lee reseated himself and waved at the other detectives that he was fine. "Sorry about that, Phoebe. An asshole that I put away a few years back."

"Put away?"

"Sent to prison."

"I'll give the two of you a chance to talk." Ed got to his feet and grasped my hand. "It was great meeting you, Phoebe. I hope to be seeing more of you."

I thanked him, and he wished me "goodnight."

"Welcome to a cop's life," Lee said, watching me with concern.

This time into which I had been plunged was not so very different from the one I had left behind. I knew not some of the words that had been uttered, but the threats behind them were clear.

"If you've changed your mind about us, I understand."

I met his gaze. "My confusion lies with the century, not you."

"You're sure?"

"You've aided me in my moment of need. Now that you require my understanding, how could I turn my back?"

A smile spread across his face. "You continue to take me by surprise."

He needed no prodding when I suggested that we return to his apartment. Once inside the door, his quiet calmness gave way to other pressing concerns. He led me over to the divan, knelt afore me, and shoved my skirt above my hips. In his haste, I thought he might forget the condom, but he carried one in his wallet.

When we joined, I no longer compared his touches to Lightning Storm's. Only the man in my arms mattered. I had been sent to this time for him. Our lives were as intertwined as our bodies. Here I was on the edge of intersecting planes of the past, present, and future. All existed simultaneously in the circle of time for us to meet.

With a shudder, I slumped against him. He held my head and kissed me. Because of the past, the future was ours for the taking.

27

Lee

RELAXED BEYOND ANYTHING he could imagine, Lee watched curiously as Phoebe sifted through his collection. Wrapped in his bathrobe, she picked up a medicine staff covered in beads, feathers, and bells.

"It's Lakota," he said. "The rattle is Cherokee."

"I don't know the Lakota or Cherokee," she replied, shaking the gourd, "but the Arrohateck had similar rattles. They also had these . . ." She pointed to the flute and tomahawk. She inspected the arrowheads. Some were made from stone, others bone. Her hand came to rest on one crafted from deer antler. "The maker was a brave warrior."

"Keep it if you like. I can't make any sense of the lot."

"I shall cherish it." Her hand closed around the arrowhead. "Lee, I can teach you the dreaming. You will uncover your own answers."

"Shae said the dreaming is nothing more than hypnosis."

" 'Tis not hypnosis." A knowing smile appeared on Phoebe's lips. "Shae requested that I not engage in the dreaming with you. I thought she feared it. Now I see the truth. With hypnosis I can recall that which I've forgotten, but the dreaming is much more. My spirit travels to aid in my healing."

"How does that explain me being there too?"

"We are connected somehow. Only time will tell us why, but Lightning Storm has chosen you to reveal that which was. If I show you the way, you can discover your own path."

Although uncertain what to make of her words, Lee was tempted. *What had happened to solid evidence?* None of it made sense. "I don't think I'm ready to fly solo, but I'd like to continue to help you. I'm learning about myself through you. For right now, that's enough." He grasped her hand.

On their way to the living room, Lee grabbed a candle from the kitchen. Whether the visions were the result of hypnosis or not, he didn't care. It had been a long time since he was drawn to a woman the way he was with Phoebe, and the dreaming brought them closer.

He lit the candle. His bathrobe opened slightly as Phoebe sat across from him, and he caught a glimpse of the curve of her breast. His will suddenly weakened. Pleasant thoughts of her naked body pressed against his intruded. "I'm not sure I'll be able to concentrate."

Picking up on his thoughts, she asked, "Was most of the night not enough?"

Her distinctive herbal scent mesmerized him. "Definitely not."

"Concentrate as if you were performing your occupation and your life relied upon it."

"If I were on duty, you wouldn't be sitting across from me in a provocative way."

She glared.

"All right. I'll try." Earlier in the evening, Phoebe had told him how she had been kidnapped by the English. She was counting on him. He sat on the floor and focused on the flame. *Absorb it.*

Nothing.

Try again.

The smoke swirled to a mist. He spotted the greyhound ahead of him. At a lope, the dog moved forward. Lee made his way through the forest, wearing moccasins and leggings to protect him from the brambles. *Where was Phoebe?* He had never seen the greyhound without her somewhere nearby.

Up ahead, the dog halted. Sheltered by cypress and sweet gum trees, Lee watched the wooden palisade from a safe distance. He resisted the urge to shoot arrows into the men when they squatted on the privy. With the women and children, he was more patient.

Still, he waited. Most of the day passed before a red-haired woman, accompanied by two other women, used the privy. He called to her in the voice of the crow.

Her head snapped around with her eyes searching the forest. He called again. She located him. For a brief moment their gazes met. Though she dressed in the manner of the English, her heart was Arrohateck. Convinced that she had understood his meaning, he would wait until he could help her make her escape.

28

Phoebe

IN THE YEAR OF OUR LORD 1609, the *Sea Venture* had run ashore on Discovery Bay. All of her passengers had safely made land. From the wreckage, the survivors built two pinnaces and arrived in James Towne in May of 1610, a full three months aft Momma and I had left the colony. Now in 1617, I wore a shift and full skirt and bound my breasts with stays. My shoes had hard soles and were made of unforgiving leather. They pinched my feet, and I had difficulty walking.

The church in the colony had fallen into disrepair, but Poppa instructed me in the ways of religion. I had been baptised as a babe in Dorset, but much of what I had learnt had been forgotten. I found the scriptures fascinating but failed to understand how God and Ahone were so very different. When commanded to say my prayers, I gave my offerings to both. The very first time I faced the four winds, Poppa struck my back with a willow stick. Thereafter, I gave my thanks to Ahone in silence.

Though the palisades were broken, the fort was my prison. I heard Lightning Storm's calls, and I bided my time for an opportunity to escape. Only at night did I dare chance responding to him with the call of the whippoorwill. I no longer tended fields, nor made clay pots. Poppa thought me unmarriageable. I reminded him that I was already married to Lightning Storm, only to feel the lash of the willow stick. He cursed me, saying no matter how large a dowry, I would ne'er find a respectable husband, because I had been soiled by an Indian.

I went about my chores, learning to cook and sew as the women showed me. My knowledge of *wisakon* was an asset to the colony. Many a woman knew the family physick. I would have shown them where the native plants grew, but Poppa feared I might run off and rejoin the Arrohateck. I felt caged, pacing the perimeter of the palisades. Whilst doing so, I discovered the breaks, so I would know which one would grant me freedom when my opportunity arose, and I signaled the openings to Lightning Storm.

Because of Poppa's lack of trust, I was always accompanied if I ventured out of doors, especially if my task was to use the privy, as it was located outside the fort. Captain Wynne frequently joined me on my outdoor excursions. He oft asked me what it was like to live amongst savages. Unlike others who spoke in hushed whispers about my previous life, his curiosity appeared genuine. When I told him the Arrohateck were anything but savage, he reminded me of their devil worship and atrocities rendered upon citizens loyal to the Crown.

I held my tongue, for I did not wish him to repeat the truth from my lips to Poppa, only for me to receive yet another beating. Instead, I smiled politely, pretending to accept the English were guiltless. Aft a time, he seemed to fancy me, and I used it to my advantage.

Three months passed, when Captain Wynne and I trod alongside the palisade. The full moon had been partially covered by growing clouds, and there was mist in the air.

"Phoebe," he said, "I'm going to speak to your father."

For a moment, I feared what I might have done now, 'til it dawned on me that he was asking for my hand in marriage. "I'm already married, Captain."

"You were ne'er married in the church."

"Then I fear my son was begotten without the benefit of wedlock."

"Phoebe . . ." He tenderly grasped my hand. "That life is behind you. In another month, I sail for England. I have land here along the James River."

Land stolen in bloodshed from the Paspahegh. Nearly panicking, I collected my wits and contained my thoughts. Captain Wynne hadn't been involved in those earlier conflicts. "Your offer is very kind, Captain. I shall need time to think on your proposal."

"Of course." He bent at the waist and kissed my hand.

My heart pounded like a war drum within my chest. Knowing the time had come to take flight, I gently withdrew my hand from his grip. His eyes glimmered, and I thought of Lightning Storm. I could feel his presence as if he were guiding me.

"I shall wait another day or two afore speaking with your father. Allow me to escort you to the house."

"I must avail of the privy first."

He guided me to the pits outside the palisade and kept watch. Many a man had been filled with arrows when tending to basic necessities, whilst a number of women had been carried off by warriors.

The Captain, with his hand poised on his pistol, peered into the mist for spectral warriors. His back turned, and I slipped off my shoes. I lifted my skirts and tiptoed away. When I gave the call of the whippoorwill, heavy footsteps charged aft me. I bolted. I uttered a loud cry, imitating a warrior the best I could. Without looking back, I kept running. The captain shouted my name to stop.

Soft moonlight filtered through the mist, but the fog thickened. Branches scratched my arms, but I would not halt 'til the colony was far behind me. When I thought my legs would carry me no further, I stumbled. I had no notion how far I had come.

I pressed onwards. Up ahead, I spied the white spirit dog. Aside him, stood Lightning Storm. Voices bellowed from behind me. I reached Lightning Storm's side, and he notched an arrow to his bowstring. I grasped his arm. "Nay. I am unharmed. My English father was responsible. He survived the sea voyage."

His muscles tensed. "Your father?"

"Aye. Do not take vengeance, Lightning Storm. You are but one warrior. He and his men will certainly kill you if you should try."

The voices grew closer, and he lowered the bow. Together, we turned and vanished into the forest.

I blinked, and Lee's face came into focus. He remained unmoving. I would narrate the memory of my escape from the colony without hypnosis to Shae at our next meeting, but I had shared the experience with Lee because of his unselfish act of wanting to help me. With each encounter, our connection only grew stronger.

He finally shook his head. "Phoebe?"

I curled upon his lap, seeking the comfort and safety of his arms. He held me close, and I lay my head upon his chest to the solace of his heartbeat. "I'm grateful for your presence."

He rolled strands of my hair betwixt his fingertips. "I'm still trying to decide how much is real." Though he shared my innermost thoughts, he still had doubts.

"All is real."

"You don't know how much I want to believe—"

I placed my fingers to his lips. "By the time I learn why I have been brought here, you shall discover your own path. 'Til then, accept what we share, not as fact, simply that it is part of us."

At my brave words, he embraced me. I kissed him upon the mouth, long and deep. How could I love him so completely whilst swirling through the unknown?

29

Lee

ON LEE'S WAY to the nursing home, his cell phone rang. "Crowley," he answered.

"*Lee. Ellen Hatfield here. I apologize for taking so long in getting back to you, but I had to consult with a colleague to pin down the dialect of the recording you brought in. It's Virginia Algonquian.*"

"Virginia? How is that possible? The language has been extinct for—"

"*Almost two hundred years. I know. Is there any chance I can meet the woman you've recorded?*"

"I'll talk to her." He thanked her before hanging up. After driving another mile, he pulled the T-Bird into the lot of the nursing home. *Virginia Algonquian—how could that be unless . . . ?* He silently rebuked himself for entertaining the thought that Phoebe might indeed be from the seventeenth century, and he went inside. There had to be a logical explanation. He dealt with puzzles all the time without going off half cocked.

He neared his mother's room, and the staff member who had stopped him on a previous visit met him in the hall. She immediately shifted her gaze and continued on, which was probably for the best. He knocked on his mother's door.

A faint voice told him to come in.

As usual, his mother sat in the wheelchair near the window with the photograph album in her lap. They exchanged hellos before he wheeled her outside for a breath of spring air. She mentioned a visit from Shae, before showing him the photo album. "I came across this photo the other day."

Dressed in stereotypical Indian garb of a feathered headdress for a school play about the "first Thanksgiving," he was about ten in the photo. "I spent two weeks in detention because I refused to wear war paint and carry a tomahawk."

She chuckled. "You won your point, didn't you?"

"Not really. It was a plains tribe headdress, and they would have expelled me if I had refused to take part in the play. I spent a lot of time in detention for my disagreements with history teachers."

With a prideful smile, she patted his hand. "I know it wasn't easy for you."

Even now he sheltered her from the extent of other peoples' prejudices. *Why?* He thought of Phoebe's offer. Should he use the dreaming to seek his own answers? He was still trying to wrap his head around the bombshell that his former professor had dropped. Phoebe spoke Virginia Algonquian.

30

Phoebe

ON TUESDAY DURING MY SESSION WITH SHAE, I was able to recount my escape from the colony without the use of hypnosis. Like Momma when I had done something that displeased her, Shae scowled. "Have you been using hypnosis on Lee again?"

My connection to Shae was not that of a friend, but a tie which I did not fully understand. "I have ne'er used hypnosis."

"Then what you call the dreaming?"

"Aye. Does it not give you the answers to which you seek?"

"It moves your story forward," she agreed, "but I don't like to see hypnosis practiced by anyone that hasn't been professionally trained." I opened my mouth to interject, but she held up a hand afore continuing, "Phoebe, your mind is playing tricks. For whatever reason, you believe you're from the seventeenth century. I know you're frustrated by how slow the progress is, but we will get to the bottom of why you're more comfortable in the world your mind has created. Meanwhile, you could be putting Lee at risk."

"Aye. If I were using hypnosis."

Shae let out an uneasy breath. "Very well. I don't wish to alienate you. I'll accept what you call it for now. We'll talk about it later. I'm also sorry to say that I need to cancel our next session, because I'll be out of town for a conference until late Saturday night. If you need to contact someone before next week, you can call my home number and talk to Russ. He's familiar with your case. Will that be satisfactory?"

I nodded.

"Keep in mind what I've told you, but if you do participate in the dreaming, be careful."

"I shall."

She smiled in a protective way like Momma oft had. Even her blonde locks were much like Momma's, and I had a sudden pang for being held in the arms of the woman who had birthed me.

On Saturday, I convinced Lee that I wished to see *more* historical sites. If, as Shae said, my mind was playing tricks and I really hailed from the twenty-first century, then why could I recall naught? More than anything, I wanted to unlock the mysteries.

Lee parked the car in a lot, where behind a gate I spied a house called Wingfield Hall. I had ne'er been in a house so grand. Like many lesser houses in Dorset, the manor was made of wattle and daub. But Wingfield Hall spread several houses wide and had a finely pitched roof, brick chimneys, and glass windows.

Once we were inside, Lee paid for our tickets. We were ushered to a darkened room to view a film on the history of the manor. When the introduction began to play, I became confused. Unlike the TV at Colwell House, the sound emanated from a different location than the picture.

Wingfield Hall was crated piece by piece and shipped from England to Virginia, where it was reassembled as it stood now. The film soon ended, and a tour guide escorted us into the great hall. The walls were wood paneled, and a tapestry with coursing hounds similar to my spirit dog adorned the wall. I tensed upon seeing the armor, ready for use.

Lee squeezed my arm. "It's nothing more than a display."

"Aye," I said, taking a deep breath. "Of that, I'm aware."

I held my tongue at the missing rushes upon the floors. In the parlor, John Gerard's *The Herbal* rested on a table. Whilst living in Dorset, *The Herbal* was the only book Momma had owned. Rarely consulting it, she oft told me that a true wise woman learnt more from observation than from reading a book written by a man with less knowledge than she in the way of physick.

We continued on. Upstairs in the bed chamber stood a hand-carved bed frame, which few could have afforded. Outside was the kitchen. Cast iron pots sat over a pretend cooking fire. A table held wood bowls and clay pottery. I had ne'er afore seen plastic food. Unlike other visits with Lee, naught triggered a memory. Aft the house tour, we strolled through the gardens, which included brick walls, courtyards, boxwood hedges, and walkways. Tulips bloomed in every color of the rainbow.

When we entered the herb garden, I bent to study a tall-stemmed plant. "Shepherd's purse. 'Tis used to stop bleeding." I continued on to a shrubby, foul-smelling five-leaf plant. "Sarsaparilla. A leaf tea cures by sweating, and roots are a remedy against pain in the joints and head." Next, I came to ginger. "It grows in Spain and aids an ailing stomach. St. John's Wort also hails from afar." I turned to Lee. "Do you think Valerie would allow me to grow a herb garden?"

With a wide smile, he crossed his arms. "I like the way you pronounce the 'h' in herb. I bet she would."

For once, no unpleasant memories surfaced. Was I growing accustomed to my situation? We ambled further 'til arriving at a yew hedge that even towered over Lee's head. 'Twas a maze. I giggled at the prospect, and together we entered. We followed the mulch-covered passageway. A sign pointed the way, only leading to a dead end.

We reached another sign.

"I won't be fooled twice," Lee muttered under his breath.

We took the opposite path and hit another dead end. I couldn't help but laugh. "I thought a cop would be used to solving puzzles."

A smile crossed his face, and he took me into his arms. "It was my plan all along to get you in here alone."

I slipped from his embrace. "We must solve the puzzle or endure seven years bad luck."

"You made that up."

"Aye." I scampered ahead, and he followed me in pursuit.

Quickly catching up with me, he caught my hand. "It's good to hear you laugh."

"This place brings no memories, except you."

He gave me a quick kiss, and we returned to the task at hand. At the center was a fountain with lily pads on the water where I felt the spray upon my face afore we began our journey through the maze to find our way out. " 'Tis much like being lost in a forest."

Worry vexed Lee's brow, and he came to an abrupt halt. "I was abandoned in the forest. Two years old, and I was left there to die. What kind of mother would do that to her child?"

Aware that he was finally unburdening his soul to me, I said, "Mayhap she had no choice, like when the English abducted me and left Dark Moon behind."

His right hand curled to a fist. "There was no evidence of any foul play at the scene."

"Because you have lived through it, you are blinded from thinking like a cop. I oft ponder the lad who vanished aft the attack on the Paspahegh town. I vowed to keep him safe, but he wandered away, whilst I slumbered. I hope someone found him, but I fear he may have died—alone."

The tautness of his brow eased. "I guess I've never thought of it that way before."

I sought his hand, and a smile slowly crossed his lips. Together, we journeyed through the maze, as we would follow the confusing path in order to seek how I had come to be here.

31

Lee and Shae

BECAUSE OF HIS REVELATION to Phoebe earlier in the day, Lee sought the dreaming. To help Phoebe would in turn lead the way for himself. As the mist surrounded him, he expected to see the shape of a greyhound. The dog failed to appear, and he fumbled through the fog. He had to take a deep breath to keep from panicking. "Phoebe, something's wrong. I'm lost."

"Nay. You're finding your own way."

Darkness everywhere. "But the dog—"

"Is my protector. Focus on finding yours. Do you see it?"

"No." But he heard the flapping of wings. "I hear a bird flying."

"Good. You can move towards the sound, or allow it come to you."

Still uncertain what was happening, Lee waited as the sound of flapping wings approached him.

The mist thinned. He heard a caw and spotted a fan-shaped tail. A large black bird settled on a nearby branch. "It's a crow."

"The spirit will guide you through the mist."

The bird's eyes were a dark brown, but the beak, legs, and feet were black. Lee had never noticed the metallic violet gloss on the otherwise black feathers before. The crow preened its feathers. When it took flight, Lee followed.

The mist cleared, and he suddenly felt dizzy. He collapsed to the ground. Strong hands were helping him, lifting him. They placed

him on a mat-covered pallet. His throat burned, and he struggled
for each breath.

A woman's gentle hand touched him, and blue-green eyes
looked on in concern. "You're raging with fever," she said.

A gourd went to his lips, and she helped him drink. It was difficult to swallow. He managed to choke out, "Phoebe—"

"Lightning Storm, you have ne'er used my English name."

Lightning Storm? In his muddled thoughts, he seemed to recall
Phoebe saying Lightning Storm had chosen him. *For what?* He felt
a cool cloth on his forehead. The refreshing feeling spread from his
neck to his chest as the cloth trailed over him. "Phoebe—"

"Save your strength, Lightning Storm."

Weariness and worry registered in her eyes. He drifted in a feverish daze, floating in a foggy dream.

Dripping water woke him. Phoebe was beside him, and her
touch returned. The cloth was cool and wet, and the haze lifted with
her deep, tender strokes. She turned him to his stomach, and he felt
long and soothing massages on his back. Once flat on his back again,
her touches reached his groin. He smiled in fond remembrance.

"You mustn't die, Lightning Storm."

But he wasn't Lightning Storm. He reached a hand to her face
and stroked her cheek. "Phoebe. It's me. Lee."

She hushed him. "Many have been ill. The *kwiocosuck* have tried
to appease Oke, but the sickness spreads."

Her words made no sense, and he drifted once more. The crow
had brought him here. How did he return? His throat closed, and he
could barely breathe. He fought for another breath. Struggling for
air, he shot to a sitting position and seized Phoebe's wrist. "Nooo!"

He blinked. He *was* in his living room.

"Lee?"

He let go of his grip on Phoebe. "What did I just see?"

"Lightning Storm nearly died from throat distemper."

A vision from Lightning Storm's life. He went into the den to
the computer. Phoebe peered curiously over his shoulder as he performed a quick search for throat distemper. The first couple of web-
pages led him to historical epidemics. The symptoms were similar
to what he had experienced in the vision, but they failed to name a

modern term. He clicked onto a third page. "Diphtheria. It's rare in this country now."

"The name matters naught. It spread throughout the Arrohateck, killing many, especially amongst the children." Phoebe's face paled.

"What's wrong? You hinted that Lightning Storm survived."

"I recall now. Dark Moon did not." With a throaty sob, she sank to the floor. "My son is dead," she repeated over and over.

Lee drew her into his arms and held her as she sobbed on his shoulder.

When Shae arrived home from the conference in Washington, she looked forward to a late dinner of Russ's fabulous almond-butter chicken. Instead, she caught him rushing out the the door.

"It's Phoebe," he said.

"What's wrong?"

"Get in the car. Lee was pretty upset."

Although exhausted from the drive, she did as he requested. If Lee was distressed, Phoebe must be in serious shape. "When did he call?"

"A few minutes ago." Russ pulled the car out of the drive and revved the engine. "He said that he can't calm Phoebe. Something about the loss of a child. I heard her crying in the background."

Another interesting development. She was also willing to bet they had been dabbling with hypnosis again. Ready to read Lee the riot act, Shae had difficulty sitting back for the thirty-minute drive to his apartment.

When they knocked on the door, no one answered. Shae tried the handle. Locked. She would have been shocked if Lee had forgotten. "Are you sure this is where you were supposed to meet him?"

"Positive. You stay here, while I get the super to open the door."

"Lee, open the door." She kept shouting and knocking. Had she heard a cry from inside? *Russ, please hurry.* A few of the neighbors gathered around her, inquiring what was wrong. She deflected them as best as she could.

By the time Russ returned with the superintendent, her knuckles had turned black and blue. The super unlocked the door, and they went inside. Afraid of what they might find, Shae held her breath.

"Lee," Russ called out, "where are you?"

"In here."

Lee's voice had been low, almost too soft to hear, but it had come from the room off to their left. Russ grasped Shae's wrist and led her in that direction. Shirtless and wearing sweat pants, Lee sat on the floor, holding Phoebe, clad in an oversized bathrobe. To Phoebe's muffled sobs, he rocked her, telling her that everything would be all right.

"How could you blatantly ignore—!"

"Shae," Russ interrupted, "your patient."

Shae raised a finger but caught herself. *See to Phoebe first.* She bent down. Phoebe's face was tear streaked. "Phoebe . . ." No response. "I think it would be best if we get her back to Colwell House." She reached for Phoebe's arm, but Phoebe clung tighter to Lee.

"Phoebe . . ." Lee took her face between his hands. "Shae thinks you should return to Colwell House." Even he wasn't reaching her.

"I could call in a psychiatrist," Shae suggested.

Lee shook his head. "I don't think that's a good idea."

He was probably right. Any of the psychiatrists she was personally familiar with would want to commit Phoebe, rather than sedate her. Unwilling to give up on Phoebe just yet, Shae was determined to try again. "Phoebe, we're all trying to help. Russ told me that you have lost a child. Is that true?"

Phoebe gave a weak nod.

Good, at least she's listening. After twenty minutes, they were able to coax Phoebe from Lee's arms. A small step. It might take half the night to return her to Colwell House. *What of Lee?* His stoic face revealed no hint of emotion, but Shae was painfully aware that he was hurting. She would speak to him after Phoebe was settled. Suddenly understanding what Valerie meant on the night of the party, she realized her initial concerns of him becoming involved with Phoebe had been for Shae's own selfish reasons, thinking no one could replace her. He hadn't had a steady relationship since their divorce, because he hadn't found the right woman.

* * *

On Monday, Shae visited the police station. It was the first time she had stopped by for personal reasons since the divorce. At the front desk, she asked for Lee. Nearly half an hour passed before he greeted her with a cup of coffee in hand and escorted her to an empty interrogation room. "How's Phoebe?" he asked. The lines near his eyes warned her how much sleep he had likely gotten.

"She's grieving. Lee, you were vague the other night. What triggered the memory this time?"

He motioned for her to have a seat. "Can I get you anything?"

"I'm fine," she said, taking a seat at the table. "You were saying..."

He sat across from her and sipped his coffee. "It's my fault this happened. I ignored your warning. I thought I was helping her find out what happened."

"You engaged in the dreaming with her."

He nodded. "Lightning Storm nearly died from what she called throat distemper. I went into the den to check the computer and discovered she meant diphtheria. She said many of the children had died. That's when she collapsed, crying that Dark Moon was one of them."

"In other words, you're saying she remembered the event without hypnosis?"

Another nod.

"I've reminded you on more than one occasion that her memories are very near the surface. Your *session* with Phoebe set off a cascade of memories in an uncontrolled environment."

His concern for Phoebe was written all over his face. "Thanks, I needed the extra guilt trip."

"Sorry, that wasn't my intent. Both Russ and I believe that she must have indeed lost a child. Her level of grief is consistent with such a loss."

"You still don't believe the dreaming is anything more than hypnosis?"

"It's not," she insisted.

"If that's the case why would I suddenly be susceptible? You said I wasn't a good subject. "

"Normally you're not, but Phoebe has tapped into the one place where you seek answers—your adoption and the circumstances surrounding it, which makes you vulnerable to suggestion."

He shook his head in frustration. "In the visions, I've always seen her seventeenth-century world, not anything from thirty-odd years ago."

"That doesn't make any difference. Not long ago I heard you spouting off about the Paspahegh and Arrohateck. You sounded like a fricking textbook. Her world gives meaning to those textbook responses. The Paspahegh and Arrohateck come to life in your mind. In turn, it lends you a sense of identity."

He rubbed a hand over his chin, as if mulling over her answer. "I'm skeptical, but let's say for the sake of argument you're right. How does the use of hypnosis help Phoebe?"

"Until this story of hers plays out to a conclusion, we're not going to be able to identify who she really is or where she's from. She trusts you because you're searching for something similar. Overall, your help seems to benefit her. My only concern . . ."

"Go on."

She hated the way he noticed any sort of hesitation. "If you continue to use hypnosis in an uncontrolled situation, it may harm you as well."

Relief spread across his face. "I'm touched that you still care."

"Lee," she grumbled. "I'm serious. If you start believing her story as fact, it may damage you psychologically. Hell, you're a detective. Can't you use a more standard method for uncovering who your biological parents are?"

His eyes narrowed. "And how do you propose I do that? The goddamned trail went cold over thirty years ago."

She waved at him to calm down. "I only meant there might have been some clue that you have overlooked. You may never find them, but I honestly don't think the road you've chosen will lead you to the answers you seek."

"I'll keep everything you've said in mind."

"Very well." Shae stood, and Lee automatically got to his feet. "Will you do me a favor?" she asked.

"If I can."

"Keep an open line of communication. If you have any questions or concerns, please don't hesitate to call me."

"I will," he assured her, "if Phoebe ever talks to me again. She doesn't answer my calls."

"Give her time."

Lee escorted her to the door. "Who would have thought that we could finally bury the past and be friends?"

"Why would you find it surprising? We were friends before. We just needed to get past the awkwardness."

"Like the memories of our wild escapades right after the divorce. Sometimes, I wondered why we had gotten divorced. You were—"

"Shut up before your colleagues find it necessary to arrest me for assaulting a police officer. That chapter of our lives is closed and has been for years."

He snorted a laugh. "Ah, but the memories will remain with me always."

"Fine. Keep the memories. You just wanted to see if I'd blush or squirm." She held out her arms. "See. I'm not blushing, nor am I squirming. We had sex after our divorce—it's hardly uncommon. We fought, then made up in bed. I think we've both learned that it takes more than good sex to make a marriage. So when you're wandering down memory lane, just make certain you recall the entire picture." Now she *was* blushing. She felt the telltale signs of heat in her cheeks. Lee's partner, Ed, had joined them.

32

Phoebe

FOR DAYS I COULD NOT RISE from my bed to do the simplest of chores. If indeed I had lost Dark Moon long ago, hadn't I already cried my tears? Lee called twice a day, but I would tell whoever answered I did not wish to speak to him. Shae visited frequently, and I overheard whispers betwixt her and Valerie that they might have to commit me. I presumed they meant taking me to an asylum. I had sunk to the darkest of depths and cared not.

On the tenth morn, Meg barged into my room and shoved the curtains open. Sunshine streamed through the window. "I've had it, Phoebe. You're getting up today. Get dressed."

I squinted away the bright sunlight and hugged my pillow. "I don't wish to rise."

She tugged on my arm, pulling me to a sitting position. "Get up."

"Nay." I fell back to the bed.

"I've already told Lee not to call here anymore."

I sat up under my own power. "Why would you do that?"

"Because you don't give a damn how he must feel. You're being selfish and only thinking of yourself."

Her words stung. "My son has died."

Meg sat aside me. "Phoebe, I can't even begin to imagine what you must be going through. If I ever lost Tiffany..." Tears filled her eyes and streaked her cheeks. She brushed them away with the side of her hand. "All of us are trying to help. Valerie says she'll have no choice but to regard you as a Colwell House failure if you don't start contributing soon. The rest of us have taken on your chores. Carol is already fed up and ready to send you packing. Personally, I don't mind a few extra chores. You're in a lot of pain, but you reject our efforts outright. If you want to cry on my shoulder, I'll sit here and hold you. We'll cry together, but please stop shutting us out of your life."

Her words spoke the wisdom of an elder, but I remained unsure. "What if I falter?"

"One of us will pick you up. You'd do the same for us."

As I stood, my knees trembled. "I shall get dressed."

Once again, tears welled in Meg's eyes. "That's a great start."

I defied the desire to return to bed. "Did you really tell Lee not to call?"

"I told him you aren't well enough to speak with him yet."

"Meg..." I hugged her. "You're a true friend."

"Sometimes, we all need a little kick in the butt. When I was doing drugs, I hit an all-time low. If Valerie hadn't come to my aid, I would have lost Tiffany. Not like you did Dark Moon, but a court would have ruled that I was an unfit mother and adopted her out."

Like Lee. Though I remained weak, I held renewed determination. "Meg, aft I get dressed, I shall come downstairs. I will see to my chores today."

"Good. That herb garden of yours will look like a weed patch if it doesn't get some tending. I've never had a green thumb."

Perplexed, I held out my pale thumbs and compared them to her dark brown ones. "Neither have I."

"Get out of here, girl," she said with a laugh.

Though her words made little sense, I trusted her, almost as much as Lee. *Lee.* I had forsaken him and worried how I could make amends.

In 1619, I was again heavy with child. Each new moon I traveled to the river and said prayers for the health of my child. One mist–filled morn, I drank slippery elm bark tea mixed with other roots and herbs to encourage an easy delivery when the time arose. Alongside

Lightning Storm and a *kwiocos,* I proceeded to the river. I carried a white doeskin, white string, and two beads, one black and one white. The black bead symbolized the spiritual realm and the white, life.

Upon reaching the bank of the river, Lightning Storm and I spread the skin on the ground. We knelt. The *kwiocos* held the black bead in his left hand and the white bead in his right. He extended his arms and recited a prayer to the unborn child's health as the beads moved betwixt his forefingers and thumbs. "Your child will be a lass," he said. "She will . . ."

I caught his hesitation and feared I would lose my unborn child, as I had Dark Moon.

"She will survive her childhood."

I breathed out in relief, whilst Lightning Storm strung the beads on the thread and wrapped them in the cloth. He handed the bundle to the *kwiocos.* Then, I retched from the slippery elm mixture. The act rid me of any malady that might harm my child.

33

Shae and Lee

A SMALL STEP, BUT PHOEBE was speaking about the past again. Two weeks had passed since the discovery of her having lost a child, and Shae silently thanked Meg for her bold move. Phoebe was moving forward again. "What about your everyday activities?" Shae asked.

"I perform my chores at Colwell House without fail and attend to my studies."

"And Lee?"

Lowering her gaze, Phoebe clasped her hands in her lap. "I have not seen him. He calls to inquire how I'm faring, but I'm uncertain what to say."

"Phoebe, he's concerned about you. Just tell him that you'll talk to him. The rest will work out. I'm certain of that." Shae was hit by a wave of nostalgia. At one time, she had felt the same for Lee. "Is there anything else you'd like to talk about before we call it a day?"

"Nay."

"Just remember to call me if you need anything before our next session."

"I shall. Thank you, Shae."

Shae escorted Phoebe to the door and breathed a sigh of relief. Phoebe was her last patient of the day. After a goodbye, she returned to her desk and looked over her calendar for the following day, when her receptionist buzzed her. "There's an Ed Bailey here to see you."

What could Lee's partner want? "Send him in."

The door opened, and Ed entered. "Shae, I hope I haven't inconvenienced you by dropping in."

"Not at all," she said, standing.

He approached the desk and shook her hand. "I was hoping to catch you before you left for the day."

She motioned for him to have a seat. "What brings you here? I admit, I'm a bit puzzled."

He pulled up the chair to the desk and sat. "It's about Lee."

"If it's in reference to a couple of weeks ago . . ."

With a wave of his hand, he said, "I wish it were that simple. He's been preoccupied lately. In one instance, he mishandled evidence, nearly jeopardizing the entire case. On another case, he put himself in an unnecessary situation that could have gotten ugly real fast. I trained him myself. He's the best. It's not like him to make rookie mistakes. I know the two of you haven't been together for quite sometime, but I didn't know who else might know anything."

"I don't see how I can help."

"Have you met Phoebe?"

"I have."

"Is she the cause of his distraction?"

"Possibly."

Frustration wrinkled his forehead. "And you're not going to say any more."

"Ed, you know I can't."

"Can you at least speak to Lee? The last time I saw him this distracted by a woman . . ." His gaze met hers. "I shouldn't have said that, but it was you, when you asked for the divorce."

She nodded in understanding. "I'll let him know your concern."

"Thanks." He stood, and they shook hands again.

As he exited, Shae blew out an exasperated breath. When she had initially taken Phoebe's case, she would have never guessed where it would lead. *Regret?* Not in the least. Phoebe continued to intrigue her.

* * *

When Phoebe had finally agreed to see him, Lee debated whether or not he should go. For two weeks he had kept calling her, only to be turned away. If he wasn't on duty, he spent the time nursing a beer until he lost count of how many he had consumed. Drunken Indian, drunken cop. He had two strikes against him.

Sober again, he refused to sink to the same level he had after Shae left. When Meg called, she said Phoebe didn't want to talk on the phone, but to meet him face to face. He had nearly said "no," but who was he fooling? He wanted to see her, even if she only wanted to see him to part ways.

With some nervousness, Lee knocked on the door at Colwell House. It cracked open.

"Lee . . ." The door widened, and Valerie allowed him to enter. Her hands trembled. "I'm glad you're here."

"What's wrong? Is it Phoebe?"

"Phoebe's fine," she gulped. "Phoebe and Meg are upstairs, trying to calm a situation."

"What kind of situation?"

"Carol's boyfriend is upstairs. He says he's not leaving without her."

"Does he have a weapon?"

"I don't think so, but I've heard Carol crying."

He didn't wait to hear more. Male visitors were strictly forbidden upstairs. He charged up the stairs two at a time. Near the landing, he overheard Phoebe and Meg begging Carol to come out of her room. He reached the top and waved the women away from the door. Heated voices came from inside the room. As a patrol officer, he had hated handling domestic disputes. As a detective, he got the call when someone was severely injured or dead. Standing to the side of the door, he knocked. "Carol, I'm Detective Crowley with the county police. Are you all right?"

Behind the door, she choked on a sob but gave an affirmative.

"Open the door and let me see that you're all right." Nothing happened, and Lee tensed with his hand near his gun. "Carol . . ."

The door slowly opened, and a man with a tattoo that had a heart and Carol's name on his right arm held his arms away from his body to show he carried no weapons. He knew the procedure, which meant he likely had run-ins with the law before. Lee remained alert.

The woman squinted as if in pain but bore no physical evidence of abuse.

"Do you want to press charges?" Lee asked.

Shaking her head, she cried into a tissue.

Lee reached for the man's arm. "I'll escort you out of here."

"I'm going," he said, jerking free of Lee's grip.

They left the room, and Phoebe and Meg went to check on Carol. With relief spreading across her face, Valerie waited at the bottom of the stairs. Lee accompanied the man outside and made certain he was leaving before returning to the house. "He'll be back," he told Valerie.

Still visibly shaken, she swallowed hard. "He's the one I told you that I had a feeling about being trouble from the start. I came downstairs to call the cops when you arrived."

"If you can give me his name, I'll run a check on him. I'll also see if the patrols can swing by more often."

"Thanks." She closed her eyes. "His name is Kevin Fletcher."

"Are *you* all right?"

With her hand on the banister, Valerie took a deep breath and gave some semblance of being in control. "I need to see how Carol is."

"I'm willing to bet Fletcher hit her, but without obvious bruises, I had no probable cause to arrest him. I was hoping she'd press charges."

"Few of them ever will." She started up the stairs. "I'll send Phoebe down."

As Lee went into the parlor, he phoned in the details on Fletcher to the department. When he finished, he heard someone enter the parlor behind him. He turned.

Phoebe stood in the entryway with her eyes gleaming. Around her neck, she wore the arrowhead he had given her on a leather cord.

"I didn't get a chance to say 'hi' earlier," he said.

She ran toward him and threw her arms around his waist.

He responded with a kiss to her lips. "I missed you."

Tears were in her eyes. Unashamed, she brushed them away. "I love you, Lee Crowley."

Her words caught him off guard. He didn't know how or why— only that they *were* connected. "I love you, Phoebe Wynne."

34

Phoebe

FROM THE FIRST MOMENT UPON SEEING Lee again, I realized I had been mistaken in withdrawing from him. Though I could not recall how long ago Dark Moon had died, my grief had eased. I would always ache from the memory of my loss, but he had traveled to the afterlife, where he joined his ancestors. The *kwiokosuk* had comforted me by letting me know that he would grow up there. In time, I came to know peace.

I had much yet to uncover from my past, but I could now go forward without fear. My confession of love to Lee seemed so natural that I had given it little thought when uttering the words. Upon hearing the same returned to me, my heart sang. I knew not what our future held, only that I cherished our time together.

In haste, we returned to his apartment and "made love." The expression for what we shared seemed gentler than the English phrase "to fornicate." Whilst I dare not say our unions were always docile, they were gratifying and not given to the pious shame that had been drilled into me during my brief visit to James Towne.

Afterwards, we lay with our naked bodies pressed together, each breathing in the other's scent. I longed for these moments of contentment to ne'er end. Still, I had left something unsaid and did not wish for it to linger betwixt us. "I shouldn't have shunned you."

He twisted a few strands of my hair betwixt his fingers. "You needed a little time and space. We all do, every so often."

"I behaved shamefully."

"You didn't." He kissed me upon my lips. "You were grieving for your son. As someone who has had to deliver the news to parents that their child is dead, I can't even begin to think of what it must be like to be on the receiving end."

"You have no children of your own?"

"By the time Shae even considered the prospect, we split."

I detected sorrow in his voice and recalled the joy of carrying Lightning Storm's children. "Mayhap, I can give you a child someday."

"I think it's a little soon to be discussing kids, when we have no idea who you really are or where you're from. What if you're still married?"

I had not stopped to broach such a question. My memories were of Lightning Storm, yet I had a Welsh surname. In my heart, I could ne'er have loved Lee so freely if I truly believed Lightning Storm were alive. The only Wynne I could recollect was Captain Henry. Was it possible? "If I am, I shall divorce him."

Lee took my head in his hands and held it. "It may not be that simple."

"This century allows it," I protested. "I love you."

"I love you too, but . . ."

I withdrew from his embrace for I did not wish to hear anything that might give me pause. I got up to dress.

He grasped my hand as I slipped from under the bed covers. "Phoebe, you can't keep doing this."

I turned to him. "I don't understand."

"Anytime you recall something uncomfortable or painful, you run from me. Do you want to discover the answers on how you came to be here or not? You need to decide what's more important and face the consequences, whatever they may be."

I traced a finger along the side of his face. "I'm afraid."

"That's understandable, but aren't we stronger when we stand together?"

Part of me wished I could remain blissfully unaware of the past. I could love Lee without any thought for the morrow, but I would not be whole. "Aye, I must know what happened."

"I thought you'd say that."

"Will you . . ."

"Go ahead."

He already knew what was in my thoughts. Why did he make me utter the words? "Will you join me in the dreaming?"

"If you promise me that no matter what happens, you won't run. We'll work through it together."

"I shan't run." With my vow pledged from the heart, I clasped his hand, intertwining our fingers. The answers I sought would bind us, not separate us.

Flame, smoke, mist. The fog engulfed me, and the white dog appeared afore me. Something that could ne'er happen in Shae's office, Lee walked aside me. Because of our connection, he could cross into the spirit world with me. Though he did not carry a bow, in this realm, he was bare-chested and wore a breechclout. He had the heart of a warrior, and I saw him as such.

My belly was so full with child that I had difficulty walking. The child wriggled within my womb, kicking me wildly. I placed Lee's hand against my abdomen, as I had with Lightning Storm. Pressing his hand on my bare skin, he smiled at the child's movements.

But my task ahead was part of a world that allowed no men, for I was about to give birth. The women would watch over me 'til I had my babe.

Momma approached me. "Phoebe, it's time."

Momma always reverted to my English name during emotional moments. "Momma, I wish for you to meet Lee Crowley."

Confused, she narrowed her eyes. "Irish name, but you appear . . . What tribe do you hail from, Master Crowley?"

"I don't know."

"Have we made acquaintance afore?"

I grasped Momma's arm. "Come, Momma. Lee has accompanied me whilst dreaming. You cannot have met him afore. He hails from the twenty-first century."

The century formed on Momma's lips, but she uttered no sound.

I guided her to the mat-covered house, where I would give birth, for the blood was more powerful than that of the moon time.

We stepped inside the house, and Momma spoke, "Phoebe, I wish to know more about Master Crowley. The twenty-first century? How is that possible?"

"I know not the answers. Somehow I made my way there, and Lee is helping me to discover what happened here. Momma, I must know, do you regret leaving the colony?"

Momma licked her lips. "Sometimes I wonder what might have been, but... Nay, I gave you a chance for life, and you will soon be presenting me with my grandchild. I also wouldn't have had Sly Fox or known Silver Eagle's love." She frowned in a troubled way.

"You can speak of Poppa, if you wish."

"There is a part of me that says I should not know such love, for I am guilty of adultery."

"You were properly wed in Paspahegh tradition."

"But I was also wed to your Poppa, which makes no allowances for divorce."

"You thought he was dead."

"Aye, and I fear he will return to claim you."

A shiver ran through me, and I rubbed my belly. "Let us think of my child. The *kwiocos* has predicted that she will be a girl."

Momma smiled. I was comforted that she was near. When Dark Moon had been born, I had been unable to travel the river to reach her. His birth had come sooner than anticipated. For another day, the women brought me food and attended to my needs. When my pains began, a *kwiocos* entered the house and said a prayer in each corner. He then circled the room to ward off vengeful spirits.

Aft he departed, I drank snakeroot tea to ease the pain. Turtle Shell, a renowned midwife, was in attendance, and I was comforted by her presence.

As my pain grew stronger and more frequent, Momma spoke to focus my thoughts on her voice. I refused to shame myself by complaining. I had a task ahead—to birth my daughter. Turtle Shell prepared more tea, which I drank with relish. We sang and prayed to the health of my child.

Momma held my arm, and I paced the floor. The pain increased. I took deep breaths but kept from crying out. Soon, I knew the time had come. With Momma on one side of me and Turtle Shell on the other, I knelt. I took deep breaths, whilst Momma rubbed my back. Turtle Shell pressed on my belly, attempting to force the child out.

The pain became so intense that I gritted my teeth. Turtle Shell spoke comforting words. I felt like I was on fire and closed my eyes. Warm blood trickled down my legs. The child was coming. Turtle Shell urged me on. I strained with the pain, and a blood-covered child slid into Turtle Shell's arms. As predicted, my daughter had arrived.

35

Lee

THE CROW FLEW AHEAD OF LEE, leading him out of the mist. He blinked. The candle had burned down to a nub, but he was back in his apartment. He looked across at Phoebe. "What did you name her?"

"You saw the birth?"

"I did."

The blood drained from her face. "I should not have involved you."

"Why? Do you think I'm going to get queasy from seeing a baby born? I assisted once when I was on patrol duty."

She touched his face and relaxed slightly. "You were not harmed?"

"Why would I have been? The mother was quite happy that I happened along. She tried driving herself to the hospital, but the baby came a little sooner than expected. I called for an ambulance, but the baby wouldn't wait to meet the new world. There really wasn't much for me to do besides keeping the mother calm until the paramedics arrived."

"Things are very different in this time. I could ne'er have fathomed a man helping to birth a child."

"It's fairly common. Even if they're not helping, many men are present when their wives deliver."

Her face wrinkled. "I was raised that it was bad luck for a man to be present."

"Even if it were, I wasn't actually present when your baby was born."

She forced a smile. "She was named Little Hummingbird."

"That's a pretty name." Sometimes he regretted that Shae and he had never gotten around to having kids. He stood. "It's time that I take you back to Colwell House."

She got to her feet.

He pulled her close. "I wish we had more time together than a day or two a week."

"As do I." With a shiver, she pressed a hand to his chest. "Lee, I fear that what you have viewed during the dreaming is an ill omen."

Her arms had broken out in goosebumps. He wished he could ease her mind from old wives' tales and gently rubbed her arms to help warm her. "I'll be fine."

Seemingly unconvinced, she drew away. Her face remained sad as he collected his keys and gun. Once they were on the drive to Colwell House, Phoebe asked, "Is there not some way you can locate your tribe?"

Wondering why her question had arisen now, he responded, "I've already explained to you that I was dumped. Even if that weren't the case, adoption records are closed."

"Closed?"

"The government seals the records so that adoptees can't easily find their birth parents, unless the parents wish to be found."

"Are you not a detective?"

First Shae, now Phoebe—the discussion nearly made him miss a red light. He screeched the T-Bird to a halt. "If you're asking me whether I can cut through the bullshit red tape, yes, I know ways around it. My adoption papers say that I'm Indian, but I have no real comprehension of what that means."

"And you have no desire find out?"

The light changed, and he hit the gas pedal. "I do, but as I explained to Shae, the trail went cold over thirty years ago. Even if I managed to get hold of the records, which is highly unlikely, they wouldn't tell me anything I don't already know. Not only do I not know my tribe, I have no idea what my actual birthday is either. My foster parents adopted me and decided my birthday was in August because that was the month some hikers found me curled up by the trunk of a tree in a forest. Then, they wondered why I had no desire to celebrate the date that was assigned to me."

" 'Tis sad. Everyone should know his ancestors."

"In an ideal world, I'd certainly agree. When I get a few days where I can actually sit down and look over the records I have, I'll check to see if there are some clues that I've missed in the past."

"Do not wait too long. Time is not always on our side."

He didn't like the way she had an ill omen and now worried about time growing short. For him? Or herself? "Maybe so, but the time needs to be right before a person undertakes such a pursuit."

"Aft Arrohateck lads go through the *huskanaw* to become warriors, their allegiance shifts from their family to the good of the tribe. Your tribe does not benefit 'til you know who they are."

"Doesn't my allegiance to society by trying to clean the scum and assholes from the streets mean anything?" He pulled alongside the curb in front of Colwell House. "Phoebe, the first thing I had to learn upon becoming a detective was patience. Even if I get lucky and wrap up a case in short order, the judicial system crawls. You said we're connected. I believe you. If we're patient, the answers will reveal themselves for both of us."

The corners of her lips tipped slightly into a smile. "You are right."

He parked the car and went around to open Phoebe's door, but she got out before he reached it. "I'll see you to the door." By the door, he gave her a goodbye kiss. "I need to see Valerie before I leave."

"I shall fetch her." Unlocking the door, she showed him the way inside.

As she started down the hall, he grasped her hand and drew her back, kissing her once more. "I'll call you when I can. "

"I shall look forward to our next meeting."

He watched her until she vanished into the next room. God, he was an idiot. After his split with Shae, he had sworn to himself to never love another like he had her. At least Shae had known she was from the twenty-first century. Maybe he loved Phoebe because of the highs. Between the sex and what she called "the dreaming," he fought the urge to blow his vacation time and spend all of his days with her. *Patience.* He had to live by his own words.

"Lee?" Valerie entered the hall from the parlor. "You don't need to stand here by the door."

"It's before visiting hours," he reminded her.

"After last night, I think we can bend the rules this one time."

"How's Carol?"

"Shaken but fine. You were right. He had been a little rough with her."

"I ran the check on Fletcher. He's had a couple of minor drug arrests and a speeding ticket, but the fact that he's taken up stalking suggests that he probably hasn't given up the drugs. Because he's already assaulted Carol and resorted to threats, his behavior is only likely to escalate. Try and convince her to involve the police."

"I will."

Due in court, Lee said his goodbyes and drove to Richmond, spending more than two hours testifying in a murder case. It was nearly one by the time he arrived at his desk, where Shae waited for him. When she stood to greet him, he noted an engagement ring on her finger. "To what do I owe the pleasure of two visits in one week?"

She glanced around at the desks of the other detectives. "Can we go somewhere to speak?"

He escorted her to the cross-examination room, where they had talked the other day.

"Phoebe canceled her appointments with me. I thought you might know why."

He shrugged that he didn't know the answer.

"Then you haven't seen her?"

"I didn't say that. I dropped her off at Colwell House this morning, but she didn't say anything about canceling her appointments."

Her face reddened as she got more excited. "I just got her speaking about the past again, and now this. Lee, she's not ready to go out on her own. She still requires extensive therapy. If she's no longer comfortable with me, then let me help her find someone else."

"Let me talk to her. I'll let you know what she says."

His composure seemed to calm her. "That's not the only reason why I needed to speak with you," she said.

"I thought not."

"Ed dropped by my office the other day."

That wasn't what he had expected to hear. "Why?"

"He's concerned about you. He says that you've become preoccupied lately, making mistakes that you wouldn't normally. I said that I'd speak to you, but I can easily guess the source of your distraction."

"What if I told you that a linguist has confirmed Phoebe's language to be Virginia Algonquian?"

"I'd say that you're trying to distract me." She blinked. "You're serious, aren't you? How can that be? Hasn't Virginia Algonquian been a dead language for several hundred years?"

"Two hundred."

The number formed on her lips. "There has to be a logical explanation."

"I'm sure there is. Phoebe could be a linguist herself, but why would no one have reported her as missing? She could have been abducted by space aliens, or she just might be—"

"No." Shae furiously shook her head. "And if you're even considering the possibility she's actually from the seventeenth century, then I'm willing to bet that she's continuing to hypnotize you. You're not the gullible sort. Dammit, Lee, think with your head, not your prick."

Narrowing his eyes, he crossed his arms. "I think you know me better than that."

"I probably shouldn't have said that, but if she's hypnotizing you, you may not be thinking rationally. I recently read of a case where an actress was hypnotized by a stage hypnotist. She was highly hypnotizable and found the experience highly erotic, so she volunteered again. The experience led to a personal relationship, then a sexual one. When he learned she was from a wealthy family, he used hypnosis to coerce her into marrying him. He kept re-hypnotizing her when they had sex. They got married and divorced within a year. He, of course, landed himself with a nice alimony payment."

Aware that Shae held little regard for stage hypnotists, he thought her story over. "You've repeatedly stated that I'm not a good subject." She opened her mouth to add something, but he continued, "Yes, Phoebe knows where I'm vulnerable, and I admit I find the experiences fascinating. But she has never tried using 'hypnosis' while we were getting it on, nor do I have any money to speak of."

She flinched from his bluntness. "Don't believe me then, but there are too many unknowns about Phoebe Wynne. You know it as well as I do, and it's affecting you, personally and professionally. Even your partner has noticed it."

"I'm properly forewarned. Thank you, doctor. Is there anything else you'd like to tell me before we adjourn?" He glanced at the diamond on her left hand.

"I was going to tell you the other day, but the timing didn't seem right. I hope you're not angry."

"Why would I be angry? You deserve to be happy, Shae."

She brushed away a brimming tear, obviously hoping he hadn't seen it. "You mean that, don't you?"

"Hell, I'll even come to the bachelor party if Russ will invite me."

Breaking the tension, she laughed. "You just want an excuse to drink beer and drool over naked women."

"Damn. I didn't know I needed an excuse for such activities."

Laughing harder, she finally caught her breath and headed for the door. Before reaching it, she faced him. "Thanks, Lee, and don't forget to speak to Phoebe."

"I won't," he assured her. As she closed the door behind her, he wondered how he was supposed to feel. He had loved her. Maybe he still did—in a different sort of way. Shae was right. They were better friends now than when they had been married.

Lee concentrated on the flame. Each time he participated in the dreaming with Phoebe, he entered the "other" state faster. Phoebe was counting on him to help her find answers. Instead of sighting the crow, he watched a streamlined shape of a falcon soar overhead. Attired in a mantle, loin cloth, and leggings, he saw the world through Lightning Storm's eyes. Slung over his shoulder were two dead turkeys. Near him, other warriors carried fish and furs. They climbed the dirt path to the fort on the precipitous ridge until reaching the palisade with corner watchtowers.

The guard greeted them with a familiar wave and motioned for them to enter. The falcon stayed with him, until it suddenly shifted direction and swooped after a thrush. The songbird attempted to move out of reach by flying higher. The predator used speed to its advantage and remained carefully poised above its prey, and then it made a headlong dive. Brown thrush feathers scattered on impact.

The falcon's hunting success was a good sign for the coming day. Along with Two Wolves, Lightning Storm went to the mud and daub cottage of William Powell to trade. Powell's wife, Mary, smiled upon seeing the turkeys he had brought. Two Wolves offered catfish and shad. She invited them to sit at the wood table, where she served a dish the *tassantassas* called gruel, consisting of oatmeal and boiled milk.

As on any other trade morning, Powell and his wife jested and laughed, while Two Wolves and he exchanged hunting stories. Walks Through Mist had taught him the *tassantassas'* language, and Powell comprehended some Algonquian.

After the meal, Powell stood. "I must tend to my fields soon. Let us finish our trade."

Even if he overlooked the fact the land had once belonged to the Arrohateck, he failed to understand why Powell plowed and planted like a woman, when he should be hunting game. He and the other warriors provided the *tassantassas* with their main supply of meat.

Two Wolves sighted Powell, which left the woman for Lightning Storm. Mary had a nervous smile, as if knowing why they were here. Walks Through Mist had informed him the name Mary was bestowed upon *tassantassas* little girls in honor of their savior's mother. He had never killed a woman before and cursed the *tassantassas* for bringing dishonorable warfare to their shores. The orders had been clear. On this day, no one would be spared. *Absolutely no one.*

Detecting something amiss, Powell reached for his musket. Two Wolves charged him. The gun went off. Powell fell. Before Mary could scream, Lightning Storm seized a knife from the table and slit her throat. Blood spattered his hands and chest. With remorse, he caught her to break her fall. She gasped one final breath in his arms. Gently, he lowered her body to the mud floor and said a silent prayer.

Forever, the shock and surprise imprinted on her face would haunt him. *Women and children.* Shamed by the action, he would harbor his torment in silence.

With loud whoops, Lightning Storm and Two Wolves overturned the table, sending a lantern crashing. Wounded cries shrieked from outside the door. They had not worn warpaint to lull the *tassantassas* into believing that it was a normal day. Now the *tassantassas* were all dying or running for their lives.

Unable to continue, Lee blinked back the image. He rubbed his hands together but couldn't wipe the blood from them. Clamping his eyes shut, he lowered his head.

"Lee . . ."

Phoebe touched him on the shoulder, and he trembled. "He was too ashamed to tell you."

"A wife knows when something ails her husband."

"March 22, 1622. My parents called it a massacre. Why is it always called a massacre when Indians kill whites, but not the other way around?"

"Lee . . ."

The blood and the woman's face . . . .

"Lee . . ."

He finally opened his eyes. The blood had vanished from his hands. For the first time in his life he had viewed *his* history—not the one he had been raised with—through Lightning Storm. "I now understand. The attack wasn't meant to annihilate the English. Paramount chief Opechancanough organized the attacks to remind the colonists of their place. At what price? It cost them their honor, and the waves of colonists kept coming, demanding more land. It only gave the English more reasons to kill, burn, and rape."

Phoebe gave a weak nod.

Invigorated by the dreaming, Lee placed a hand under Phoebe's chin and tilted her head until her gaze met his. "Why did you cancel your sessions with Shae?"

She looked away. "You are the one I must share with. I cannot explain any better. Shae listens because 'tis her occupation. She does not believe. You are uncertain, but you listen with your heart."

"She's trying to help."

"For now 'tis as it must be. Lightning Storm will only reveal what happened through you, from one warrior to another. I must know how he died."

Lee stroked her cheek. "Then you're certain . . . ?"

"Aye. I could not love you as I do otherwise."

He drew her trembling body into his arms. Phoebe kept her promise and didn't withdraw from him. He worried though. After the loss of Dark Moon, how would she react when she learned the truth about Lightning Storm?

36

Phoebe

A T COLWELL HOUSE, MY TUTOR, Liz Sedgewick, instructed me in what she called the three Rs, "reading, writing, and 'rithmetic." Even though I puzzled over the phrase, she said I was a fast learner and suspected that I had some education in the "basics" previously. I could not recall ever having been taught in such a fashion, but I was thrilled by my newfound abilities, especially when it came to reading books. My thirst for knowledge ne'er ran dry.

Whilst studying history, Liz glossed over the founding of James Towne, as she did not wish to debate with me what was written in the book. It mattered not that I could speak the Algonquian language as was spoken afore the English arrived. When she moved on to other periods, I learnt of the Revolution for Independence from England, a Civil War that had erupted betwixt the states themselves, along with two world wars and several political wars.

I was in turmoil. Was this my past or future? And did people of the twenty-first century contemplate anything aside waging wars? Indian warriors oft fought amongst other tribes but not with the intention of annihilating them. To try and help me understand, Meg and Carol showed me pictures of a town called Appomattox.

At first, I expected to see familiar longhouses. Instead, there was a red-brick building called a court house, several other brick buildings, including a gaol, and wood structures. "But the Appamattuck is a tributary tribe of the paramount chief, Opechancanough."

"No, Phoebe," Carol said gently, "it's the town where the Civil War ended."

Ever since Carol's incident with Master Fletcher, she had taken an interest in my progress. Alongside Meg, she oft befriended me and helped me with my studies.

"Have none of the tribes survived?" I asked. "Lee said they have."

Meg squeezed my hand. "Lee's right. It's been a struggle, but some have survived."

Breathing deeply, I relaxed slightly. "I feared you were going to say they are all gone. Then why can I not meet with them?"

Meg and Carol looked at each other but had no answer. Meg returned to the book, showing me pictures of red, white, and blue flags, muskets that were not much different from matchlocks, and uniforms. Upon seeing the drum, I could hear its beat, signaling hospitality, afore gunfire and screams erupted. Houses burned, and Crow in the Woods wandered away. I had tried to save the lad.

"Phoebe . . ."

At the sound of Meg's voice, I blinked, and the smell of smoke faded. "I was reminded of the Paspahegh."

Meg closed the book. "I think that's enough for one morning."

But I could not rid myself of the ill feeling. *Lee.* "I must speak with him."

"Who?" Meg asked.

"Lee. I fear something has happened to him." I could not get to the phone fast enough. In my haste, I forgot how to dial.

Carol took the phone from me and dialed as I recited his cell phone number. With a shaking hand, I put the receiver to my ear. I held my breath as it rang once, twice, thrice.

"Crowley."

Hearing his voice was like music to my ears, and I let out my breath. "Lee, you are well?"

"I'm fine. What's wrong?"

My hand continued to tremble, as my foreboding hadn't abated. "I have a feeling that you are in trouble."

"I'm fine," he reassured me again. *"Listen, Phoebe, do you mind if I call you back later? I'm in the middle of an investigation right now."*

"Be careful," I whispered as I hung up the phone. I feared that I would lose him as I had Lightning Storm.

37

Lee

Puzzled by phoebe's call, Lee pondered it for a moment. Could it be intuition? Uncertain how much he believed, he joined Jan Kelsey, a forensic anthropologist, and her assistant, Mike, beneath the protection of a leafy canopy that sheltered them from the mizzling rain. Lee explained the situation to them. "The property owner was doing renovations, when he noticed disturbed soil in the family cemetery. A decaying finger poked through the surface, which the owners thought most likely didn't belong to the grave's occupant. Their assumption was correct. The original grave belongs to Carrie Anderson, a woman who died in the late-nineteenth century. My crew has enlarged the hole to gain access, but we've left the body and what may remain of Mrs. Anderson for you to examine. We're hoping you can give us some leads as to who was buried on top of Mrs. Anderson."

"What better way to dispose of a body," Jan muttered. "Dump it in an already occupied grave. Does this sort of thing happen often?"

"It's my first," Lee replied, gesturing the way to a slight rise of the family graveyard.

As they trekked to the hill, they pulled their rain gear tighter against the heavier rain. Uniformed officers stood upwind of the grave site. Even a heavy piece of plywood covering the hole failed to mask the putrid scent of decomposing human flesh. Nothing equaled the smell of a rotting corpse. A distinct odor that was never forgotten. Lee had seen seasoned investigators turn away and vomit when confronted with the stench. Even his stomach churned, but somehow he got past it. He always did.

Jan and Mike pulled away the plywood cover, and most of the officers took a quick step away to evade the stink. At the bottom of the hole, about four-feet deep, was a decaying corpse. As Jan went down into the grave pit, Lee saw Indian warriors beside him, covered in black and red warpaint. Crouched low, they crept silently through the dense forest.

He blinked. *A vision—why here?* Jan cleared away more mud. She began handing bone and sinew to her assistant, one piece at a time. Mike positioned the decomposing pieces in skeletal order on the plywood.

Several hours passed.

Without warning, Lee's arms were poised on a bow, ready to fire an arrow. In the pouring rain, an unearthly yell filled the air, and the warriors rushed forward with arrows sailing. Shrieks of pain surrounded them as he shoved through the dense underbrush.

The vision faded.

Jan climbed from the pit. "You're looking a little mystified, detective."

Lee shook his head to clear it. *Where am I?* A reconstructed body lay on the plywood. "I'm amazed how you can fit the pieces together."

She smiled. "All in a day's work. Your victim is obviously male, mid- to late twenties, around 180 pounds."

A minute passed before he absorbed her words. "How long has he been dead?"

"I'm getting to that." With a pocketknife, she cut into what was left of the flesh on the corpse's thigh. "Around six months to a year."

Lee felt a sharp sting in his abdomen. He staggered back. Blood covered him. An armored *tassantassas* aimed a musket directly at him. He swung his tomahawk. The man went down.

Another gunshot, and fiery pain spread throughout his body. He fell to the sloshing mire, gasping for breath. *What was real?*

A man stood over him. In a challenge, he met the man's gaze. A musket butt rammed down on his chest. Bones snapped. As his strength ebbed, his mind grew foggy. Death was preferable to following the *tassantassas'* rules. What of Walks Through Mist? Part of both worlds, she would adapt.

He coughed, nearly choking on the blood. *Soon.* He only wished he could tell her how much he loved her.

"Detective?"

Lee blinked, finding himself standing over the corpse and Jan staring up at him in puzzlement. "He was shot twice, in the abdomen and chest. You'll find broken ribs."

She examined the rib cage. "I don't see any evidence of broken ribs. Let me get him back to the lab and see what I can find out."

Lee mumbled his thanks, but his mind was on Lightning Storm's death. Here—on a similar rainy day in the seventeenth century—Lightning Storm had died on this very ground. He was honored the warrior had trusted him with his final thoughts. Phoebe's ill omen had been for Lightning Storm, and he now understood her fear of guns.

38

Phoebe

IN THE BACKYARD THE FOLLOWING AFTERNOON, Carol aided me in weeding my herb garden. Unlike Meg, she worried not about possessing a green thumb and called it "puttering." The cohosh already budded with greenish-yellow flowers, whilst most of the herbs would flower later in the season. I checked the comfrey, sarsaparilla, and poppies, but I continued to think of Lee.

Throughout the night, I had barely slept. Yet I resisted the temptation to call him again, as I didn't wish him to think of me as a burden. I had learnt such patience from the Arrohateck. The women would go about their daily tasks, comforting each other as the men were oft hunting.

"He'll be fine." Carol said, plucking a weed from the red soil.

Carol no longer seemed sullen, and I thanked her for her kind words. In turn, she asked me about the herbs and their medicinal uses to distract me.

"Phoebe," Meg called from the landing by the back door. "Lee's here."

Delighted that he had chosen to surprise me, I brushed the dirt from my hands onto my work jeans.

With a smile, Carol squeezed my arm. "I'll finish here, should you decide to stay the night."

I expressed my appreciation and made my way to the house.

"He's waiting in the parlor," Meg said.

With my anticipation rising, I hurried in that direction. Upon my entrance, Lee stood. He was attired in comfortable trousers and

a T-shirt, signaling that he was off duty. Unable to restrain myself,
I rushed to him. We kissed, longingly. I ne'er wanted to part from
him.

"Would you like to go for a ride where we can speak in private?"
he asked, drawing away.

"Aye. Allow me a moment to change..."

"You look fine."

His voice had been urgent. I grasped his hand, and he led me
to the car. With months behind me, I had grown somewhat accustomed to the strange coaches, especially when I was in Lee's presence. I climbed in, and as he drove away from Colwell House, I
could see the tension on his brow. "What is wrong?"

Speeding through the streets, he grunted a response but failed to
elaborate.

I feared his ire for having called him whilst at his job. "I beg
forgiveness."

"You haven't done anything wrong. I'll explain, but not here."

"Lee..."

He held up a hand. "Soon. I can't talk about it while I'm driving."

I settled back. With each passing day, I was less astonished by the
hoards of people, the stately buildings, and even the planes that flew
overhead. I oft dreamt of what it must be like to be a passenger in
such a magnificent flying coach. But not today. Troubled by what
Lee had to say, I could not get comfortable.

We passed from the city to a wooded area, where he halted
the car. Aft parking, he showed me to a dirt path leading through
the oak and sycamore trees. A doe with her spotted fawn bounded
across the trail. I patiently waited for Lee to speak, only to continue
walking the path in silence.

Finally, he turned to me and grasped my hands. "He loved you."

My throat constricted, and I tightened my grip on his hands.

"Lightning Storm. He loved you."

"Aye," I managed to utter.

"Phoebe, I saw him."

I could no longer ignore his meaning. "Saw him?"

"His last thoughts were of you. I saw him, like in the dreaming.
He wanted to tell you how much he loved you."

My thoughts were in turmoil. I swallowed. "The other warriors told me that he had died bravely, but I was not aware of his final thoughts. Thank you for the message."

Lee stroked my cheek in a gentle caress. "I can't turn my back on the truth anymore. There's a reason why we can't find any clues as to where you come from. You *are* from the seventeenth century."

Suddenly, my mind was at ease. I didn't know whether to laugh that Lee finally believed my tale or to mourn Lightning Storm's death. But he had died long ago, and I was certain I had already cried my tears over his loss.

"I'm puzzled though," he said. "Why are you here? Am I supposed to help you return?"

His questions struck unexpected terror in my heart. "Return? I cannot return. Pray don't make me."

He embraced me. "Don't worry, Phoebe. I have no such powers. I thought you knew. I want you to stay here with me—forever. Once you've learned all you can at Colwell House, we can find a place in the country. You can have a greyhound and grow an herb garden. But for now, we need to know the hows and whys in order to make sense of anything else."

How different he was from those of my time. People in the twenty-first century followed a clock for every action—to rise, to eat, to sleep. "Are you saying I can return to the seventeenth century?"

"I don't know, because we have no idea how you got here."

"Then I shall resume my sessions with Shae. Like the dreaming, hypnosis helps me recall what happened." My arms circled about Lee's waist, and I lowered my head to his chest. With his and Shae's help, I would discover why I had been brought to this time. What if I was meant to return? I couldn't. For I wouldn't lose Lee as I had Lightning Storm.

Aft Lightning Storm's death, I grieved. I could not imagine ever loving another as I did him. During that disconsolate time, Little Hummingbird and I traveled downriver to live with Momma and Silver Eagle. Once again, I sought comfort from the woman who had borne me.

It grieved me further when my moon cycle arrived twenty-eight days from the last. I had hoped that I could preserve Lightning Storm's memory with another child. Normally, I sought refuge at the moon lodge, but this time, I felt banished.

Bringing me food and water, Momma came to soothe me. Whilst I had told her about Poppa surviving the *Sea Venture*, we had ne'er spoken further about him. "Phoebe," she said in English, "you must be cautious. Your Poppa will not rest 'til he has you married to a proper English gentleman."

My appetite had waned upon Lightning Storm's death. Even now the scent of turkey stew made my stomach churn. "What *gentleman* would have me? He claimed I was soiled because I had fornicated with an Indian."

"Please eat, my child."

With a clam shell, I ladled some stew to my mouth.

Momma smiled in satisfaction. "There are few English women in Virginia. Men are looking for mates and will overlook your past 'til more gentlewomen arrive on these shores. I'm certain you are already aware, but 'tis within their nature. Their rutting rituals bear little difference than that of the deer. They will fight for what they believe they possess."

I set the clam shell next to the turtle shell bowl. "And Poppa . . . ?"

"He can overlook your transgressions because I am the one to have led you astray. You are his daughter, and he means to fulfill his claim."

The truth was more unsettling than I could have fathomed. With Lightning Storm dead, Silver Eagle welcomed Little Hummingbird and me into his house, but the women oft gathered food and firewood away from the town. Like afore, my father would lie in wait 'til I was defenseless.

39

Shae and Lee

RELIEVED THAT PHOEBE had rescheduled her appointments and was really talking again, Shae had listened to the progression of her story with interest. "I still think we'll be able to work out what happened to you in time."

"Lee believes my story."

Normally, Lee wasn't the sort to humor a person. *God, he must have fallen head over heals for Phoebe.* "I'll see you next week, then?"

"Aye."

Shae exchanged goodbyes and ushered in her next patient. After her last patient, she checked her calendar for the following day, but Phoebe's case kept intruding on her thoughts. She had no doubt that Phoebe and Lee were dabbling with hypnosis again. She had given them ample warning. There was little else she could do.

"Knock, knock."

With a smile she looked up at Russ, approaching her desk.

He tapped his watch. "Didn't we have a date?"

"Date?"

"Dinner and the theatre."

"Oh my God, I forgot. I even brought in a skirt with me this morning. It'll only take me a moment to change."

"Let me guess, you were thinking about Phoebe."

Shae retrieved her long black skirt from the coat rack. After making certain the door was closed, she removed her slacks and slipped on the skirt. "She says Lee believes she's from the seventeenth century."

"Lee may be many things, but gullible doesn't strike me as one of his traits."

The skirt fit a little too tight, and she had difficulty zipping. Her jacket would cover her less-than-lean belly as long as the zipper didn't burst. She sucked in her breath and got the skirt zipped. "You're right." She finished dressing and tickled Russ on the cheek. "I was worrying for nothing. Let's go and have a relaxing time."

He grasped her hand, and they walked out of the office.

After a long day, Lee headed the T-Bird in the direction of Colwell House. He would have preferred returning to his apartment, but he had promised Phoebe to drop by. By the time he arrived, darkness had settled and his watch read 8:04. Visiting hours were over, but he had to let Phoebe know she hadn't been stood up. He hurried to the door and knocked.

The porch light went on, and Carol opened the door. Valerie joined her. "I'm sorry, Lee," Valerie said, "but visiting hours are over. I wish I could make an exception, but—"

"I understand. Just let Phoebe know I dropped by. I couldn't get here any earlier."

"I'll tell you what. I'll have Phoebe meet you outside."

Carol stepped outside as Valerie closed the door. "I didn't get a chance to thank you."

"Have you seen Fletcher again?"

She lowered her gaze to the porch floor.

He continued, "I realize you think it's none of my business. It's not—yet. But you should be aware that stalkers escalate their actions. That's when it becomes my business. If you really want to thank me, let me escort you downtown to get a protective order against him."

"That won't be necessary. I haven't seen him."

Why did he bother? They never listened. "Carol . . ." When she looked up, Lee didn't see the hardened gaze of a streetwise woman—only the naiveté of youth. He handed her his card. "Stalkers don't change. Feel free to call me if Fletcher bothers you again."

"Thanks."

Phoebe appeared on the doorstep, and Carol vanished inside. Phoebe's arms went around his neck. They kissed, and he straightened. "I'm sorry I'm late."

"I have yet to fully understand clock time."

"If you haven't already had dinner, I can take you out for a quick bite to eat."

"I should like that."

He escorted her to the T-Bird. Normally when Phoebe was with him, he'd bypass fast food, but having missed lunch, he was famished and chose the closest place to Colwell House. After collecting their order, they found an empty booth. Phoebe told him about her session with Shae, while he polished off two pieces of crispy fried chicken, mashed potatoes, and a side order of corn.

"Lee, will you join me in the dreaming tonight?"

He checked his watch—a little past nine. "Unfortunately, I'm usually regulated by clock time. I have an early morning."

"I'll arrange for Meg or Carol to pick me up so you needn't drive into the city again."

She had only nibbled on her chicken, and he gestured to it. "Are you going to eat that?"

Phoebe shoved the plastic plate to his side of the table. "I've already had dinner."

"You should have warned me." He dug into a drumstick—not his favorite piece—but he was finally beginning to satisfy his hunger. "There's no need to bother Meg or Carol. I'll be coming into the city for court." What had he just agreed to? Under normal circumstances, he got little enough sleep. *Oh hell, I'll do what I always do: dose up on coffee.* He was eager to discover how Phoebe had arrived in the twenty-first century.

Lee stared at the candle until the mist surrounded him. Following the flight of the crow, he walked along a riverbank until meeting a man wearing breeches, a slashed-sleeved doublet, and a plumed hat. A sword was at his left hip and a pistol on his right. Lee checked his own hip. His Glock wasn't there.

The man bowed slightly. "Captain Henry Wynne. Phoebe wishes for you to see what was through me."

Like Lightning Storm. But how could he identify with an Englishman? "Where's Phoebe?"

"Nearby."

Henry Wynne had been the man who had abducted Phoebe and taken her to her father in Jamestown. Lee narrowed his eyes. "You're not afraid of sharing with a savage?"

Wynne laughed. "Nay, and you shall understand in time, should you decide to continue."

Did he have a choice? He had agreed to help Phoebe. "All right."

The crow cawed from a branch, and fog engulfed him. When the mist cleared, Phoebe stood across from him, and his hands clamped around her wrists.

She struggled with a strength uncommon for a woman. "Unhand me!"

"Phoebe, allow me to bring you to your father. I assure you that you and your child will be unharmed."

She spat at him, continuing her fight. "Like Lightning Storm was unscathed."

"I was not responsible for your husband's death. I was in England at the time. Search parties have been sent, unable to find you afore now, but your father will spare naught to see that you are returned to him." She stopped struggling, and he released his grip. "Run from me as you have afore. Your father will only send someone else. The next man may not concern himself about you or your daughter's safety."

"Why do you care, Captain Wynne?"

The sword was at Lee's hip. He wore breeches and the doublet. He *was* Henry Wynne. The feel of a full beard was an odd sensation. He'd never had much in the way of facial hair.

"You must continue. You have seen Lightning Storm. You must also come to know Henry Wynne."

It had been Phoebe's voice, but the words hadn't come from the woman before him. Lightning Storm's death remained vivid. He had felt the warrior's love. It was part of them. What would he have in common with Henry Wynne?

"Lee, pray continue."

He had promised. He concentrated on the woman before him.

"Why do I care?" asked Henry, lowering his hat. "I was sincere in my request. Whilst I may not be the richest, you could do far worse. And I would raise your savage daughter as a Christian."

"Little Hummingbird is not a savage."

He did not debate the statement. "My land is far enough away from the main colony that I can look the other way should you desire to visit your mother on occasion."

Flight faded from Phoebe's eyes. In its place, he saw compliance. Not many men would have accepted her into their households other than as a whore.

Distaste lingered at seeing the world through Wynne's eyes, and Lee blinked. Usually he was on the receiving end of blatant bigotry. A moment passed before he was able to collect his thoughts. "You were forced to marry Henry Wynne?"

"My father had vowed my hand to Henry. He would have made his threat good should I have chosen to ignore Captain Wynne's warning. I had already lost one child. I obliged him for the sake of my daughter."

"In other words, yes."

Avoiding his gaze, she said, "He treated me kindly."

"Then he wasn't the one to whip you." It was a statement, not a question. They would need to continue with the dreaming to discover that answer. "And you didn't love him."

"Nay."

"How does my seeing what happened through Henry's eyes help you? I can't relate to him like I could Lightning Storm."

"He loved me."

To that statement, he had no argument. "I'll continue as you wish me to."

She hugged him, and he hoped he wouldn't disappoint her.

40

Phoebe

IN MAY OF 1623, I married Captain Henry Wynne in James Towne. Following the ceremony, Little Hummingbird was baptized as Elenor in honor of my momma. During the baptism, Poppa scowled, and I did all that I could to keep from weeping. Now married to a man that I did not love, my heart was heavy with remorse. Though I had rejoined my kinsmen, I was severed from the people I loved. Long ago fallen into disuse, my English was garbled, and I sometimes had difficulty making my thoughts known. And my daughter would ne'er hear her father's voice, nor lay her eyes upon his countenance.

In the years since my arrival, more horses had been brought from England, and James Towne had a cartway. Beyond the colony, most transit remained by ship. I had vowed to ne'er set foot upon a deck again, yet here I was climbing the wood plank in pinching leather shoes, longing for my moccasins.

Once the ship set sail upriver to Henry's plantation, I grew ill to my stomach. For the first time, I saw an African. Contrary to the woodcut I had seen as a wispy lass, he was fully clothed, wearing a linen shirt, breeches, hose, and a ruff collar like many English men. His skin was nearly the same shade as tar, and his black hair twisted in tight spirals about his head.

I gaped 'til Henry introduced us. "Mistress Wynne, I'd like for you to meet our indentured servant, James."

"Forgive me for staring. I have ne'er met an African afore."

He bowed. "A pleasure, missus."

His English was almost musical, but broken, much like my own. I wondered if he also had family elsewhere.

"I shall obtain a female servant afore I set sail for England," Henry said.

Had he secured James to keep watch over me so that I wouldn't run off to the Arrohateck whilst he was away? I had a few months afore the fall of the leaf to form a plan. My stomach calmed, and I cast my eyes to the Powhatan River, renamed the James by the English. Many of the tall trees near the colony had been cut to make way for tobacco fields. Due to paramount chief Opechancanough's attacks the year afore, many a field lay idle and brimming with weeds.

"Do you not fear Indians, Henry?" I asked.

He narrowed his eyes. "Nay, for you speak their language."

"If warriors are set upon attacking us, I can do naught, for the English have taught them how to kill women and children too."

"Phoebe, 'tis our wedding day. I only want you to be happy."

Then return me . . . I held my tongue. Taking my wrath upon Henry would be for naught. Love reflected in his eyes. Why could I not feel it too? "I have pledged my vow. I shall honor it."

Tobacco fields gave way to hickory, tupelo, and cypress trees. Occasionally, we passed a palisaded plantation, most of which lay abandoned. I spied no dugouts, nor any other sign this had once been Paspahegh land. How could the world have changed so vastly in a mere span of thirteen years?

Near sunset, the ship rounded a bend. Cleared land once again came into view. Through the palisade, I could not catch a glimpse of the house. Sailors secured the mooring. I scooped Elenor into my arms, and soon we descended the plank to our new home. Henry led me through the fortified gate.

The house built of wood had a pitched roof for a loft with brick chimneys at each end. Glass being too costly, the windows were shuttered. Inside, there were two rooms: a parlor and a hall. The kitchen was in a separate building. Only two sturdy beams separated the rooms. A table spread across the hall, with a bench on each side and chairs at the ends. A cup board held pewter plates. There was even a looking glass.

On the opposite side, in the parlor, was a pallet with a rope lattice and straw mattress. A four-panel coffer with punch carvings on the sides sat at the end of the bed. A trundle bed was neath ours for Elenor. I had ne'er been in a house so grand, and here I was, the lady.

"You honor me, Henry."

He smiled. "When Elenor gets a little older, she can sleep in the loft."

Though melancholy about what had come to pass, the Arrohateck had taught me that any woman could be taken captive. I set about to making the house my own. I first opened the shutters to let a cool breeze fill the rooms. The sight of the palisade reminded me 'twas as much of a way to hold me prisoner as keeping Indians out. Henry had not merely hired a servant, but soldiers guarded the gate.

"I shall fetch some wood for the fire," I said.

"Phoebe, that's what James is for. He'll help with the heavy work."

"I'm perfectly capable of—"

"I insist."

I bowed my head slightly. "Whate'er you say."

He instructed James to collect the wood, whilst I checked the larder in the loft.

"Phoebe . . ." Henry grasped my hand. "Chores can wait 'til the morrow. Let us ready Elenor for bed, so that aft James returns, we can celebrate the occasion in our wedding bed."

Trembling, I pulled the trundle bed from neath ours. I dressed Elenor in a shift and sang her an Arrohateck lullaby.

"English," Henry insisted.

"I do not know the English words."

"Then find a new song."

My thoughts were in turmoil. I barely recollected the songs Momma had sung to me. In my head, I translated the words, but could not form them into music. "Forgive me, Henry." I gave my precious one a goodnight kiss upon her cheek. Her black hair and brown skin reminded me of Lightning Storm. I ached for him to take me into his arms and sat aside Elenor 'til she fell asleep. Even then, I lingered.

Behind me, I heard the pounding of wood near the fireplace. I turned and caught James's eyes as he stacked the firewood. He was as much of a captive as I, and with Africa an ocean away, he would ne'er see his homeland again. I opened my mouth to express my sorrow, but caught myself—not in front of Henry. And how soon would Henry trust me afore I could visit Momma?

Aft James bid us good eve, Henry's look changed to that of a man's hard stare when thinking of a woman. Gulping back a deep breath, I focused on his green eyes. I had ne'er noticed the flecks of brown in them afore. He approached. Lowering my head, I shifted uneasily upon my feet. I had ne'er lain with any man aside Lightning Storm.

His hand went neath my chin, and I spied a hunger that I did not feel, yet he was my husband. My duty was to oblige him. I forced a smile.

Unlacing my bodice, he kissed me upon the lips. When I felt his tongue, I closed my eyes to hide my tears. My skirt and bodice tumbled to the floor. Only my shift remained. He lifted it over my head. I had ne'er been shamed of my body afore, but my heart thumped as he touched and fondled.

Hurriedly, he undressed and showed me to the pallet. Praying he would be gentle, I lay upon it. With his body atop mine, he kissed and touched as a man caught in a raging fever. He forced my legs apart and entered my person. Like a chaste virgin, I winced, but so caught up in his rut, he failed to notice my discomfort. Panting loudly, he grunted and groaned.

If I thought of Lightning Storm . . . . I could almost feel his long hair brushing against my shoulder. Responding to the sensations, I opened my eyes to Henry's face. *He is my husband.* Struggling to accommodate him, I attempted to match his rhythm, when he howled in delight. Satisfied, he rolled to my side but continued to grope me. Afore long, he was ready to fornicate again.

I blindly went through the motions. Poppa had called me a whore for loving Lightning Storm. I had ne'er felt as such, but I certainly did now. One more time I reminded myself that Henry was my husband. The pattern continued several more times throughout the night. Finally fulfilled, he rolled over and fell asleep.

Bedazed by Henry's abruptness, I lay with my legs spread wide. My entire body ached. I pressed my face to the pillow and sobbed. Had Momma felt similar when she married Poppa? Resolved to follow her example and remain unflinching for Elenor's sake, I dried my tears and gathered my courage. I would be a good wife to Henry, as I had vowed.

41

Shae

CONVINCED THEY HAD MADE significant progress, Shae watched Phoebe blink from the hypnotic state. "I think we've learned a lot with this session."

"Aye."

"Was Henry the one who whipped you?"

Phoebe shook her head. "I don't recall, but in my heart I know 'twasn't Henry."

"Why do you say that? He forced you to have sex."

"I was fulfilling my obligations as his wife."

Shae remained silent for a moment. Although the idea was repulsive, she understood the historical context of arranged marriages. There had to be a connection to Phoebe's fantasy world and the reason why she accepted abusive treatment. How did Lee fit into the grand scheme of things with Lightning Storm supposedly dead? Everything was intertwined somehow. If only she could make the connection, she had no doubt Phoebe would recall what had put her on the road in February before she had been struck by the car.

42

Phoebe

THE FOLLOWING EVE, Carol drove me to Lee's apartment, where I made preparations for our meal. He had given me a key, allowing me entrance at my whim. Carol stayed long enough to make certain I had the ingredients afore bidding me farewell. I set about to fixing supper, using Meg's grandmother's fried chicken recipe. I hoped to excel at the meal Lee seemed to enjoy at the restaurant. Along with the chicken, I made fresh corn on the cob and baked beans.

Around 7:30, I heard a key rattle in the door.

Lee entered and sent me a tired smile. "You're a welcome sight to come home to."

I was gratified by his greeting and gave him a kiss. We lingered. I had come to take great comfort in his embrace but reluctantly withdrew to check on the food afore it burned. "Supper is nearly ready."

"Do I have time to change?"

"Aye."

Removing his tie, he vanished into the bedroom. Unable to find a platter in the cup board, I put the chicken on an earthenware plate. When I had the table nearly set, I felt Lee's lips upon my neck.

"To what do I owe the pleasure of your visit?" he asked, brushing my neck with his lips once more.

With a smile, I turned. He was attired more comfortably in a T-shirt and jeans and wore no gun upon his hip. "I had hoped to speak with you afore the weekend."

"Your session with Shae?"

I nodded, and he retreated towards the refrigerator. "Would you like a beer?"

"Aye, I'll take an ale." Afore I could be seated at the table, Lee was behind me, helping me.

He sat across from me and helped himself to the food I had prepared. "How did the session go?"

" 'Tis one of the reasons I wished to see you."

Aft a few ravenous mouthfuls, he said, "Go on."

Making certain to use my fork, I placed a chicken thigh on my plate. "I hope 'tis to your liking."

He muttered a positive response and wiped the grease from his fingers onto the napkin near his hand. "Phoebe, you know you can tell me about it."

"Eat first. Tell me of your day. I watched a program last night with Meg and Carol. They said it would help me understand your work."

Taking a sip of ale, he leaned forward with interest. "What's the name?"

"*CSI.* Meg said that stands for crime scene investigation."

He nearly choked on his ale. "It does. I'll make a deal with you. I'll tell you more about my job, if you only watch TV for entertainment. There's a reason it's called fiction."

Whilst we ate our supper, Lee shared the events of his day, and I began to comprehend his amusement. Afore long, I spoke of my session with Shae.

Upon telling him about my marital bed encounter with Henry, his hand tensed, forming a fist. "You said he was kind to you."

"He was," I said.

"But he raped you."

I grasped his clenched hand. "How can a husband despoil his wife?"

"How? Let me take you to the station, and I can show you the pictures how."

" 'Tis not the same," I insisted. " 'Twas foolish of me to behave as a chaste virgin."

"And you want me to continue to get into this guy's head? Phoebe, his attitude against Indians and blacks is abhorrent enough, but the way he treated you is—"

"Lee, 'twas a different time. If you do not wish to see what happened through Henry's eyes, then I only ask that you accompany me."

With my words, Lee relaxed his hand. "You know I will, as long as I don't have to witness any scenes like the one you just described. I'd challenge Henry to a duel, and I might not fare very well with a sword or seventeenth-century pistol."

"You cannot change what was through the dreaming."

"Now you tell me."

I detected his sense of humor returning and set about to making preparations. The dreaming was as much a part of him as 'twas me. I only hoped that he would eventually seek the answers to his own questions, as I had. Once the candle was in place, a sparkle entered his eyes.

I had come to know his thoughts. "Later, my love." I kissed him upon the lips, then lit the candle.

To my suggestion, he agreed. Grasping his hand, I focused on the flame and absorbed it. Mist engulfed me. The hound was in the lead, and Lee was aside me.

When the mist vanished, I found myself within the palisade of my home with Henry, and Lee was no longer within sight. "Lee . . ."

Momma stood afore me. She handed me wild yam root in a wooden bowl. "Come fall of the leaf," she said, "you must harvest your own."

I calmed myself. Lee would show himself afore the dreaming had completed. "Come fall of the leaf, Henry will sail for England, and I shall not need the root tea."

"Does he intend on staying in England fore'er? You will want a supply upon his return, or are you planning to escape when he takes his leave?"

Momma spoke the truth. Over the months, I had come to regard him as a man of his word. Most men would have viewed Momma as a traitor and not allowed her to visit. "Nay, I do not wish to shame him."

She gestured to the bowl containing the root. "Yet, you refuse to bear him a son."

"I gave Lightning Storm a son, and now, have none."

Momma nodded in understanding. "Silver Eagle has come to see you, but the guards would not allow him through the gate."

"I shall go to him." Thrilled at the prospect of seeing Silver Eagle, I set the wild yam on a table and walked along the path to the gate with Momma. The guards allowed us to pass. Aside Silver Eagle stood a warrior—Lee. Nearly forgetting myself due to my glee, I raised my arms, ready to embrace him. I caught myself and lowered my arms and gaze. "I'm pleased to see you, *Nows*," I said.

A hint of a smile crossed Silver Eagle's lips. "How are you keeping, *Amesens*?" Daughter.

"I'm well. Henry forbids me to bring Little Hummingbird outside the gate."

"He does not trust you."

No answer was necessary. Henry knew Elenor was the key to controlling my actions. All the while we spoke, Lee stared at me in familiarity. I began to wonder whether his presence was real or merely the figment that had accompanied me during the dreaming.

Finally, Silver Eagle said, "This is Little Falcon."

"I'm honored," I said with a slight bow of my head.

"As am I," he responded.

Why did he not speak to me in a less formal fashion? Afore I had a chance to say anything further, Silver Eagle and Little Falcon notched their arrows to bowstrings. A party of English men, with Henry in the lead, aimed their muskets at the warriors.

I raised my hand and moved betwixt the two parties. "Wait! Silver Eagle is my father."

Neither party lowered their weapons, but Henry's gaze softened.

"Henry, you've met my momma afore. This is Silver Eagle and his friend Little Falcon."

Henry ordered the men to lower their weapons, and the warriors did the same. He thrust out a hand. "I'm honored, sir."

"Shake his hand, *Nows*," I said to Silver Eagle. "He's offering you a truce."

With some hesitation, Silver Eagle shook Henry's hand. Little Falcon did the same.

Henry nervously wetted his lips. "Phoebe, invite your family in."

"The guards refused them entrance," I explained.

"That order shall be overridden immediately. 'Twas ne'er intended for members of your family." He bowed and motioned for everyone to enter through the palisade.

With that simple gesture, I came to care for Henry in a way that I had not previously. Mayhap, I would not resort to using wild yam. An honorable man such as Henry deserved to be blessed with a son.

As we walked towards the house, my eyes met with Little Falcon's. I still could not shake the feeling that on this journey, he was Lee. I nearly called his name, when the mist formed ahead of us. At the center was my guardian, the hound.

A moment passed afore I fixed myself to my surroundings of Lee's apartment. Lee held a stare on his countenance. "Lee?"

He blinked, taking a look around the room. "What does it all mean?"

"You saw the dreaming through Little Falcon's eyes?"

"I did," he admitted.

"You keep viewing the world through the eyes of a warrior."

"Is that surprising?" He held his hand next to mine. "What difference do you see?"

Puzzled by his question, I replied, "Your hand is larger and darker compared to mine."

He lowered his hand. "I doubt even Shae or my mother would have admitted the skin color difference. Both are what is called color-blind. The thing is, the world isn't color-blind, and even if it were, it strips away who I am. I may wear a suit and tie and cut my hair, but none of it makes me white."

Finally comprehending, I squeezed his hand. "I, too, am caught betwixt worlds. Like me, you must make peace with your past. If not through the dreaming, then in your own way. Only you can find the right path."

He agreed, but he didn't reach out to me in the way I had hoped. Whether his reasons were fear or a wish not to burden me, I did not know. I had to believe my words. If the road in seeking his past included me, he would tell me so.

43

Lee

THE FOLLOWING EVENING, Lee dragged himself into his apartment. He felt more exhausted after a day in court than from writing reports and following up on the usual complaints. Part of him had hoped that Phoebe would surprise him with another visit, but with an allowance of two overnights per week, he doubted he'd see her again until the weekend.

After grabbing a beer from the refrigerator, he spotted the answering machine light flashing. The nursing home had left a message first thing in the morning. His mother had fallen. He put in a quick call.

A nurse came onto the line. *"Nothing's broken, but your mother took a fall when showering this morning. Instead of waiting for assistance, she tried to return to her wheelchair by herself. At first we thought her arm might be broken, but she's fine. She has a few bruises. Nothing more."*

"Why was she left unattended in the first place?"

"She wasn't."

"You just suggested she was."

"The aide was reaching for a towel, when your mother took it upon herself to return to her wheelchair."

"Stark naked, and she decides to take her wheelchair out for a spin. That doesn't even make sense."

A heavy sigh came across the line. *"Mr. Crowley, she's not always mentally coherent. Dementia patients can be unpredictable."*

An easy excuse. He left that thought unsaid and double checked his cell messages. He hadn't missed any. "Why didn't someone call my cell number?"

"I thought they had." He heard a shuffling of papers. *"I'm sorry, Mr. Crowley, that must have been overlooked. It wasn't my shift when your mother had her accident. She's fine. That's the important thing."*

"And the next time?"

"I've made a notation on her chart to be certain to call your cell number. If you'd like, I can have Mr. Shreve give you a call in the morning."

First, deny what happened; then pass the buck. Typical. "You do that."

Lee hung up before he said something he regretted. Not once had the nurse referred to his mother by name. She was nothing more than a faceless aged body, and he didn't have the goddamned resources to do anything about it.

He tossed his tie and suit jacket over the back of the sofa. After a quick change into his sweat pants and a T-shirt, he sipped his beer and flopped in a chair. He picked up the TV remote and went channel surfing. *CSI.* It must be some sort of marathon week. Thinking of Phoebe, he laughed.

A candle remained on the table where they had participated in the dreaming. *"Only you can find the right path."*

The right path. Sometimes he wondered if there was such a thing. He switched off the TV and gulped down his remaining beer. The dreaming had shown him a side to himself that had been missing. Could it provide him with answers to his own questions?

He stared at the candle. Phoebe had shown him the way. All he had to do was embrace it. *Oh, what the hell.* After lighting the candle, he sat on the floor and stared at the flame. *Absorb it.* Nothing happened.

Why could he make the transition easily when Phoebe was present? He reminded himself the first couple of times *had* been difficult. Lee tried again. Like on the first occasion, outside noises kept distracting him. Think of Phoebe. On second thought, that hadn't been such a good idea.

He focused on the flame. The crow flew overhead. Mist swirled around him. He heard a woman crying. Unable to locate her, he stumbled through the thick fog. Her sobs emanated from all around him. Deeper and deeper, he went in search of her. Gunfire surrounded him, but his Glock wasn't at his side. He was lost. *Nooo!*

Covered in sweat, Lee blinked back the image. Sick to his stomach, he lowered his head until the nausea passed. Uncertain whether he'd try the dreaming again on his own, he wondered the significance of the meaning. Like most police officers, he had nightmares of his gun not firing when his life depended on it, but this experience hadn't seemed quite the same.

His hand trembled. He had definitely been afraid.

44

Phoebe

FOR THREE YEARS, Henry's plantation grew. Tobacco, hemp, and corn were planted, along with my own garden of beans, squash, and herbs. Some herbs, such as mallow and poppy, Henry brought from England. As captain of a ship, he usually sailed during fall of the leaf and returned to Virginia in May. Our house swelled with luxuries like wood stools and a red rug, and the windows had pane glass.

During the long months of Henry's absence, I ran the household. I now had two female servants, Bess and Jennet, to help with my chores, but the responsibility rested upon my shoulders. Jennet hailed from England, but like James, Bess came from Africa. Her skin was the color of ebony, and her prominent cheekbones were adorned with tribal scars. As indentured servants, their contracts belonged to Henry, but I looked the other way when James and Bess fell in love. Laws against such pairings during servitude had been firmly established, and I encouraged Bess to make use of the wild yam.

Despite my prompting, Bess got with child, and if Henry discovered the truth, he would lengthen the duration of her contract. She was able to conceal her pregnancy in the early months, and the child, thankfully, arrived in early May, afore his return. I had ne'er birthed a babe alone and gave Bess snakeroot tea to ease her pain.

I pressed my hand against her overly large belly. The babe squirmed neath my fingertips, affirming that it was very much alive.

I touched further. I believed the child was positioned correctly, head down in the womb. Without a knowledgeable midwife, I distrusted my judgment. Matters were made worse when Jennet attempted to assist me, crying and sniffling every time Bess moaned from the pain. Her hysteria grated upon me, but Turtle Shell and Momma had taught me patience. I heeded their advice 'til I could take no more.

"Jennet, tend to your other chores."

Instead of taking offense at my dismissal, the servant seemed relieved and hastily fled the house. I did my best to make Bess more comfortable by helping her walk about the room. When she rested, I faced the four winds and prayed the same words as the *kwiocos* had afore Elenor's birth. I circled the room to ward off rancorous spirits, whilst sending appeals to the Virgin Mary, as Momma had taught me.

When Bess's waters came down, I knew her birthing time was near. To my instructions, James had made a birthing chair with a slanted back and a horseshoe-shaped seat. I helped Bess into the chair and spread straw neath it. As her pain increased, so did her groans. I prepared more tea, which she gulped betwixt spasms.

"I shall use the wild yam next time," Bess moaned.

I hushed her and pressed on her belly to help force the child out. "Save your strength for birthing."

Blood gushed, and I got spattered.

"I'm going to die," she cried, again and again.

"You're not dying." Against my better judgment, I called for Jennet. I could not birth the babe without aid.

Aft telling the servant to mop up the blood from the floor, I knelt afore Bess. I pulled her hips towards me and spread her legs wide. As the babe's head crowned betwixt Bess's legs, she gasped as if she were burning alive.

"The babe is almost here." A blood-covered beast, looking more like a squiggling newt than a babe, slipped into my arms. He opened his mouth and wailed. He was a rich chestnut color with black hair.

Counting my blessings that Jennet had calmed from her earlier hysterics, I handed her the babe. The servant flinched at taking the bloody bundle into her arms. Ignoring her display, I pushed on Bess's belly once more to present the caule. " 'Tis a lad, and he was raring to enter the world."

A frantic knock came to the door. "Mistress Wynne, Mistress Wynne."

"Bess and the lad are fine, James," I shouted over my shoulder.

But the insistent rapping continued. "Mistress Wynne, word from England."

"Tell James that I shall speak to him when I can," I said to Jennet, "and let him know that he has a fine son."

Aft Bess had a few more spasms, the caule soon followed. I packed it in a pouch for burial, and then I cut the babe's navel cord with sharp scissors. Whilst Jennet saw to Bess, I washed the blood from myself. Once clean, I checked on Bess. She nursed the lad on a pallet in the parlor.

Satisfied that all was well, I went outside to speak with James. "Bess and the lad are in fine health."

With the news, he grinned, revealing large white teeth.

"Now, what is it that you wanted to tell me?"

He handed me a parchment. "A missive from England, Mistress Wynne."

"From Henry," I said, eagerly opening the letter. "Go see Bess." But why would Henry send a letter? He usually showed up at the gate in the spring. My joy was short lived, and my throat constricted as I began to read. 'Twas slow going, as I had to sound out each letter to string them into words. Henry had been stricken with the small pox. He would not be returning in the spring—if ever.

I floated through the layers and emerged from the seventeenth century into Shae's office.

"Did Henry eventually return?" Shae asked.

Though I recalled Henry's letter in my hand, I could not remember if he had survived the malady that kept him from sailing to Virginia. "I don't know. I thought myself to be a widow."

"Understandable."

From the beginning, Shae had not believed I hailed from the seventeenth century, yet I could not deny that our sessions helped me recall what happened. There was something else in my thoughts, but I could not quite grasp what it was.

"You look puzzled."

During the dreaming, Lee had identified with Little Falcon for a reason. "When I thought Henry dead, I shared my sorrow with Little Falcon."

"I take it that you mean in an intimate sense?"

"Aye."

"And you remember nothing else?"

I would need to share my next memories with Lee. "Nay."

"I think that's enough for one day."

Folding my hands on my lap, I agreed. As always, I looked forward to telling Lee.

45

Lee

AFTER MULLING OVER PHOEBE'S SESSION, Lee debated whether to share his own experience. *Not yet.* Phoebe sought answers on how she had arrived in the twenty-first century. His own questions had already waited thirty years. A little longer wouldn't hurt. Funny how a person could find solace by discovering the distant past. Where would it lead? He had no doubt that once Phoebe learned the truth, she would aid him in his own quest.

During the dreaming, he sought out Little Falcon. The warrior agreed to him seeing the world through his eyes. When the mist faded, his body was intertwined with Phoebe's on a straw mattress. Naked on the bed, they touched and caressed. Her cries drove him further until he surrendered to her.

Satiated, he moved to her side and held her in his arms.

"I love you, Little Falcon," she said in Algonquian.

"And I, you, Walks Through Mist. Leave this place and come back with me. You are Arrohateck. Let Little Hummingbird know her father's people. Your English husband is dead."

"But my English father is not. He will hunt me down if I run off again."

He wiped the tear streaking her cheek from her face. "I will protect you."

Shaking her head, she gripped him tighter. "You don't understand. There are far more English than you could possibly e'er fend off."

In time, he would abate her fears and convince her to return with him. Until then, he rejoiced in the time they shared. In each others' arms, they rested, and he finally slept. Near dawn, he hovered between the worlds of sleeping and waking.

A door creaked. Instantly awake, Little Falcon reached beside the bed for his tomahawk. In the shadowy light, he silently sprang for the intruder. Up close, he made out the features of the black servant and relaxed.

"Visitors coming, Mistress Wynne," James said, only now seeing Little Falcon and gasping in a quick breath of surprise.

Rushed by James's unexpected entrance, Phoebe put on her shift. "Go, Little Falcon." Little Falcon returned to her side, and she shoved him away. "Go! I'll be fine. They won't harm me."

He quickly adjusted his breechclout and laced up his leggings. After gathering his bow and arrows, he slipped out the door. The low-early morning light greeted him. The fact that the sun hadn't fully risen was to his advantage. He heard the tread of footsteps outside the palisade gate. Only leather shoes tramping against the ground would make such a sound—definitely *tassantassas*. He estimated around ten to twenty men.

In an effort to avoid them, he moved to the side gate. He unbarred it and slipped into the forest. Branches creaked in the wind. Overgrown with brambles, the trail was nothing more than a deer path. He forged forward, swiftly and silently.

Up ahead came voices, and he halted. *Tassantassas.* More voices behind him. Given no choice, he would fight. He raised his tomahawk and club.

46

Phoebe

I HURRIEDLY FINISHED DRESSING and set about to making my house every semblance of normal. Satisfied there were no signs that Little Falcon had spent the night with me, I went to greet the English soldiers. The guards opened the gate. Along with several musketeers, my father entered astride a strapping bay stallion. He now had more gray in his hair than blondish-red. Wrinkles lined his forehead and the skin around his mouth, as well as his eyes. Though he ne'er smiled, his grim features seemed all the more unforgiving.

"Phoebe, how could you shame me?" he asked, dismounting.

My mouth went dry. "I don't understand, Poppa."

He held up a long black lock of bloody hair.

Little Falcon! Suddenly weak, I sank to my knees and wailed my sorrow.

Soldiers surrounded me and seized my wrists, wrenching me to my feet. To no avail, I fought against their grip. Even when I tripped over a root, they failed to halt and dragged me to the nearest tree. Nearly pulling my shoulders from their sockets, they lashed me to an overhead branch. Stretched out on my tiptoes, I barely reached the ground. The bindings seared my skin, but I struggled against their hold. Behind me, one of the soldiers gripped my hair, snapping my head back.

Poppa stood afore me. "You have shamed me and the memory of your husband. You have replaced one Indian for another." He pressed the scalp lock to my face 'til I could barely breathe. "Fornicate with your savage now. You're to be punished for not having resisted his advances." He dropped the scalp lock to the ground, where it came to rest upon my toes.

Little Falcon's blood stuck to my face, and I spat on my father.

He wiped the spittle from his eye. "You will be taught proper manners."

A sharp blade barely missed my skin and traveled the length of my back, cutting laces and ripping through to my shift. Rough hands tore the fabric further and bared my back. Blood stained my sleeves from my struggles with the ropes. Defeated, I halted my futile resistance. "Do what you will with me, but I shall always send my prayers to Ahone."

He raised a hand. I thought for certain he would strike my cheek, as he had in the past, but he lowered his arm and stepped aside. "Proceed."

A whip cracked against my bare skin. I gritted my teeth to keep from crying out, only to feel another lash. And another. Tears entered my eyes, but I refused to render my father with the satisfaction of a pain-filled wail.

The whip struck me again. I lost count the number of times it pounded across my back. Blinded by pain, I thought of Little Falcon. I would meet my fate bravely, as he had his. A mist arose, and he stood afore me. In spite of the thrashing, I smiled. "Little Falcon, you're alive."

His arms went around me. "It's me, Phoebe. You've seen enough for now. Come back."

Come back? Caught betwixt the cracking whip and the misty world, I howled from the pain and slumped against the ropes. My father had won.

47

Lee

AN EMPTY STARE crossed Phoebe's face. She swayed, and Lee called her name. Before he could catch her, she sank to the floor with a thump. "Phoebe?"

She murmured in Algonquian.

Why could he no longer comprehend? Only moments ago during the dreaming, he had spoken and understood the language fluently. He checked her breathing and pulse. Normal. Thank goodness for small blessings. "Phoebe? Are you okay?"

She muttered, still in Algonquian.

After a quick check to make certain she suffered no broken bones, Lee gathered her in his arms and carried her to the bedroom. He helped her to bed and covered her with a blanket. Climbing in next to her, he held her in his arms.

Soon, he drifted.

"Lee?"

He blinked.

Phoebe looked at him with a curious stare. She stroked the side of his face and his lips as if making certain he was really beside her.

Still groggy, he stretched. "You worried me that time."

Her index finger traced along his jawline. *"You* brought me back." She hugged him.

In their embrace, he felt the deep ridges on her back where the whip had bitten into her skin. "Now we know where you got some of the scars."

"Aye." Still afraid, she tightened her grip and cried.

Lee brushed away her tears, telling her everything would be all right. She continued to sniff back the tears, and he handed her a Kleenex.

She sobbed into the tissue. "You don't understand. The dreaming is symbolic. Through Little Falcon, I have witnessed *your* death."

"Mine?" No matter what he said, he was unable to convince her otherwise. He held her until she finally calmed down and slept.

48

Phoebe

L ATE MONDAY AFTERNOON, I called Shae and canceled my appointment for the following morn. Though thwarted by my action, there was little she could do.

"If there's something wrong, I wish you'd confide in me."

" 'Tis not that easy."

"Phoebe . . ."

I hung up the phone.

"Phoebe?" came a gentle voice from behind me. I turned, and Valerie stared in bewilderment. "You've been on edge ever since returning this morning. Did something happen between you and Lee?"

How could I explain? She had indulged my whims when I last had such a feeling, only for everyone to discover that Lee was fine. "Lee and I are still courting. I shall see him later this week," I said, hoping that my voice hadn't wavered. "I have some chores to tend to afore supper."

"Phoebe, you know we're here for you if you need to talk." She squeezed my arm. "Let me know if there's anything I can do."

"I shall."

With my nagging foreboding, a plate slipped from my fingers and shattered on the floor whilst I helped prepare supper. I bent down to pick up the shards and cut my forefinger.

"Phoebe," Meg said, entering the kitchen, "let me help." She knelt aside me and started collecting glass fragments.

I held up my bleeding finger. "I fear that Lee is in trouble."
Her brows knitted together. "Because you cut your finger?"
"Nay. I simply know."

"Have you talked to him? Sometimes that helps our fears."

He had held me long into the night, comforting me, yet I could not shake the feeling. "I told him my fear."

Meg placed the shards on the counter. "What did he say?"

"He said he'd be fine."

A large grin appeared on her face. "And he will be. Why don't I finish cleaning up this mess, while you take care of that finger? Afterward, call Lee. You'll see that he's okay."

When I faltered, one of the women from Colwell House always supported me. With me hailing from the seventeenth century, it couldn't have been easy for any of them. I hugged Meg and told her how much I cared for her.

49

Lee

FINISHED TRANSCRIBING HIS NOTES for an assault report, Lee had
the sudden feeling something was amiss. He trusted his gut and
dialed the number for Colwell House. Meg answered and immediately passed the phone to Phoebe. "Are you all right?"

"Aye."

"I had a weird feeling and thought I had better call."

She remained silent.

"Phoebe, what's wrong?"

" 'Tis what I saw in the dreaming."

"Just because Little Falcon died doesn't mean I will too. I've had
a rather uneventful day, writing reports mostly."

"You're sure?"

"Positive." Lee checked his watch. "In fact, I'm just about ready
to head home." Ed tapped him on the shoulder and showed him a
murder call that had come in. *So much for heading home.* He motioned
to his partner that he'd be right with him. "Listen Phoebe, I have to
go, but call me if you need anything."

"Lee, pray be careful."

"I will," he promised. With her words, he had an overwhelm-
ing sensation of coldness. Quickly dismissing the feeling, he told
Phoebe goodbye. He had barely hung up when his cell phone rang.
Thinking Phoebe had forgotten something, he said, "Phoebe . . ."

"Lee, it's Carol."

"Carol? Is Phoebe okay? I just talked to her . . ." Ed sent him an
impatient wave.

"She's fine. You told me to call you—"

"Carol, can I call you later? I really can't talk now."

"Sure."

Lee joined Ed for the drive to the crime scene and worried that something had happened. *Phoebe would have called.* But he couldn't shake the feeling. He put in a quick call to Colwell House. When Valerie answered, he told her about the odd calls from Phoebe and Carol.

"Everyone is accounted for. Phoebe's worried about you, and Carol called to reassure her."

Logical explanation. Lee thanked Valerie. He needed to mentally shift gears, but the nagging inside his head wouldn't vanish.

Upon their arrival at the upscale apartment complex, Lee took several photos and noted the time, before passing under the yellow tape to the uniformed police officer for his report.

" . . . mother and daughter, side by side."

The most gut-wrenching cases were those involving children.

After hearing the officer's account, the detectives went into the living room, where the sectional sofa with plump cushions sat in front of a bay window. Magazines were neatly arranged on the coffee table. In one corner of the room stood a wooden doll house. Beside the doll house was a red child-sized rocker and a bookcase filled with children's books. The only telltale sign that anything was amiss was the blood splattered across the white carpet. In the middle of the red pool was a three-foot body. Her mother lay a couple of feet away.

Lee swallowed, keeping the bile and his rising fury down. The girl's face, or what was left of it, was an unidentifiable bloody mess from the close-range, execution-style gunshot. For a second, he envisioned a brown-skinned woman in a deerskin apron, weeping with a small child in her arms.

"Lee," Ed asked, "you okay?"

The image faded, and he suppressed the building rage. What kind of lowlife wasted a child? He faced Ed. "No, I'm not okay. She couldn't have been any more than four."

Ed cleared his throat. "I know, but we have a job to do."

By the time they finished their examination of the bodies, photographing and sketching the scene, one of the detectives reported back from canvassing the building. "I think it might be worthwhile to question the neighbors further." He handed Ed his notes.

Ed passed the report to Lee. "Ready, partner?"

After a quick scan, Lee nodded. They went into the hall. Apartments were separated by five feet of a pale marble mosaic tile that had the appearance of being freshly scrubbed—all the way to the next door. For a brief instant, Lee saw an armored soldier looming over him.

Not again. The vision distracted him. *What am I doing?* He blinked and stared at a door. *The investigation.*

Ed knocked. "Police."

The door opened to an auburn-haired woman of about average height and maybe twenty-five years old. Both detectives showed their badges and identification.

"I've already told the cops what I know—twice," she said in an unsympathetic manner.

"I'm Detective Bailey," Ed replied, "and this is Detective Crowley. We want to make certain nothing was missed, ma'am. Two people were murdered next door. One was a four-year-old child."

She opened the door, inviting them in. "I didn't see anything."

Lee confirmed her identity from the previous detective's report before asking any questions. "Did you hear gunshots?"

She shook her head.

After a few more routine questions, he added, "According to my report, your brother also lives here."

A man equal in height to Lee's entered the room. "I do."

Lee noted the man's holey and worn athletic shoes were sparkling white. Exchanging a glance with Ed, he knew his partner had made the same observation. Lee went ahead with his questioning. The sister vowed that her brother hadn't been out of the apartment all day, yet he spotted hesitation in her eyes. He suspected spraying Luminol in the hall would trace blood from the victims' apartment directly to the athletic shoes.

Without warning, Lee heard voices. Frightened screams surrounded him, along with the smell of smoke. Crawling on his hands and knees, he escaped the worst of the suffocating fumes. Guns fired, and he called out. *To whom?* More screams. Blind in the smoke, he was lost. Heat from a flame nearly burned him.

The vision faded to a gun in the perp's hand. Lee drew his own at the same time. Gunfire exploded. He felt a sharp sting and heard a snap in his left thigh. His leg crumpled from beneath him, knocking him flat on his back. Blood spurted. Lightheaded, he sank to the floor. He thought of Phoebe before darkness engulfed him.

50

Phoebe

SITTING UPRIGHT IN BED, I AWOKE in a cold sweat with my heart pounding. *Lee.* Once again, I had an overwhelming feeling that he was in danger. I resisted the temptation to call him. 'Twas well past ten and outgoing calls were strictly forbidden 'til the morrow. I would have to answer to Valerie if I tried.

I lay back. Unable to sleep, I struggled to get comfortable. Amongst the Arrohateck, I had been known as Walks Through Mist. Why did I not follow my instinct? The last time that I had felt this way . . . .

Recalling the day in my mind with shocking clarity, I curled to a ball and let out an unearthly howl.

"Phoebe . . . !" came Meg's voice from the hall. Her fist hammered on my door. "Phoebe! Answer me! What's wrong?"

I sobbed into my pillow.

The door swung open, and comforting arms went around me, holding me like Meg so oft held her young daughter. Soon, Carol and Valerie joined her.

"He's dead," I cried.

"It was a bad dream," Valerie said, shoving my hair from my eyes and hushing me.

Her words failed to soothe me, and I continued to weep, repeating the god-awful truth, "He's dead."

51

Shae

THE PHONE RINGING IN THE MIDDLE of the night woke Shae. Russ fumbled for the light switch before answering, "She's right here." He handed her the phone. "It's Valerie."

"Shae, we can't console Phoebe. She keeps crying and repeating, 'He's dead.' "

"Who's dead?"

"Lee."

Surely she would have heard something if that were true. "What set it off?"

"A dream, I think, but she's in bad shape. She believes it's real."

"I'll be right there." Shae switched off the phone. "I've got to go. For some reason Phoebe thinks Lee is dead, but she's inconsolable."

Russ grasped her elbow as she got up to dress. "Do you want me to come with you?"

"I'll be fine." The phone rang again. Russ reached for it, but Shae got to it first. "Valerie, I'm on my way just as soon as I—"

"Shae?"

But it was a baritone voice, not Valerie's. The phone nearly slipped from her fingers upon recognizing Ed. "Oh God, Lee *is* dead."

"No, he's not dead, but there's been a shooting. I'm sorry to bother you, but he never changed his emergency contact."

Her mind blurred as Ed relayed the details. *So much for being hit by a truck.* And Phoebe had felt him die. "I'll pick up Phoebe and be right there." Why had her voice seemed to come from outside of her body?

"Thanks, Shae. They don't know yet whether he's going to make it."

Even Ed's voice had sounded shaky. The line went dead. "Lee's been shot. That goddamned bastard. I divorced him. Why does he keep dragging me into his life?"

Russ hugged her. "Are you angry at him or yourself, for still caring?"

She struggled to keep from crying and forced a smile. "I should have known better than to become engaged to a psychologist."

"How is Lee?"

"Ed said he was in surgery. They don't know whether he'll survive. I need to calm Phoebe down and get her to the hospital."

"Let me drive you." He pulled on his pants. "Lee's tough. He'll pull through."

"Thanks." That was why she loved Russ. No matter the circumstances, he was always there.

52

Phoebe

M EG AND CAROL STAYED WITH ME. Struck numb, I had cried all
my tears. I heard voices in the hall but took no notice of what
they were saying. The voices came closer, and I felt the bed shift.
Meg and Carol left my side, as if they had been instructed to do so.

"Phoebe, get up and get dressed. Lee needs you."

Hovering over me, Shae's face came into focus. I saw fear in her
eyes. "Lee's alive?"

"He is, but he's in serious condition. I'm going to take you to
him." She took my arm, forcing me to my feet, and helped me to
dress.

"Lee's alive," I repeated, not knowing whether to allow myself
to hope.

Shae finished dressing me and guided me to the door. "We'll
talk about it later. Right now, I need to get you to the hospital."

I focused on her words. "What has happened?"

"I don't know the details, only that Lee's been shot." She led me
down the stairs and outside the door.

A car waited by the curb, where Shae's betrothed kept the engine
running. Shae slammed the car door behind me, and Russ whisked
us through the night-lit streets, only for me to recall a time when
the lights aft dark had been the moon and stars.

Though I prayed for Lee, I yearned for Lightning Storm. He,
too, had been shot. I had wrapped his battered body in mats. I blackened my face with charcoal and wailed as he was placed on a scaffold.
Months later, he was buried with his bow, for he would need it in
the afterlife.

The *kwiocosuk* existed no more. I had to find my own way to appease Oke's wrath and present offerings of tobacco and bloodroot. If I did so, mayhap Lee would be spared and not suffer the same fate.

Russ screeched the car to a halt outside the hospital. As Shae ushered me through the halls, nurses and uniformed police officers pointed the direction. Finally, we reached a waiting room filled with people. Ed emerged from the crowd. "Phoebe, thank God you're here. Shae, thanks for bringing her. There's been no word yet."

"Take me to him."

He shook his head. "They're not going to let us in. He may not even be out of surgery yet."

Confused as to why I had been summoned if I was not allowed by Lee's side, I looked at Shae for guidance.

"What happened, Ed?" she asked.

He ran a hand through his thin hair. "He saved my life. We were questioning a suspect. Lee saw the gun before I did. He drew his fire. I should be the one in there, not him."

"It's not your fault, Ed. The blame belongs to the man with the gun."

"He murdered a woman and her young daughter. Small comfort, but we got him. I don't know which one of us sent the fatal bullet."

Like most warriors, Ed attempted to hide his true feelings, but an intuitive woman could see beyond the appearance. I touched his hand and felt a surge of grief.

Uncomfortable with the revelation that I was aware of his sorrow through a mere touch, he said, "Let me get you some coffee while we wait."

Shae guided me to a chair, but I had difficulty sitting still and waiting. She picked up a publication called *Prevention* and thumbed through it, pretending to read. If only I had some solitude in which I could face the four winds and send my prayers to Ahone.

Ed returned with a cup of coffee. I did not wish for him to think his efforts were in vain, but ne'er having acquired the taste, I sipped the bitter drink and nearly choked. He quickly apologized, when a doctor attired in a bluish-green material entered the waiting room. The doctor singled out the three of us and led the way to an office. "Detective Crowley isn't out of the woods yet, but because of his excellent health and conditioning, I think he'll make it. However, the next twenty-four hours will be critical."

Was this good news? The doctor's inflection suggested that it could be, but I failed to comprehend why Lee was in the woods.

"He's in the ICU and probably will be for a few days. The bullet fractured his left femur, and a bone fragment nicked the femoral artery. He's lost a lot of blood. We're giving him transfusions and fluids to help compensate. I didn't see any sign of nerve damage. He was in a lot of pain when he was first brought in, but thankfully, he was able to move his toes. Any questions?"

Where to begin? "What is a femur?" I asked, raising my hand, as my tutor had taught me.

"The thigh bone." He pointed to a chart of a skeleton. "The femoral artery is the main artery in the leg. More than likely, Detective Bailey saved his life by applying direct pressure to stifle the bleeding until the medical team arrived."

As a healer, this explanation I understood. "May I see him?"

"Of course. He's been asking for you. I do want to limit the number of visitors to two at a time while he's in ICU."

I glanced to Shae, and she instructed me to go ahead. Following behind the doctor, Ed escorted me to the ICU. I imagined this to be the woods that he had spoken of, but it looked similar to the hospital room I had been in upon arriving in this century. A blue curtain separated the beds, and tubes trailed everywhere from Lee's body. A mask covered his nose and mouth, and there was a screen that resembled the TV at Colwell House.

Though Lee was awake, his eyes were glazed. Careful not to hit any of the tubes in his arm, I grasped his hand. His face brightened upon seeing me, and he squeezed my fingers.

"You were lucky, Lee," Ed said. "He killed that mother and her little girl."

Lee's gaze followed Ed's voice.

"We got him, partner. He won't hurt anyone again."

Lee's grip tightened on my hand, and I stroked my fingers through his hair. He closed his eyes, but I had already felt the rush of emotion. As best as I could, I hugged him, whispering my love, whilst behind me, Ed slipped out of the room. He had delivered the message that Lee needed to hear. Unlike Lightning Storm, Lee would live, and I would tend him.

53

Shae and Lee

THE FOLLOWING DAY, Shae canceled her appointments and drove to the nursing home. After parking the car, she went straight inside. Upon entering, she notified the receptionist that she had an appointment with Mr. Shreve, one of the management staff workers. Soon, she was escorted into an office, where a portly man with a pale-blue button-down shirt greeted her. He motioned for her to have a seat. "What can I do for you, Dr. Howard?" he said, seating himself behind the desk.

"I was wondering if Natalie Crowley has been informed about her son."

"The hospital hasn't kept us very well informed."

"In other words, 'no.' Mr. Shreve—"

"Dr. Howard, we *have* told her, but I'm not certain how much she's absorbed. We're short staffed, and I'm actually quite relieved that you're here. As a psychologist, you're much more qualified to explain the situation."

Not really—dementia wasn't her specialty. "I'm going to take her to see him."

"As I had hoped. I'll make certain the paperwork is ready when you are."

At least they were being cooperative. "Thank you."

"If there's anything else I can do—"

"I'll let you know. Thanks again." Shae made her way into the hall and went in the direction of Nat's room. Except for a few cousins, Lee was the only family Nat had among the living. And now— *Don't think that way. Lee will live.*

Stopping before the door to Nat's room, she wondered if she was ready for this. How did you tell a mother that her son had been gunned down? Lee faced these situations in his job. She'd handle it as well. Shae knocked. When no one responded, she poked her head into the room. "Nat?"

As usual, Nat sat in her wheelchair near the window. "Shae?"

Shae pulled a chair next to Nat's wheelchair. "I'm here."

Tears filled Nat's eyes, and she gripped her hand. "They told me . . ." She drifted, obviously having difficulty thinking of which words to use. "Lee . . ."

"I'm going to take you to see him."

Though infirm, Nat's grip tightened. "He's alive?"

"Very much so," Shae said in as much of a reassuring voice as she could muster. "He's in critical condition, but you know how pig-headed he is. He'll pull through."

The wetness of Nat's tears spread to her cheeks. "I knew you would come."

Shae took a tissue from the nightstand and wiped Nat's face. Damn Russ for being right. Although her relationship with Lee had changed, she couldn't deny what had gone before. "I've never stopped caring for you or him."

More tears. "Thank you."

Shae wheeled Nat toward the door. On their way out, she said a silent prayer that not only would Lee be alive by the time they arrived, but that his condition had improved.

In a morphine haze, Lee was semi-conscious of people filing in and out of the room. Police officers, some he hadn't seen in years, since he had been on patrol duty. All of them sent their best wishes. They were like a tribe. When one of them was down, all shared the pain. He felt the camaraderie only understood by those who lived behind a badge.

Shae visited. Even while drifting in and out of the drug-induced fog, he saw that she fought the tears.

"Damn you, Lee. You said you were more likely to be hit by a truck."

Had she really uttered the words? Aware of why she had divorced him, he hoped Russ could give her what he had been unable to—a stable life. She deserved it, and he held no animosity that she had sought it.

What of Phoebe? He'd bring her the same grief, if he loved her. Too late, he already did.

Vaguely cognizant of a feeble form in a wheelchair beside the bed, he struggled to lift his head. "Mom?"

She hushed him to take it easy, as if he had skinned a knee, and he lowered his head back to the pillow.

"Lee, there's something I must tell you." A fragile but loving hand touched his. "You already know that your father and I couldn't have children of our own. We were at the age where we should have been thinking of grandchildren, but when the hikers found a toddler in the woods . . . well, it was like having a gift delivered from God. I tried my best to teach you about your heritage, but I had no guidance . . ."

"You did your best."

She hushed him again. "I need to finish, or I may lose my nerve. I was so happy to have a child of my own, but I was angry too. Angry at the woman who had left you to die alone in the woods. Our attorney knew a compliant judge who got you labeled as abandoned. I didn't want to lose you. After the media circus died down, we stopped looking for your birth parents. I let my anger rule, and we rushed the adoption through. Over the years, I began to think about your birth mother. I don't know why she wouldn't have responded to the newspaper reports or gone to the police, but what if there was some reason that had prevented her? Maybe she was sick and never saw the reports. Maybe she was injured. Lots of maybes. And what if she hadn't found out about you until it was already too late? You know how they seal adoption records. If she did abandon you, may the Lord have mercy on her soul, but I can never forgive myself if there was a legitimate reason that I separated a mother from her son."

Lee had difficulty focusing on his mother's wrinkled face.

She patted his hand. "Please, don't hate me."

"Mom . . ." But he couldn't break the dizzying effect of the morphine.

When Lee woke, she was gone. He was flat on his back. Sound asleep in the chair beside the bed, Phoebe rested her head in her arms. She had on the green dress that she had worn to the party. *How long ago? A week? Or a month?* He couldn't recall. She wore the arrowhead he had given her. When he was on his feet again, he'd have to buy her a real necklace.

Exhausted beyond anything he could imagine, he stretched, then clenched his teeth against the pain. He reached a hand toward Phoebe's reddish-blonde curls. "I thought of you before . . ."

Her eyes opened, and tears of joy filled them. "I was afraid that I might lose you as I had Lightning Storm. Right now, you're not to worry about anything but getting better, and I shall tend you."

He liked the sound of that and hugged her close.

Shae hadn't planned on visiting Lee in the hospital again, but circumstances required her presence. When she entered the room, Phoebe and a nurse were helping him into a wheelchair. "I'd like to speak with you," she said.

He looked in her direction. "You're always complaining to me about no 'Hi, how are you?' "

"Alone, please."

He nodded, and the others left the room. "I presume your visit is about Phoebe."

"She's left Colwell House. What's gotten into you? She's not ready for the world."

He shifted his weight in the wheelchair and grimaced. "In case you hadn't noticed, I'm not going anywhere anytime soon. Her tutor has agreed to work with her at my place, and I'll show her what she needs to know."

"Of all the asinine . . . ," Shae muttered, attempting to keep her temper in check. "Are you certain you didn't break more than your leg? You used to think rationally. Have you given any thought as to how she'll manage when you return to duty?"

"I'm on extended medical leave. I won't be going back to work for several months."

"And you just avoided the question. I had to call in favors to get her into Colwell House—"

"She promises me that she'll keep in contact with her friends there." Shae opened her mouth to protest, but he continued, "Shae, this is none of your concern."

"The hell it's not. Phoebe is still my patient."

"I thought you had said she canceled her appointments."

"Lee . . ." She held up her hands in surrender. "I only want what's best for Phoebe, okay? Nothing more. In my professional opinion, I think it's too soon for her to move out of Colwell House, but if both of you insist on this, I'd like to work with you to help make it a smooth transition. Can we agree on that point?"

His features softened. "We can."

"Good. Then can you please try to get her to return to her appointments?"

To this, he agreed.

"I do wish the two of you the best of luck, but it's not going to be easy."

"Tell me—what in life that's worth pursuing is easy?"

He had a point, and her shoulders sagged. "Call me sentimental or unprofessional, but I don't want to see either of you getting hurt."

"Your concern is appreciated." His face contorted.

"And don't pretend you can hide that you're in pain."

He caught his breath. "Is this an 'I told you so,' doctor?"

She gaped at him in disbelief. "I wouldn't be that cruel. I thought you knew me better than that."

His gaze met hers. "I do. Forgive me."

"We've come a long way, haven't we?"

"Definitely. And I'd like to thank you for bringing my mother."

"You're welcome. She's always treated me well."

His face clouded in thought.

"Don't judge her harshly," Shae said. "She did what she thought was best for you and her."

"It's nothing like that. I had often wondered if there were things my parents hadn't admitted to. So my adoption was one of the many that falls into a gray area, legality wise. Minimum waiting period, an all-too-willing judge ready to label a woman an unfit parent, even though most of the facts are unavailable, and she's forever shut out of her child's life. Nothing ever changes. Why didn't my mother tell me before now?"

"For a cop, you can be dense sometimes. What usually keeps people from revealing the truth?"

Fear. He nodded in comprehension.

"I'll get Phoebe." She turned and said, "I expect to see you walking soon. The wedding is in August."

"I may be on crutches, but I'll be there."

She left the room.

Phoebe waited outside the door. "Are you angry with me, Shae?"

"Of course not. I know how much you love him. Phoebe..." Shae caught herself. Let Lee talk to her. "Lee's waiting for you."

Phoebe's eyes sparkled before she vanished into Lee's room.

Shae had no doubt that Lee was in good hands. If only she could worry a little less about Phoebe.

54

Phoebe

UPON TAKING UP RESIDENCE IN LEE'S APARTMENT, I began by seeing that he was resting comfortably in bed, and then I set about
to straightening up the clutter by picking up the clothes thrown
across the divan. Aft finishing that task, I placed empty ale cans in
the recycling bin. Meg had told me that bachelors were oft messy.
My experience had been that 'twas true of men from any century.

Throughout the day, Lee ne'er complained of pain, but he woke
in the middle of the night drenched in sweat. I held him 'til he finally slept. In the morn I phoned Meg. She and Carol brought me
to a shop where I could purchase herbs. The few I had grown at
Colwell House were unready for harvesting. Used to growing my
own, I expected a visit to an apothecary, but the shelves were lined
with bottles, jars, and packages. Teas and salves were already formu-
lated, overwhelming me on how to choose the best medicines.

Confused by the labels and unable to read them in their entirety,
I had the women assist me. I failed to comprehend the twenty-first
century physicks—the remedies prescribed from the doctor seemed
to hinder Lee's wellbeing more than they aided him. The yellow
dandelion pictured on a bottle made my initial selection an easy one.
I would make a tea to aid his digestive woes. I then proceeded to
choose comfrey, sarsaparilla, and lobelia. The powdered roots would
make a poultice for the swelling in his leg.

Though I searched the many shelves, I could find naught to relieve his pain and became distraught that I was unable to locate a

suitable remedy. Carol assured me that she would drive me to another shop, as Meg needed to return to her daughter. Aft taking my
purchases to the sales counter, I carefully counted out the currency,
as Liz had shown me. I mistook a nickel for a dime, and Meg shook
her head. I checked one more time, found the dime, and Meg nodded.

Afterwards, we returned Meg to Colwell House, but the next
shop produced the same results. In defeat, I got into Carol's car.

"Listen, Phoebe. I might be able to help."

I raised my head. "Do you know of yet another shop?"

"No, but . . ." She withdrew a plastic bag containing dried herbs
and handed it to me. "You can have this if you don't tell anyone
where you got it from."

I inspected the bag. The leaves had distinctive jagged edges.

"Do you recognize it?"

" 'Tis bangue."

"Whatever. Can you use it?"

"Aye. I can simmer it in butter and add it into soup. Why could
we not find it in the shop?"

Carol twisted a lock of hair around her finger. "They must have
been out of stock. It's popular for pain relief, and stores are always
running out."

Though I detected hesitation in Carol's voice, her answer made
sense. Satisfied that I had what I needed to make Lee comfortable, I
told Carol to return to his apartment.

Once again, I was a prisoner in my home. Bess tended to the
wounds upon my back, but the scars of my being failed to heal.
I had lost many loved ones—Lightning Storm, Dark Moon, Little
Falcon, even Henry. Poppa locked the gate, instructing the guards
to not allow me outside the palisade. Cut off from Momma and Silver Eagle, I feared I would not have been able to carry on if it had
not been for Elenor.

With Henry presumed dead and having no male heir, his land
was bequeathed to me. If I had truly understood the meaning of
my newfound wealth, I could have ordered Poppa to leave the plantation, but having been raised Arrohateck, I failed to comprehend

how land could be bought and sold. With each passing day, I went aimlessly about my chores, as I had always done whilst Henry was at sea.

On a cool day the following May, I performed my morning ritual of bathing in the spring. Upon completing my task, Poppa stood afore me. Immediately, he averted his eyes, and I pulled on my shift.

"Phoebe, I wish you would wear your shift when you bathe."

I finished dressing. " 'Tis the way of the Arrohatek."

He grumbled under his breath about the futility of daily bathing, but his usual lecture of how I would burn in hell if I didn't mend my heathen ways wasn't forthcoming. Instead, he glared at me. "I've decided to return you to England."

"I shall not go!"

"You have no choice in the matter. I am your father, and as long as you remain here, you're at risk of running off to the Indians."

"I vow that I won't run off if you will allow me to stay. Virginia is my home."

"I've reserved passage for you and Elenor." He put his arms loosely about me. "I only want what's best for you."

Amongst the Arrohatek, I had been taught to honor my elders. Though I had been borne from this man's seed, he was not my father. I could not bring myself to reciprocate his hug and vowed to myself that I would somehow escape with Elenor.

55

Shae and Lee

RELIEVED THAT PHOEBE had rescheduled her appointments, Shae had listened to the progression of her story with interest. "I'm pleased you're seeing me again."

"Lee thought it best," Phoebe acknowledged.

Thank goodness she'd had that chat with Lee. "How is he doing?"

"He doesn't bemoan his injury, but he is melancholy. He doesn't know how to 'take it easy.' "

No surprise. Even when they were married, Lee had never been the sort to sit still. "I'm sure you're making certain that he does."

"To the best of my ability."

"That's good. I'll see you again on Thursday."

After a round of goodbyes, Shae let out a breath. What a frustrating, tormented patient. If only she could get to the bottom of Phoebe's troubles. She sifted through the possibilities. With Lee on medical leave, maybe he'd be open to the idea of attending a session or two with Phoebe. Something about him connected Phoebe to the twenty-first century.

Between Phoebe's poultices and other medications, Lee's pain and the swelling in his leg were decreasing. Sometimes, he woke in night sweats, but they were steadily lessening in both frequency and intensity. With massage, stretching, and Phoebe's dedicated care, he had quickly graduated from a walker to crutches.

Annoyed at how long it took him to get anywhere, he went into the kitchen. Phoebe stirred something in a pan on the stove. Unable to put weight on his left leg, he moved slowly but finally reached her.

When he kissed the back of her neck, she turned to him with a smile. "I heard you coming."

"I didn't think I could sneak up on you. What are you cooking this time?"

She stirred some butter with a wooden spoon and added a dried herb. "I simmer bangue in the butter before adding it to soup. It aids in ridding your pain."

Leaning on his right crutch, Lee took a closer look at the herb. *Holy shit.* "Phoebe . . ."

Her eyelids flickered with wide-eyed innocence.

"What did you call it?"

"Bangue."

"This is what you used in the seventeenth century?"

"Aye. Farmers used differing varieties of hemp. Some for fiber for linen and cordage. The leaves and flowers of this type made medicine."

Lee swayed slightly. He'd already been on his feet for too long. "We need to talk."

Seeing his difficulty, Phoebe helped him to the recliner in the living room. Besides the bed, it was the only place he could get comfortable.

"In the twenty-first century, bangue is called pot, marijuana, and at least a dozen other street names. For reasons that are a bit lengthy to go into right now, it's illegal. You could be arrested for merely possessing it."

Confusion crossed her face. "Even if I'm using it for medicine?"

"In the state of Virginia, yes."

"And you . . . ?"

"I could lose my job."

She frowned. "I did not mean to bring you shame."

He stroked her cheek. "You were only trying to help. I can easily guess that it was either Meg or Carol who gave it to you."

"Carol," she admitted. "She said the apothecary shop was 'out of stock.' "

He also bet that Carol was still seeing that asshole Fletcher, who would probably like nothing better than to see a cop lose his job for doing dope. "I'll have a little talk with Carol."

"Is that essential?"

"I think so." Pain stabbed him in the left thigh, and he muffled a groan. The phone rang, giving him a headache as well.

Phoebe rushed to answer it and handed him the receiver. "Shae wishes to speak to you."

"*Lee . . . ,*" came Shae's voice before he barely got the receiver to his ear. "*I was wondering if you could do me a favor?*"

"Need I remind you that I'm not moving too well these days?"

"*All I'm asking is if you would mind accompanying Phoebe for a session or two? You can't use the excuse that you have to be on duty, and I honestly think your presence will help her sort out her thoughts.*"

Aware that Shae didn't believe Phoebe was from the seventeenth century, he had serious doubts. "Won't that be a conflict of interest, doctor?"

"*If you're worried that I'll pry into your personal life, I won't. Lee, I've come to think of you as a dear friend, and I hope we can always keep that. I only want to help Phoebe, and you may be the key to doing just that.*"

"I'll ask Phoebe what she thinks."

At the mention of her name, Phoebe looked at him with interest.

He muted the phone. "Shae wants me to come with you to your next session. She thinks it may help."

Concern crossed her features. "Are you feeling well enough?"

"I'll be okay."

She nodded her approval.

Lee unmuted the phone before returning the receiver to his ear. "I'll be with her."

"*Good. Thanks, Lee.*"

After a quick goodbye, he switched off the phone. Even he had to admit that he was worried about where Phoebe's story might lead. "I've been thinking. Once I'm on my feet again, we can start looking for that place in the country. I know I said you could have an herb garden, but promise me, no bangue."

"I vow that I shan't grow any bangue. Will you join me in the dreaming?"

"I don't know how . . ."

She moved a table beside the recliner. "I can place the candle atop the table, so that you shan't need to move. The experience should be curative."

With some hesitation, he agreed.

Phoebe went into the kitchen to get the matches, while he struggled to get comfortable. A sharp pain stabbed through his leg. What an ass he was. Why had he agreed?

When she returned, she lit the candle.

He tried to focus on the flame, but the pain distracted him. *Absorb the flame.* He shook his head. "I'm having difficulty concentrating."

She grasped his hand. "You shall get there, if you seek it."

Squeezing her hand, he tried again. Like the first time, and when he had been on his own, every little noise distracted him—the clock, people shouting outside, and cars on the street. *Concentrate.* He felt himself sinking, and suddenly he was surrounded by a familiar mist.

Henry stood across from him, and Lee narrowed his eyes.

"You have e'ery right to hate me. My ship brought conquerors, then goods to supply the colony, including guns to kill your ancestors. But *I* no longer think of Indians as savages. My presence is merely to show you what was."

Lee relaxed. "I don't hate you. That, too, is part of the past."

Henry bowed slightly. "Then view the past through me for better understanding."

To this, Lee agreed.

Henry swayed in a rocking motion. *Back and forth.* Wind ruffled his hair as he cast his eyes upon the land. *Virginia.* At long last, his voyage would soon end, and the sea air faded behind him. They set into port at James Towne, where his goods would fetch a high price. In a hurry to be en route to his own plantation, he shouted orders to the crew to unload the cargo as quickly as possible.

Within a day, he sailed a smaller pinnace up the James River. Betwixt the forests, plantations dotted the banks with fields of tobacco. Six years afore, he had brought Phoebe along the same route as his bride. Three of those years, he had been absent entirely. First, he had hovered betwixt life and death with the small pox. By the time he had recovered sufficiently to write a letter, he was ready to sail.

Round the bend, a palisade came into view. His heart skipped a beat. *Home.* He craned his neck to see if he could catch a glimpse of Phoebe. The gate was closed, and he worried there might have been trouble from the Indians.

He ordered the lads to drop the anchor and secure the mooring. As soon as the gang plank lowered, he disembarked to the dock. The guards opened the palisade gates. Surprised that no one greeted them, he stepped towards the house. When he heard a squeal, he quickened his pace.

"Henry!" With outstretched arms, Phoebe bounded towards him.

They embraced and kissed.

"Poppa said that he booked passage on a ship to England. I thought you had come to take me away. I was going to escape, but... Henry, you're not here to take me to England, are you?"

He hushed her. "I'm home. Everything will be all right now." With a huge grin, he stepped back. "I missed you." Then, he noticed her pallor. Normally, she was nearly as brown-skinned as an Indian, but she was as pale as those in England. She had also become very thin. "My God, Phoebe, what has happened to you?"

A moment passed before Lee regained his bearings. His apartment came into view, and the pain in his leg was once again part of him. "You cared for him."

"Aye, but not the way I do you. With Henry's return, Poppa couldn't carry out his threat."

Henry had been right. Lee saw things more clearly by viewing the world through the other man's eyes. Henry *had* loved Phoebe. But what if his own connection to Phoebe was to help her return to her time?

Thankful that Ed was willing to drive him to Colwell House, Lee told his partner to remain in the car before he hobbled up the brick walk on his crutches. The stairs proved even more challenging. Once, Ed got out of the car, but Lee waved at him to remain where he was. Finally reaching the door, Lee caught his breath and knocked.

The door opened, and Valerie blinked in surprise. "Lee, I didn't expect to see you around here again. How's Phoebe? How are *you*?"

"We're both fine. Valerie, I'd like to see Carol, and if you don't mind, I'd really like to sit down while waiting for her."

She stepped back, allowing him to enter. "Has Carol done something wrong?"

With a groan he seated himself in the chair beside the door, rather than struggling into the parlor. "I'd just like to speak with her."

"Lee—"

"Just get her, please."

While Valerie went up the stairs, he fidgeted to get comfortable. Carol crept down the stairs. "You wanted to see me?"

"Forgive me for not standing," he said, motioning to his crutches, "but I think you know why I wanted to speak to you."

She remained standing but avoided his gaze. "I presume it's about Phoebe."

"Why don't we cut to the chase? I'm not in narc, so I don't give a damn where you got the pot. I can easily hazard a guess, but if you *ever* involve Phoebe again in your little drug deals, you'll lose your sanctuary here at Colwell House."

"I—" She cleared her throat. "I don't know what you're talking about."

Suddenly pissed, Lee stood. *Mistake.* He collected himself before speaking again. "Carol," he said evenly, "I've seen a lot of women like you. You deserve better than how Fletcher treats you. Dump him. Get a warrant and an Emergency Protection Order before he involves you in something that causes you to wind up doing time or worse. Let Valerie help. She only wants the best for you, and I don't want to investigate your death because some addict has found your body on the streets."

Sheepishly, she looked up at him. "Kevin's not like that."

With her response, he silently cursed himself. "You called me. Carol, I'm sorry. I forgot."

Her gaze shifted to the floor. "That's all right. You had other things on your mind."

"Was it about Fletcher?"

She shook her head.

"Carol, let me help. If you're uncomfortable talking to me, I can give you the name of a female detective."

"That won't be necessary."

"Then why did you call?"

She chewed on her lip. "Phoebe was afraid something was going to happen to you."

That might have been the story she had given Valerie, but Lee didn't believe her. He had blown his chance of reaching her by jumping down her throat. "Call me if you change your mind and want to talk."

"If you don't mind, I have chores to take care of."

Lee made his way back to the car. When he reached the stairs, he looked over his shoulder. With a lost expression, Carol stared at him. Maybe Shae could help.

56

Phoebe

L IFE RETURNED TO THE WAY it was afore Henry's leaving. Unlike in the past, he did not sail to England in the autumn. Having ne'er spent a winter in Virginia, he had difficulty adapting to the cold. With nowhere else to go, Poppa stayed in the loft during the winter. We formed an uneasy truce betwixt us. I did not reveal his connection to my whipping, and he remained silent about my love for Little Falcon. Henry truly believed us when informed that I had been caught trying to escape to the Arrohatek.

By spring, Momma was once again allowed to visit. I weeded my garden, having adapted to planting in rows like the English, instead of in mounds like the Arrohatek. When I first spotted Momma, I thought she was a specter. Startled by her sudden appearance, I dropped my hoe. "Momma?" Overjoyed that she was real, I ran to her and embraced her.

"Phoebe, let me look at you." With a proud smile, she stepped back and coughed. "And Elenor?"

"Let me fetch her."

"First, I have a gift." She handed me the softest deerskin mantle, decorated with shell beads in the shapes of soaring hawks. "A welcome home for Henry."

Afore she could speak further or I could alert her to Poppa's presence, Poppa joined us. His eyes followed the length of Momma's body.

Though Momma had ne'er bared her breast in the tradition of most Arrohatek women, she wore a fringed deerskin skirt and a shell-bead necklace. Her long blonde hair, nearly gone gray, hung in a single braid down her back, and dogwood blossom tattoos encircled her upper arms.

Poppa staggered slightly. "Good God, Elenor."

"Robert," she replied evenly.

His eyes fixed upon hers. "How could you have brought shame to our family like this?"

She stared at Poppa. "We thought you were dead," she replied in slow, but clear English. "Our daughter was starving. What choice was I given?"

"But to the savages!"

"You see the Indians as savages. I see them as people. Even though they had little food to spare during the starving time, they shared what they had. I have more freedom than our daughter, and my husband loves me. You ne'er once spoke a kind word or shared a caressing touch—"

"Enough!" He struck her squarely on the cheek with the flat of his hand.

"Poppa..."

Afore I could step betwixt them, Momma raised her hand for me to keep silent. I bowed my head and allowed her to continue. "Silver Eagle has ne'er touched me, except in tenderness. I *know* which of you is the savage."

His nostrils flared, and he clenched his fists.

This time, I did step betwixt them. "You will not touch her as you have me."

"Phoebe?" came Momma's voice from behind my back.

I felt her light touch on my arm, but I did not turn. Poppa relaxed his hands. With his eyes seething, he about faced and stormed to the house. He would inform Henry of what had come to pass, but 'twould be to no avail.

"Phoebe..." Momma now stood afore me. "What has he done to you?"

" 'Tis not important."

Momma searched my face. Realizing that I would remain firm, she spoke of the reason for her visit. "The small pox has come to the town. Many are ill. The *kwiocosuk* are at a loss what to do, and I know not what local herbs may help."

I trembled with the thought. Henry had nearly died. "I have some saffron. Henry brought it from England. 'Tis not much but should be enough to aid a few."

Nearly in tears, Momma clasped my hands. "Bless you, daughter."

Little did I know, I would give away the very medicine my own family would need.

57

Lee

AFTER TWENTY MINUTES OF LEAFING through out-of-date magazines, Lee tossed the previous year's August issue of *Time* aside. If he hadn't already known that most of Shae's clientèle was female, he would have easily guessed. After sifting through a *Southern Living, Vogue,* and *Cooking Light,* he finally uncovered another *Time.*

Meg stared at him.

"What?" he asked.

She couldn't hide her smirk. "Nothing."

He'd be glad when he could drive again. Depending on others was already growing tiresome.

"I doubt Shae gets many law enforcement officers through here, so she doesn't subscribe to *Gun Digest,* or whatever it is they tend to read."

"Very funny," he mumbled.

"Lee . . ." She didn't continue until he glanced over at her. "I'm glad that you're going to make a full recovery."

"Thanks. You'll make an excellent nurse."

"I'm glad you think so." She beamed with pride in her accomplishment. "I graduate this summer."

The door to Shae's office opened, and Shae beckoned him inside. "Lee, we're ready for you."

As he gathered his crutches together, he hoped his attending a session was a good idea. He hobbled into the office. Phoebe sat near Shae's desk. He attempted to make himself comfortable in the chair next to her, while Shae sat across from them.

"Phoebe would like to share what she's remembered today."

He listened to her as she recounted her tale. Smallpox before people knew that contact with others transmitted it. And no vaccines. It had decimated most of the native people. He had a fair idea where her story would eventually lead.

When Phoebe finished, Shae stared at him. "Your reaction?"

"I'm wondering how my presence now makes any difference than if I had heard it later, like I usually do."

Shae had a pinched smile. "At least you're honest."

"Would you have expected anything else?"

Shae sent him a scorching look. "Please try and cooperate."

"What do you want me to say? I nearly busted my balls getting here—"

"You agreed to come here in an effort to help Phoebe," Shae interrupted. "Lee, let's start over. Maybe I shouldn't have rushed ahead with this appointment. Don't pretend to hide the fact that you're in pain. Have you taken anything for it?"

"Tylenol," he replied. "Everything else messed with my head too much." He exchanged a glance with Phoebe. He hated to admit the pot had helped with fewer side effects than anything the doctors had prescribed.

"I should have asked before arranging this meeting if you felt up to it. My apologies. Would you prefer to reschedule?"

At least she sounded like a doctor again, rather than the ex-wife. "I'm good."

"Then how do you feel about what Phoebe's told you today?"

Besides wanting to lock up her father or to beat him to a bloody pulp? He kept the thought to himself. Shae didn't believe Phoebe's time travel story. He chose his words carefully. "I think I can see where her story is heading, but I fail to understand how my presence here can make a difference."

"You remind Phoebe of someone she once knew."

And loved—Lightning Storm. He met Phoebe's gaze once more.

"Somehow you're the key to unlocking her memory."

Returning his attention to Shae, he asked, "How?"

"If I knew, I wouldn't have to ask what seem like silly questions. I'm doing much the same as you in your work, searching for clues."

To this response, he nodded. "I'm not certain we'll know any-thing for sure until her story plays out."

"That could be, but you're Phoebe's connection to the present." She glanced in Phoebe's direction.

"Aye, 'tis so."

"Lee, I know you've shared continuations of the story with Phoebe. When you do, I don't need to use hypnosis to get her to reveal the next installment, for lack of a better term. Your participa-tion moves the story forward. What is your role in all of this?"

"I'm not sure I know what you mean."

"Are you an observer or are you actively involved?"

"Usually actively involved."

"In what way?"

Uncertain where she was leading, he answered, "As one of the people in the story."

"Who?"

"I've been Lightning Storm, Little Falcon, and most recently, Henry." All were Phoebe's lovers. Unconsciously, he had known as much, but having it pointed out was another matter. *What is the connection?* It was almost as if he had known Phoebe.

"Keep going," Shae said, prodding.

"You said you wouldn't pry."

He half expected Shae to protest, but she merely let out a disap-pointed breath. "I'm sorry for bringing you in here. I really thought we'd make progress using this approach."

"That's it?"

"You're obviously uncomfortable. I don't think it's wise to pro-ceed. Thanks for trying, though." Shae turned her attention to Phoebe. "I'll see you next week. We'll continue as we have in the past."

Phoebe collected his crutches and waited while he got to his feet.

"Lee, have you visited your mom recently?" Shae asked.

"I haven't been much of anywhere, except physical therapy. Why?"

"She's not well. I hope you'll make the time."

Phoebe spoke up. "I shall see that he visits."

After Shae muttered a "thanks," he lingered.

Shae looked up. "Was there something else?"

He motioned for Phoebe to continue ahead of him. After she left the room, he said, "I was hoping you might be able to talk to Carol."

"Carol?" she asked, arching a brow.

"Before the shooting, she called me. I didn't have time to talk, and Valerie had reassured me that everything was okay. Then, I was laid up. I didn't remember her call until the other day. To make a long story short, she's doing drugs, and I suspect Kevin Fletcher is behind it."

"I would ask how you know all this, but I don't doubt what you say. You do realize, though, unless a person *wants* help, there's nothing I can do."

"She wouldn't have called if she didn't want help. Now she's afraid to talk to me. She might find you a little less threatening."

"You know I'll do it, but you will have to fill me in on the details."

"Should I call you later?"

"I've got a few minutes before my next patient."

He was afraid she might say that. Lee got off his feet, setting his crutches beside him. A smile crept across her face as he told her about Phoebe mixing marijuana with butter. Her grin faded as he continued. Maybe the time off had done him a world of good. People rarely listened when he sent them warnings like he had with Carol, but Carol *might* listen to Shae.

58

Phoebe

A FORTNIGHT LATER, Poppa alternated betwixt shivering and sweating. I ministered yarrow tea for his fever. Three days later, a deep red flush crept across his face. 'Twas either measles or the small pox that ailed him. Aft Momma's warning, my heart thumped wildly.

Jennet kept Elenor and Bess's lad away from the sickroom in the loft, whilst Bess helped me tend Poppa. If the malady was indeed the pox, Poppa couldn't have been in finer hands. In Africa, Bess had treated many so afflicted. 'Twas naught we could do but wait.

The following morn, red spots formed, mostly upon Poppa's forehead. As the day passed, the rash spread from the top of his head to his toes. The flecks enlarged to pustules. 'Twas as I feared—the pox.

Two morns later, I climbed the ladder to the loft and found Bess bent over Poppa's form. Poised with a sharp knife, she made a small slice into one of Poppa's pustules.

"Bess, no!"

"I must. I ain't goin' to let my son die." Poppa groaned as she ran a piece of thread through the open wound.

Intrigued, I moved closer as she bandaged Poppa's hand. "What do you mean?"

"I do the same to my son. He gets a mild form of the pox."

Skeptical, I asked, "You've done this afore?"

"Aye. 'Tis the way in Africa, as 'twas done to me."

If she would risk her own child with such an undertaking, then the African medicine must be strong. As one healer to another, I trusted Bess. "I have not had the small pox. Start with me. Be certain to include Elenor for I cannot lose another child."

Bess bade me to hold out my arm. "Roll up your sleeve."

I did as she instructed. She raised the knife, and her black eyes met mine. Gritting my teeth, I nodded that I was ready.

She made a quick, modest slit that I barely felt in her expert hands. My blood seeped, and she buried the infected thread in the channel. She placed lint and a piece of a rag over the scratch, afore she bandaged my arm.

"Now what?" I asked.

"We wait for you to get the pox." Bess returned to Poppa and started the process over again.

Aware of what I had done, I suddenly had misgivings. Would I become like Poppa? But as I watched Bess carry out the same procedure on her son, I knew that my family had a chance for survival. When Bess returned a third time, I took the knife from her hand. "I shall attend to Elenor." I grasped my daughter's arm and pushed up her sleeve. Hadn't the *kwiocos* said she would survive her childhood? I must believe. "I want you to be brave, Elenor. Momma's going to make a small cut in your arm. 'Twill keep you from getting the pox like your grandfather."

'Twas more difficult for me to minister aid than usual. My hand shook. What sort of momma cut her own daughter? Had I not seen Bess infect her own? I bit my lip and proceeded. Elenor winced afore letting out a cry when I sliced into her skin. Like I had seen Bess do, I placed a small thread in the cut. I patched her, dried her tears, and hugged her, all the time praying that I had chosen the right path.

"Phoebe?" came Henry's voice.

I turned.

"What have you done?"

"Bess says 'tis the way in Africa. We won't die from the small pox."

Knowing there was naught he could do, he furrowed his brow. He had already suffered the malady and could only wait to see which of us lived or died. "When I was in England, I saw families lose all of their children . . ." He cleared his throat and fell silent.

At moments like these, I felt tenderness towards Henry. I touched his cheek. "You survived, and so shall we." From the loft, I heard Poppa groan. Immediately, I went to his side. Upon entering the sickroom, I smelt the sickly sweet odor of death.

"Phoebe, I ne'er blamed you. Can you e'er forgive me?"

"Poppa, I will tend you, but you ask too much."

The pustules on his face had shrunk and turned to rosy spots. "Your Indian lover—"

"Little Falcon?"

"We didn't kill him."

Was he simply trying to gain my sympathy out of fear that he was dying? "Then what happened?"

He swallowed with some difficulty. "The lads had already collected two scalps on our journey and wanted to add another. I told them to let your Indian go. He would have died bravely, but I told him your husband lived. We let him go with that knowledge, and he has ne'er returned."

"You knew that Henry— Poppa, why did you deceive me so?"

"For your obedience. 'Twas the only way to keep you from running away with the one you call Little Falcon. One of Henry's mates told us that he was indeed alive in England."

I didn't know whether to be elated or furious at Poppa. Little Falcon had survived.

"Phoebe, can you e'er forgive me?"

'Twas not the time to bear malice. "Can you accept Elenor as your granddaughter?"

He sent me a broad smile that I had ne'er seen the likes of afore. "A brush with death reveals to a man the error of his ways. I'm honored to have Elenor as my granddaughter."

"Then you admit that Lightning Storm is her father?"

"Aye," he said, lowering his voice.

I sat on the pallet aside him and clasped his hand. "I forgive you, Poppa. I hope someday you can find it within your heart to forgive Momma too."

He withdrew his hand from my grip. "Ne'er."

As I had suspected, 'twas Momma he blamed. We had made progress, and for that, I said a silent prayer to Ahone's goodness. As the day wore on, all of Poppa's pustules changed. According to

Bess, 'twas a good sign, but later in the eve, the spots darkened to purple with angry red rings.

Our hopes were dashed, and Poppa's breathing grew labored.

"The pustules are inside his throat," Bess explained.

Throughout the night, I sat with him. Near dawn, I helped Poppa to the pisspot. Instead of yellow, his stream was scarlet red. Since I had given Momma my saffron, I could only treat Poppa's symptoms. Henry had brought mallow from England. I made Poppa some tea to help ease his breathing and lessen his bleeding. I held the flagon to his lips. When he sipped, he choked and coughed up blood.

Early in the morn, Bess examined his spots and confirmed my fear. "They're blood-filled. 'Tis the bloody pox."

Hour by hour, the pustules enlarged 'til his face was naught more than a red, raw sore. Red streams streaked his cheeks as if he cried in blood. I held a linen cloth to his nose, but blood seeped faster than I could wring the cloth. He started retching—more blood. In my effort to help him, I brushed against his bare arm. His blistered skin peeled, and he let out a tortured shriek, reminding me of Master Collins being burned at the stake.

Except for those who had already survived the pox, 'twas the fate that could await us all, if Bess's ministerings failed. I took heart and focused on Poppa. In spite of his torment, his mind remained clear. 'Twas a curse, more than a blessing.

Again, I helped him drink, talking soothingly as I did so. In spite of his swollen tongue, he managed a few drops. He weakly patted my hand. "For . . . give," he rasped.

Ne'er afore had I wanted to embrace him, and now, I could not. To do so, would only bring him agony. "Poppa, I've already told you that I forgive you. I meant it."

His head moved slightly, but he didn't have the strength to shake it. "El . . . nore."

"Momma?"

"Tell . . . her."

"I will, Poppa." The sickly, sweet odor of death strengthened. "Poppa . . ."

He coughed, spraying blood on me. Incapable of swallowing, he choked. Unable to catch his breath, he gasped and sputtered. I closed my eyes against the sound as he drowned in his own blood. Finally, his muscles relaxed. The man I had wanted to hate for so long was dead.

59

Shae and Lee

CONVINCED THAT PHOEBE'S difficulties stemmed from the abuse
she had likely suffered at the hands of her father, Shae mulled
over the turn of events on her drive to Colwell House. There were
a number of instances where people had created fantasy worlds after suffering abuse as children. The scars on Phoebe's back proved
someone had whipped her. But Phoebe's case didn't quite fit any
textbook model. Even Russ was perplexed as to why she never
slipped from the seventeenth-century persona while under hypnosis.

Turning her thoughts to Carol, Shae parked the car along the
curb in front of Colwell House. She went up the walk and knocked.
Carol answered. "Valerie's not here."

Carol nearly slammed the door in Shae's face. "It's you I've come
to see."

The door cracked open a little wider. "There's nothing to talk
about."

"Lee told me about what happened."

"He had no right."

"Would you rather he had spoken to his police buddies instead?"

Carol widened the door enough for Shae to enter. "It's not what
you think."

"Carol, I'm not here to lecture you, and while you're not my
patient, I will respect your privacy as if you were. Lee said you called
him before the shooting. He's sorry that he forgot about it until

talking to you the other day. Trust me, he wouldn't have asked me to speak with you if he truly didn't want to help."

Swallowing nervously, Carol motioned for Shae to follow her. Out back, herbs flowered in yellow and pink blossoms, alongside bright red poppies. "This is Phoebe's herb garden. I continued tending it after she left."

"Are you saying she grew the marijuana here?"

"She only grew seeds of what she could easily find."

"I don't understand."

"She told me how to make medicine from poppies."

Think historically, Shae reminded herself. *Poppies were for making laudanum, and the basic ingredient of laudanum was*— "Opium. Carol, you don't need to fall into this trap."

"He says he loves me."

That was the connection Shae had been waiting for. "If Kevin truly loved you, would he ask you to do things you're uncomfortable doing? Things that are illegal and could send you to jail?"

Tears entered the other woman's eyes. "He tells me I'm pretty and smart."

"You are both of those things, but what does Kevin do when you disagree with him?"

No answer.

"Carol, why did you call Lee?"

Carol brushed away her tears. "He said he could help."

"He can. You simply had the misfortune of bad timing. Will you let us help now?"

Carol inched away, but then she gave a weak nod.

"Why did you give Phoebe the pot?"

"So Lee would take notice. I didn't think he'd arrest me, because he got it from Phoebe, but I didn't really care. I also thought he could probably use it after what he'd been through."

"A risky way asking for help, but I'm glad you did." Admission of a problem was the first step in solving it. Shae had high hopes for Carol's recovery.

* * *

When Lee visited the nursing home, he found his mom sitting beside the window with the dreaded photo album in her lap. This time, the album was opened to a photo of his dad. "Mom?"

She failed to look in his direction.

Not a good day. "I brought a friend," he said, trying again.

Phoebe moved beside his mother, and he made the introductions—for all the good it did.

His mother's face brightened with a smile. "Shae, I knew you'd come."

Ready to apologize to Phoebe, he needn't have worried. Phoebe bent to his mother's level. "Mrs. Crowley, I'm Phoebe. Shae won't be visiting today."

Bewilderment crossed her face. "Phoebe?"

"I'm a friend of Lee's."

"Lee." Suddenly panicked, she searched the room. "There was a shooting—"

"He's fine. He's right here."

Instead of balancing on crutches, Lee sat in the chair near his mother. "I'm not moving as fast as I used to, but I'm here."

Her knobby fingers reached for him and touched him on the wrist. "After what I told you, I didn't know whether I'd ever see you again."

He finally understood Shae's words. "Hell, Mom, did you really think I'd desert you because you rushed the adoption through? You didn't tell me earlier because you were afraid. I see it all the time, and I suppose it's good to know. But I wonder . . ." He broke off before voicing his thoughts aloud.

"I'm sorry," she said, barely above a whisper.

Even though he'd been off work for a few weeks, he hadn't given much further thought to his birth mother. Had there been a reason why she couldn't locate him? Or had she left him alone for some protective reason? If that was the case, she likely hadn't been thinking straight. More children than he cared to recall were left in cars *for a few minutes* during the summer and didn't make it. "There's nothing to be sorry about. You did what you thought was best. Not many couples would have adopted an Indian child during that era. Who knows where I would have ended up otherwise."

She patted his hand and turned her attention to Phoebe. "You've known Lee for a long time, haven't you?"

"Though it seems like I've know him fore'er, we met in February."

Amazed as they conversed, Lee leaned back in the chair and made himself comfortable. Phoebe and his mother chatted on and on—the weather, shopping, tales of when he was growing up. He hadn't seen his mother act so alive or coherent in years. He should have known she'd take a liking to Phoebe. She had never been the sort of mother who thought any woman he introduced to her wasn't good enough. He nearly laughed to himself. The only other woman he had brought home to meet his parents had been Shae.

When their visit ended, Phoebe waited until they were outside his mother's room to speak. "Lee, your mother hasn't long to live."

"The doctors have been saying that for two years now."

She gestured to her nose. "I could smell it."

Like in the dreaming. At a loss for words, he leaned on his crutches.

"The Arrohateck always cared for their elders," she said. "To shelter the wise ones away is disrespectful."

"Don't you think I hate seeing her waste away in here? What would you have me do? I'm not exactly in a position to take her out, and I can't afford a better facility."

"Let me care for her as I have for you. I can let her retain her dignity in her final days."

He searched her face. No words were necessary. She was deadly serious. Both of them had witnessed death many times. While he viewed it as part of a puzzle, she saw it as progression in the circle of life.

60

Phoebe

FOR THREE WEEKS, I suffered headaches and fevers. Pustules erupted over my skin. Bess tended to Elenor and her son. The children were barely affected. Bess's African treatment had saved them. In my delirium, I walked through endless mists. Stumbling along, I was lost in the forest and could not find my way. Waving my hands afore me, I struggled through the brambles as they tore through my flesh.

"Phoebe..."

'Twas Henry's voice. I searched and searched but could not find him. "Henry, where are you?"

"Right here. Phoebe, please don't die."

His voice seemed to come from everywhere and nowhere at the same time. Why could I not see him? I staggered further 'til my feet grew weary and sore. How far had I come? The fog remained around me. When I feared I could go no farther, the spirit dog appeared afore me. He would guide the way.

I latched onto his collar and continued walking. The hound stepped surely and soundly through the forest. Ne'er afore had I traveled so far without the fog clearing. Again, I stumbled. The dog waited 'til I could get to my feet.

Finally, the mist lessened slightly. Up ahead, I could make out a shadow of a man. As we got closer, I saw that he wore a breechclout. The right side of his head was shaved. On the left, his black hair stretched the length of his back and was adorned with osprey feathers.

"Lightning Storm." I let go of the hound's collar and ran towards him with my arms outstretched. But he wasn't Lightning Storm. I stopped short. "Lee?" I *had* seen him afore meeting him in the hospital.

He reached out and called my name.

My arms went around his neck. Unable to contain myself, I murmured my love in his ear.

"Phoebe, oh Phoebe. Thank God."

I woke with a start. Henry bent over me, stroking my hair.

"Henry?"

He touched my forehead. "The fever's broken. I thought I was going to lose you."

The tenderness that I felt for him had ne'er been stronger. If only I had not been forced into marriage, I might have been able to love him.

"Phoebe, when I count to five, you'll wake up."

To Shae's count, I drifted through the layers. I blinked. I *had* loved him, but not with the passion I had Lightning Storm or Lee. It had taken Shae's probing through my memories to discover that fact. Only then did I truly realize that in this time Henry was dead. What were my last words to him? I hoped I had not said anything that would have caused him distress.

"Phoebe?"

"Except for Poppa, we all survived the small pox." Due to Bess's treatment, I had few pock marks. I extended my arm, revealing a deep white scar on my forearm. "I got it from the pox."

"There hasn't been a case in the entire world since the seventies. Phoebe, I don't mean to disbelieve you, but you're too young to have suffered from smallpox."

No matter the evidence I presented, Shae did not believe me. 'Twas unimportant. I rested comfortably with the knowledge that, like Lee, she would eventually come to accept who I was. I thanked her for the session and retreated to the waiting room.

Meg looked up from a magazine. Her skin was a light nut brown compared to Bess's deep ebony, but how she reminded me of my faithful servant. 'Twas the reason I had instantly liked her. "Vow to me that once you are a nurse, we shall remain friends."

"I promise. You might want to think about taking up nursing yourself. You'd be a natural."

I hugged her, all the while thinking that I had ne'er dreamt it possible to have an occupation.

61

Lee

AFTER TWO MONTHS, LEE HAD GRADUATED to the use of a cane and was driving again. At least another couple of months would pass before he could return to work. Even then, he would likely be assigned to desk duty at first. He thought he'd be growing restless, but the time he spent with Phoebe had changed his entire way of thinking. Time moved slower, and he found himself cherishing every minute. Had his brush with death influenced the feeling or was it solely due to Phoebe's presence?

As they walked along the edge of the James River, the summer sun reflected a soft sheen in her red hair, while a gentle breeze ruffled it slightly. Waves lapped against the bank. He had difficulty keeping up with her. When she noticed, she slowed her pace. "Everything is familiar, yet 'tis different."

"That's not too surprising given how many years have passed."

"I want to know where the Paspahegh and Arrohateck lived, where they died, and if anything remains of Henry's plantation."

A red-winged blackbird called from nearby reeds. For some reason, thinking of the tribes that had died gave Lee pause. They were a part of him as much as Phoebe. "I've looked at the maps. It's anyone's guess as to where Henry's plantation could have been. There's a historical marker for the annihilation of the Paspahegh, if you'd like me to take you there. The Arrohateck were east of Richmond."

"I'd like that."

"Phoebe, there's something I've been meaning to tell you. Before the shooting, I entered the dreaming on my own."

A small smile crossed her face. "Did you find any answers to your questions?"

"Not really. The images weren't very clear."

"In time you shall discover the meaning."

Lee liked the sound of that, and for once, he believed it. As they headed back to the T-Bird, his cell phone rang. The caller ID belonged to Colwell House. "Hello," he said, answering.

"Lee . . ." Valerie whispered. *"Carol wanted me to call you. Kevin Fletcher is here. He's upstairs, threatening her."*

"Valerie, don't take any chances. Call the police, then get everyone you can out of the house. Don't put yourself at risk. I'm on my way."

Phoebe sent him a worried look.

"Fletcher's at Colwell House." Returning to the car, he put in a quick call to a detective he had worked with on a number of cases in Colwell House's district. After Lee explained the situation, the fellow officer assured him that he would check the scene.

They reached the car. Like so many times when Lee had been on patrol duty during an emergency situation, time crawled. Would help arrive soon enough? He gunned the engine. The faster he went, the slower time seemed. Lights and buildings passed in a blur. They were still a few miles away. He avoided turning up the police radio to protect Phoebe from any potentially unsettling news.

They neared Colwell House, and a horrible feeling wrenched in his gut. Around the corner, police cars were out front with lights flashing. Ready to jump into the fray, Lee leaped out of the car. Pain shot through his leg. He gritted his teeth to keep from crying out. *Slow down.* Many capable officers were already present.

He collected himself and grabbed his cane. "Stay here," he said to Phoebe.

Near an ambulance, he spotted Valerie with an EMT checking her over. Beside her, Meg clutched her sobbing daughter. Lee showed his badge to the attending officer. "Is everyone all right?"

Valerie's eyes teared. "I got everyone out of the house like you said, except . . . There were gunshots."

Carol. Lee glanced in the direction of the house as officers combed the property.

"Lee, a detective has talked to us, but he wouldn't say what's happened to Carol."

Without looking back, he started for the house. "I'll see what I can find out." Why hadn't he taken the time to escort Carol personally to get a warrant and an Emergency Protection Order against Fletcher? He had detected all the telltale signs, but he had been too cocksure that she wouldn't listen.

Lee flashed his badge to the officer keeping watch by the door.

"Detective Pierson has been expecting you," the officer stated.

Anticipating the worst, Lee went inside. Another officer motioned the way upstairs. Although negotiating stairs was difficult, he fought the urge to forge ahead. Acting foolish wouldn't help Carol. *Not now.* Finally, he reached the landing.

The door to Carol's room was open. Blood spattered the wall and a body lay on the bed. His colleague bent over Fletcher. Pierson indicated with his hand to look at the opposite end of the room. Beside Carol, an EMT checked her vital signs. Her face was streaked with tears and makeup, but she was very much alive. "Carol . . ."

Her head tilted up, but her expression remained blank. She blinked as if coming out of trance. "Lee?"

"Detective," the EMT interrupted. "She refuses to go to the hospital."

Lee nodded that he understood and moved in their direction. Unable to bend down to Carol's level, he feared she might perceive him as a looming figure intent upon harming her again. "Carol," he said in a low, sympathetic voice, "it's best if you go to the hospital and let them check you over. Your friends are waiting outside. I'm sure one of them would be happy to accompany you."

No longer refusing the EMT's aid, Carol accompanied him out of the room.

Pierson instructed a forensic team before speaking to him. "The medical examiner has ruled Fletcher's death as a probable suicide. He roughed the girl up and apparently tried to kill her too. I need a statement from you."

"Of course." Lee went on to tell Pierson the approximate time that Valerie had called him, alerting him to the situation. His colleague asked him a few questions on how he had come to know the women at Colwell House. Once finished with the routine, Lee retraced his steps.

Outside, Phoebe had joined Meg and her daughter. Valerie was absent, and he presumed she had joined Carol in the ambulance. They were a strong group of women. If anyone could help Carol through the crisis, Valerie could.

62

Phoebe

UPON MY RECOVERY from the small pox, Henry and I sailed up-river in a shallop to the fall line. To contact any Indians was forbidden by English law. But Henry, as dedicated as he was, risked his life and livelihood for me to discover how badly affected the Arrohateck had been from the malady. Near the bank, two men jumped from the boat, and with a hefty heave, they brought it to rest on solid ground.

Henry gave them orders to wait for two days, and we set out for the Arrohateck town. Nearly seven years had passed since my last travels along familiar paths through the forest. Then I had worn leggings and fine doeskin. Though I had long ago grown accustomed to skirts and leather shoes, I wished for my moccasins to make the journey more swiftly and continued to worry about what we might find.

By midday, as we got closer to the town, Henry readied his musket. I spotted fear in his eyes. "They will not harm us," I assured him.

He lowered the musket. " 'Tis been a long time since I've traveled in Indian country."

" 'Twas once all Indian country, but I speak Algonquian. You need not fear."

As we went further, I grew more and more uneasy. We approached the town, and no warriors greeted us. No children played. No women sang whilst sewing, making pots, or tanning hides. No men made arrows or readied fishing nets. No cooking pots. No fires. Mats on the longhouses were falling off. Other dwellings were in equal disrepair.

I peered into the first house. A man covered in pustules mumbled in delirium. In the next house, a mother hummed, whilst cradling her dead child. The pox were just beginning to erupt on her forehead. "Where are the *kwiokosuk*?" I asked.

Without looking up, she continued to hum. More houses revealed much the same. No one paid us any notice. I barely recognized the faces—gaunt, weary, and beaten. In a mindless manner, those who were healthy tended the sick. Amongst them, I expected to find Momma, doing what she could. I searched further, 'til coming to Momma and Silver Eagle's house. 'Twas empty.

In the next house, a woman cried over another dead child. A man held her in his arms. Though years had passed since I had last seen him, I recognized my brother's broad shoulders. He had gone through the *huskanaw* and had taken the name Charging Bear. He was a warrior with a family now. "*Mat*," I said. Brother.

Tears were in his eyes when he cast his gaze in my direction. "Walks Through Mist?"

"Charging Bear." I couldn't help but cry my relief and said a silent prayer of thanks to Ahone. "Does everyone have the small pox? I can help."

He blinked in confusion. "Walks Through Mist, you mustn't be here. 'Tis too dangerous."

"I've already suffered from the pox, as has Henry. Where is Momma?"

As he moved towards me, his face became an unreadable mask. "She died nearly a moon ago."

"And *Nows*?"

"The previous moon afore. Aft his death, I don't think *Nek* wished to continue living."

Dead. How could that be? The vision I had when reaching my first moon time had finally come to pass. The town burned from pestilence brought by the English. Momma and Silver Eagle were dead. I would have ne'er guessed the meaning.

Henry's hand came to rest on my arm, and I fought to remain strong. Grieving would come later, for Bess had taught me how to help the survivors.

"Phoebe."

At the sound of Shae's voice, I blinked. I wondered how we could meet in her office week after week, yet she continued to believe my story as naught more than a fantasy.

"Lee told me about what happened to Carol," she said.

"She received some bruises but will recover."

"Physically, maybe, but emotionally might take a little longer. How are you holding up with the added stress of this and Lee's mom moving in?"

"I do what I must. I'm a healer. 'Tis my chosen life to bring comfort to those that I can."

Shae smiled. "I wish more medical personnel felt the way you do."

On that note, we concluded the session, and I reflected on my latest discovery. At least now I knew how Momma had died.

63

Lee

Lee woke to the sound of a loud thump and a crash, coming from the den. Phoebe was out of bed and had on her robe before he could get his feet underneath him. He tugged on his sweat pants and reached for his cane, moving as fast as he was capable. By the time he reached Phoebe, she was in the den examining his mom, who lay sprawled on the floor, groaning.

A red welt formed on his mother's cheekbone.

Phoebe muttered in Algonquian. Her tempo sounded like a prayer, and it was almost like he could make out the words. When she spoke to him, she switched to English. "Fortunately, she missed hitting her eye. Let us aid her to bed, and I'll tend to her cheek."

Though he had difficulty bending down, he managed to get a hand under his mother's arm. She barely weighed a hundred pounds. With Phoebe on her other side, they helped her back to the bed they had set up in the den.

Once his mother was safely tucked in, Phoebe straightened her nightgown and propped a pillow behind her head. "Lee, could you fetch the Solomon's seal?"

"Sure." Phoebe was trying to save his mother some dignity. He had already noticed the scent of urine, but he took his time. Not that he moved very fast anyway. He first stopped off at the bedroom to put on a T-shirt. Afterward, he went into the kitchen, where Phoebe kept her herbs in the cabinet. As he checked through the bottles, he imagined her collecting roots and plants in the forest.

By the time he returned to the den, Phoebe had his mother clean and was ready for the herb. Lee sat in the chair beside the bed with his mother while Phoebe went into the other room to prepare a poultice. Her withered hand came to rest on his arm. "Thank you," she whispered.

He nodded.

"Lee, I've heard the language she spoke before."

"Phoebe's?" he asked. "That's not possible."

"But I did."

He hushed her. "You just rest. You've had enough excitement for one night. The next time you need to go to the bathroom in the middle of the night, call one of us. You could have broken some bones. Trust me, it's not a lot of fun."

With a little laugh, she patted him on the arm. "A mother can't ask her son to help her to the toilet."

"Ah hell, Mom, I've seen a lot worse than someone taking a—" Lee caught himself. "If you're uncomfortable with my help, then call Phoebe."

"When are you going to marry that girl?"

He should have known that would be the next topic. Her lack of protest about their unwed status spoke loudly about the nursing home conditions when they had brought her out. "If and when the time is right," he finally said.

"That's not an answer and you know it."

"It's the best I can do for now. I'd rather not repeat what I went through with Shae."

She patted his arm again. "You won't."

"I'm glad to hear it."

"I've already given up hope of living to see grandchildren."

"Give it a rest," Lee said, struggling to keep his voice even. How he managed to calmly deal with murders and rapists, yet allow an eighty-two-year-old woman get under his skin, he would never know. "I'll make certain you're the first to know when we've set a wedding date."

Without hearing Phoebe return, he looked up at her, standing beside him. As she applied the poultice to his mother's bruised cheek, she smirked.

"If it would make you happy," Lee said, "I can propose to her now."

"Lee Crowley," his mother responded in a firm tone. "I may be old and forgetful, but there's no need to be condescending."

When he mumbled an apology, Phoebe laughed but quickly caught herself. "I can see to Nat if you would like to return to bed."

"I can sit with her for a while. You get some rest."

"You're certain?"

"Yes. Now get some sleep."

"Be sure the poultice stays on her cheek. 'Twill absorb the bruising."

He promised that he would follow her instructions. Before Phoebe left the room, she sent him a radiant smile. Wishing he could return to the bedroom with her, he thought of her unclad body pressed next to him.

His mother's voice intruded on his reverie. "I may be half blind, but I can see how much you care for her."

Hoping to keep her quiet on the subject once and for all, he said, "If you must know, my thoughts were more animalistic than altruistic."

"Lee!"

Once again, he apologized. "If you're not going to get back to sleep anytime soon, can we change the subject?"

"Then please just tell me about Phoebe."

He detected annoyance. Rightly so. In her own roundabout way, she had merely been asking about the woman who had cared enough to see her with dignity through her final days. Without going into too much detail, he told her that Phoebe came from Dorset and had been married twice before. Conveniently leaving out anything about the seventeenth century, he made her sound like a New Age healer and mentioned how her knowledge of herbs had mended his leg much faster than it would have healed otherwise.

In turn, she told him tales of the "good ole days" of when he was small. He had always felt like an outcast at the family reunions that she recalled so fondly.

"My cousins used to give war whoops and scream that I'd scalp them," Lee admitted absentmindedly.

She raised her head slightly from the pillow, and the poultice slipped from her cheek. "Why didn't you tell us?"

Motioning for her to lie back, he adjusted the poultice. "You and Dad were color-blind. You know how kids' minds work. I guess I was afraid that if I pointed it out, the two of you would think you were harboring a savage. Back then, even the historical markers called the Indians savages, so I half expected a Mr. Hyde to leap out at any given moment."

"We only wanted the best for you."

He regretted bringing the topic up. If his mother was truly dying, the last thing he wanted was to give her any sense of guilt. "I know, but I still have no idea who I am."

"Your cousins, Bruce and Charlene were along with the hikers on the day they found you."

His cousins had been with the hikers? "Why didn't you tell me?"

"I thought I had. Oh dear, I've gotten so forgetful. It was a small group of school kids. Charlene was the reason we initially found out about you, and since we were a qualified foster home, we managed to keep you out of the institutions. After all you had been through, you didn't need that too."

While Bruce was likely to have been too young at the time to recall much of anything, Charlene must have been around ten or so. But a thirty-three-year-old trail? Hell, many of his cases didn't get solved if they went past a few days. Would he bring grief to his mother by following the lead? "I don't want to hurt you. If I contact them about it . . ."

She smiled. "I want you to uncover what you need to know so you can marry Phoebe."

He didn't chide her this time. While the trail was certainly a cold one, he might uncover some sort of clue that could help him discover what tribe he belonged to, or if his biological parents had truly abandoned him.

64

Phoebe

WHEN LEE WASN'T TENDING to his own recuperation, he helped me care for his infirm mother, and in doing so, I spotted something wondrous. As I had hoped, their bond renewed in Nat's final days. She glowed with pride at Lee's accomplishments, not just as a mother but as a friend too, and he came to fully comprehend how she had tried to teach him about his heritage but had no counsel herself.

On the morn of her death, I felt something amiss. Dawn had yet to arise, but Lee was already gone from our bed. I found him in Nat's room, combing her thin, gray hair. On her face was a blissful smile. The odor lingering in the room had changed from sweet to the stagnant scent of death.

When I entered, I thought of Silver Eagle and Momma. How I wish I could have been with them in their last moments of life, but 'twas not meant to be. Momma had ne'er returned to Dorset to see her kinsmen, and she had been buried in her adopted home, where her bones had long ago turned to dust. She had followed the path to the afterlife with Silver Eagle.

I went over to Lee and held him. He buried his face in the depths of my robe. "Thank you," he whispered.

"She has rejoined your father."

He nodded and looked up. His eyes glistened. Like so many warriors, he refused to shed a tear. "You gave her what you had hoped—death with dignity."

"Not just I. You, too, gave her much in these final days. She got to know you and you, her—in ways that wouldn't have been possible if you hadn't taken the time."

He seemed to take comfort in my words, and I knew in time that he would be fine.

65

Lee

Dᴜʀɪɴɢ ᴛʜᴇ ꜰᴜɴᴇʀᴀʟ, Lee had spoken with his cousin, Charlene. Her sandy-colored hair and blue eyes reminded him how different he was from the rest of the family. She provided him with little new information. A couple weeks after his mother's death, he drove Phoebe to the place where he had been found as a toddler. Instead of woods with hiking trails there was a strip mall.

After he had turned twelve, his parents had brought him to this place. That was before the trees had been cut, and they had walked through the forest talking about inconsequential day-to-day activities. Never knowing exactly how he was supposed to feel, he had learned early to bottle his thoughts. His parents occasionally prodded him to open up, but he had eluded their questions, never letting on that he had been terrified they might leave him there like in the stories of his birth parents.

The August sun on the pavement made the day seem all the hotter. Thirty-three years to the date since he had been found. As Lee stared at the gas station and supermarket, he wondered what he had expected to find. His birth mother wouldn't be lingering around, and after all this time, no clues that she might have left would exist. Did she hug him before leaving? Had his biological father been nearby? He only wished he could remember her face when she had said goodbye forever.

"Lee?"

Phoebe's voice pulled him back to the present.

"I became a cop because my dad was one," he said. "I wanted to be like him. He would have been proud if he had lived to see me make detective, but there was always something missing."

"When I was a lass, I oft thought of my kinsmen in Dorset. 'Twas not because I wanted to return, but I wondered what had happened to those left behind. E'en now, I seek the answers of my past for the sake of discovering what's gone afore, but I do not wish to be anywhere else." She squeezed his hand.

"I've talked to everyone who might know something about how I got here."

"Have you held counsel with the tribes?"

"The tribes?"

"Mayhap someone amongst them may recall the events."

Why had he avoided talking to the tribes? If he thought in his usual manner, it would have been his first step. Plain and simple—he had lived almost totally in the white world and feared rejection. He would set aside his fear and speak to them with confidence.

66

Phoebe

HENRY RETURNED TO THE PLANTATION, whilst I stayed on to lend aid to the Arrohateck. I gave Bess's treatment to as many as I could. Those who received it lived. Many were already in the final stages of the pestilence. I could only comfort them as best as I could afore their inevitable fate.

Amongst those I tended was Little Falcon. I had difficulty believing the warrior covered in blood-filled pustules could be the same man I had loved. I did not tell him of the ruse Poppa had used to gain my obedience. None of that mattered now. I gave offerings of tobacco to Oke in order to appease his wrath.

My mind went numb from the grief. I had few supplies and even fewer medicines. My gentle touch calmed many a panic-stricken person. I dared not look into their eyes, or I'd see their hope in my abilities. These were my people, my tribe. I had grown to womanhood, married, and birthed my children amongst them. And now, there was naught more I could do to save them.

As more died, my numbness spread. Grief must wait, or I would be of little use to the living. Bending aside Little Falcon, I placed a water-filled gourd to his lips and helped him drink. We ne'er spoke of our love. In the years of our separation, he had married, and his wife, with their young daughter, remained by his side. I prayed that I had treated his family in time.

Poppa had spared Little Falcon, only for him to suffer a languishing death. "Your spirit will soon be set free, Little Falcon," I whispered for his ears alone.

His gaze met mine in understanding and acceptance. He was at peace.

When I stood, his wife came nearer, looking hopeful.

"There is naught I can do. He will be dead afore day's end."

How many times had I delivered the words of late? I had lost count. As I left the longhouse, Little Falcon's wife wept. I felt helpless, only to be reminded that I had saved some. So few would survive that my heart was heavy, but I continued on, doing what I could.

Another moon passed afore Charging Bear took me downriver in a dugout. I worried about my brother's welfare. I also grieved for Momma and Silver Eagle, but he had lost two children as well. He and his wife were young, but most of the Arrohateck were gone. Like the Paspahegh, they had been killed or displaced by the colonists, or died from their pestilence.

He brought the canoe up on the river bank a few miles from Henry's plantation.

"Are you sure you won't join me, *Nemat*? Henry has always welcomed my family."

"I cannot. My people need me."

I studied his countenance, for I feared I would ne'er cast my eyes upon his face again. I could no longer refrain myself and embraced him. "I shall miss you, Charging Bear," I whispered in his ear.

"And I, you, Walks Through Mist."

When I stepped back, I forced a smile. He shoved the dugout from the bank and jumped in. I waved. "Goodbye, Charging Bear."

He returned my wave and began to paddle. I stayed on the bank and watched him 'til the forest appeared to swallow him. Elenor needed me. I set out on my venture. Whilst away, I had taken to dressing as Arrohateck again. I regretted that I must soon return to skirts and stays. At least I had my moccasins for my journey to the plantation.

Alongside the river, I made my way through the forest trail and spied thunderclouds ahead. In times past, I would have sought refuge afore the storm reached me, but I thought of Elenor and walked towards the tempest. Soon, the river churned to a rapids and thunder rumbled. As angry clouds unleashed their fury, I feared I had vexed Oke with my decision to willingly return to Henry.

Wind gusts nearly blew me from the trail, and rain pelted the ground. I no longer had a choice and sought refuge in a hollow, covering myself with leaves.

When the storm passed, I brushed the leaves from my doeskin and returned to the trail. Though wet, I was prepared to finish my journey. Only a few more miles and Elenor would be in my arms once more. I picked up my pace.

Afore long, I stood outside the palisade. Smoke drifted from the chimney. I was home. I approached the gate, and a crow cawed overhead. Suddenly wary from the sign, I hesitated. The guards were nowhere to be seen. Cautiously, I peered through the gate. *Soldiers—drinking ale.* Retracing my steps afore they saw me, I sought cover of the forest. When I reached its safety, I breathed in relief. How would I get Elenor? What of Henry?

Keeping watch over the palisade 'til darkness fell, I waited. My heart pounded as I crept forward with only moonlight to guide me. I reached the gate, opened it, and slipped inside the palisade. Candles burned in the house, and I heard drunken laughter. I edged alongside the wall, wondering how I would ever find Elenor.

I fought the urge to rush ahead and carefully negotiated my way over to the house. I crouched neath a window. The laughter from inside grew more raucous. Was Henry amongst the soldiers? And what had happened to the servants? I huddled against the wall, thinking over what I should do next. Panic nearly overcame me. My only weapon was a knife I used for cleaning game. *Think.*

I caught hold of my growing fright. Taking a deep breath, I peeked inside. Four soldiers, but no sign of Henry or Elenor. Thinking they could be in the loft, I hugged the ground. I would wait 'til the soldiers had fallen into a inebriated slumber. Determined to free Elenor, I held my position. My muscles ached from remaining bent for so long, but finally, I heard loud snoring.

As I sneaked inside, the door creaked. I waited 'til I was certain I'd roused none of the soldiers. I edged towards the loft. I reached the ladder and nearly tripped over a man sprawled on the floor. He snorted but didn't waken. Carefully stepping over him, I climbed the ladder.

I held my knife ready. From the pallet, a lass muttered. *Elenor!* I lowered the knife but soon realized someone was with her. "Henry?" I said in a low whisper.

"Phoebe?" came a sleepy voice. Awakened fully, he continued, "Phoebe, you mustn't be here. They're waiting for you. Run. They already have Bess."

"Why?"

"To be tried as a witch. Now go. I'll see that Elenor remains safe."

"But Henry—"

He kissed me upon the lips. "Do as I say. Go."

More than anything, I wanted to hug Elenor and say goodbye. I turned. *Where am I to go?* Most of the Arrohateck had already disbursed. Mayhap, the Chickahominy would take me in. Many of the Paspahegh had sought refuge there.

With new resolve, I scrambled down the ladder to the first floor. On my tiptoes, I made my way through the snoring soldiers. Near the door, I halted. So many years ago, my family had fled Dorset, only for Momma and I to run from James Towne. Afterwards, we barely escaped with our lives when the Paspahegh town was burned. Tired of running, I held up my hands and spread my fingers to show that I bore the witch's mark. "I'm here," I announced. "Take me!"

Snorts and muffled mutterings surrounded me.

"I'm here!"

Footsteps clambered and stumbled. Soldiers tripped over the other, shouting blasphemies. A lantern was lit, and muskets aimed in my direction.

"Phoebe, no!" Henry called from the ladder.

"You have imprisoned the wrong woman," I said in Bess's defense. " 'Tis me. I am guilty."

The nearest soldier seized my arm, whilst the next brought iron shackles. They pressed against me, and I smelt the ale on their breath. I did not fight them as the massive shackles were clamped about my wrists and ankles.

"Phoebe . . ." With his arms outstretched, Henry rushed towards me, but the soldiers blocked him afore he could reach me.

" 'Tis the way it must be, Henry. I cannot let Bess suffer for my sins."

The soldiers led me away, and Elenor cried from the loft. "Momma!"

My heart broke, for I could not tell my sweet daughter goodbye.

67

Shae and Lee

WITCH TRIALS—IN VIRGINIA? Shae withheld her skepticism. Because the patient believed something, that didn't make it true. But she felt they were getting to the source of Phoebe's problem. "We're making good progress. How is everything else in your life?"

"I'm still studying my reading and writing. Liz says my history lessons have almost reached current affairs."

"And you've kept in contact with your friends at Colwell House?"

"Aye. Meg's graduation is a fortnight away. She drove me today. Valerie says she'll be sad to see her leave. Carol remains melancholy, but she's looking forward to Meg's graduation party. There's also a new woman, who took my room. I don't know her very well."

That left one topic. Although Shae had seen Lee on the day of Nat's funeral, she noted that he hadn't driven Phoebe. In recent times, he often had. "What about Lee?"

Phoebe frowned. "He no longer participates in the dreaming."

In that respect, Shae was relieved. "I'm sure it has something to do with the difficult time he's been through lately."

"Aye," Phoebe replied.

Shae gave Phoebe the usual instructions of calling her before her next appointment, if necessary. In that sense, they had definitely made progress. Phoebe never called anymore. Escorting her patient to the outer office, she found Meg leafing through a magazine.

Upon seeing them, Meg stood.

They exchanged goodbyes before Shae returned to her office. Thank goodness Phoebe was her last patient of the day. Instead of gathering her files together, she checked her computer for witch trials in Virginia. To her surprise, there had been a few, and she wondered why so much attention had been given to Salem. As it turned out, Virginia claimed the dubious honor of holding the first witch trial on the North American continent.

Website after website mentioned the "Witch of Pungo," better known as Grace Sherwood. She had been a healer and midwife. Was that who Phoebe had modeled herself after? Shae clicked onto another website. She scanned through the names: Joan Wright, another midwife and fortune teller; Katherine Grady, the only woman to have been executed; and William Harding, bewitched a cow. Her eyes widened. The name Phoebe Wynne stared back at her.

Over a beer in the living room, Lee listened to Phoebe's story that she had recalled while under hypnosis with Shae. He should have shared with her in the dreaming like he used to, but of late, he had been unable. *Why?* Then, when she reached the part where she had left her daughter behind . . . he nearly broke down in tears. Had his mother been faced with no choice as well? "Do you still think of her?"

"Elenor? Aye, but what choice was I given? I may ne'er know whether she grew to womanhood, married, had children of her own or . . ." Her voice wavered. ". . . died."

Lee wondered if his mother could have been in a similar situation. Had he passed her on the street without ever knowing? Or was she long dead? He frequently saw the missing persons reports. Many people vanished due to foul play. Yet he couldn't shake the police reports that no such evidence had ever been uncovered at the site where he had been found.

The phone rang. Lee checked the caller ID and answered, "What's up, Shae?"

"Hi, to you too, Lee." He detected her usual annoyance. *"I'd like to speak to you, but not over the phone."*

"When and where?"

She suggested a bar and grill not too far from his apartment. *"And please, come alone."*

"Okay. I'll see you in about thirty minutes." He hung up the phone. "For some reason, Shae wants to meet with me."

" 'Tis about me, isn't it?"

"I honestly don't know. She didn't say, but sometimes she helps me with some of my cases."

"You're not at work now."

"No, but she might have found something that I can pass on to Ed." Even he didn't believe the words, and when she wrinkled her brow, he knew that she hadn't either. "If she says anything about you, I'll let you know when I return."

This seemed to satisfy her. With regret that he had to leave her after such an important revelation, Lee made his way to the car. He arrived at the bar and grill ten minutes late. He spotted Shae's silver Acura in the lot. Bypassing the handicapped section, he parked the T-Bird next to the Acura.

Once inside, he looked around the room.

Shae waved at him from a booth.

When he reached the booth, he was glad to get off his feet. "Sorry I'm late, but I'm not moving as fast as I used to."

"And I bet you were too stubborn to use the handicapped parking."

"I doubt that you invited me here to prove how well you know me."

She gave him a smug grin. A waitress in black pants and a blouse stopped at the booth and asked them if they needed a few minutes yet to order. Lee told Shae to go ahead, and she ordered chicken fingers and fries. When he only ordered a non-caffeinated soft drink, Shae sent him a look of mock horror. "I've already eaten, and I don't depend on caffeine these days," he explained.

"I guess I don't know you as well as I thought. I remember when you wished caffeine came in an IV drip."

"That was when I was on patrol. Right now, any kind of caffeine keeps me awake at night. You can bet I'll be indulging again when I return to duty."

She chuckled. "Glad to hear that some things never change."

"Shall we get down to business? What's so important that it couldn't wait until the morning?"

The waitress returned with their drinks, and Shae took a sip of Chablis. "Has Phoebe told you about her latest experience while under hypnosis?"

"She has."

"I presumed she would, but I needed to ask."

He nodded that he understood.

"I became curious after hearing her story about witch trials in Virginia. I did a computer search and discovered something interesting." She passed a folder to his side of the table.

He looked inside at the papers she had printed out. There were only a few scattered, incomplete records, but the pages concurred. A woman by the name of Phoebe Wynne had been tried as a witch in 1630. Oh God, he knew what was going to happen next in Phoebe's story.

"Well?"

"What do you want me to say?"

"Phoebe obviously has read these."

"How is that possible, doctor, when she just recently learned to read?"

Flustered, Shae rested her elbows on the table. "You may recall that she was perfectly capable of reading. It's writing that she supposedly learned a mere few months ago."

Her tone signaled that she was pissed, but both of them remained silent when the waitress returned with Shae's meal. "Is there anything else I can get you?"

Shae pasted on a smile. "No, thank you. We're fine." She pounded the ketchup bottle. Ketchup splattered over the fries.

"I'm surprised you chose to meet me in a dump like this when you could be home savoring one of Russ's meals."

She narrowed her eyes in annoyance. "Leave Russ out of this, and quit changing the subject. I think you know the truth about Phoebe, but for some reason, you've decided to keep me in the dark. Is she in the Witness Protection Program or something?"

Suddenly enjoying Shae's bewilderment, Lee leaned back in the seat and crossed his arms. "If she were, I doubt the Feds would inform me. I'm merely a detective—on medical leave, no less."

"Lee, stop it. Is Phoebe in some sort of trouble?"

Her captors were long dead, and in that sense, he could relax his guard. No one would be coming after her. "Not anymore."

She indulged in a French fry. "Why all of the mysteriousness?"

"Because you wouldn't believe me if I told you."

Munching on a chicken finger, she said, "Try me."

"She told you long ago who she is and where she's from."

She rolled her eyes and took another bite of her meal. "A cunning woman from the seventeenth century. I'm trying to help a patient, so please stop toying with me. She has dissociative—"

"Forget all of the psycho-babble," he said, growing annoyed, "and ask yourself, has she ever recalled anything about this century before we visited her in the hospital?"

"Besides amnesia, what does that prove? You used to be a stickler for the evidence. Where is it?" She picked up a fry, but replaced it in the basket. "The hypnosis that she calls the dreaming? For Christ's sakes, Lee, that's not real. I've already explained to you how dangerous hypnosis can be if it's used improperly. See what it's done to you. It's opened a wound that had healed, but now it's got you searching for biological parents that you were unconcerned about before."

He reached across the table and gripped her hand. "That's where you're wrong, Shae. Haven't you ever wondered why I don't trust very easily?"

She yanked her hand from his grip. "You're a cop. It goes with the goddamned job."

He laughed slightly. "Denial? I would have thought a trained psychologist could do better. You're afraid to admit that what went wrong between us goes much deeper than my job."

She took a few breaths and calmed herself. "Lack of trust isn't uncommon in adoptions of older children, international, cross-cultural, or cross-racial. I guess I never thought of you—"

"And therein lies the problem. I've been denied my heritage."

"Phoebe saw it. That makes her perceptive, not a time traveler."

"I warned you that you wouldn't believe me."

"Evidence," she repeated with a sigh.

"She can speak Virginia Algonquian. There hasn't been a native speaker in at least two hundred years."

She appeared to mull over his words as she nibbled a chicken finger. "That's not a lot to go on, but you have a point. Okay, for the sake of argument, if she's not fantasizing about the seventeenth century, how did she get here?"

He shrugged that he didn't know. "We haven't reached that part of her story yet. She'll tell us. Just give her the chance."

Her eyes flashed. "Damn you. Here I am listening to a cock-and-bull story like it's fact. Sorry I called. I really thought you could help me with the breakthrough I need in Phoebe's case."

"We're done here." He placed a couple of bills on the table to cover his drink and his portion of the tip. Phoebe had been tried as a witch. He had been so absorbed about the hows and whys of his adoption that he had avoided the dreaming. Now, he sought it.

68

Phoebe

WHEN LEE RETURNED from his counsel with Shae, we made love with a fever that had been missing since the shooting. We kissed, fondled, and frolicked 'til tumbling to the bed in exhaustion. His playfulness reminded me of Lightning Storm's, and I rebuked myself for making the comparison. But Lee had probably thought of Shae, and I wondered if his meeting with her had provoked his vigor.

On this night, the past was unimportant, only our love and its expression. To the steady rhythm of his heartbeat, I fell peacefully asleep in his arms. Though he had yet to inform me what he and Shae had discussed, 'twas the first time I had ever truly felt safe. I prayed it wasn't an illusion.

In the early light of dawn, I woke to Lee's smiling face. He gave me an intimate good-morning kiss, whilst his fingertips brushed my cheek. "Good morning, Phoebe."

I gently stroked the expanse of his chest. " 'Tis a beautiful morn."

He took the arrowhead I wore round my neck betwixt his fingers. "I'd like to take you shopping for a proper necklace."

"This one is special. You gave it to me." He muttered that he understood, and I said, "I shall fix you breakfast."

We parted with another kiss, and he delighted in watching me as I dressed. Though I preferred the simple attire of the Arrohateck, I had grown accustomed to modern garments. In this culture, 'twas perfectly acceptable that I wear trousers. Lee's eyes gleamed as I wiggled into the tight-fitting material. I had yet to adapt to the breast binder, but again, Meg had said 'twas a woman's choice. Relishing the freedom, I chose to go without.

Finished dressing, I blew Lee a kiss as I had seen Meg do with her daughter. I went into the kitchen and began by scrambling eggs. By the time Lee hobbled into the room, the eggs were ready, and I scooped them onto plates afore setting them on the table. He winced when he sat.

"Mayhap we should have restrained our passion last eve," I said.

He waved at me that he was fine. "It's worse in the morning."

I sat across from him. His brow wrinkled ever so slightly. Anyone less familiar with him would likely have missed it. "Something troubles you."

"Thank you for not asking about what Shae and I discussed last night."

" 'Twas not my place."

"But it was." He picked up his fork and scooped the eggs onto a piece of toast. "Shae showed me some printouts of historical records—seventeenth century. I'd rather participate in the dreaming with you again than explain the details."

"You have discovered something about me?"

"I think so."

Confused, I asked, "Why do you not wish to share your findings with me?"

"If I stick to police procedure and make no disclosure, then Shae will eventually become a believer too. In the long run, her total support and understanding will benefit you. Because you can speak Virginia Algonquian, she already has doubts. I saw it on her face."

Though uncertain why my ability to speak Algonquian made a difference, I trusted Lee, and I enjoyed the thought of exploring the dreaming with him once again.

As I walked through the mist, I breathed easier, knowing that Lee would accompany me on the journey. The hound guided me to my fate. The windowless gaol was dark and damp. With my arms and legs shackled, I sat in a bed of moldy straw with a rat squeaking near my feet.

My hair was unkempt and greasy, and my skin was layered by filth. Used to daily cleansing, I scratched from the lice. The cell reeked from my own wastes, and my stomach rumbled with fits of hunger. 'Twasn't the first time. During the intervening years, James Towne had grown from a few hundred colonists to a couple of thousand. The Paspahegh were now gone and would not rescue me from starvation.

At peace with myself, I was ready to join my family—Lightning Storm, Dark Moon, Momma, and Silver Eagle. Poppa, in spite of all of his sins, would be admitted to heaven. I, on the other hand, was considered to be in league with the devil. I laughed aloud at the irony. Unable to face the four winds, I said a silent prayer to Ahone and Henry's God, hoping that one of them would hear my plea.

At least, I had succeeded in my mission. Bess had been absolved of all charges for being a witch. She would help Henry care for Elenor. *Oh, Elenor.* I closed my eyes, thinking of my darling daughter. I hoped that she could someday find it within her heart to understand. "Forgive me."

"If you have a contract with the devil, there shall be no forgiveness."

Through crusty eyelashes, I raised my head to the voice. A matron alongside a gaoler stood outside the door. The bearded man unlocked the cell, and the heavy door creaked upon its hinges. The gaoler came towards me and unlocked the shackles about my wrists. As he attended to the restraints about my ankles, he fondled my leg and whispered in my ear, "I've already told ye I can make things more pleasant for ye."

His hand reached my thigh, and I swatted it like a fly.

"Suit yerself." He seized my arm and forced me to my feet.

My legs were wobbly from being left in the same spot for nearly a week, and I toppled. The gaoler caught me, making certain that he touched my breast as he did so. I elbowed him in the ribs. The resulting strike to my cheek knocked me to the bed of straw. This time, he grabbed both of my arms behind my back and jerked me to my feet.

All the while, the matron sent me a disapproving look. We neared her, and she said, "Harlot. If I had my way, we'd burn the likes of you."

In horror, I thought of Master Collins, the smell of roasting flesh, and his screams. *Did they burn witches?* "I have done you no harm."

"Bring her," she said in disgust. "We can expect little from her. She was raised by Indians."

The gaoler fixed shackles about my wrists and ankles that allowed me to walk. They led me from the cell to the outdoors. Light pierced my eyes. I had been in the dank cell long enough that the brightness was painful. I faltered, only for the gaoler to wrench on the chains to keep me moving.

When my vision adjusted to the light, I grew conscious of eyes following me from passersby. *Were they taking me to my trial?* I knew not what to expect. They led me to a wood frame house similar to the one I had shared with Henry. Once inside, I counted eleven women greeting me with their glares. Determined not to give into my fear, I followed Momma's example upon meeting the Paspahegh warriors and held my head high.

The gaoler removed my chains and retreated outside.

"We are here to examine you," the matron said.

"Examine me?" I asked, looking from one to the other.

"To see if you bear the devil's mark. Now, disrobe."

Whilst I had always been comfortable bathing in the river or wearing but few items of clothing when others were round me, to undress in front of these women intimidated me. Hoping that I might be spared the indignity, I held out my left hand and spread my fingers to reveal my conjoined digits.

One woman near the front of the group gasped. Another moved forward. Gray hair peeked from under her white cap. She pressed the webbing betwixt my fingers 'til it pinched. I refused to yield to pain and did not cry out.

" 'Tis not very sensitive," she announced to the group.

"I said disrobe," the lead matron repeated, "or I shall recall the gaoler to assist us. I will not be responsible for what actions he might take upon your nakedness."

Fully realizing her threat, I began to unlace my bodice. Aft I removed the garment, I let my skirt fall on top. Soon, I was down to my shift and stockings. The matron motioned for me to remove those as well. I obeyed. They brought me to a chair that looked more like a birthing stool and told me to sit.

Self-conscious, I again followed their instructions. As fingertips sifted through my hair, I closed my eyes and thought of the men who I had brought joy by my natural state. Their images faded as fingers poked and prodded my ears and nostrils. I was told to open my mouth. One woman lifted my arm. Two more examined the webbing betwixt my fingers, squeezing harder than the first woman had. I held my tongue.

Hands reached my breasts, inspecting them for extra teats. Another woman bent afore me and spread my legs. Her hand probed my secrets, and then two fingers thrust into the neck of my womb. I bit my lip to keep from crying out. Their faces blended, and I struggled to keep the tears away.

One woman found the webbing betwixt my toes. Again, my flesh was pressed 'til I nearly screamed.

"Stand," the matron demanded.

As I did so, she motioned for me to turn around. I obeyed. Hands inspected my back.

"Grab you ankles."

I hesitated.

The matron went to the door. "I shall call the gaoler if you do not obey."

Reluctantly, I clutched my ankles, and the women probed my inner depths.

When the examination was completed, I was allowed to stand and face the lead matron. Refusing to bow under to their affront, I held my head proudly.

The matron's arms were crossed and her look of disapproval hadn't left her face. "Is it true that you are left handed?"

"Aye."

"And those devil markings." She pointed to the tattoos about my arms and upon my breasts. "Where did you get them?"

"The Arrohateck women regard them as a thing of beauty."

"Now, you may dress."

Numb from the humiliation I had endured, I reached for my shift. Even afore I could slip it over my head, the gaoler returned. I hurriedly dressed, but his desire swelled neath his breeches. He leered at me as he shackled my wrists and ankles.

Once outside, he tugged on the chains so hard that I fell to my knees. "Get up!" Afore I could regain my feet, he grabbed my arms and forced me upright. "I'll have ye, witch."

Exhausted, I had so little fight left, but I met his gaze. "I shall die afore I allow you to touch me."

A wicked smile appeared on his face. "That can be arranged." He gave the chains a sharp tug and led me to my cell. When the shackles held me against the wall, the gaoler sent me another leer. "I can help ye. Get ye away from here."

I spat, and he struck my face.

"Yer trial is on the morrow." He slammed the cell door behind him, and the key rattled in the lock. As his footsteps retreated, he doused the lantern. Like so much of my life, I was alone. In the dark, I surrendered to my fear. A cold tear slid down my cheek, then another.

"Phoebe . . ."

'Twas *his* voice. I raised my head and searched for him. "Lightning Storm?" I struggled against the chains. "Lightning Storm? Where are you?" But no one answered my pleas. Resigned that his voice had been naught but my imagination, I leaned against the wall. Would I even know when the morrow arrived? I embraced ending this ordeal.

I closed my eyes, but rats scurried and squeaked about the cell.

"Phoebe . . ."

I disregarded him.

"Phoebe!"

"You're not really there. Stop tormenting me."

"I'm here, Phoebe. Look."

At his bidding, I opened my eyes. I spied a misty light. At the center was a white hound. Aside the dog was Lee, attired in a breechclout and moccasins. I tried to stand, but the shackles held me fast. "I cannot move."

The fog spread, totally engulfing me. As Lee's strong hand helped me to my feet, the chains melted. Together, we walked through the mist. A moment passed afore the surroundings of Lee's apartment came into view. He sat across from me, staring at the candle betwixt us. "Lee?" I touched his face, and he blinked.

He rubbed his temple as if in pain. "I tried to reach you before, but couldn't. I wanted to spare you . . ."

"Thank you, but 'twas necessary for you to see as 'twas for me to recall." I should have known Lee had been the one who had tried to spare me from the horrors of the past. Lightning Storm would have used my Algonquian name.

69

Lee

LEE HAD CONTACTED THE PAMUNKEY and Chicahominy tribes because they were located nearest to the area where he had been
found as a toddler. Although more than one phone call was usually required before he could locate someone who might be able to
help him, the answer turned out the same. No one was aware of
a small child that had been lost or kidnapped. There were several
more tribes to check, but what if his birth mother hadn't originated
from any of them? She might have been traveling through the state
and have been a member of a tribe from across the country.

He studied the scrapbook that his parents had prepared for him.
He leafed through the news clippings about him being located in
the woods as a toddler. The story had made the headlines. As with
Phoebe, no one had known who he was or where he had come
from.

For the first time in over twenty years, he actually read through
the articles. How odd to be reading about himself in such a way.
Police found no signs of foul play or abuse, except for a few cuts and
scratches, which were consistent with a toddler stumbling through
the woods. As a matter of fact, he seemed to have been well cared
for. A follow-up article claimed that he had been abandoned. The
two didn't add up.

Lee couldn't help but feel that something must have happened
to his birth mother and the evidence had never been uncovered. Or
was it wishful thinking? No one liked the idea that they might have

been unwanted. Perhaps he'd had a deadbeat dad, who had fallen behind on support, and his mother had no longer been able to make ends meet. But if she had abandoned him, wouldn't she have left him in an area where someone would have been more likely to find him? The fact that the hikers had stumbled upon him was nothing less than miraculous.

He read further. A Deputy Frank Kulp had given the statement to the press. While Lee had been found in a different county than the one he currently worked for, it shouldn't be too difficult to find out if the deputy was still on the force. A lot of years had passed. It was a long shot, but it was the only clue he had never pursued.

Or he could try the dreaming again. Without Phoebe's help, the results had been less than satisfactory. He'd wait until she discovered how she had arrived in this century before asking her. For now, he'd follow the more solid leads.

70

Phoebe

As I was led into the courtroom, my gaze met Henry's. He had not been allowed to visit whilst I was in gaol. For the first time in our marriage I longed to hold him and tell him that everything would be all right. But would my words speak the truth? I was on trial for my very life.

A row of justices all dressed in black sat behind a long table. In the middle was the presiding judge, an eminent elderly gentleman with a neatly trimmed beard.

"Phoebe Wynne," came the magistrate's voice, "a jury of women hath searched your person for marks of the devil. The able jury hath found webbed skin betwixt your fingers and toes. Do you agree with their assessment?"

My skirt safely hid my shaking knees. "Aye."

"You also stated to the jury that you are left handed?"

"Aye."

"Let it be recorded on this day, the ninth day of September, in the year of our Lord 1630, by your own admission, you bear marks of the devil. You now stand afore this court accused with a sundry acts of witchcraft. How do you plead?"

I cleared my throat. "I am innocent."

A collective gasp went through the courtroom. The justice arched a brow. "Mistress Wynne," he said sternly, "you have a long record of consorting with the Indians. Is that not true?"

"I have lived amongst the Paspahegh and Arrohateck," I replied, struggling to keep my voice even. "I have learnt their ways of healing, prayed to their Gods, but I have ne'er practiced witchcraft."

Loud voices spread over the courtroom, and the justice called for order. "You admit to healing, using the ways of the savages, and praying to their Gods but not to practicing witchcraft. How is that possible?"

" 'Tis simple. The Paspahegh and Arrohateck are not savages."

The courtroom voices grew loud and angered. The magistrate pounded a gavel to restore order. "Your father, Robert Knowles, rescued you from the savages, yet you ran off to rejoin them. Is that not true?"

No matter how hard I was pressed, I refused to call the people I loved savages. "I rejoined the Arrohateck."

More loud murmurs. Once again, the justice requested order. "Was your daughter begotten by an Indian?"

Elenor. Let them do anything to me, but I had prayed Elenor would be spared. "I was married to an Arrohateck warrior."

"Married? In a Christian ceremony?"

"Nay," I replied.

"Then you declare your daughter was begotten through an act of fornication. Even aft marrying a law-abiding citizen of the Crown, did you not continue to consort with the Indians, as well as administer aide to them?"

"My mother was married to a Paspahegh warrior. She called upon me on occasion, and when my family was overcome by the small pox, I gave them aide. They had no prior knowledge of the malady."

The judges bent their heads and deliberated amongst themselves. 'Twas not long afore they reached a decision. The presiding justice pounded the gavel. "Phoebe Wynne, you freely admit to consorting and fornicating with the Indians. Due to the said influence by devil worshippers, we believe you hath been unduly bewitched by them. You are found not guilty of witchcraft. However, you are found guilty of fornication and consorting with the Indians. For those crimes, you shall receive twenty stripes. Aft punishment is carried out, you will be returned to England, where any temptation of rejoining the Indians will be an impossibility."

The sound of the gavel marked an end to the proceedings.

71

Shae and Lee

WITH SOME DOUBT IN HER MIND, Shae listened to Phoebe as she recounted her involvement in a witch trial. "You're certain Lee told you nothing about our meeting the other night?"

"Aye. He was insistent that I know naught about what you spoke of. He said he would 'stick to police procedure.'"

That certainly meant no disclosure. Aware that Lee must be ready for another confrontation, Shae remained unconvinced. He had driven Phoebe to her appointment. "If you don't mind, I'd like to talk to Lee for a few minutes in private."

"I shall fetch him." Phoebe left the office.

A few minutes passed before Lee limped in. She motioned for him to have a seat. He sat across from her and rested his cane next to him. "I take it Phoebe has told you about the trial."

"She has," Shae agreed. "Lee, why are you doing this?"

"Doing what?"

"Stop it. You know I don't like it when you answer a question with a question. You don't allow it in your line of work. Don't bring it into mine either."

"Sorry," he quickly apologized. "After we had our meeting, I knew what was about to happen next in Phoebe's story, but I didn't want to influence her. It's important that you believe her."

His near-death experience had affected him more than she had imagined. Shae wrote a name on her notepad. "You've been under a lot of stress lately. Many good cops break under the pressure." She tore the sheet from the pad and handed it to him. "If you won't see your department's psychiatrist, here's someone I recommend."

After a quick glance, he crumpled the paper and tossed it to the side. "Shae, you know me better than that. Don't pretend otherwise. I also recognize fear when I see it."

"Why would I be afraid?"

"Because you saw Phoebe as an intriguing case when you took her on. You thought I was in over my head, but the tables have reversed. You're afraid that she just might be telling the truth."

She fidgeted with her pen. "You still haven't presented me with an ounce of evidence. You, of all people, know what holds up in a court of law."

"We're not in court."

She threw up her hands in frustration. "Why is it so important for me to believe?"

Fed up, Lee got to his feet. "You wanted a breakthrough in order to help your patient. What better breakthrough is there than learning the truth? Oops, I just asked a question. Forgive me. It was an oversight on my part." He withdrew a business card from his wallet. "If you won't take my word for it, here's an old professor of mine, Dr. Ellen Hatfield. She's in the linguistics department and can verify that Phoebe speaks Virginia Algonquian. I'll let her know that you might call. Did you want to see Phoebe again?"

"No, we're finished for the day. Tell her that I'll see her next Tuesday."

Grasping his cane, he made his way out of the office.

That had gone poorly. She sighed. In spite of their disagreement, she managed to collect herself for her two remaining patients. By the end of the day, she was beat. After a quick call to Russ that she'd be home soon, she picked up the card Lee had given her. He wasn't the sort of person to make up stories. But Phoebe couldn't be from the seventeenth century. What harm would there be in giving the professor a call?

Shae picked up the phone and began dialing. It rang a few times before a woman answered. *"Ellen Hatfield."*

"Dr. Hatfield, this is Dr. Shae Howard."

"Lee said you might call. I presume this is about your patient Phoebe Wynne?"

"It is. Is it true that she can speak Virginia Algonquian?"

"I've never met Ms. Wynne. Lee brought in a tape. I immediately recognized it as Algonquian, but it took me a couple of weeks to uncover that it was indeed the Virginia dialect. I was hoping Lee would bring her in. A native speaker is a rare find."

"Why is that?"

"Previously, we believed the last native speaker had died at least two hundred years ago."

Two hundred years. That fact didn't prove Phoebe was from the seventeenth century. "Can you tell me what tribes spoke the language?"

"There were several. The remaining descendants are the Mattaponi, Pamunkey, Nansemond . . ."

Shae quickly cut her off. "What about the Paspahegh and Arrohateck?"

"As a matter of fact, yes, they were Virginia Algonquian speakers, but both tribes were annihilated in the 1600s."

The seventeenth century. How could Phoebe, an Englishwoman, have learned a dead language? Unless—

No, the thought that Phoebe might be from the seventeenth century was too implausible.

"Dr. Howard, would it be possible to meet Ms. Wynne? As you might guess, I'd like to speak with her."

"I'll see what I can do." They exchanged goodbyes, and she hung up the phone. Witch trials had taken place in Salem, not Virginia. She had already uncovered documentation to the contrary. Suddenly curious, Shae wondered if an in-depth web search might turn up more information. The name Phoebe Wynne came up in several searches but with few details. She could always see if any of the Jamestown historians could trace the records.

To what end? She was reacting like she might actually believe the story. But nothing else seemed to fit. Phoebe had never slipped in mentioning the twenty-first century until February, when she had supposedly arrived. And the fact that she spoke a dead language fluently . . . .

Shae *would* give Jamestown a call.

* * *

Retired Deputy Frank Kulp was more than happy to meet with Lee. Along with his wife, he now lived in a ranch house in the suburbs of Richmond. After exchanging introductions, Lee was quickly escorted to a modest living room. Frank told him to have a seat on a sofa with overstuffed cushions covered with a hand-embroidered throw. The former deputy mentioned reading about Lee's shooting in the newspapers and was pleased to see that he was well on the road to recovery. "What brings you here, Lee?" he asked, seating himself in an easy chair that matched the sofa.

"You stated over the phone that you remembered a case from 1975 where hikers happened on a small child in the woods a few miles from Jamestown."

"That case made the headlines. It's not likely I'd ever forget. Has something new come to light after all these years?"

"Not really. My interests are personal."

Suddenly curious, Frank leaned forward. "In what way?"

Usually Lee had no difficulty answering questions, but something held him back. He swallowed. "I was the child the hikers found."

"I see." Frank sat back once more and tapped his fingers on the arm of the chair. "How can I help? Everything was in my report."

"I've read it, but reports often leave out the human element."

"Spoken like a seasoned police officer. What do you want to know?"

"I know it's been a lot of years, but if you can just tell me what you remember, I'd appreciate it."

"We got the call around eight. I can remember the time because when we arrived it was dark. A group of hikers had found you. You were a bit on the skinny side and not wearing a stitch, but otherwise, we found no evidence of abuse or foul play. We thought maybe your family had been out swimming, and you had wandered off. We scoured the area, even brought in the dogs, but couldn't locate anyone. In spite of whatever you had been through, you were in good spirits—a friendly child, but not overly so—if you know what I mean. Definitely not shy though."

"I guess I haven't changed much."

"Undoubtedly. Because of your build and physical coordination, we guessed your age around two, maybe two and a half. You sounded like you were stringing words together, but nobody understood you."

That point intrigued Lee. "Could I have been speaking another language?"

Frank rubbed his chin. "A child psychologist examined you later, but she determined that your language development was in fact late, and you were what they call babbling. As soon as you were in foster care, I got the word that you were speaking like any child of your age."

He recalled that his former professor had said few people tended to recognize the Native American languages. "Could I have been speaking an Indian language?"

"Hmmm..." Another chin rub. "I'm not familiar with any of the tribal languages myself, but I suppose it's possible."

Since the local tribes had spoken Virginia Algonquian in the past, Lee automatically eliminated them, but like Phoebe, he might have reverted to a language he had been familiar with. The Cherokee language was very much alive. If only they had recorded what he had said back then, he might be able to trace it.

"There was one other thing..."

"Go on."

"The hikers gave us an arrowhead. They said it had been clutched in your hand when they found you."

An arrowhead? "Do you know what happened to it?"

"Initially, I believe it was held as evidence, but I suspect it was eventually turned over to your foster family."

Could the arrowhead have been one of those in his collection? "Is there anything else you remember?"

Frank shook his head. "We followed standard procedure of the time to see if anyone knew who you or your parents were. No one ever showed up. My gut as an officer of over twenty years told me that some sort of foul play was involved, but I had nothing to prove it."

At least his own hunch had been substantiated, and he had a couple of slim leads. Lee grasped his cane. "Thanks, I appreciate you taking the time."

"For whatever it's worth, I'm glad you stopped by. I had always wondered what happened to you. I also hope you find whatever it is you're looking for."

Lee repeated his appreciation, and they shook hands. No wonder the local tribes didn't recall him. His mother had likely come from elsewhere.

72

Phoebe

ON THE MORN FOLLOWING MY TRIAL, I was led from my cell to the town square. My hands were bound to a post. For the second time in my life, I was to be flogged for fornication. Only this time, Elenor would also bear my supposed shame. I held no regret, for Elenor had been begotten in love by my husband.

A crowd gathered, hissing and shouting "harlot." Some threw dirt, stones, and rotting vegetables. A rock struck my face, barely missing my eye. I refused to give them the satisfaction of hearing me cry out.

A knife slit my bodice down the back, ripping through to my shift. Fabric tore, and I felt the cool air upon my back. In preparation, I gritted my teeth. Then, I spotted Henry. I focused on his face, and his eyes misted. *Be strong, Henry.* The whip cracked against my bare skin. And again. Thrice. Soon, I lost count. I writhed from the pain, but the bindings held me fast. Finally, I could take no more and wailed.

The crowd cheered and began chanting, "Die, witch!"

Another lash, and I cried. More chanting.

"Phoebe..."

'Twas *his* voice, and I smiled. The mist formed, but the whip struck me again. Dizzy from the pain, I fainted.

When I awoke, I remained tied to the post. The fog that had so oft saved me had vanished. Passersby laughed and spat. The wounds upon my back festered, and the sun grew warm. My legs were weak, and I slumped.

I thought of Lightning Storm. So many years had passed, I could barely recall what his voice had sounded like. Hadn't he been the one calling to me from the depths of the mist? Nay, 'twas . . . "Lee?" I had entered the dreaming but couldn't find my way out. Delirious with pain, I laughed.

By nightfall, the gaoler untied my bindings. Only when I was returned to my cell and shackled to the wall did I receive food and water.

"Phoebe . . ."

I looked up at Henry, standing on the other side of the bars.

"Forgive me, Phoebe, for being weak. I could not watch you suffer."

"You needn't beg my forgiveness, Henry. For you have done naught wrong. My only regret . . ."

"Pray tell me."

"That I could ne'er be the wife you wished of me. You're a kind man and deserve better."

He gripped the bars. "You mustn't berate yourself. I have always known there was another afore me in your heart. E'en now, I see it in your eyes. I saw them as savages. You have educated me otherwise. Your father should have ne'er returned you to civilization. You were meant to remain Walks Through Mist. Afore your ship sails, I'll find a way for you to rejoin your tribe."

At his words, I bowed my head and wept.

73

Shae and Lee

AFTER SHAE'S LAST PATIENT, SHE GATHERED her files together and shoved them into her briefcase. A knock came to the door.

"Shae?" came a male voice.

"Come in, Lee."

The door opened, and Lee entered. Even though he moved slowly, she could see that he was getting stronger with each passing day. "Is something wrong with Phoebe?"

"She's fine." He sat in the chair across from her, resting his cane against the desk. "It's nothing like that. I've come to ask a favor."

Relieved that Phoebe was fine, she laced her fingers together. "Okay."

He let out an uneasy breath before continuing, "I want to recall what happened."

"Recall?" A moment passed before she grasped what he was asking. "Lee, first, you're a lousy subject for hypnosis. Second, childhood memories are often unreliable."

"If Phoebe has been hypnotizing me all this time, then I must not be as difficult of a subject as you claim."

"We've already been over this."

"Shae, I have nowhere else to turn."

She studied him a moment. "I'll give you the bottom line. A highly hypnotizable subject is more likely to get results if a skilled hypnotist asks the correct questions. But those subjects are also the ones who often produce false memories. I've had enough experience with forensic hypnosis to know to stay away from leading questions, but what you're asking is to recover a memory from when you were two years old. Although some people have recovered memories as early as the age of one, full recall is rare before three. Early memories are usually poorly organized. On top of that, you've heard stories from family members about the day you were found. Stories like that create fictitious memories that come out while a subject is under hypnosis."

He was silent a minute, obviously thinking over what she had said. "What I'm seeking happened before any of the family stories."

"Fair enough. Let's suppose I do what you're asking, and we're successful in recovering the memory. A childhood trauma might be involved. There's a reason why our memories often forget trauma. It protects us. I can't risk unleashing something that could scar you permanently."

"Does that mean you're saying 'no'?"

Thankfully, he seemed to understand the situation. "It does."

He grabbed his cane and stood. "I guess I'll have to find someone else. Thanks, Shae."

So much for understanding. "Wait, Lee. You're serious?" His determined expression warned her that he was. "You're more likely to be screwed up if you go to some fly-by-night hypnotist."

"That's why I came to you."

"I'll do it—on one condition. If we uncover anything traumatic, you'll agree to psychological treatment. I've got several colleagues that I can recommend, depending on what we find."

He nodded that he would do as she asked.

What had she agreed to? If it had been anyone else with the request, she would have never reconsidered. "Just let me call Russ to tell him that I'll be a little late." Her hand shook as she reached for the phone. Not a good sign. Was she more worried that her subject was Lee or about what they might uncover? She glanced over at him and forced a smile. "I hope you realize you're making me a nervous wreck. Hypnotizing an ex is highly unethical. Just think of all the mean-spirited subconscious suggestions I could give you."

"I have confidence in your abilities. Besides, you're not a mean-spirited person."

"Thanks for the vote of confidence. Make yourself comfortable on the sofa, and I'll be right..." Russ came onto the line. What should she tell Russ? The details could wait until she got home.

As Shae made her phone call, Lee sat on the sofa.

After she hung up the phone, she joined him. "You're certain about this?"

"I need to know what happened."

"If we don't learn it here?"

"I'm no worse off than I was before."

Shae furrowed her brow. Usually, she wasn't the nervous sort.

He reached across and grasped her hand. "I'm not expecting miracles."

"I think I'm more worried about what might surface. I don't think using the induction method like I used with Phoebe when you first brought her to me would be best for you. Settle back and get comfortable."

He leaned back. "I already am."

She waved at him to keep quiet. "Close your eyes."

He obeyed.

"Good. Now relax. Breathe in. Now out. Breathe in once more and hold it for a count of three. One. Two. Three."

In the distance, Lee heard Shae's voice as they went through several breathing exercises. "Become aware of the sounds around you ... the sounds in the building ... out on the street."

Like his first experience of the dreaming, he heard people's voices and cars honking.

Shae led him through several relaxation exercises. "As you relax deeper, listening to all of the sounds, you become aware of your body. Your legs are getting heavier ..."

He opened his eyes. "It's not working."

"Lee ...," she said in annoyance.

"Sorry."

"Contrary to what I may have said, your susceptibility hasn't gotten any better. You said a few months ago that Phoebe uses a candle to induce hypnosis. Can you give me the specifics?"

"I stare into the flame and concentrate. When I see a mist, I walk through it, and I'm part of the story."

"That's the oldest induction technique. The movies like to use the clichéd dangling watch or the crystal ball. I don't have a candle handy, but we can get you to focus on one in your mind. Okay, let's try again, and for your information, when childhood memories are achieved, clients don't curl up, pretending to get smaller, like on TV. Are you ready?"

Once more, he got comfortable.

"Think of the candle in your mind. Do you see it?"

In the new environment, he had difficulty imagining a candle. He struggled, but finally saw a candle and flame. "Yes."

"Good. Focus on the flame."

Absorb it. He heard Phoebe's voice.

"Soon you will take a journey . . ."

Shae's voice faded as he concentrated on the flame. Nothing happened until he heard the sound of wings flapping. "I hear a bird flying."

"Go with it. Concentrate on the sound. The bird is getting closer."

The flapping wings approached him. He heard a caw, and a familiar black bird settled on a nearby branch. "It's a crow."

The crow preened its feathers before taking flight again.

Follow it. Again, he had heard Phoebe.

With the bird overhead but slightly ahead of him, he walked along a path through a forest. First, the trail went to the left, then the right. He found himself alongside the James River. In the gentle breeze, waves lapped against the bank. He breathed in the air. The motion of the waves made him feel like he was drifting.

The crow circled overhead before heading downstream. He followed the path beside the river. As he traveled further, he spotted Shae standing beside the path. Her blonde hair draped over her shoulders, looking much the way she had when they first met. He reached out to her, but the crow continued on.

"You feel yourself getting smaller and lighter," came Shae's voice. "Your arms and legs are getting smaller. You're getting younger and younger . . ."

Shae vanished from the path. Further downriver, the crow landed in a nearby tree.

"You are eleven or twelve, and you see a happy scene."

A tent was pitched, and he smelled fish roasting over the campfire.

"What's going on, Lee?"

"My dad took me camping."

"How old are you?"

"Eleven."

"Clear your mind."

The crow spread its wings and was airborne. Farther and farther, he followed the river. Near a bend, he saw a playground with green grass. Children swayed back and forth on the swings.

"How old are you?" Shae asked.

"Five." But the crow continued onward. He had difficulty keeping up. No longer near the river, he stumbled and fell to the ground. Frightened and alone, he called for his mother. Struggling to his feet, he made his way through the hemlock and cypress trees. Why did he hurt? His arms and legs were covered in cuts and scratches from the brambles.

Suddenly, the bird gave a panic-stricken caw, and he was plunged into billowing smoke. His eyes burned, and he couldn't see where he was going. Screams surrounded him. A woman clutched him to her body. No matter how hard he tried, he couldn't make out the features of her face.

"Lee, what are you seeing?"

"Fire—all around me. Screams. People running."

"Try and focus on the details."

The people were like shadows, fleeing through the smoke. The woman holding him screamed, and he felt himself falling. He hit the ground, and his shoulder hurt. She barely missed landing on top of him. He clung to her skirt. *His mother.* She lay still and unmoving.

"Lee . . . ?"

"I think she's dead."

Scared and alone, he crawled along the ground. The smoke nearly choked him, and he coughed. Still on his hands and knees, he crept blindly, not knowing where to look for safety. The smoke drifted, and he saw a kind face. Another woman—no, a girl. She pulled him to her. His body began to shape itself to her, and he clung to her. His grip tightened, and he cried on her shoulder.

Shae counted backwards, slowly returning him to the present. The memory faded, and Lee blinked. "I couldn't see things clearly. It's almost like I was an adult and a child at the same time."

Shae stared at him in concern. "Everything you describe is common for hypnotic memories from such an early age."

"How much was real?"

"There's no way of telling for sure. That's why a lot of hypnotists don't like using age regression."

"You warned me. I accept the results." Had there really been a fire? And the people—were they his family?

"Lee, we might be able to get a clearer focus of what you saw, but not today. You need time to recover first."

Surprised she would suggest continuing on, he thanked her. "It's weird."

"In what way?"

He grasped his cane. "For so long, I've dreamed about what my birth mother was like. Now, I don't know whether that was really her or something I've made up."

Shae smiled. "You'll figure it out—in time."

Thirty-three years ago, his life had changed drastically at such a young age. He had no idea how much was real of what he had seen, but he had a feeling that his birth mother had died in a fire.

A historian had helped Shae locate documents on Virginia witch trials. The only transcript available was of Grace Sherwood. But they had located a few references to Phoebe Wynne's trial and made copies for her use. Seventeenth-century English wasn't the easiest thing to read. The documents verified that Phoebe Wynne had received twenty stripes as punishment.

Lashes? Looking up stripes in the dictionary didn't help. Shae cross-referenced to the *Oxford English Dictionary*. She had been correct. Stripes in the 1600s equated to whipping. Phoebe had been found with healing wounds on her back. *Not real.* The evidence, though circumstantial, was adding up.

She continued reviewing the documentation. There was a handwritten letter at the bottom of the pile of papers. She had difficulty making out the words. Requiring help to decipher the letter, she nearly gave up in frustration, but the signature caught her eye. *Henry Wynne.*

She made her way back to the reference desk. A woman with shoulder-length hair smiled. "I thought you might be back after I helped you find the documents."

"I was wondering if you could help me make out what this letter says."

The archivist took her copy and began to read. "Henry Wynne was Phoebe's husband. He claims he hadn't known about her witchcraft. He also says that he is innocent in helping her escape. She vanished in a mist."

"A mist?"

She showed Shae the letter and pointed to the word. "M-Y-S-T. A common spelling during the era. Isn't it amazing what they used for testimony then? But they truly believed in witchcraft. Usually it was along the lines of bewitching a neighbor's livestock, but I bet Henry Wynne did help his wife escape. For what reason, I don't know. Virginia didn't hang witches like New England, so why go to all the effort?"

Because she was going to be returned to England? "Is there anything else?"

"More about the mist, but I really can't make out the details." She returned the copy to Shae.

"Thank you for your help." She was definitely looking forward to her next session with Phoebe.

74

Phoebe

IN THE GAOL CELL, I COULD TELL little difference betwixt night and day. I prayed for Henry's swift return, but he failed to show as he had vowed. On the morrow, I sailed for England. Aft all these years away, how could I possibly adapt?

The gaoler brought me a bowl of a thin pottage. As he set the bowl on the floor next to me, I heard the cry of a crow. I raised my head. *Could it be?* Like the time I had escaped from Henry, Lightning Storm had given the sign of the crow.

He smiled a toothless grin. "I told ye I'd have ye, witch."

Again, the crow cawed, and I returned the gaolers smile. "You said you would help me."

His grin widened. "Ye must make it worth my while."

I lifted my left arm. "Unshackle me."

He helped me to my feet. "Only aft lending me a sample of what I may expect."

Up close, I smelt the rum on his breath, and his greasy, unwashed body. He kissed me. Fighting every urge to pull away, I held fast, feigning to savor his sloppy, full-of-spittle kisses. His hand ran across my bosom. As I touched his hard form through his breeches, I bit my lip to keep from retching.

He stepped back and unshackled my ankles. The crow called once more, and he unlocked the irons around my wrists. He pulled me to him but crumpled in a heap from a blow to his head.

"How did you know I was here?" Henry asked, lowering his musket.

"Did you not signal me?"

"Nay." He grasped my hand. "I have a shallop waiting."

'Twas Lightning Storm, sending me a sign. Relieved to know that his presence had ne'er left me, I went along with Henry. Under the cover of darkness, he led me to the river. In amongst the trees where no light penetrated rested the boat. Henry helped me in. Aft he cast off, I rowed alongside him. For two nights, we traveled the river. On one occasion we came ashore to evade a search party.

Henry hoisted the shallop onto the bank. "I've sent word to your brother. You should meet him on the morrow. I'll send Elenor when the sheriff is convinced you have fled for good."

Aware that I would ne'er see Henry again, I hugged him. "I can ne'er repay you."

"You already have, Phoebe. May God go with you."

We shared a parting kiss. "I'm sorry, Henry."

He placed two fingers to my lips. "Just go."

Though I could not see his face through the darkness, I detected a waver in his voice. I turned to seek shelter for the night, so that I might start my flight anew in the morn. I barely went a hundred paces when I heard loud voices, questioning Henry. I bolted, nearly tripping over a tree root.

Calm. I evened my breath and pushed deeper into the forest. Afore long the sound of the lapping river was behind me. Branches scraped my arms, but I continued forward. My skirt protected my legs from the brambles, but my hands were sliced.

When I had traveled far enough to elude my pursuers, I sank to the ground in exhaustion. I drifted into a fitful sleep, only to be awakened by the light of torches. On my hands and knees, I scrambled along the forest floor. Only when the torches grew distant did I regain my feet.

No moonlight alighted my path to aid me. Halting to catch my breath, I focused on the night sounds. Branches, with rustling leaves, creaked in the wind, a screech owl trilled a mournful melody, and midges hummed past my ear. Upon hearing rushing water, I reasoned that I could follow its course and escape those who sought my death.

Unless the hounds were sent aft me, the advantage was mine. Unlike my pursuers, I had been taught to move swiftly and silently through the forest. Reaching the bank of the stream, I kicked off my leather shoes, for they were a hindrance. I dipped my toes into the water and felt the cool and slippery moss-covered rocks. Near me, a fish splashed. On the path behind me, I heard a familiar voice, hailing me and assuring me that no harm would come to me.

For a moment, I turned, contemplating whether I should continue on or turn back. Always steadfast in his devotion, Henry would not harm me. But was he alone? My back stung from the whip's lashes. Like spiders waiting in their webs, those close to him could have spun a trap.

He called to me once more. I quivered with irresolution, when a voice inside me urged me to continue forward. Though my life with Henry had ne'er been true, I feared what lay ahead.

"Do not fear it. You will be reunited with what once was."

'Twas *his* voice. So many years had passed that I had nearly forgotten the sound of it. Unashamedly, tears sprang into my eyes. Disregarding those who followed me, I called out to him in the tongue that had been forbidden to me for so long.

"Forward," he urged.

Heeding his advice, I forded the stream. The water churned around my feet whilst fish kissed my toes. Near the middle, the water swirled about my waist. I slogged through it and reached the far bank, when suddenly I was lost.

Trees were everywhere. I stumbled my way through the gigantic roots. Ne'er having felt confused and alone in a forest, I cried, "Where, my love? Where am I to go?"

Raging shouts came from the opposite stream bank. My heart pounded at their nearness. If I did not seek refuge, the mob would be upon me. I could now see their torches, and my breaths quickened. In the breeze, my beloved whispered, and I followed his voice 'til an elegant white hound stood afore me. I now knew what I must do.

The dog's body was made for coursing, but he kept a slower pace in order to guide the way. Deeper and deeper into the forest we traveled. I sought shelter in a dark opening within the roots of an immense oak. Instead of blackness surrounding me, a thick mist engulfed me. The clammy dampness upon my skin raised the hairs on my arms. The hound was my salvation, and I latched onto his leather collar.

On and on I faltered through the fog with the dog tracing a huge circle. I felt the rough, bare wood of a rocking and swaying ship neath my feet. A wave of nausea overcame me, and I clutched my stomach with my free hand. The hound failed to break stride. Onwards.

From a nearby branch, a crow cawed. Suddenly, I thought of a tiny lad vanishing in a similar mist, ne'er to be found again. Assured that my pursuers would reason that I suffered from the same fate, I continued walking along the arc.

When my beloved's voice returned, I signaled the hound to halt. He kept going, and the loving voice faded. With a twinge of remorse, I thought of Henry. He, too, had loved me. A love that I could ne'er return, for my heart had always belonged to another.

The mist grew thinner, and *he* whispered in my ear for me to follow the light. Up ahead, I spied what looked like thousands of torches. As I emerged from the fog, the dog vanished. I blinked in disbelief. How could so much light be possible in the night sky? I scanned about me. Lights upon lights, swarming with people. And clattering noise. I pressed my hands to my ears to block the racket. The thoroughfare had a surface the likes of which I had ne'er seen. *Where am I? Which lights should I follow?*

I stepped into the road to escape. More lights chased aft me, blinding me. I froze in my path, deafened by a piercing sound and sudden screeching. The earth trembled, and I was flying afore striking the pavement. I closed my eyes to the pain. *Soon, my beloved, I will join you.*

Recalling all that had happened, I gasped.

Shae gazed at me with a mixture of fear and relief upon her countenance.

"Lee!" I sprang from the chair, shouting his name again and again. By the time I reached the door, it opened and I was in his arms. " 'Twasn't Lightning Storm who summoned me here . . . but you."

"Me? How?"

I stepped back and fought the tears. "You are the lad who vanished in the mist, Crow in the Woods. Along with my momma, your mother, Snow Bird, taught me the art of *wisakon*. You are Paspahegh—the last of your tribe."

"The last..." Confounded, he stared at me. "That's not possible."

"It is," came Shae's voice. "Think about what you saw, Lee. The fire, terrified people running, and your mother. I found Henry Wynne's letter dated 1630 in the archives. He said Phoebe vanished in a mist."

His gaze came to rest upon me, studying me as if finally making sense of all that had happened. "*Netab,*" he said. "In the hospital, you were asking if we were friends." He grasped the arrowhead round my neck. "And this... was my father's."

With a kiss to his lips, I placed my arms about him. Henry had vowed to return me to my tribe. Even he could have ne'er known that Crow in the Woods had traveled in the mist afore me. For me, Walks Through Mist, my journey was complete.

75

Phoebe

L ATER THAT AUGUST, SHAE MARRIED her betrothed. 'Twas a small
gathering of family and friends with Lee and I included. I no
longer see Shae in a professional capacity. We both know who I am
and where I am from and have now become friends.

In December, she reciprocated the favor and attended my wedding with Lee. Ne'er afore had I experienced a honeymoon trip,
but Lee granted me two of my wishes by taking one. For the first
time in my life, I flew on a plane. The discomfort in my ears was
a minor annoyance compared to the months of nausea at sea. How
small the ocean seemed when transversing it in a few hours.

Aft our arrival in London, Lee rented a car, and we continued our journey to Dorset. We traveled along the hedgerows and
winding lanes. Stone cottages dotted the countryside. Whilst there,
we visited the giant man, carved into the chalk hillside. Though
time had a way of bypassing Dorset, little seemed familiar to me.
Deep down, I realized 'twas the closest I could come in transport-
ing Momma back to the land of her kinsmen. As I gazed upon the
hills, I knew she had found peace.

Upon our homecoming to Virginia, Lee returned to active duty
as a detective. I worried about the danger of his job, but the Arrohateck women had taught me to focus on day-to-day affairs and not
to try to change the heart of a warrior. I followed their wisdom, and
our love continued to blossom.

Over the months, I kept up with my studies. Meg and Valerie
were invaluable in aiding me to achieve my goal of acquiring a GED

diploma by the following summer. In my prior life, I had ne'er dreamt that an education was possible for a woman. I looked forward to college and becoming a nurse like Meg, but aft the first semester, my coursework was interrupted, when I birthed a little lass.

We called her Heather, giving her a connection to England as well as the Algonquian name, meaning Snow Bird. Her hair was black, and her eyes were dark brown. She reminded me so much of my Elenor that my heart ached.

Lee noted my melancholy, and once again, we joined in the dreaming. The mist became an impenetrable fog, engulfing us. With the spirit dog guiding the way, I latched onto his collar and Lee's hand.

As we traveled, Lee was no longer aside me. I called out. "Lee?" I spied him in the distance with Ed at his side. Across from them was a man in sneakers. Gunfire surrounded me. My heart pounded as my beloved fell. "Lee!"

A crow cawed, and the bird took flight, whilst a gentle squeeze came to my hand. "I'm here, Phoebe. That's part of the past."

I drew a relieved breath and continued forward. Lee was fine, and the hound began tracing along a circular path. Bright lights filled the night sky. Then came the sound of cars racing to and fro. The walkways were crowded with people. 'Twas the site where I had been struck by a car. Not wishing to relive the event, I clenched Lee's hand all the tighter to reassure myself that he remained aside me.

As we walked, I felt a long skirt against my legs. Up ahead, the mist thinned, and when we emerged, I found myself standing on the bank of a river.

Attired in breeches and a linen shirt, Lee said, "It's the James, but I don't recognize the landmarks."

Trying to discover our whereabouts, I cast my gaze about. The gentle roll of the land appeared familiar. *It couldn't be.* I bolted, following the river downstream.

"Phoebe!"

Lee easily caught up with me, but I did not stop running 'til I was winded.

The palisade had long been torn down, and the pitched-roof house was no longer built of wood, but brick. Out front stood a man. I drew closer. His hair had some gray, and wrinkles had formed near his eyes. "Henry . . ."

He blinked in disbelief. "Phoebe? How is this possible? You look the same as when—"

"As when I vanished?"

He nodded and glanced at Lee.

" 'Tis through the dreaming that I appear afore you. This is my husband, Lee Crowley. He is Paspahegh."

With tears in his eyes, he kissed my hands and shook Lee's.

"I'm honored to meet you, sir," Lee said.

Thrilled by the chance I had been given, I could no longer hold back. "Where is Elenor?"

"She's fine, Phoebe. You'd be proud. She cares for me now. Come." He waved the way inside. A hall with wooden floors divided the house. A table was to one side with candles atop it and a looking glass above. Instead of a ladder to the loft, a staircase with a black walnut handrail wound the way to the second story.

In the parlor, a black-haired woman was bent over a spinning wheel. She looked up as we entered the room.

"Elenor, we have guests."

She stood, slowly came closer, and studied my face.

Unable to keep my tears at bay, I ran over to her and hugged her. "Elenor, I've thought about you e'ery day. I ne'er meant to leave you behind."

"Momma?"

We embraced and cried in each others' arms. "Poppa told me what happened. If you hadn't taken the witchcraft charges for Bess, she would have certainly been hanged."

I stepped back and dried my tears. Of course, she would think of Henry as her poppa. 'Twas proper.

Aft another round of introductions, we sat in the chairs around the parlor, where Elenor introduced me to my grandchildren. Tall and ungainly, Christopher was named aft his poppa and was nearly seven. He had Elenor's black hair. At five, Elsa looked a lot like myself, with her blue-green eyes, reddish hair, and freckles. With light-brown hair and blue eyes, Nicolas was two. Elenor said he took aft his poppa.

Upon seeing me, Bess shrieked with joy and joined us.

My melancholy faded as Henry told me that he had remarried, but she had passed on a few years afore. He also had a son by the name of David. He, along with Elenor's husband, was a merchant, and both were presently in England. They told me of my brother Charging Bear. Living farther up the river, he oft brought them venison and fish in exchange for English goods.

In turn, I went on to tell my family how I had come to meet Lee. Their eyes widened when I mentioned the twenty-first century, and they had all sorts of questions. Whilst we chatted, hours passed without our noticing.

Sad that our time together had to end, I felt a fullness in my breasts. Heather needed my attention, not Elenor. I hugged each and every one of them goodbye, except for Elenor. My daughter accompanied Lee and me outside.

Near the mist-covered river, the waves lapped against the bank. Lee gazed upon the water. No words were necessary. I knew he thought of how the land had once belonged to the Paspahegh. He held his hands out afore him, palms facing up. My eyes filled with tears. At long last, he understood the sacrifice of the woman who had birthed him.

The fog on the river enlarged and spread beyond the bank. The hound stood off to the edge, and I knew the moment had arrived. One last time, I embraced Elenor and whispered, "If you e'er need me, contact me through the dreaming."

She nodded in understanding. Like myself, and my mother, and her mother afore her, Elenor is a cunning woman.

Author's Note

Throughout much of European history, the cunning folk were the healers of society, using herbs and magic. Some had familiars, like Phoebe's greyhound, and were essentially the shamans of European society. Although I have read about the Virginia Algonquian-speaking people—often referred to as the Powhatan—having visions, the records are obscure and generally written from an English-biased perspective. Rather than misrepresent another culture's belief system, I chose to draw on another portion of history that tends to be ignored in the history books. The dreaming is meant to represent one cunning woman's shamanic journey.

During the seventeenth century, doctors were fairly uncommon in English society, and few people could afford them. Those who could often didn't trust them. Like healers of any time period, some were excellent, others were charlatans. People would travel many miles to seek the aid of a renowned healer. While a number of historians state the majority of cunning folk were men, many were women. In the patriarchal society of the time, clashes resulted. Although the cunning folk were not the most frequent members of society to be tried as witches, such charges against them weren't unusual, and as might be guessed, women were more often suspect.

In the United States, Salem is most noted for witch trials, but Virginia has the dubious honor of being the first to hold such a trial on the North American continent, in 1626. Thirteen women and two men are known to have been tried as witches in Virginia, but records for others have likely been lost. Unlike in Salem, in Virginia only one woman is recorded to have been executed. In 1654, Katherine Grady was hanged at sea en route from England to Virginia.

I have uncovered no records of cunning women in Virginia, but due to their prevalence during the period, I have no doubt they were in the colony. I sincerely believe at least two of the women tried as witches were cunning women. In 1626, Joan Wright often foretold the future and was a midwife, and the most famous witch trial was that of Grace Sherwood, beginning in 1698. She fully admitted to being an herbalist, healer, and midwife.

Many of the historical accounts portrayed in *The Dreaming* are accurate. Throughout the early colonization period, the conditions were harsh. Jamestown was located in an area where many died of salt poisoning from drinking the water. The colonists encroached on the land of the Paspahegh, a tributary tribe of the paramount chief, Powhatan. The Paspahegh resisted the infringement and were labeled as hostile. As a result, conflicts ignited.

In 1609, the first group of English women arrived in Jamestown. Unfortunately, their arrival coincided with the harsh winter known as the "Starving Time." Sixty of approximately five hundred colonists survived the winter. Depending on shipments from England for supplies, they had grown no food for themselves, leaving them ill prepared. They had slaughtered all of their livestock. Colonists were reduced to eating rats, and some dug up corpses. One record indicates a man killed and ate his wife. For his crime, he was burned at the stake.

Colonist George Percy wrote in *Trewe Relacyon* that "many" ran off to the Indians, never to be heard from again. The fact that such an act became punishable by death suggests that it was more common than many historians care to admit.

The scene where the colonists attacked the Paspahegh is a fictional account, in which I combined the actual raids on the Paspahegh and the Kecoughtan. The English military used the same tactics as they had in Ireland, and both tribes were annihilated. Until that point in time, the killing of women and children was unknown among the Algonquian people, as it was considered a law against nations. The action permanently changed the nature of their warfare.

The blond-haired boy living among the Arrohateck was real. In 1607, George Percy described him in his log as being approximately ten years old. Beyond that, there is no other mention of him in the historical record. Several theories exist as to who he might have been: a "lost" colonist's child, a genetic anomaly, or a child fathered by a Spanish or English sailor prior to colonization. I chose what I thought to be the most believable.

Throughout the colonization period, a number of diseases were brought from Europe and Africa. Epidemics, to which the indigenous population had no resistance, were mentioned in the written record, but oftentimes not the specific diseases. In that sense, I took liberty as to which one occurred at any given time.

The event of March, 22, 1622, goes by several names. The English of the era called it a massacre. Some historians call it Opechancanough's uprising or coup. I chose "organized attacks," as the outlook portrayed in the story would have been from the Arrohateck point of view. Some tribal aspects, such as Jamestown never having been in danger during the attacks, are frequently ignored by modern historians.

Variolation is the form of inoculation that Bess and Phoebe used to fight smallpox. While I have found no circumstances in the written record that it had been used in Virginia, medical historians state the technique made its way to Egypt in the thirteenth century. The date for North and Western Africa is in question, but it was definitely known by the late seventeenth century and, most likely, much earlier. Because the exact timing is in dispute, I took liberty that Phoebe could have learned the technique from Bess, as Cotton Mather had from his African slave in Massachusetts later on in the century.

Hemp was first introduced by Sir Thomas Dale in 1611. It was used for paper, cordage, fiber for linen, and, of course, medicinal uses. The First Virginia Assembly encouraged colonists to grow the plant. *Culpeper's Complete Herbal,* first published in 1653, states that hemp "is so well known to every good housewife in the country [England], that I shall not need to write any description of it."

Little information on the Virginia Indians survives from the 1600s. I have read as much as possible from the period-biased sources, plus archaeological and contemporary sources, to try to recreate a semblance of their daily lives. In addition, I have consulted with modern-day tribal sources. Even so, gaping holes exist. As a consequence, the scenes depicted are entirely my own interpretation, and any mistakes are not the fault of my consultants.

For some Powhatan scenes, I have drawn from texts about similar tribes. Again, this was merely to fill in some of the gaps, and, hopefully, I have portrayed the Paspahegh and Arrohateck as accurately as possible.

Around a thousand words from the Virginia Algonquian dialect have survived to modern day. Numerous spellings seem to exist for many words. I tried to use the most accepted spelling for any given word.

Acknowledgments

A special thank you goes to my editors, K.A. Corlett and Catherine Karp, my cover designer, Mayapriya Long, historical consultants, Deanna Beacham and Angela "Silver Star" Daniel, and law enforcement consultant, Michael Gibbs. All scenes depicted in *The Dreaming* are my own interpretation and any mistakes are not the fault of my consultants. And, of course, I wish to thank my family: my son, Bryan, and especially my husband, Pat; both are now concerned that I may continue to retreat further through the centuries.